Maggie Mason is a pseudonym of author Mary Wood. Mary began her career by self-publishing on Kindle, where many of her sagas reached number one in genre. She was spotted by Pan Macmillan and to date has written many books for them under her own name, with more to come.

Mary continues to be proud to write for Pan Macmillan, but is now equally proud and thrilled to take up a second career with Sphere under the name of Maggie Mason.

Born the thirteenth child of fifteen children, Mary describes her childhood as poor, but rich in love. She was educated at St Peter's RC school in Hinckley and at Hinckley College for Further Education, where she was taught shorthand and typing.

Mary retired from working for the National Probation Service in 2009, when she took up full-time writing, something she'd always dreamed of doing. She follows in the footsteps of her great-grandmother, Dora Langlois, who was an acclaimed author, playwright and actress in the late nineteenth–early twentieth century.

It was her work with the Probation Service that gives Mary's writing its grittiness, her need to tell it how it is, which takes her readers on an emotional journey to the heart of issues.

Also by Maggie Mason

Blackpool Lass
Blackpool's Daughter
Blackpool's Angel
Blackpool Sisters

As Mary Wood

An Unbreakable Bond
To Catch a Dream
Tomorrow Brings Sorrow
Time Passes Time
Proud of You
All I Have to Give
In Their Mother's Footsteps
Brighter Days Ahead

MAGGIE MASON

A Blackpool Christmas

SPHERE

First published in Great Britain in 2020 by Sphere

1 3 5 7 9 10 8 6 4 2

A CIP catalogue record for this book is available from the British Library.

ISBN 978-0-7515-7718-1

Typeset in Bembo by Hewer Text UK Ltd, Edinburgh
Printed and bound in Great Britain by Clays Ltd, Elcograf S.p.A.

Papers used by Sphere are from well-managed forests
and other responsible sources.

Sphere
An imprint of
Little, Brown Book Group
Carmelite House
50 Victoria Embankment
London
EC4Y 0DZ

An Hachette UK Company
www.hachette.co.uk

www.littlebrown.co.uk

For my brother Christopher Olley –
You made me laugh.
You made me believe that I could achieve my dream.
You were simply the best.

PART ONE

TORN APART

1916–17

ONE

Babs

A week to go till Christmas. Such a different Christmas to the one Babs had thought she would have. She pulled her shawl around her and, despite her bulk, quickened her steps. She was on a mission. They needed some holly branches with lots of berries on to decorate the house with.

Getting as far as the barn, she stopped and rubbed the ache in her side. Her body seemed full of aches and pains that had come with being pregnant. The child in her womb kicked as if in protest at Babs standing still. 'Eeh, lad, behave for once.' Patting her stomach, she smiled, but the smile didn't reach her inner self. 'Well, your da said you were a lad,' she told the bulk as she rubbed the place where her baby's foot seemed stuck, causing her discomfort. Somehow, though, physical pain was a relief to her as it bled some of the pain from her soul. *Oh, Rupert, I miss you so much.*

Putting her hand out to steady herself, Babs reeled at the memory of the awful day when she and Rupert, her doctor husband, were working on the ambulance train in France and came under an attack. A direct hit destroyed many carriages. None of the brave wounded and dying soldiers on board made it and neither did many of her colleagues, including her lovely friend Cath. But worst of all was finding that her darling Rupert had been killed.

Theirs had been an unlikely love. She, a lost soul, had been brought up with her twin sister Beth by the gypsy couple Jasmine and Roman, who'd stolen them from their lovely ma, and Rupert was a man of high birth – the son of an earl.

But then, war was a great leveller and love could conquer any social divide. Not that it had conquered Rupert's parents, as they'd disowned him once they'd heard about his marriage to her.

The sound of the door to the farmhouse opening cut into Babs's thoughts. She looked up to see Eliza, her half-sister – the second child Ma had had during the time she and Beth were missing – coming out of the house. Eliza waved. A tentative wave that made Babs realise how unsure Eliza was of her.

Ma had told Eliza from birth about the twin sisters she had and what had happened to them, and had brought her up to love them even though she didn't know if she would ever get to meet them. Now, suddenly they were here, and yet the happiness Eliza thought they would bring hadn't arrived with them. Poor girl didn't know how to be when around them.

'Eeh, Eliza, lass, you look bonny in that coat. It's a lovely red, and suits you. Have you come to give me a hand?'

Babs quickly wiped her eyes where tears had brimmed as Eliza came up to her, her stride surer now. 'Aye, Ma said I was to help you as I knaw where the best places are to find the holly.'

Similar to her and Beth, in that she had the same curly, raven-coloured hair and dark eyes, Eliza's face was more the rounded shape of her da Tommy, who Ma had married and found happiness with. 'Well, I'll be glad to have you along, and you can keep me going by telling me tales about Ma Perkins. You allus cheer me up.'

Eliza's smile widened. A born teller of funny tales that made you laugh, she was almost fifteen years old and training to be a baker, though Babs thought when she tasted the cakes Eliza baked that they didn't tell of anyone who needed training – they were the best she'd ever eaten.

Babs felt her mood lighten as they crossed the bottom field of the farm that Ma and Tommy owned and she listened to Eliza telling of how Ma Perkins wiped the tops of the iced buns. 'Eeh, never buy one of them. You knaw how they show the dust in the icing if you leave them out? Well, Ma Perkins had some on a stand and they'd been there all morning. I were in the back getting a batch of tarts out of the oven when I heard her say, "Eeh, look at them buns." I went in to see what was making her cross and caught her licking her finger and wiping the tops of them.'

'Ugh!'

'I knaw, Babs. I were that angry I stamped me foot and gave her what for.'

Babs was astonished at this and let out a giggle. From what she'd already been told about Ma Perkins, she thought her a tyrant that you would never challenge.

'I told her that were a filthy thing to do, and she should throw them away as she'd tainted them. But then I realised what I'd done and trembled with fear. But do you knaw, she promptly put them in the bin and said, "There, does that suit you, Miss Prim and Proper? Well, see if this does: get mixing and make some more!" And here I were about to come home an' all. Eeh, she's a one that one.'

Babs burst out laughing. And with the feeling this gave her, her heart lifted. Putting her arm around Eliza, she pulled her to her. 'Eeh, lass, you're a card.'

The conversation between them flowed easily after this as they gathered the holly. Eliza was a little chatterbox. 'Ma Perkins says that the holly being laden with berries shows that we're to have a hard winter.'

'Aye, I've heard that saying from Jasmine and Roman. The gypsies follow the signs of the earth and they are never wrong.'

'What was it like living with gypsies, Babs? I knaw I shouldn't ask and Ma'd skelp me if she heard, but I want to understand how it is that Beth can't give them up. To my mind they were wicked taking you from Ma. Ma suffered so much ... I – I mean, well, I shouldn't have said owt ... Don't take notice of me. Ma said as there's naw one nosier than I am, and I knaw as she's right. I seem to want to knaw everyone's business.'

Again, Babs laughed. 'You and me both. I'm allus curious as to what's behind every closed door. Well, I think as you have a right to knaw. You're having to live with the atmosphere Beth's caused as much as me and Ma does.'

'It just seems funny – naw, wicked – that Beth wants Jasmine and Roman in her life, when it causes Ma so much pain.'

Not wanting to stand up for Beth, as she herself felt cross with her, Babs was still careful not to open the rift wider than she could already feel it was from Eliza's words. Naturally, Eliza would be cross at Beth. She'd lived with a grieving ma all her life, and now when Ma should be full of joy, she had more heartache to deal with.

'It ain't an easy situation, Eliza, but we have to try to see it from Beth's point of view. Since a very young age, Jasmine and Roman have been the only parents she knew, and they were loving and caring to us.'

'But you didn't stay with them, did you? You ran away and tried to find Ma.'

'I did. But it wasn't a sensible thing to do. I were only a young girl and I went through hell. Things happened to me that should never happen to anyone, yet alone a young 'un. But I can't talk of it all, lass. It's too painful.'

'But why didn't Beth leave with you?'

'Beth was allus the weaker of us two and allus relied on me. She was too afraid to go. She begged me not to. I think after I did, she was loved and given into even more by Jasmine and Roman. After all, the gypsies don't believe in education, and yet Beth got her wish to have a tutor, and to learn to speak proper, and to take her training to become a nurse.'

'Aye, and in that she got her punishment.'

'Eeh, Eliza, you shouldn't say that, lass. Naw one injured in the war is being punished for owt. Beth were doing a job that took courage and in conditions near to what hell must be like. She were trying to save the lives of our brave soldiers, many miles from home across the sea. That ain't easy, I can tell you. And she didn't deserve for that shell to hit the tent she were working in, nor to lose the ability to walk from the injuries she sustained.'

'Eeh, I'm sorry, Babs. Me feelings were so cross that I let me tongue wag without thinking. Ma says as I'm a one for that an' all.'

Babs wanted to laugh, but what Eliza had said, despite her apology, hung between them. They were quiet as they walked back across the field.

The weak December sun gave off a little warmth, and was winning the battle with the overnight frost. The ruts in the field were hardened with it, but its white layer was beginning to melt.

'Babs, I didn't mean what I said. It really did just pop into me head and out of me mouth. I love Beth. I were just trying to understand.'

Babs found it impossible to be angry with Eliza for long. She smiled at her and accepted the hand Eliza offered. Together they walked hand in hand till they reached the fence. 'You climb over and I'll pass you the basket, lass. Then I'll walk to the gate. I don't think I can get this bulk over the stile.'

As she climbed over, Eliza voiced something that often occurred to Babs. 'Twins allus seem to do things together, even if they aren't with each other. Look at you and Beth, both having babbies, both being nurses, and both having worked in France looking after the soldiers.'

'Aye, I knaw, even though we spent years apart, our lives have gone like that.'

When she dropped down on the other side of the fence, Eliza became solemn. 'I were sorry to hear about your Rupert. And now Beth's Henry is away at war an' all. He will come back, won't he?'

'Aye, he will. He's not in any danger, thank goodness. Where he is, attached to a hospital in Paris, he's doing vital work. His research has given him knowledge that will mean that many a soldier will make it home, and won't suffer the disabilities they would have. He's a fine doctor from what I've heard, and I can't wait to meet him.'

'He's lovely. I loved him the minute I met him. He's posh, but has naw side to him.'

'Naw, when it comes to us all being in the same boat, we find out that the posh are just like us really.'

They were walking along each side of the fence and had reached the gate. As Babs came through, Eliza said, 'Babs, I wish your Rupert hadn't died. I knaw I would have loved him an' all. Just because you did. And in my book that makes him a lovely man.'

Babs caught her breath and swallowed hard. Before she could say anything, Eliza had dropped the basket and had flung her arms around her. 'Eeh, Babs, the young 'un inside you makes it hard to cuddle you.'

'Ha, you can cuddle him an' all then.' With this, Babs put her arms around Eliza and held her as close to her as she could. 'Eeh, lass, it's lovely having a little sister. I knaw we haven't known each other long, but I love you as if I've known you all me life.'

'And I love you, Babs. You're all I dreamt you would be, all them years that I longed for you to come back to Ma.'

This touched Babs, and for the first time she understood how hurt Eliza was that Beth refused to live with them and carried on seeing Jasmine and Roman, who had followed her up to Blackpool from Kent where they and Beth had lived – Beth in her own home that she'd set up with Henry, and they with their wagon parked close by and working on a nearby farm.

Now Beth lived in a ground-floor flat in Blackpool, just along the promenade from where Ma had her basketware shop, cared for by the lovely Peggy, when it should have been Ma and Babs caring for her.

'Babs, is it bad out in France?'

Just as Eliza asked this, Babs caught sight of Phil, the farm-hand and son of Florrie, one of Ma's best friends, coming out of the cowshed, and she knew what had prompted the question. Eliza was sweet on Phil and he on her, and being nearly sixteen, he was talking of joining up. Though he was still too young to be conscripted, age wasn't a barrier for many young lads who wanted to go to war as the government carried out few checks, or just turned a blind eye to a willing lad's age, such was the need for soldiers.

'Aye, lass, it's bad, but think on, it might be all over before Phil gets the chance to go. And you're to be proud of him for wanting to fight for us.'

Eliza squeezed Babs harder. 'Eeh, Eliza, give over! Babby's protesting at being held so tightly.'

'Sometimes I feel that scared, Babs, that I want to hug the world and make it safe.'

'You've a lovely soul, lass.'

They stood a moment longer in the hug that was bonding them until the cold began to seep into Babs's bones. 'By, the clouds have taken what little sun we had. I'm chilly now, so let's go inside and start to decorate the living room, eh? Christmas is a time for happiness, and spreading good-will to all men – we should do that, no matter what's in our hearts.'

They parted then and walked towards the lovely farmhouse. Covered in ivy, it's low thatched roof added to the feel of this being a home. And that's what it was – made so by Ma.

As Babs thought this, Tilly opened the door. 'Hey, you two, I were thinking of sending a search party out for you. Where've you been? You must be frozen stiff.'

'We've been putting the world to rights, Ma, and finding our love for each other.'

'Awe, me Babs and me Eliza, that's grand to hear. Come in the warmth, I've kettle on.'

Tilly hurried in, but not before Babs saw the tears brimming in her eyes. Babs understood. For she had been through hell just as her ma had, and knew that at moments when things happened that touched you, it was hard to keep strong.

Babs didn't know anyone stronger than her ma. What she'd been through since Babs and Beth's da died while he was working on building the Blackpool Tower would have floored a lesser woman. *For Ma, me and Beth turning up was the salvation she has always longed for, but even more than that, coming just after she'd lost her son, Ivan. A lad I would have loved to have met. Our return home must have been like an answer to her prayers.*

With this thought, Babs felt renewed anger at Beth for spoiling that homecoming.

'You just bristled, Babs, are you all right?'

'Bristled?'

'Aye, you knaw, shuddered as if in a temper.'

'Eeh, lass, I told you that you've got a good soul. Well, you've got insight an' all. I had a moment when I wanted to make everything right for Ma. Come on, let's get this Christmas started, for who knaws what's around the corner, eh? Maybe sommat'll happen that'll open Beth's eyes and then everything'll be as Ma would want it to be.'

How Babs hoped that her words would come true. But this morning had been a good start. She and Eliza were true sisters now. This gave her a nice feeling as Eliza said, 'Aye, I've a lot of baking to do, so you and Ma can get from under me feet and do the decorations.'

They were laughing as they went inside and the warmth of the kitchen embraced their joyfulness and love.

Tilly turned towards them from the pot sink where she was stood, holding on to the side as if it would stop her from falling. 'Eeh, me lasses, that's a lovely sound.'

'It's Christmas, Ma. It gets into all the corners and makes the sad bits happy. Now, I've a lot to do. Me cake is waiting to be iced, I've bread proving, and I want to make some of them mince tarts for you. Ma Perkins made some the other day and by, they were good.'

'Well, that's us told, Babs. I think we'd better leave this baker to it!'

They all burst out laughing, and then spontaneously went into a hug.

'We're going to be all right, me lasses.'

'We are, Ma. We have each other, and we'll help each other through.'

'Aye, Babs. We will. And Beth will be here for Christmas day an' all.'

'And our Ivan, Ma. He wouldn't miss a Christmas. He'll have a lovely time in heaven, but he'll come to visit us an' all. I can feel it in me bones.'

Babs's laughter following this from Eliza nearly split her side. She never thought to laugh again, but this sister of hers came out with such things that tickled you. Her ma was right when she said that Eliza should be on the stage. But all she dreamt of was having her own little cake shop.

As they set about their various tasks the mood lifted. Ma began to sing a carol and they all joined in. Christmas was always a healer, and this one, her first back in Blackpool with her ma, was going to do that for her. Babs knew that, and wished for it with all her heart.

She gently stroked her bump. *Eeh, lad, we'll get through all of this, me and you, son. We will. And we'll never forget your da. He should have been an earl, you know, but he were willing to give all that up for you and me as I'd have never fitted in with his family.*

Whether you'll ever knaw your grandparents on his side, I don't knaw, but you won't miss them as you'll have the best of grandparents in me ma and her Tommy, and two lovely aunties in Eliza and Beth an' all. Then you have an Aunt Molly – well, not a proper aunt, but a grand woman who's a friend of Ma's, and all her family. And if God's willing, and Henry comes home, you'll have him, and his and Beth's child will be your cousin. By, we're going to be all right, you and me. I promise.

TWO

Tilly

Tilly lay awake not feeling the usual excitement at this being Christmas Day. She closed her eyes, trying to get a spark of how she knew she should feel.

The best room looked lovely. The fireplace framed with holly was laid ready for lighting and the ceiling was draped in the paperchains that Babs and Eliza had made. The Christmas tree that Tommy had cut down for them was laden with bows and tiny hanging lamps, each holding a candle. The crib stood on the dresser and already, delicious smells of roasting cockerel and steaming puddings floated on the air. Eliza must be up and working away in the kitchen. The lass so wanted this Christmas to be the best ever. Tilly knew the reason. Eliza suffered so much with missing her brother Ivan and did anything to keep herself busy and distracted.

Tilly mentally shook herself. Afraid of sinking into her grief for her son, she tried to think of how he was at last out of pain. A brave soul, he'd coped with being disabled, he'd had a cheerful manner and had been a joy. He must continue to be that in her heart, otherwise she would sink under the weight of her longing for him. Ivan wouldn't want that.

Making her mind up that she would do all she could to make this first Christmas for many a year with her lovely twin daughters a happy one, she stretched and reached out towards Tommy.

Tommy stirred and made a funny snorting noise. She knew he'd been up with the lark and seen to the animals, milked the cows, and bedded them with fresh straw in the barn. He'd have broken the ice on the trough for the animals to drink from and fed the chickens and the pigs. All would have been tended to before he'd crept back into bed, something he only did on Christmas morning. And he would have collected the eggs – something she usually did, even on work days. *By, it's getting harder for me to get up and out of bed these days.* Not one to admit anything like that, this thought surprised Tilly as did the truth of it. Always she'd been one for being up with the lark, looking forward to going into the shop, planning in her mind what she was set to make that day while she did the few chores that needed doing before she left the house.

She still loved to weave her wicker and cane, and made an increasingly wide variety of items other than baskets, even big things such as basket chairs and frames for tables that would be set with a glass table top. Many of these were commissioned, since she'd done some work for Malcolm, a designer from London who had come across her shop while he was in Blackpool doing up one of the large promenade houses owned by a rich family. Not for them to live in, mind, but to use for their holidays. *Eeh, how the other half live. They don't*

15

know they are born. They want to try life as we mere mortals live it. That'd shake them up.

Thinking of work brought to mind the way that Beth showed talent for making baskets and how quickly she was mastering some of the intricate patterns that could be achieved with different shades of wicker. The thought made her smile. The hours they spent together in the shop made up for a lot. It was nice to pass on her skills to one of her lasses. Aye, and to spend time with Beth.

At these times Tilly made herself forget Jasmine and Roman were still a big part of Beth's life. She couldn't change that and didn't want her feelings about it to spoil how she was building a relationship with Beth – something she had to work on, but wished she didn't have to; she wanted it all to be as simple as it was with Babs. For her to be the central figure in both her twins' lives. Sharing Beth with those wicked, scheming gypsies was breaking her heart.

Snuggling into Tommy's warm body, Tilly felt her pain lessen. Tommy had been her saviour, and she loved him dearly. Their meeting, twenty years ago, in the asylum where Tommy had worked as a gardener and handyman and where she'd been taken after a drunken episode, wasn't a good memory for her to have. Tommy hadn't behaved well towards her, but he'd been given the wrong impression of her. Once he realised her true nature, he became the man of her dreams. Despite herself, Tilly shuddered. That was a time in her life that she wanted to forget. It was in the past. But then, maybe it was timely to think of it as it reinforced her resolve not to touch even a drop of sherry this Christmas. She knew if she did, it would be fatal as she couldn't stop at one. There was a demon inside her that turned her into a different person when she took a drink.

Making an effort to dispel all these thoughts that were putting her in the doldrums, Tilly sat up. *Today is going to be a happy day, despite everything. You'll help me make it so, won't you, my Ivan?* The curtains flickered and a beam of light from the gas lamp that Tommy would have lit in the yard fell across the bed. It may be fanciful, as there were many draughts in this old farmhouse that could have caused it, but Tilly liked to think that Ivan was answering her and telling her that he would. *Eeh, lad, Eliza says as you'll 'ave a lovely day in heaven an' all, but I wish you were here with us.*

With this thought, Tilly flung the bedclothes back and braved the cold as she shuffled her feet to find her slippers and slip them on, then ran shivering to the armchair in the corner and gathered up her dressing gown. When she opened the bedroom door she was bathed in light and warmth. Tommy must have stoked the fire for Eliza and lit all the fires for the usually freezing landing to be this welcoming.

Feeling thankful for it, Tilly took a deep breath. *Right, best foot forward. I'm to make this a day to remember.*

As the fog-filled air lightened and the sun broke the mist into swirls that floated above the fields, Tilly sipped her tea. Eliza had told her she didn't want her under her feet, not for at least an hour. So, she'd taken herself into the Sunday best room – the room at the front of the house, which earned the name due to it only being used on high days and holidays. She loved this room with its big, comfy furniture in deep red, and its beige carpet with swirls of red woven into it. It had a special atmosphere and opening it meant it was time to celebrate. She hoped the feeling it always gave her would help to dispel this misery that lurked in her heart.

Her grief was always there but days like today were the hardest to cope with, so it was a relief to hear Babs come into the room.

'Eeh, Ma, what're you doing sitting in this half-light? Shall I light the mantel?'

'Aye, lass. Then come and sit next to me.'

With light now bathing every corner of the room, Tilly brightened. The sofa sank as Babs joined her. 'My, you're a lump.'

'Ma! That ain't nowt you should be saying to a mother-to-be.'

Tilly laughed as this had been said with a mock indignation. 'I expect you're feeling fed up by now, love. Once I passed six months of carrying, I was ready for it to be over.'

'I am and I ain't. In a funny way having me lad inside me is like carrying me Rupert around with me.'

'Awe, lass, that's lovely. But you worry me with being so sure this babby is a boy. What if you have a girl?'

'Eeh, that'd be strange, as I've thought on me little one as being a boy from the beginning. But I'd not be disappointed, a little girl would be lovely an' all. I just want whatever it is to be healthy and, well . . . to look like Rupert.'

'He sounds as though he were a lovely man. And him being a toff an' all. I wish I'd met him.' With this Tilly put her cup down on the occasional table and took Babs's hand. 'We've been through the mill, lass.'

Babs's head came down on her shoulder, and the worst tears of all spilled – silent tears. Tilly didn't say anything, just reached her arm around Babs' shoulder and held her. What was there to be said? Words were sometimes empty. She knew there were few that could comfort herself, so it was the same for any grieving person.

They sat, allowing their grief for a moment. The door opening and Eliza bustling in made them both straighten. Neither wanted to upset Eliza; she didn't deserve that after all the effort she was putting in.

'By, it's warm. I've worked meself into a sweat. I'm just going to get me shawl and go into the yard for a bit. Now don't go interfering in me kitchen. I knaw where I'm at with everything, and when I come back in, I'll get some breakfast on the go.'

'Yes, Matron!'

'Ha, I were a bit bossy. Is that what your matron used to sound like, Babs?'

'Aye, and she were lovely, just like you, but when she took on her boss role, we all stood by our beds. Come here, lass, I need a cuddle.'

Tilly helped Babs to rise, then had a warm feeling as she saw her lovely daughters embrace and heard Babs say, 'Eeh, Eliza, you bring the sunshine into the room. Happy Christmas, sis.'

'Ta, Babs. And you've brought me a lot, you knaw. You're like a replacement . . . naw, I didn't mean that as you're special on your own, the bestest big sister I could wish for, but, well, you knaw.'

'I do, Eliza, as you're the same to me. You've filled a large part of a deep hole that was in me heart. Let's have a happy day today, eh? I knaw all our loved ones would want that for us.'

'They would. Well, I knaw as Ivan would, wouldn't he, Ma? He loved Christmas. He'd allus make sure we had a . . . stocking! Oh, Ma . . . you've put them up, and eeh, look at mine, it's brimming!'

Leaving the circle of Babs's arms, Eliza ran over to the fireplace where six stockings – old socks of Tommy's – hung from the mantelshelf, each held in place by the tab that Tilly had stitched to them, which was weighted down by a large stone painted white by Tommy and with a piece of holly stuck on the top. Below the holly was painted each person's name – Tilly, Eliza, Babs, Beth, Tommy and Peggy, Beth's lovely nurse.

'Naw, lass.' Tilly laughed as she said this, and the laughter did touch her cold heart and melt the pain that had hovered there. 'Naw touching them till we are all together. Your da's fetching Beth afore breakfast. Then when she's here, we'll all see what Santa Claus has left us.'

This didn't stop Eliza squeezing the one with her name on. 'Eeh, Ma, there's so much in them and I never saw you fetch owt into the house. I thought we weren't going to have them this year.'

'Eeh, it ain't Christmas without a stocking. Naw, I'd not let you all miss out on that treat.'

'Ta! Awe, Ma, ta ever so much.'

Eliza nearly knocked Tilly backwards when she bounded over and hugged her. To Tilly, it was as if Eliza was a little girl again, but then she soon dispelled this. 'Right, I'm to go and get me wrap. Phil will be in the yard and I want to wish him a happy Christmas. I wish he was spending it with us, but he wants to go home.' Eliza reached the door as she finished speaking, meeting Tommy coming through it.

'Well, me little lass, aren't you a lovely sight on a Christmas morning. Merry Christmas.'

'Eeh, Pappy, you've already wished me that.'

'Wasn't that in the middle of the night, wee one? Well, now it's Christmas proper, and I'm wanting a hug.'

Eliza went into Tommy's arms. As Tilly watched, memories assailed her of another father, her Arthur, cuddling Babs and Beth as little girls. It didn't come with pain, but with a nice feeling that all of her children had been lucky to have known a good da, for she knew that both Babs and Beth remembered little things about Arthur, and all of it was good. It couldn't be anything else, for he was a kind man, and a loving husband.

'Hey, Eliza, you can't hog all of Da, I need a Christmas hug an' all.'

Tilly saw Tommy's look of surprise at Babs saying this. A look which quickly turned to a smile of joy. 'It is that I have three daughters now, Eliza, and have to give them all a greeting.'

Eliza looked shocked. Tilly didn't think she'd thought of her half-sisters as wanting to share her beloved pappy. Babs hesitated, but Tommy took charge. He held Eliza from him and looked into her eyes. 'Now, I was for being outside the door a few minutes ago until nature called me. And I heard a little bit of conversation. I heard you say to Babs that she was like a replacement, but not like one at all. Well then, it will be that you'll be understanding that me and Babs can be that for each other too. Am I right?'

Eliza was quiet. Tilly could see she was struggling with this. Tommy was her adored pappy and she'd lost so much that

Tilly could see she was finding it hard to give a piece of him away.

Babs stepped forward. 'I had a lovely da, Eliza, so I knaw how you feel. I didn't want him to leave me and go to be with God in heaven as me Ma told me had happened. I wanted him for me and Beth, not all those angels as I'd heard about. But you knaw, naw one can ever take him from me. They can share a bit of him, but he's here in me heart and I knaw as me and Beth are in his. But it would be lovely to have a replacement da. And I can think of naw one better than Tommy to be that. It would be the best Christmas present ever if you could give a part of your pappy to me to share.'

'Awe, Babs. Of course I can. Eeh, what am I thinking?'

'Nowt as we wouldn't all think, lass. You've a good soul as I'm allus telling you.'

With no more said, Tilly saw three of the people she loved most in the world go into a group hug. The sight lifted her heart until it soared and her thought was that now, she knew she could make this a Christmas Day to remember.

Tilly smiled as she got up and went into the kitchen to see Tommy off and caught sight of Eliza and Phil. Though they weren't touching, they seemed to her to be joined, as Phil, a tall lad, looked down into Eliza's eyes, and she up into his.

'I tell you, me wee Tilly, not many years will pass before it is that we'll see them two wed.'

'Naw, Tommy, she's only a young 'un as yet. Phil is just a fancy. They've known each other that long that they're like brother and sister.'

'Ha, it is for suiting you to think so, but that's not a look of a brother to a sister. As young as they are, it's for being plain to see that they're meant for each other, and that does me heart good. For won't we be able to leave the farm in Phil's capable hands when the time comes for us to retire? And won't that be when he is our son-in-law and pappy to our grandchildren?'

'Tommy! For goodness' sake! You're an old romantic. Well, I think you should get the notion out of your head. If it happens, then we'll all be over the moon. By, Phil's the son of one of me best mates, and nowt would be better than Florrie's son marrying me daughter, but we have to keep an open mind. What if, when she's properly grown-up, she falls for someone else? We've to be ready to welcome him, just as much as we are to welcome Phil. And, aye, it could happen the other way an' all. Phil could meet someone. They're so young and this is what me old aunt used to call puppy love. Wait and see is what I'm saying.'

'Where will he meet anyone? He is for going from here to home and back again, and that's it. There's no fair maiden on the road to Lytham when he cycles back and forth.'

'Tommy, you knaw as he still talks of going to war. Please God, he never does, but he seems set on doing so.'

'Aye, it is that you're right. I'll get Babs to talk to him. It is that she can scare him off that idea, I'm sure of it. Now, I'm to get on the road to fetch Beth and Peggy. And you should get that bacon in the pan. Old Bessy would be proud to know as we are eating her on Christmas morning.'

'Tommy! Eeh, don't. Bessy were a lovely pig, I don't like to think of the bacon coming from her.'

'It was her place in life to provide food for us, so it was. We gave her a good life while we fattened her.'

'Oh, Tommy, stop it.' But Tilly couldn't help laughing at him. Tommy was a farmer through and through. Brought up on his

23

father's farm in Ireland, a falling-out with his brother had brought him to England. But after she and Tommy had married, Tilly had gone with him to take over the farm on the death of his brother. It was a sad and frightening time when they became caught up in the unrest in Ireland and had to flee to Blackpool. Even now, Tommy yearned to go back and reclaim his farm, but he knew the impossibility of doing so. The discontentment still brewed; they were just distracted from it by the war. And they had no idea how the land lay there. Someone may have taken his farm over. Maybe, one day in the future, they would find out.

A sigh came from Tommy as he pulled her into his arms and somehow she knew similar thoughts to her own had passed through Tommy's mind. 'Eeh, me little lass. Life has it's funny turns.'

'Aye, Tommy. It does.'

'I just need to say this the one time, me Tilly, but me heart is for breaking that our Ivan isn't with us today.'

Tilly held him tighter, wanting to get comfort for herself as much as to comfort him. 'I knaw, lad. But he is, you knaw. He's here with us and'll allus be. We just have to think on how he was suffering. How his breathing was so laboured that he struggled to take air in at times. And of the pain in his limbs. He was a grand lad – the best son we could have had – and we have to give him up graciously and be thankful he is naw longer in that pain, and is at peace.'

'Tilly, you are a special person, so you are. A strong woman. You make surviving anything possible. With you by me side, it is that I will get through.'

Tilly wiped the tear that had trickled down Tommy's face. 'We will, love, we will.'

Tommy smiled and, as always, cheered up in an instant. 'Aye, and I've gained a daughter today. What about that?'

'Ha, I might just share her with you. Now, go on and get Beth, and you never knaw your luck, lad, you could gain another daughter in her. I can see that she loves you, but poor lass is wary of us with how things have panned out.'

'She is, but as ever, you make that situation the best it can be. I love you, me little Tilly.'

His kiss awoke a desire in Tilly. She wanted to run with him to the barn just as they used to when they were younger, and make love in the fresh-smelling hay. Shaking herself for having such a notion, she came out of his arms, and saw the same desire in Tommy.

'Away with you, lad. There's a time and a place. Let's get this Christmas started.'

With this Tommy turned hastily from her, but not before he thrilled her by squeezing her bottom and giving her a look that held a promise.

Tilly had no time to dwell on the feelings Tommy had awoken in her as Eliza came back in at that moment. 'Eeh, Ma, I could eat Phil sometimes.'

Laughing, Tilly told her, 'I will in a minute, if you don't get the breakfast started. Come on, lass. We've to get the pan on.'

'I'll do it, Ma. I want to. I want to keep as busy as I can, and I love to. You go and be with Babs, she needs you.'

'Aye, lass, you're right.' As she went out of the door, Tilly wondered how much of her there was to give to all those who needed her. Into this she included Eliza, for though seeming to be strong, she was really Tilly personified. Showing a strength that she didn't always feel. Of her three daughters,

Eliza and Babs were the most like her in nature. Beth wasn't so. And in this, she had to remember that Beth would need her more than any of them as when disaster struck Beth, she couldn't cope.

It came to her then that this was the reason that Beth had clung to Jasmine and Roman. They had been her strength when she found out that she may never walk again. They had supported her through an illness she'd told of that had struck her down when she was younger, and they had helped her to realise her dream to become a nurse. Beth just couldn't see that they had no right to that privilege, or that they had stolen from her the right to have all of that provided by her real ma.

She could only pray that one day, Beth would come to see that. And although she would never wish the extreme pain that she had felt at losing the twins on anyone else in the world, she did wish that for Jasmine and Roman. It was a pain that Tilly had lived with for years – one that they were prolonging by still being in Beth's life – and she hoped that at some point in the future they too would experience that loss with both of her girls walking out of their lives once and for all.

THREE

Tilly

By the time breakfast was over, the merriment Tilly wanted this Christmas had truly descended on the house. Eliza skipped into the best room. 'Time to play Santa, Pappy. Eeh, I remember you dressing up when we were little and me and Ivan thought you were real. We believed that you would come in from the fields later, and that Santa was in the living room.'

'I know, me wee one. And I put on me best Norwegian accent for you. Ahh, your wee faces.'

Tilly intervened before this got too much to handle. 'Well, you're not dressing up again, so you can both stop fantasising about days gone by. I want to see what we all have in our stockings.'

'Oh, Ma, you daft apeth, you made them up, so you knaw what's in them.'

'Aye, but not mine, and anyroad, knawing what's in them's not the same as when I see them through your eyes. It's like I didn't knaw and every one's a surprise.'

And this is what happened for Tilly as she clapped her hands in glee as they all were overjoyed with what she'd got for them. Peggy's and the girls' stockings contained items from her shop – lavender bags made by Molly, a wonderful seamstress, who made many items to sell in the shop, from cushions to the lining for sewing baskets. These little bags made of flower-patterned cotton material and edged with lace were so pretty that it was a shame they would live hidden away in a drawer, amongst the clothes. And then there were the little baskets with a lid, for Beth, Babs and Eliza. Each one made by herself and lined by Molly. Each held a brooch of intricate filigree design bought by Tommy. These brought squeals of delight and had Eliza jumping up and down. 'It's like you are saying I'm all grown-up, Pappy. Ta, and ta to you, Ma, I'll treasure me little basket.'

Tilly laughed, but thought that Eliza had no idea, and probably didn't want to have, that her pappy did think of her as grown-up and practically had her married off.

The little jars of bath salts came out next, and this was a present that Peggy got too. These Tilly had bought from one of the stallholders.

'Oh, I love everything, thank you, Tilly.' With this the usually reserved Peggy planted a kiss on Tilly's cheek. Tilly put her arm around her. This was another woman doing the job that Tilly should be doing – looking after Beth – but the feeling for Peggy was different. She knew Peggy was on her side. She'd known the suffering Tilly had endured. Not that they had been close friends before Babs and Beth came home, but Blackpool was a place where everyone knew everyone and, aye, knew their business too.

Peggy was one of life's stalwarts. Like her mother before her, she'd never been trained as a nurse, but seemed to know how to heal people and was always there in everyone's hour of need. And though in her forties as Tilly was, she'd never married.

For the little hug, Tilly was rewarded by a big smile from Peggy. This lit her face. A face that wasn't unattractive, but wasn't made the best of with how Peggy pulled her dark hair back off her face and secured it tightly in a bun.

The last items to come out of the stockings were a lace hanky for Peggy and a ribbon and a fancy hairclip for the girls. Everything had been so well received that Tilly felt very happy with her choices.

For herself and Tommy there was a present from all four of them. For Tommy, a new pipe, some tobacco, a hairbrush and a new tie, and from Tilly, a pair of gold cufflinks nestled inside another little lidded basket. And for her, perfume spray, two lace collars that would brighten a couple of her dark-coloured frocks, lace hankies and trinkets, and then from Tommy, the most beautiful locket, which when she opened it contained a picture of Ivan on one side and a tiny forget-me-not flower embroidered on white silk on the other, which she knew could only have been made by the lovely Molly. She couldn't speak.

Eliza saved the day by clapping her hands and saying in a gleeful voice, 'I knew as our Ivan would get here somehow. Pappy, you're a genius.'

Tilly smiled and as she had thought a thousand times, this daughter had a special quality and she thanked God for it. Looking at all of her girls, Babs, Beth and Eliza, she knew that she was blessed a thousand times over, as she had been to have Ivan. Now she would forever have him with her, in her locket, because as Tommy put the locket on her and kissed her cheek, she knew she would never, ever take it off again.

As Eliza disappeared into the kitchen, refusing all offers of help, Tilly quietened them all. 'Leave lass alone, she knaws what she's doing and, aye, needs to do it. She's occupying herself every minute of the day. I think she's doing a good job in taking care of not letting her emotions run away with her, in the best way she knaws how – in the kitchen, where she loves to be. So, though it's hard, we're best to leave her be.'

Thankfully, they all agreed.

'I suggest a walk. It's a lovely morning now, and we can walk down the lane. Expectant mothers need plenty of fresh air.'

'Oh, Peggy. Take your nurse's hat off, love, and relax. By, there's none better to take care of me Beth than you, but today, you can have a day off.'

'Eeh, Tilly, I didn't mean—'

'I knaw, love, and you're not stepping on me toes. I meant what I said, there's none better, and I agree a walk is the thing, but I just want you to be yourself – part of the family, not just Beth's nurse.'

'Ta, Tilly. I've allus said it, as many more have – you're an angel. Oh, I knaw as you had times when your halo slipped badly, but you've a good soul and that shows.'

'We'll not mention me naughty times, if you don't mind, Peggy.'

Peggy looked mortified, but Tilly burst out laughing. 'By, I had some an' all, didn't I? Don't worry, me lasses knaw all about me and how I slipped a few times. Come on, coats on, everyone. We're going for that walk.'

Along the lane there was silence but for the winter-stayers of the bird families tweeting away and the grinding of pebbles under the wheels of Beth's wheelchair as Tommy pushed her. The mist had cleared away, leaving a world of white as the heavy frost lay like icing on everything. It looked magical, with the sun making it twinkle as if inlaid with a thousand lights. Lacy cobwebs hung between branches in the hedges, all picked out in white and making an intricate pattern.

A hand came into Tilly's and she looked into Babs's lovely face. 'Eeh, this is a little bit of heaven, ain't it, Ma?'

'It is, Babs.'

Tilly didn't press any more conversation out of Babs, but allowed her her thoughts. She just walked at the pace she knew Babs was comfortable with and left her to chat when she wanted to.

Peggy walked close to Beth. In the few months she had been her nurse she had become very fond of Beth. Tilly wondered if Peggy sought the love of those that she cared for to make up for not having anyone special in her life, but didn't dwell on it, as Peggy was just Peggy and no one would have her any different.

As she thought this the peace was shattered by Tommy calling out, 'What in Jaysus's name?'

They'd rounded a bend and found their way barred by a flock of Tommy's sheep trotting towards them as if they too were out for a Christmas morning walk.

'Will you be for taking the wheelchair, Peggy? I've to see to getting these sheep back into their pen.'

Peggy looked only too pleased to take charge of Beth again and Tilly realised she'd relinquished her duty not really wanting to. She sighed. Peggy was a nurse through and through and even saw today as a day when she was needed. Tilly smiled as she turned to Babs. 'Go and stand with Peggy and Beth, lass. I'll have to help Tommy.'

The sheep had other ideas than having their morning walk disturbed and went every way except for back into their pen, regardless of all the shooing she did and the cursing Tommy did. But though feeling out of breath, the sound of Babs's, Beth's and Peggy's laughter almost drowning out the noise of the bleating and angry protests of the sheep kept Tilly going.

But then another sound filled the air – the sound of a cranky old engine revving far too much for whatever gear it was in. Fear took the place of any frivolity that Tilly had felt as Molly's car came into view. Disastrously, Molly was driving – something she'd never mastered – and now she seemed unable to stop the car. Tilly saw the look of horror on her face, but no sign of it registering with her that unless she braked, she would hurtle full tilt into the sheep. Tilly wanted to scream, but no sound came as the space around her was suddenly filled with screams coming from the girls and the sheep as bodies of the animals were tossed into the air and blood seemed to rain from heaven.

Gasping in the air that had been taken from her lungs, Tilly looked back in horror as the car passed within inches of her and swerved around the girls before going on to two wheels and toppling onto its side on the grass verge. 'Molly! Molly! Oh God, naw, naw!'

Peggy reached the car before Tilly did. Both were met with Molly shouting, 'I'm all right, it's Will who's hurt.' Her voice rose. 'Help him, someone help him! Oh God, please help Will!'

Tilly's blood ran cold. She didn't register that Tommy wasn't around the scene, but tugged at the car door for all she was worth. When it opened, she and Peggy helped Molly out. 'Eeh, Molly, Molly, lass.' Clinging on to Molly, whose legs seemed incapable of holding her up, Tilly helped her away from the car, leaving Peggy to see to Will.

'Where's . . . where's Tommy? I hit him, Tilly, oh, Tilly, I hit him!'

'Naw.' The word gasped from Tilly. 'Naw, not me Tommy.'

'Ma, he's all right. Tommy's all right. His leg is hurt, but otherwise, well, he's in pain, but that's not . . . Oh, Ma, come over and help me.'

How Babs had got to Tommy's side, Tilly didn't know. The last time she'd seen her she'd been standing by the wheelchair. 'Will you be all right a mo, Molly?'

'Aye. I'm sorry, Tilly, lass. I – I didn't expect . . . Oh, Tilly, I want me Will.'

'He'll be all right, Peggy'll look after him. I have to get to Tommy. Sit quietly and try to keep yourself together. Naw one's to blame.'

Bewildered sheep milled around Tilly's legs as she tried to get to Tommy. When she did, she found he wasn't all right but was writhing in agony, his leg twisted at an angle she didn't think anyone's leg could get into. 'Tommy, me Tommy. How could this happen?'

'Ma. I need to straighten Tommy's leg. Now, this is going to hurt him, but if I don't do it, the leg will die and he will lose it. It's broken and that will stop the blood flow. I need you to hold him. Put sommat between his teeth for him to bite on. Oh, if only we had sommat with us that I could sterilise the wound with afore I start, there's so much danger of infection.'

'I – I have me flask on me, Babs, it – it's for being in me coat pocket. It has the good whiskey in it that I – I like to take a drop of on Christmas morning.'

'Oh, Tommy, me love.' Tilly felt at a loss as to what to say as she rummaged for the flask. Finding it, she had the urge to take a long swig of it, but handed it to Babs. At that moment it registered with her that Babs was kneeling on the cold, damp grass, and had taken off her shawl which she'd worn over her coat. Concern for Babs vied with her being the only hope that Tommy had. 'Babs, are you all right, lass? Don't hurt yourself, think of your babby.'

'Ma, I'm a nurse. What I'm about to do, I've done a hundred times, and, aye, I've seen the consequences of it not being done by the time a wounded soldier got to the ambulance train. I ain't going to let that happen to Tommy. Me babby'll be fine, he's made of strong stuff; his daddy was a hero and so will he be.'

This was the lightest Babs had ever spoken about her Rupert, but it came at a moment when Tilly couldn't really register the small element of healing that had taken place in Babs. She stayed quiet as she watched Babs pour what would have been nectar to herself at this moment over Tommy's gashed leg. As she did, and the blood cleared, a piece of bone could be seen protruding through Tommy's skin.

'Give the rest to Tommy, Ma. It will help him through what I have to do.'

'No, I'm not for needing it, Babs, keep it in case someone else requires it. Is everyone for being all right?'

Tilly patted his arm in a soothing gesture. 'Molly is, Tommy, but we don't knaw about Will yet. Peggy's with him.'

'Oh, Tilly, me wee lass. We were so happy. Is it that God can't bear to see us so? I feel that we turn one corner, only to be kicked in the stomach when we turn the next.'

Tilly couldn't answer him; she felt she was in the grip of a great force and wanted to scream and scream. A voice behind her steadied her. Beth had managed to manoeuvre her wheelchair over to them. 'Ma, Babs will need some splints. Go and find something in the hedgerows. Give me your shawl, Babs, I'll tear it along with mine to make bandages for you. Keep some of the whiskey to sterilise the part of the shawl that will be near to the wound.'

Tilly marvelled at these daughters of hers, and yet felt a pang of pain in her heart at not really knowing them. Before her were two professional nurses, doing a job they had been trained to do. Her pride in them was tempered by the fact that she'd had no hand in shaping them. And that caused a feeling of hatred for Jasmine and Roman to rise in her. At this moment, she could cheerfully kill them both.

Her search took her near to the overturned car. Molly still sat on the grass as if in a daze, and Tilly could see that she'd gone into shock. This worried her, and she called out to her girls. 'Molly needs help. Beth, Babs! I think she's gone into shock.'

Beth called back, 'Make sure she's warm, Ma, wrap her in your coat as well as her own. There's not much more that we can do at the moment, just hurry and get her warmed up.'

Obeying Beth's command, Tilly quickly took off her coat and lay it on the ground. Easing Molly down onto it, she wrapped it around her. 'Eeh, lass, hold on. Hold on. We're here, we just have to see to Tommy and Will.'

Not daring to look to see how Peggy was doing with helping Will, Tilly hurried along the road, praying that she would see something. Molly's voice called her back. 'Tilly, in the trunk. You'll find sommat in me trunk.'

Tilly could see the trunk that was used for carrying luggage had become detached from the back of the car and lay open on the ground. Inside it, she found some lengths of wood. They lay among a tangled mess of leather. Will was a saddlemaker by trade and was skilful at making anything out of leather, and Tilly and Molly sold some of his beautiful designs in the shop for him – footstools, picture frames and lamp stands made of glass with sleeves of leather cut into lacy patterns. He must have packed his materials with the wood. Grabbing the wood, she ran back to Babs and Beth. What she saw terrified her. 'Tommy . . . Tommy, naw!'

'It's all right, Ma. We've put him to sleep using a gypsy method.' Sweat poured from Babs's face as she tugged at Tommy's leg. 'We've only seconds to complete this before he wakes. Though the pain will be so bad that he might pass out again with the force of it.'

Tilly knew what they were talking about. A member of a gypsy clan had once used the same method to make her pass out by putting pressure on a particular point of her neck. But she'd learnt since that it was a dangerous thing to do and her anxiety increased as she saw the greyness of Tommy's face.

Suddenly the leg cracked, and in an instant looked normal again. 'Here, Babs, I've a bandage ready.'

Babs took the makeshift bandage soaked in whiskey that Beth handed to her and wound it around the open wound. 'Pass the splints, Ma. By, they're perfect. Made for the job.'

With these in place, Tommy opened his eyes. A moan came from him, then turning his head, he vomited.

'Tommy, Tommy, lad, it's done. Me girls have tended to you; you're going to be all right.'

'Let's turn him over. Help me, Ma. We don't want him to choke.'

When they turned him, Tommy was sick once more. Tilly rubbed his back and spoke gently to him. 'Me Tommy. You're all right. Oh, Tommy, I love you, I'll take care of you.'

A shout from Peggy had them all looking up. Tilly could feel the tension. 'Will's all right. He were knocked out, but he's come to now. I think his arm's broken.'

'Go to him, Babs, be for seeing to him, for the pain of a break is a powerful pain. I don't know what it is that you've done, but me pain has lessened and is just bearable now. Do that for Will.'

'I will, Tommy, if Ma can help me up. The weight of me babby is pulling me down.'

Tilly heaved Babs to a standing position.

'Eeh, Ma, me legs have gone dead. Hold on to me for a minute while I shake them back to life.'

'Come here so that I can rub them for you, Babs.' As Tilly helped Babs to Beth's side, Beth told them that she had some painkiller in her bag. 'It's not strong enough to have had an effect on the pain caused by what you had to do, but it might help Tommy now.'

'I'll give it to him, Babs,' Tilly said. 'You go to Will.'

Glad to have something to do that would help Tommy, Tilly found the medicine and left the twins. As she did, she heard them asking each other if they were all right, and as she turned, she saw them in a hug. Her heart lifted. It seemed that no matter what, her girls had a strong bond – one that she knew would overcome everything in the end.

FOUR

Babs

Babs felt a deep sense of weariness in her body by the time she got to Will. And yet, she had to find the strength to help him.

With Will having already been unconscious, she couldn't render him so again. Somehow, he would have to bear the pain.

The next few minutes were filled with Will's screams as she straightened his arm to marry the bones, and Molly's sobs as she couldn't bear the agony of hearing him in such pain. But though tortured, Will bore up well, telling her to ignore him and to do what she had to do.

Covered in blood, and exhausted not only from the effort of straightening two breaks but from the position she'd had to hold her heavy body in, Babs now found that she couldn't climb out of the car.

With her feet pressed against Will's passenger seat, Babs didn't know how long she could keep herself from falling onto him. But then with the dying down of the cries and only Molly's sobs breaking the silence, a new sound could be heard.

'There's a car coming along the lane. I'll run to the bend to warn it.'

Relief filled Babs at these words from Peggy and she prayed that whoever it was could help them as she could feel her legs cramping.

'We have help, Babs, hold on. It's a delivery van, father and son. They're on a mission to get a Christmas tree for a poor family they met at church this morning. A bit late, but like the driver said, it seemed a kind thing to do, and others were seeing to the family having food and the like. Anyroad, they're here now and are going to help you out first.'

'Ta, Peggy, please tell them to hurry.'

'We're here, lass, you'll be all right now. Me name's Pete, and me son here is Clifford, but we call him Cliff. Now, can you give me your hand?'

'I daren't let go as me legs will give way. I don't mind if you put your arms around me and heave me out, Pete, but I'm a bit of a bulk as I'm having a babby.'

'All right, lass. Hold on. I'll be as gentle as I can. By, you're a brave lass. The woman who flagged us down told us what you have done. Sounds like you've saved lives today.'

Though it was uncomfortable being dragged out and then lowered to the ground, Babs was glad to at last be standing on her shaky legs. She clung to the bottom of the car to steady herself. But then jumped when an arm linked into hers. Turning, she looked into the handsome face of a man of about her own age. 'Let me help you, lass. I've put me coat down for you to sit on.'

'Awe, thanks, but I only need a minute. Then I'm to see to me patients getting settled in your van. Well, that is if you'll help us to get them home. We only live up the lane. It ain't far.'

'Aye, we'll help you. By, you and your sister, I've never seen two women so alike.'

'We're identical twins.' Babs found him easy to chat to. 'I'm a nurse, and so is me sister. I called those injured me patients out of habit, but they're much more than that.' She told them who everyone was. 'Now, I need to get to Molly. She's showing signs of going into shock and that can be as dangerous as a broken bone.'

'I don't want to tell you your job, lass, but I reckon the best thing is for us to get you all home and then go for a doctor.'

'Aye, you're right, ta.'

With this, it wasn't long before Cliff and his dad had the car righted, and Will lifted out. By this time, Babs had recovered and rose from the ground. She wandered over to Beth and watched as the two men soon had the injured in the van along with Ma and Molly.

Babs held Beth's hand. 'Eeh, Beth, that such a thing should happen when we were all so happy.'

Beth squeezed her hand. 'When you're upset, Babs, I still get a feeling of everything collapsing around me.'

'Aye, I knaw.' Babs patted her arm. 'We should never have been parted, and I'm sorry as I went off. And I'm sorry to the heart of me that you've landed up like this, Beth. I knaw how much it affected you when you couldn't help me just then, but you did, you knaw. You kept a level head and talked through the procedures and that helped. It confirmed to me that I were doing the right thing.'

'We'll get through, Babs. Our bond is too strong for anyone to break it.'

Babs knew this was so, but she also knew that they could never be as close as they were. Not while Beth clung on to Jasmine and Roman.

Peggy interrupted them. 'I'm going to push you back home, Beth. I won't leave you.'

Beth smiled, and Babs felt a gladness in her heart that Beth had Peggy. She would always be safe with her by her side. 'Ta, Peggy. I have to go with Tommy and Will to take care of them and I'm worried about Molly an' all.'

Cliff had joined them. 'I'll push the wheelchair. We'll soon have you back in the warm, lass. But I'll help you get into the van first, Babs.'

As she walked with him, he asked, 'It's all right to call you Babs, ain't it? I heard the others calling you that.'

'Aye, it's fine and ta for all you're doing for us.'

'Glad to help. Now, I'm afraid that there's only room in the back as I put the other two women in the front. But there's a seat in there and the two men are lying on the pallets we strapped them to. I'll give you a hand up.'

Babs found Cliff to be the gentlest of men, even though his stature made him appear as if he trained to be a strong man. He had dark hair and eyes, and his face was squarish with high cheekbones, which gave him a very attractive look. Taller than her by a few inches, he gave the impression that you were safe with him by your side. A nice feeling for Babs as with Beth not really able to help and all of the others either hurt badly or in shock, it was good to have someone take charge. Cliff made it seem that what had happened was an everyday thing in his life and that everything was going to be fine. The thought occurred to Babs that if only it was the case. But now, they had even more to contend with. *And this being me first Christmas with Ma and Beth an' all. Life just isn't fair.*

Eliza came running out when they reached home. Through the windows of the van Babs saw her Ma running forward and gathering Eliza close to her. Babs couldn't wait to be let out so that she could help Ma, who she knew was using all her strength to overcome her shock and fear to reassure Eliza.

As soon as Babs stepped out of the van, Eliza broke away from her ma and came running to her. 'Babs, where's Pappy?'

'He's in the van. When Cliff arrives, that's the son of the driver, he will help his da to get Tommy and Will out and then they are going for the doctor. Tommy's all right, love, you're to be a very brave girl for him. He has a lot of worries to contend with about how he is to manage the farm and everything, besides being upset that everyone's Christmas is spoilt.'

'Eeh, Babs, that such a thing should happen.'

'I knaw, but you and I can cope, can't we? We can take charge along with Ma and make everything as it should be. The doctor will give some painkillers to Tommy and Will, and with that and a couple of stiff whiskeys, I'll bet we'll soon have some laughter around the place, just as it should be – a proper Christmas, but with a hitch. I hope the dinner is coming along and you've not been shirking.'

'I've worked me fingers to the bone, I have, Babs. It'll be ready by three o'clock.'

'Good girl. Eeh, I've said it before, but you're a lovely sister to have.' Eliza clung to her. Babs had seen the tears brimming in her eyes, and the effort she was making to stop them flowing, but she didn't mention them. Her battle with her tears was Eliza's own, and if she wanted to hide them, then Babs would respect that. Better that she gave Eliza things to do. 'Right, me little darling, this ain't spoilt our Christmas, we'll get that underway as soon as we can, but I heard of a family that Cliff and his da were on a mission to get a Christmas tree for as they've got nowt. They won't be able to do that now, so I want you to get together a basket of stuff for them. Folk from the church are taking some, but I doubt there'll be owt like your cakes and bread, and if you've any of your old toys anywhere, I want you to scoot around and find them – well, them as you don't want to keep. Can you do that, eh?'

'I can, Babs, but I'll have to ask Ma about owt of our Ivan's. She ain't shown any sign of parting with it yet.'

'I'll talk to her. You get started, lass.'

'Can I see Pappy first?'

'Aye. Speak to him through the open van doors.'

'What if it makes me cry? As I'm wanting to.'

'He'll knaw as you love him then and care about him, won't he?'

Eliza smiled up at Babs, and Babs's heart warmed. She loved this half-sister so much; her misgivings in the beginning were completely dispelled now.

Hurrying to help Ma with Molly, Babs saw Beth, Peggy and Cliff arriving. She waved, then carried on her way. 'Are you all right, Ma?'

'Aye. Well, I would be if I could stop shaking and feeling sick. But Molly's not feeling well, lass.'

'Awe, poor Molly. Get her inside, Ma, take her to the living room, but get the others into the best room. I'll need to get Molly to undress so that I can check her over. We have to make sure she hasn't got injuries that we don't knaw of yet. Check that all the fires are stoked well, and if you've any bandages, iodine or owt as will help me to dress wounds, then that will help an' all.'

'I'll do all I can, love.'

'Oh, and Ma . . .' Babs asked then about the toys.

'Eeh, lass . . . I – I don't knaw . . . I . . .'

An idea came to Babs. She'd long thought it wasn't good for her ma to keep all Ivan's things as if he hadn't left the house. 'Look, Ma, I reckon as this is Ivan's way of reaching out to you. He wants you to help those less fortunate, aye, and in his name an' all. There's a lot you can do, and you can start by helping this poor family who have nowt this Christmas.'

'Awe, Babs, you're right. Why didn't I think of that? And Ivan was a hoarder, you knaw. There's books, and there's toys that his pappy made for him out of wood, and, well, all his clothes an' all from when he were about ten – a trunk of them. He wouldn't let me throw owt away.'

'That's good, Ma. Just let Eliza knaw, but tell her to send only things that'll be good to tide them over for Christmas, and we'll sort the rest out later. Now, once you have Molly settled and have done the rest of what I've asked of you, get the kettle on – everyone will need a cup of hot sweet tea, aye, and maybe a tot of whiskey with it an' all.'

Ma laughed, and it sounded good. Babs had always found that folk reacted better to any situation if they were involved in trying to put it right.

When Beth wheeled herself over to her sister, Babs told her what she'd tasked their ma with.

'That's good to hear. I agree with you: it's not good for Ma to keep everything like a shrine. She just needs to keep a few special things and let the rest do others some good. So, what if I go with Molly, Babs? If she undresses and lies on the settee, I can manage to examine her.'

Babs knew this was something Beth really wanted to do, and that she would be able to, so she nodded. 'Right, I'll supervise the moving of the patients then. See you in a mo, Beth.'

As they sat sipping their tea, all wounds dressed – Molly was found to have a few open cuts, many bruises and a swollen wrist, which they had been able to determine was a bad sprain, and Will to have a cut on the back of his head as well as a gash on his leg – Babs found time to thank Cliff.

'I'm only glad as we came along. Think nowt of it. Me da won't be long fetching the doctor. And he said as he'll drop those things off to the family. They'll make up some for him not getting them a tree.'

Babs was sitting on the arm of the sofa that Tommy lay on and Cliff on a chair next to her that had been brought in from the dining room.

'It were kind of you to remember them too, and at such a time as this,' Cliff continued. 'Naw one else was able to sort out things for the kids, other than food, at such short notice. We didn't knaw the family. The mother was sat outside church waiting for the congregation to come out and approached us then.'

'I wish we'd known sooner; there's a lot we can do. Is the woman on her own? I mean, has she lost her husband?'

'I don't knaw. But I knaw where she lives; I can take you to her, if you like. I did see that she had a couple of lads of around ten and eleven with her, though, and the thought's just occurred to me that maybe your da could do with a hand and the eldest might be useful to him. It'd be the answer to your da's dilemma and would help the family.' Cliff turned to face her then and lowered his voice. 'Speaking of husbands, is your man fighting overseas?'

'Naw, he ... well, I — I naw longer have him.'

'Awe, I'm sorry, I shouldn't have asked. I'm a praying man and will pray for you, and ask that you're helped to cope.'

'Ta, I could do with some prayers. I send plenty up, but they're rarely answered. But don't worry about asking, you're bound to be curious. Which I am about you. Have you not been conscripted?'

'Aye, but I weren't medically fit — I've a weak chest. I'm all right at the moment, but I can have bouts when breathing is very difficult for me. I'd have given owt to go. I were prepared, like all me mates were, to lay me life down, but it weren't to be. Me da's a tree feller — well, not just that, but a healer of trees an' all.' He laughed then and said, 'Like you, only a nurse to nature. He works a lot in the Bowland Forest. I help him, but I'd rather do war work. I just haven't found owt as suits me condition.'

'Awe, I'm sorry to hear that. I expect you have to explain yourself a lot as it's the first thing folk think of if they see a fella of your age still at home.'

'Aye, I do, but I don't mind, as I'd be asking an' all if I saw one. You knaw, it's just occurred to me. Me da don't allus need

47

me help, especially in the winter. I could come and give a hand around here, if your da wants me to, and if he takes on the young lad that I were telling you about, then I could give them a lift. I've me own car you knaw.'

'Ta, Cliff. We'll manage for a couple of days, as Ma knaws the ropes and me and Eliza can help her, but the things we can't do will pile up if naw one sees to them, so I'm sure Tommy – he's me stepda by the way – will take your offer up. I'll ask him later. He's enough to contend with at the moment. Though, come to think of it, settling his worries might help him.'

With this, Babs turned towards Tommy. Though quiet, his face was etched with pain and Babs wished that the doctor would come soon.

When she told Tommy what she and Cliff had been talking about, he smiled. 'That is for easing me some. It seems that the Lord has thought on, for now he's after sending me the help that I'm going to need.'

Speaking directly to Cliff, he thanked him, and then engaged him in conversation about what he knew about farming. It turned out that he was someone who could turn his hand to most things and had always wanted to work on a farm. 'The fresh air is good for me lungs. I love being outdoors and working with me da, but I've allus said to me da that if I could get to work on a farm, that would suit me better, because I love farming.'

The doctor arrived then and the Sunday best room became a hive of activity as Babs shooed all but her and Beth and Will out through the door. 'You take Molly into the living room, Ma, and wait with her. We'll update the doctor on what we

48

have done so far, and if he wants to examine Molly, it will be better if she is ready.'

The doctor was full of praise for Babs and thought her work excellent. He'd been able to determine that there was a good blood flow to both Tommy's leg and Will's arm, and applied fresh and much firmer splints to both. Everyone else he declared as being fine, though prescribed painkillers – milder ones for Molly and stronger for Will and Tommy. And after taking a very large tipple of whiskey – the amount directed by himself – he set off, a little wobbly in his walk and with a much redder nose than when he arrived.

Cliff stood near to Babs as they saw the doctor off. They giggled together as the doctor's car swerved this way and that and Cliff joked, 'Let's hope that he doesn't meet anyone on the lane, though this being Christmas Day, there won't be many about.'

'Aye, and with the noise his car is making, they'd hear him coming a mile off . . . Oh! I just thought, the sheep!'

'Naw need to worry. Da said that most were back in their pen when he passed, though there was a couple on the verge not moving. He stopped and checked, but the poor things were dead, so he brought them back with him. We unloaded them while you were with the doctor and your Eliza told us to store them in the far barn where it is coldest. She's a good head on her that one. She said as how they would freeze in this weather and keep fresh till they could get them to the butcher. I were very impressed with her. Anyroad, me da said as we'll stop off and check the rest on our way back. We'll report back if we see that any need help.'

'Ta. You've done so much for us, I don't knaw what we would have done without you. I hope as we haven't spoilt your Christmas. Your ma will wonder where you've got to.'

'Me ma died two months ago, and me and Da haven't done owt about Christmas. We went to church, and have a bit of a stew left that I made yesterday and that's it.'

'Oh, naw. I am sorry. Look, why don't you stay with us for the day? Eliza has cooked for a dozen or more as it is, so you won't make us short. It'd be grand to have you and would be our way of thanking you.'

'Awe, that *would* be grand. But make sure as your ma won't mind first, and tell your da that we'll still go and check on the sheep.'

She didn't know why but it lifted Babs to think of Cliff staying for the day. He wasn't without troubles to bring to the table, although they all had those, but somehow it brightened her a little to know that she was going to have his company. She liked him, he was easy to talk to – someone who wasn't involved in all that was happening, or anything that had gone before. Yes, despite the accident, this could turn out to be a happy Christmas.

FIVE

Beth

'Eeh, lass, I knaw as it's only February, but it's lovely out there. The sea's like a millpond and there's some warmth in the sun. Do you want to go for a walk along the prom to see your ma? It's her day for running the shop, ain't it?'

'It is, but I don't feel up to it, Peggy. I have this niggly pain in my back.'

'Oh? Is it there all the time, or coming and going?'

'Coming and going, but when it's there it takes my breath away at times.'

'Well, lass, I'd say as you're in the beginnings of labour. It can start with a pain in your back.'

'Really? Oh, Peggy, I thought I had three weeks to go? Will the baby be all right?'

'Aye, they have a mind of their own, and they knaw when it's time to make an appearance. We can only work out an approximate date for when they might arrive but it's not set in stone.'

'But what shall I do? Should I get back into bed. I want Ma here and Babs and, oh, Peggy, I want Jasmine too.'

'Well, you knaw as that ain't going to happen, lass. It should be your ma and your sister by rights, but you've to choose. Them or Jasmine, as them three ain't going to be in the same room together and you knaw it.'

Beth hung her head. She didn't want to hurt anyone. She loved them all. Oh, she knew that Jasmine had done wrong in stealing her and Babs from their ma, but she had loved her like a ma would and had brought her and Babs up. Well, at least until Babs ran away.

Beth sighed. Why couldn't they all accept each other? Why couldn't Ma forgive Jasmine? And Babs, how could she hate Jasmine and Roman so much? She too had known their love as a child.

But then, whatever it was that Babs went through after running away from the gypsy camp had changed her. *She's no longer the sister I knew – caring of me and of my feelings. She isn't accepting or understanding, but judgemental.*

Maybe if Babs could tell them all that had happened to her, it would help her and help their relationship to get back on a proper footing. But even broaching the subject made her clam up.

Not that any of this changed the love that Beth had for Babs. She just wished that she and Ma would try to understand how she felt, and allow her to live her own life and be accepting of her wishes. Sighing, she rubbed her back. She knew in her heart it should be her ma and Babs attending her, but how could she reject Jasmine?

'Maybe it would be better if I told none of them and went through the birth with just you, Peggy. I can say that it happened suddenly and that I had no time.'

Peggy's disdain hung heavily in the air. She rarely took sides, or counselled for or against, but Beth knew what was in her mind. She knew that Peggy didn't approve of Jasmine, or Beth's association with her.

When Beth had taken Peggy on, she'd explained to her what had happened to her and, as anyone would be, she'd been appalled at Jasmine and Roman's actions. If Jasmine came around, she would make herself busy in the kitchen, and wouldn't show her face until Jasmine had left.

'Lass, I'm not sure that I can cope on me own. Oh, aye, I've attended many births, but allus there's been another woman there to fetch and carry for me, or the woman in labour has been able to do things, but lass, you can't, and with your limitations, you may need more help than I can give. You should have your ma here, and it's her right to be an' all.'

Beth felt as though the two worlds she lived in were colliding and she wasn't strong enough to ward off the consequences. *Oh, Henry, my darling husband, if only you were here. How am I going to cope?*

'Eeh, lass, naw tears now. It's said that a babby born into tears knaws nowt but sorrow. I'll tell you what, I have a friend who's helped me on occasion. I'll go and see her and ask her to pop in during the day to see how things are progressing and do owt as I need her to do, then, when it's time, she'll stay with us and keep kettle boiling and do as I ask of her.'

Beth didn't want to be left alone and wanted to ask if it was all right if she went too, but then a sudden pain clutched her, this time in her stomach as well as her back, which had her bending forward and gasping out loud.

'Eeh, me lass, you could be further on than I thought. Let me nip along to your ma. That'll only take me a mo.'

Beth couldn't protest; neither did she want to. She wanted to scream out for her ma to come, and all thoughts of Jasmine faded as yet another pain began to build inside her. 'Yes, yes, run, Peggy, run as fast as you can.'

'Good lass. But by, me running days are gone. I'll see who's passing by, and if there's anyone quicker than me who would go for me. There's a fair few taking strolls along the promenade.'

Peggy wasn't gone a moment, but when she returned, Beth was so glad to see her. The sweat stood out on her body, soaking her clothes, which felt as though they were restricting her breathing and made her inclined to rip them off. She felt so helpless. Always her inability to walk frustrated her, but at this moment, she wanted to scream against the injustice of what had happened to her.

'The milkman was out there. He left his horse and cart tethered and ran like the wind, so I don't expect your ma will be long. Let's get you sorted, Beth.'

It always marvelled Beth how Peggy handled manoeuvring her. She was a gem, and Beth had grown to love her. Wheeling her through to the bedroom, it seemed to Beth, through a haze of gripping pains, that Peggy soon had her onto the bed and was taking the clothes off her that only an hour or so before she'd helped her to get into.

Beth tried to do what she could for herself, and loved Ivan's bath chair that Ma had given her. It enabled her to get around her home, which she couldn't do with her own cumbersome wheelchair. Not that she really looked upon this flat as her home. A living room, kitchen and two bedrooms, one hers and one Peggy's, and all furnished in a style that wasn't her own – brown, heavy, practical, and not at all appealing. Relieved only by the square red rug in the middle of the tiled floor, and by the floral cushions. The latter Beth had bought from her ma's shop to cheer the place up a bit as the family who owned the house had obviously gone for practicality rather than comfort.

Beth's heart wanted to be in her ma's lovely farmhouse, surrounded by cosy homeliness and with her family around her. She always longed for the one day a week that she was picked up and taken there, and she lived for the days when Peggy walked her to her ma's shop and she sat helping to make baskets – a task she loved.

So much so that when Henry finally did come home, she intended to set up in business herself, in Margate, which was where Henry worked. And where they would live. A part of her never wanted to leave Blackpool, but she couldn't ask Henry to give up his work for her and come to work in the small hospital that Blackpool had. *Oh, Henry, Henry, my love. I so want you here by my side.*

As another pain took her the door knocker rapped. Scrunched up against the force of the agony she was in, Beth tried to listen for her ma's voice, but shock at what she heard trembled through her.

'It is that I know my Beth is needing me. I heard her voice calling to me.'

'Naw, Jasmine, you have to leave. You've caused enough heartache. Tilly is on her way. She's Beth's rightful ma, not you, you thieving rotten cow.'

A cry from Jasmine had Beth calling out, 'Jasmine, I'm all right. Peggy, don't talk to her like that. But please go, Jasmine, please, I'll get word to you later.'

'No! My Beth, don't cast me away at such a time, my heart is breaking. I need to be with you. Is it that the baby is coming?'

'Yes, but please do this one thing for me. My ma is on the way. She mustn't catch you here, please, Jasmine.'

Another voice came to her then, and Beth felt distraught. 'What do you think you're doing here, Jasmine? Go, get out! Me ma's not two minutes away. If she sees you, she'll break. You have a lot to answer for, you and Roman. I could beat you with me fists. I hate you!'

'No, Babs, my Babs. My little girl, I have longed to see you. Don't! Don't cast me out.'

'Babs, Babs, please. Oh God, someone come – the baby, my baby, it's coming!'

With this, they were all by her side.

Screaming from the pain that gripped her, Beth didn't care any more. 'Help me. Help me!'

'I have a potion, little one. It is that it will lessen the pain and relax the muscles that need to contract. Don't fight this, my Beth, go with it, help your *bambino* to come into this world.'

A pain-filled voice blotted Jasmine's pleas out. 'What? Naw! What's she doing here? Awe, Beth, how could you? How could you?'

'Ma! Ma, I didn't. Don't leave . . .' The words disappeared in a pain more severe than any of those Beth had suffered before.

'Right, all of you, stop fighting and help Beth.' Peggy's commanding voice silenced them all. 'I'll get this leg. Tilly, get yourself around the other side of the bed and climb onto it

56

and get hold of Beth's other leg. Bend it and push it towards her so that when she bears down, she has our help. Babs, get the kettle boiling – we'll need a load of hot water ready. This babby's about to enter the world and I don't want to hear you lot squabbling as its introduction.'

'Please let her have me potion. I promise it will be helping her. Please.'

'Naw! Naw gypsy concoction's going to be administered while I'm in charge, ta very much. Now, do as everyone's asked you to do and leave, Jasmine. That's the best thing that you can do for Beth right now.'

Beth wanted to cry out against the treatment of Jasmine, and yes, she wanted the potion Jasmine offered. All her life, Jasmine had helped her with the medicines she made up from herbs and wild flowers, and Beth truly believed in such healing powers that Jasmine had. As another pain ripped through her she cried out, 'Let me have the potion! Jasmine, don't leave!'

Her ma said on a sob, 'Don't do this to me, Beth. Don't, not now, me darling girl.'

She wanted to say that she hadn't asked for Jasmine to come, but at that moment the urge to bear down was so strong that she couldn't speak. Pushing with all her might, she felt her muscles in her neck expand, and her head felt as if it would burst.

'It's coming! I can see its head. Eeh, Tilly, look at that hair, just like yours. Ha, another as is going to look like you, lass, it's only and *true* grandmother.'

Beth knew these words were aimed at Jasmine, but she couldn't do or say anything as she pushed again, and again, the third time on a scream as a ripping pain shot through her. 'Help me! The potion, please, please. I know it will help me.'

As she said this, she smelt Jasmine's violet perfume and knew she was near. She turned her head to see Jasmine leaning over offering her a bottle. But her ma turned and swiped it away, letting out a terrible screeching tirade of abuse at Jasmine, and kicking out at her, while still holding Beth's leg. Beth felt that her heart would break. To see these two women that she loved and who were so dear to her in such a state nearly undid her.

She registered Jasmine leaving the room, and called out to her, 'I'm sorry, Jasmine, so sorry.'

But then her strength left her, and she flopped back onto the pillow.

'Naw, lass, don't give up. One more push and I'll get the babby's head and be able to help your child into the world. You can do it, Beth. Forget everything else, concentrate on bringing yours and Henry's babby into the world.'

'Aye, Beth. I'm sorry, lass, I'm sorry. Please, Beth, we'll sort it all out afterwards, but get your child born.'

At this from Ma, Beth knew that nothing would ever be sorted out between her and Jasmine, and if anything, it was all much worse than it had been. An arm came around her and she looked into Babs's face. 'Come on, me Beth, we can do this. Let me help you. By, I've to do the same soon and here I was thinking that I'd be first.'

Gripping Babs's hand, Beth once more felt a pain building. She gasped against the intensity of it. 'Help me to sit up again, Babs, its co – oo – ming!'

'Good, lass. Eeh, I've got him – aye, it's a lad!' Peggy's cry sounded triumphant. 'I'll just get him to take his first breath, hang on there.' In no time a cry filled the room and Beth's heart swelled. 'Oh, Ma, Ma.' Sobs racked her body as her ma held her, rocking her backwards and forwards.

'My Beth, my Beth.'

'Now then, none of that, Tilly, Only happy tears. Let's give lad a happy welcome. By, he's bonny. You'd never think as he'd been squeezed by sommat akin to a vice!'

Beth heard her ma laugh out loud at this from Peggy, and a giggle bubbled up inside her. Babs's body rocked with laughter as she held her, and Beth knew a happiness like none she'd ever known soar through her.

'Here you are, Beth, lass. He needs a bath, but you can hold him first. Rest him on your tummy, that will help to push the afterbirth out for you.'

Looking into the ruddy face of her son, Beth knew her world was almost complete. If Henry was here, she would have been whole, but as it was, she had their beautiful son in her arms and she felt how this moment joined them together even though they were apart.

'Right, Babs, get a pot of tea made.'

'It's already brewing, Peggy. And there's plenty of hot water for bathing Beth and the babby.'

At that moment, Beth felt the afterbirth arrive. Peggy massaged her stomach, saying she needed to make sure it was all out, then picked up the old newspaper it had landed on and handed it to Ma. 'Now, Tilly, put it on the fire, and count the cracks as it burns – that'll tell us how many children Beth's going to have.'

Her ma's laugh was the best sound that Beth had heard in a long time. She lay back trying to dispel from her mind the ugly scenes that had taken place. But they played over, as did the pain she knew Jasmine would be feeling. An urge came to her that she wanted to go to Jasmine, take her son to her, and let her perform the gypsy ritual over him, but she said nothing and clung on to him. Maybe he would bring about the bonding between Jasmine and her ma that she hoped for, but something told her that it wouldn't be so, as both would want equal shares of him and that, she knew, wouldn't happen.

As Peggy took her son from her, saying she was going to clean him, Beth turned to Tilly. 'So how many children am I going to have, Ma?'

'Oh . . . Eeh, lass, it cracked that many times, I couldn't count.'

An alarm rang inside Beth. She had the feeling that Ma wasn't telling the truth – not that it mattered as the whole thing was an old wives' tale anyway, and she knew that Henry wanted to have at least four children. At this moment, Beth didn't want any more, not to go through that again. But then another saying was that you soon forgot the pain. She wondered at this, and thought it was more likely to be that the joy a new baby brought made you not care about what you had been through to bring him into the world, and yes, she knew she would do it all again to get her precious bundle.

'Anyroad, what are you going to call him, lass?'

'Benedict, Ma. Henry asked me in one of his letters to call our son that after his late father, and I want Arthur after mine. So, Benedict Arthur Freeman. To be known as Benny.'

'Eeh, lass, that's lovely. A fitting honour to Henry's da, and to your own da. As I've told you many times, he was the loveliest man you could meet. Tommy has a lot of his ways. Happy in his life and his work. Nowt pleased your da more than being able to put bread on the table for his family. Eeh, and that were naw easy feat in them days.'

Beth thought of the struggle she remembered her ma had to put bread on the table after she lost Da, and suddenly she felt so very sorry for all her ma had been through. 'Ma, oh, Ma, I'm sorry. I missed you every day, I did. I love you, Ma, I love you.'

'I knaw as you do, lass. Don't take on.'

Her ma's arms came around her. Beth felt a tear plop onto her hair. 'Everything will be all right, Ma. I promise.'

It was then that they both became aware that Babs was missing as Peggy said, 'Eeh, lass is taking a long time with that tea. I'll go and see what's holding her up.'

'Naw, I'll go, Peggy. You're busy.'

Beth lay back on the pillows, but there was no time to rest as Benny let out a squawk and Peggy brought him over to her. 'There, he looks a lot better now, but eeh, he's a pair of lungs on him that one. I'll put him to your breast, Beth. The sooner they suckle the better, and it'll comfort him and encourage your milk to come in, lass.'

The feeling was like no other Beth had experienced as Benny suckled on her nipple. A little sore, but not only did the first liquid that would soon be milk flow into her son with the action, but her love did too, and she knew that she would protect him with her life.

Looking down at him, she smoothed his dark hair back off his forehead, and saw how like Henry he was. *If only I could share this moment with you, Henry, my darling. Keep safe, for us, Henry. Come back to us.*

SIX

Babs

Babs clung on to the side of the pot sink in the kitchen, trying to steady herself and control the emotions that were trembling through her. With the birth of Beth's son, so much of her pain had become raw again.

For some reason Cliff popped into her head. He came to the farm most days and had been a salve to her; he had a way with words that calmed her and helped her to see another way. She wished he was here now as she would cope better with his strength helping her. He never asked questions of her. It was as if he knew that she wasn't ready to talk, and yet she knew she would find it easy to tell him everything. It just didn't seem right to do so yet. They were still building a friendship – one that Babs instinctively knew would be special even though he was a man and she'd never had a close male friend before. But already, it sometimes felt like she was with Daisy when she was with Cliff as the companionship between them was just as easygoing. Lovely Daisy, who'd she'd met in the convent for wayward girls and who was now a nun, had been like a sister to her.

The door behind her opened and Ma's anxious voice asked, 'Babs? Oh, Babs, what is it?'

'Ma, I – I can't tell you, not now. I'll be all right. Let's get back to Beth. I'm sorry, I just needed a moment.'

'But you're crying, lass. Eeh, me love, you've a lot on your plate. You need to talk to us. Tell us what happened to you before you became a nurse and after. Let us share it with you, me Babs.'

'Aye, I do, Ma, and I will. But trying to hold meself together is taking all me energy. The tea's ready. Let's take it through.'

She watched her ma pick up the tray, but though she knew it was heavy, laden as it was with a full teapot, cups, milk and sugar, she couldn't offer to take it herself as she was afraid that she might drop it.

Babs hadn't shared everything that had happened to her with Ma yet, even though she'd been home for months now, but she knew the time was on her. She needed to talk of all she'd been through and of her lost baby, Mario, too, and make it so that Beth and Ma knew Rupert as if they'd met him in person. But she also needed to take heed of the pains that had begun a few minutes ago and not will them away as she'd been trying to do. She knew what they were, but she wasn't ready.

In one way she was, of course, as she and Beth and Ma had sat for hours knitting and sewing, and Ma and Beth had made wicker cots and Aunt Molly had lined them. And they'd made baskets for holding everything the babbies would need. But she didn't feel mentally ready to welcome her child.

Holding herself as upright as she could against the onslaught of yet another pain, Babs walked over to Beth. 'Eeh, he's bonny. Has he the look of Henry? He has our hair colour and dark eyes, but there the similarity ends.'

'He does, he's the image of Henry. Oh, Babs . . .'

'Awe, I knaw. Better than most, I knaw the pain of missing your man, Beth. But we've to be brave for our young 'uns, they'll need us now.'

'I know, but it's hard. I want nothing more than to see Henry walk in that door.'

Ma interrupted them, bringing the conversation round to practicalities. 'Look, babby's asleep now. Let me put him in his cot, and you have your cuppa. Then me and Peggy will wash you down and make you comfortable, Beth.'

'Thank you, Ma. That'll be a distraction, and something that I'm longing for. I feel all hot and bothered.'

'I'll fetch some nice warm water, Ma. I should manage that . . . Ooh . . .' A pain that took her breath away and had her clutching the end of the bed for support stopped Babs in her tracks.

'Babs! Eeh, Babs, what's to do, lass . . . ? Naw! Not you an' all?' Ma gave an astonished laugh.

'What! Your babby's coming an' all?' Babs looked up to nod her head as the pain subsided and nearly giggled as Peggy's and Ma's faces were a picture.

'Oh, Babs, Babs.'

'It's all right, Beth, don't fret.' With the pain now subsiding, Babs felt able to straighten herself. But another attacked her and bent her double again. 'Ooh, help me . . . Eeh, Beth, Ma, I'm sorry . . . I didn't mean . . .' Gasping against the ferocity of the pain, she cried out, 'God, help me – e – e!'

A frenzy of activity happened then and before she knew it, Babs was laid on the bed next to Beth. 'I can only hold your hand, Babs, but grip on as tight as you need to. Oh, Babs, I can't believe this. Both of us and on the same day!'

'Aye, and in the same bed an' all, and before I've had time to clean it up. It's like a production line as you hear about in them factories.' They all laughed at this from Peggy, who was busy putting on a clean pinny and seemed to be in her element.

Babs's own laughter relaxed her and she looked into her ma's beloved face on the one side of her and her lovely twin sister, Beth's, on the other and felt a sense of peace enter her. Rupert would have wished this for her as he couldn't be here, she knew that, and drew comfort from the thought. But as she did, another pain took her into its depth, and she cried out.

Barely aware of her clothes being removed, she wriggled against the restrictions Peggy was putting on her as she prepared her for the birth. *Be with me, Rupert. Get me through this, me darling.* The thought came to say to him that she would soon give him a son, but as it did, she knew that if the child was a girl, she would be equally happy. She just wanted it here and to be out of this pain. A pain she knew so well.

At the cry of her child, Babs's world splintered into the fragments that were happy and those that held deep sadness. Her body heaved a huge sob. She heard the words Peggy repeated about crying bringing sorrow down on her and the child and thought to herself that there could be no deeper sorrow than loss. Loss of her Rupert, and yes, she would let in the loss of her first born too.

Ma was holding her. 'Babs, me darling girl, don't, don't. Your babby's fine. You're fine, me little love.'

'Aye, you have a lovely boy, Babs.' These words from Peggy allowed a joy to filter into her. 'And he's a big 'un an' all. I'd say a couple of pounds heavier than Benny. He's lovely, look at him, love. Hold him, he needs you.'

Holding her arms out to take her son from Peggy, but unable to speak for the sobs racking her body, Babs felt a love surge through her and her heart swell with joy as she held little Rupert to her.

'Babs, what is it? Aye, I knaw as this moment's brought your Rupert to you and your heart is breaking, but there's sommat else, I knaw there is. I've known it these past months since you've been home. Tell us, darling, tell us.'

'Oh, Ma, Ma . . .'

'Is it my fault, Babs? Have I upset you?'

'Naw, Beth, naw.' Through her tears, Babs saw the image of Rupert etched on her son's face. 'Me little babby, I love you.'

A sigh came from her ma, who until then must have thought she was rejecting her baby, but she'd never do that, never. He was her world. *He is going to put me together again. Through him I'll be near to his da, and aye, near to me little Mario.*

With this thought, Babs was able to tell them all that had happened to her – the rape, her imprisonment, and finally, the birth and loss of her darling Mario.

All cried for her and with her. Ma, still kneeling on the bed beside her – the stance she'd taken during the birth – held her, rocking her as if she was a baby, her tears soaking Babs's hair. Beth held her hand, sobbing her sorrow at the pain her sister had been in and, Babs knew, for her own pain too. Peggy dabbed at her eyes, and as only she could, not being a member of the family, voiced her disdain of Jasmine

66

and Roman. 'Them bloody gypsies. Look what they caused! By, they need stringing up. I knaw what you went through, Tilly, everyone knew. All them as have known you talked about your courage, but now, you've to put up with still having them around.'

Though she agreed with this, Babs knew how hurt Beth would be by it and felt her flinch beside her as if someone had slapped her. 'Aye, they did wrong,' Babs said, 'but you've to remember, they never harmed us, and I truly believe as they thought they were doing right by us.'

'Don't.'

This from Ma cut into Babs. She stretched out her hand and took Ma's in hers. 'I'm not saying they did right, Ma, I hate them with a vengeance, but, well, I was just trying to help Beth out.'

Ma squeezed her hand and smiled a tight smile. Babs hated this division and knew there was only one way that it could be resolved, but she wondered if Beth would ever give Jasmine and Roman up.

Peggy cut into her thoughts. 'Eeh, I'm sorry, I let me anger run away with me. I had no right to speak me mind. Me tongue wags without me giving it permission to at times. Forgive me, Beth. I love you like me own, lass, and I wouldn't upset you. I just had a fit of temper on me for a moment.'

Beth sighed. Her cheeks were unusually red, and she looked lost. Babs swallowed hard as she handed her baby to Beth in an attempt to lighten the atmosphere. 'Here, little one, this is your lovely Aunty Beth.'

Beth smiled a weak smile and looked up at their ma. 'Well, Ma, two grandchildren on the same day, eh?'

'Aye, never was there a luckier mother than me. They're grand lads. I'm going to enjoy spending time with them.'

Ma was smiling too now. The moment had passed. Hurts were in the open. Babs only hoped that in the last hour, Beth had learnt what pain was being caused by her actions.

'Right, I need to knaw as I'm forgiven for me outburst, then me and you, Tilly, need to clean up the new babby and these daughters of yours.'

The appeal was to Beth and Babs held her breath.

'There's nothing to forgive, Peggy. I know what you mean. And I know that you are right. I just need time. Will you all give me that? Then I'll handle the situation, I promise.'

This was the best news that Babs had heard. It was a start. She looked over towards Ma. Ma was nodding her head. 'Aye, lass. I understand. Take all the time you need but come back to me. Really back, I mean.'

Babs slipped her arm around Beth and hugged her to her. Her son stirred in Beth's arms but hadn't yet been demanding of attention. She knew as she gazed at him that he was going to be easy to look after. The thought came to her that he'd probably have his da's nature, placid and accepting of all.

When at last they were all cleaned up and drinking their first cuppa, the one Babs had made having gone cold, they asked Babs what name the child would have.

'Rupert Mario Arthur.'

'Eeh, that's lovely. I'm in a tiz about all this. Two grandsons and, like you said, Beth, both coming on the same day. By, I'm blessed. But eeh, Babs lass, Rupert's a bit of a posh name for around here, ain't it?'

'I knaw, Ma. Like I said, my Rupert were the son of an earl, so he would have a posh name.'

'Did he have a nickname?'

'Naw. Eeh, it's a dilemma, I want him called after his da, but . . .'

'Maybe call him Art. He has his grandfather's name in his, and that's a short form of Arthur.'

'Aye, that's a good idea, Beth, and that suits him an' all. Art it is. But to me, he'll allus be little Rupert.'

The two babies proved a salve to everyone's hurts. The days following their births saw Tilly visiting regularly and the two new mothers helping each other out as much as they could during their confinement to the one bed.

Peggy fussed over their every waking hour, till it was a relief when she said goodnight and they had some time together.

This was a time to talk, to renew all they had once shared, and Babs felt that though they didn't touch on the subject of Jasmine and Roman, it being too emotive, Beth was beginning to feel a sense of peace and was making decisions regarding them.

'By, Beth, it's good to find that despite your posh way of talking you're still the same, though I think with us being apart, you've grown in your confidence. I naw longer feel that you need me to look out for you.'

They were both feeding their babies, sitting up in bed, the half-light of the oil lamp creating an atmosphere of cosiness and calm.

'Yes, I was lost when you left, but did grow in confidence. In some ways it was good for me. And, though it seems bad to say it, it gave me more of a say in my own destiny as Jasmine feared that I would go too. With that fear, they were more inclined to treat me as different from them, and make provisions for me to follow the path that I wanted to, instead of forcing me into their ways.'

'Aye, I was surprised that you were educated, and made your own way, and can see that it made you think more of them for allowing it.'

'It did. I no longer felt like a captive and built on the love that both you and I had for them. But I know they did wrong. I look at my little Benny and cannot bear the thought of anyone taking him from me, and that has made me see Ma's side, and to grieve for her.' On a huge sigh, Beth asked, 'Oh, Babs. What am I going to do? How am I going to break ties with Jasmine and Roman? And why haven't they been back to try to see me? I have to admit, I am worried about them since Jasmine was made to leave.'

'I would leave it to Peggy and Ma. Let them deal with them.'

'No! Oh, Babs, you don't think ... What if Jasmine has been back and Peggy has sent her away?'

'If she has, it can only help matters.'

'No. It can't! I have to do this, and in a way that causes the least hurt. I don't know if I can give them up totally. I thought that if they went back down south, when Henry comes home I can go down there and see them without Ma knowing, then no one would be hurt.'

'Eeh, Beth, I can't understand you, I can't. You just said how much hurt it would cause you to lose Benny. Well, Jasmine and Roman caused that hurt to our ma. She has said to me that although her pain cut her in two, it was easier to lose Ivan than it was to lose us. And that's because she knew Ivan was gone forever, and to a better place and hadn't really left her, but us, we were out there somewhere, gone and yet not gone. Her agony was a daily grinding of pain. You have to do the right thing and threaten Jasmine and Roman with us going to the police if they ever try to contact us again. That will solve it. They will disappear into the night and that will be that.'

'But they will be so hurt.'

'Good!'

With this, the gulf between them that Babs had thought had disappeared opened up once more, and she felt overwhelmed by a sense of despair and an urge to get away from Beth that she never thought she would feel. So strong was the feeling that she got out of bed and, though shivering from the cold, went into the living room.

There the remains of last night's fire still glowed in the grate. Lying Art down on the sofa, she stoked the embers with sticks and coal from the scuttle next to the hearth and watched as they spluttered into flames that lit the room and sent warming rays out to her.

But the warmth didn't touch her heart. Never in her wildest dreams had she imagined being at odds with Beth, and now, she didn't know how she was going to bear being so. Because she knew she could never come around to Beth's way of thinking.

By morning, Babs had decided that she had to leave Beth's house and get back to her ma's. It took a lot of persuading Peggy to go along to the shop to arrange it, but seeing her distress, Peggy at last agreed.

It was Molly who came to the house. 'Eeh, lass, I met Peggy on the way to the shop and said that I'd come to try to talk to you. What's to do with the pair of you? Happen it's the after-babby blues. They take us all around three days after the birth and God knaws as you two lasses have more than your share to sadden your hearts. But that's all the more reason for you to be together and to help each other. Aye, and your ma too, as she has a lot to contend with. You knaw as Tommy is taking a long time to heal and isn't a good patient.'

'I knaw, more than most, Molly, but me and Beth just can't bridge the gap that divides us.'

Molly said that she understood, but surprised Babs by telling her that she also understood Beth. 'You both need to think of the other in this. Aye, and think of how it is that at last you're all together again. Your ma is so happy and she has this idea that Jasmine is no longer a threat to her.'

'Aye, because Beth has led us to believe that. But now she tells me that she is only planning on getting Jasmine away from here with promises that she'll see her often when she goes to live down south. I – I thought she wouldn't do that, I – I thought she'd stay here with me and Ma.'

'Eeh, me love. Nothing is forever, and I knaw that more than most. I have me little Gerry here to remind me every day of how me son – his da – was taken in the war . . . By, lad seems to knaw I'm talking about him. Look, he's waking. I'll get him out of his pram. He's crawling now, you knaw.'

For a few moments they were taken with Gerry crawling over to Babs and putting out his hand to Art. Uncannily, Art stretched out his hand and the two boys held each other's hand as if in a gesture of friendship.

72

'Awe, that's lovely. Gerry's a gentle soul who doesn't ask much of life, other than the love of all those around him. Sadly, Mary, his Ma, is grieving so badly for his da that she cannot see the attention this little one craves.'

'I suppose he's been a salve to you, Aunt Molly? Your Gerry was lovely. I was so sad that we couldn't help him when I tended to his wounds. Everything seemed all right but ... Look, I wanted to ask before, did he have a weak heart or owt?'

'Naw, not that I knaw of. He was never as strong as his younger brother, our Brian. Gerry used to succumb to owt as was going and allus had it much worse than any of the other kids, measles and the like.'

'What about rheumatic fever, did he ever have that?'

'Aye, he did. Why? Are you thinking that his injury didn't kill him? And talking of that, naw one has ever told me exactly what happened and I haven't liked to ask you, Babs.'

'Well, if you're sure you want to knaw?'

'Aye, I am. I need answers and so does Mary, bless her. Maybe you'd talk to her once you're over the birth? She could do with a friend as understands and you having lost your Rupert, she'll knaw as you do. Oh, aye, Gerry were me son, but that's not the same as what Mary went through losing her man.'

'Of course I will. Anyroad, Gerry were brought in with a bad injury. His leg was almost blown off.'

At the gasp from Molly, Babs stopped. 'Eeh, I'm sorry, Aunt Molly, I can only tell it you as it was.'

'Aye, I knaw, lass. And I want you to.'

Babs told Molly as gently as she could how Rupert had amputated Gerry's leg. 'He did a wonderful job and both of

73

us thought that Gerry would make a full recovery. Neither of us knew why he didn't recover, but if he had rheumatic fever, then he could have been left with a weak heart.'

Molly was silent for a long moment. When she spoke it was with a strong voice. 'By, I feel strangely better for knawing. And you say as he didn't die in agony?'

'Knaw, I promise you. It was more of a slipping away, and he'd have felt nowt of the surgery. Like I said in me note, he told me of his love for you and his da and brother and especially Mary. He was happy that he had a chance to come home now.'

'And he has in a way. Through you, he has come home, Babs.'

They hugged each other close, both feeling the pain of this horrific war – Babs knowing it first hand, and Molly having suffered, and continuing to suffer, as her second son Brian was still fighting on the front line.

'Right, lass. Knawing the pain of loss, don't let it happen again, nor to your ma. Make it up with Beth and find a way that you can go forward as friends. This problem isn't going to go away, you knaw.'

Babs nodded, but she wondered if she could. Beth felt like a different person to her and not the twin sister she'd so longed to be with.

SEVEN

Tilly

Tilly stood by Ivan's grave with Babs by her side, carrying her little Art. The keen early April wind whipped their woollen skirts around their legs. 'Ivan, lad, this is Babs. She wanted to come and visit you even though it's cold enough to freeze your lugs off today.'

'Awe, Ma, I feel so sad for you – and for everyone. The whole world is full of misery with this terrible war raging. But I feel closer to Ivan being here, it makes all Eliza's tales of him seem real.'

'He was a grand lad. Anyroad, let's get back and into the warmth, we'll catch our death.'

'Aye, but it's a toss-up as to what'll get us, the cold or your driving.'

Tilly laughed and playfully hit out at Babs. As she did, she had an urge to hold her to her. Babs came willingly into her arms. 'Eeh, me little Babs. What would I do without you, eh?'

'Ha, you knaw as I get under your feet. But, Ma, I love you. You're me world, along with me little Art.'

'He's a good lad. Always placid. Not like his cousin. Poor Beth has a time with Benny. He's demanding is that one.'

'I reckon it's because Beth is allus anxious and on edge, he picks up on it. For all I hate the gypsies and me forced time with them, they are full of wisdom and that's one of the things they say: that a babby can pick up on a mother's mood. We need to try to calm Beth and help her to cope better.'

'Aye, we do. How about we go around there and spend an hour with her? I'll take a chance on Jasmine not being there.'

'But what if she is?'

'Then, for Beth's sake, I'll just be polite and hopefully she will leave.'

'Awe, Ma, do you reckon you can do that? I mean, it's a big step, but would be a grand one for Beth.'

'Well, let's just hope that it doesn't happen, and I'm not tested. But I don't see why I should be the one afraid to call on my daughter. Come on, let's just do it.'

'By, it's good to see you both.'

'Hello, Peggy. I see little Benny's having a turn.'

'Aye, Tilly, I'm having a job with him, and with Beth. She's very upset today. She's had a letter from Henry and it allus upsets her, and yet poor lass lives for them to arrive.'

'Ha, that's us womenfolk for you. Where is she?'

'She's in the bedroom. She said she needed to change as this one had been sick on her, but I think she just needed a moment.'

'By, you've a nice fire going there, Peggy.' Babs, who'd been listening to this exchange but hadn't commented, now suggested, 'Let's lay a rug out and you put Benny on it and I'll put Art with him. Art might settle Benny some; Benny loves it when he's near to him.'

As if by magic, Benny stopped crying the moment Art lay next to him. Both lay on their backs but had their heads turned towards one another, making little gurgling noises. For all the world they looked like two little old men having a natter. The three women laughed out loud.

The sound of a tinkling bell had Peggy dashing for the bedroom door.

When Beth appeared wheeling her bath chair, her tear-stained face looked drawn, but brightened when she saw them. 'Ma! Babs! Oh, it's good to see you.'

Running to her, Tilly and Babs flung their arms around her and the three huddled together.

'Eeh, that's a sight for sore eyes. I'll leave you to it and put the kettle on.'

With Peggy out of the room, Tilly stood back and gazed down at her beloved Beth. 'Awe, me Beth, you don't look well, love. What's to do, lass?'

'I'm just tired, Ma. I'm not sleeping well, and little Benny is very demanding in the night hours.'

'That'll soon pass,' Babs reassured her. 'Anytime now he'll be sleeping through. Art has for a week now, hasn't he, Ma?'

'Aye.' Tilly nodded as she also sought to reassure Beth. 'But no two babbies are the same, even if they're siblings like you two – chalk and cheese you are. But I'm sure it won't be long now before Benny's sleeping through the night too, Beth. Anyroad, come near to the fire, lass. And how's your Henry? Peggy said you had a letter from him.'

Beth burst into tears.

'Eeh, lass. Me poor lass.'

'Oh, Ma, I just want him home. I . . .' The sound of the front doorbell stopped Beth in her tracks. Tilly saw her anguish turn to fear and guessed that Beth knew who this would be.

Peggy was out of the kitchen and shot by them towards the hall. 'I'll get it and I'll send whoever it is packing.'

Tilly took hold of Beth's hand; her own muscles had tightened with the tension that seemed to have gripped them all. 'Don't worry, Beth. It'll be all right.' But inside, she knew it wouldn't be. Looking over towards Babs, she saw the concern in her eyes.

Peggy's raised voice came to them. 'You're not welcome at this moment. Mrs Freeman has visitors. Kindly go and come back another time.'

'But it is that my Beth is distressed. I need to see her. Just for a moment.'

Tilly looked towards Babs. 'How does she knaw? That woman's uncanny.'

'She does have insight into a lot of things, Ma. She tried to teach me and Beth her ways, but it seems to be a gift that the gypsies have, especially the Romany gypsies.'

Jasmine's voice came again. 'I have a potion that will help me Beth and settle the little one.'

'I've told you before, Jasmine, we'll have none of your witchcraft in this house, ta very much.'

Even Tilly had to giggle at this, but as she did so, she realised how Beth was squeezing her hand to the point of causing her pain. 'Beth? Beth, lass, if you want to see her, me and Babs can go into the kitchen.'

'Oh, Ma, I'm sorry. I had no idea.'

'It's all right, Beth. Me and Ma said as we'd just accept it if Jasmine came at the same time. We love you too much, lass, to have you upset any more.'

'Oh, Babs. I do need Jasmine's potions, they've always helped me, but Peggy is so against them. I've been brought up on the natural healers of the land. I don't want the sedatives that Peggy gets from the chemist. I think they are making me worse.'

'Eeh, lass. Is that what's she's doing?'

'Yes, Ma. She means well, but they just make me drowsy and unable to cope.'

The argument at the door was still going on as they spoke. Tilly took a deep breath. She had to put aside her own feelings for the sake of Beth. 'Just a mo, Beth.' With this she strode determinedly towards the door and out into the hall. 'Beth does want the potions, Peggy. It's what she's known all her life and she has faith in them.'

As Peggy turned in astonishment, Tilly caught sight of the hated Jasmine and had the urge to spring forward like a cat after a bird and claw her still beautiful face. But she just stared at the woman, unable to speak.

'Tilly, it is that I only wish good for our Beth.'

Tilly gasped.

'She needs us both, Tilly. I can help her. She is descending into a gloom she won't be able to rise up from. For her sake, Tilly, take me potion.'

Swallowing hard, Tilly held herself stiff against the onslaught of pain radiating from the presence of this woman. 'Peggy, take the potion.'

'Ma, are you all right?'

'Babs, me Babs! I must be speaking with you. It is that I have to warn you.'

'Naw, stop! Don't speak to me, Jasmine.'

'But it is that you must be careful. There are forces that are working to take your *bambino* from you.'

'What! What are you saying? You're evil, Jasmine. You should go on your knees and pray to God for forgiveness, you and Roman.'

'Naw, Babs. Think of Beth. We said we wouldn't do this. Come on, me lass. Let it go.'

'Babs, take heed of my words, get away from here with your son.'

Tilly went cold. It was as if the frosty air had frozen her from the inside out. She grabbed Babs and ushered her back into the living room.

'What can she mean, Ma? Who can hurt me and Art?'

'Naw one. She is just trying to get her revenge. Take naw notice. She can't bear it that you won't have owt to do with her so is trying to scare you into doing so. She thinks this will make you seek her out for her help. Forget it.'

'Ma?'

'It's all right, Beth, me little lass, don't fret yourself. I told Peggy to take the potions for you.'

'But what has upset you, Babs? What's this about you and Art?'

Babs ran over to Beth and held her hand.

'You're trembling, Babs. Oh, Babs, what is it?'

Tilly listened to Babs telling Beth. Her heart felt heavy as she could see the fear in both of her girls and knew that they believed what Jasmine had said. 'My poor darlings, you've

80

been steeped in the folklore of the gypsies for so long. But listen to me, me lasses. It is just that sommat as the gypsies think they knaw, but they cannot possibly.' Though she sounded confident, memories came to Tilly of how the gypsies had predicted that her lovely Jeremiah – the only gypsy that Tilly had ever met that had been good and kind to her without any other motive than love for her – wasn't long for this world and how that came true. An urge to protect Babs had her running to the door again.

'She's gone now, Tilly, lass. Though I reckon as these potions should go down the sink!'

Disappointed that she hadn't been able to tackle Jasmine on her meaning, Tilly rounded on Peggy. 'Naw. You're to give them to Beth, Peggy. It's her decision. Poor lass cannot do a lot for herself, but we mustn't take everything out of her hands. She's cleverer than the lot of us and can make her mind up as to what she wants to take and to give to her babby. That's not for us to decide for her.'

'Well! I consider meself told off, but I only have Beth's interest at heart, you knaw.'

'Oh, Peggy, lass, I knaw. But that interest should take into account her wishes, that's all I'm saying, love.'

'Aye, you're right. I've done wrong. I'll apologise to her later. I thought I knew what was best for her. I'll listen to her in future.'

'That's good. And, Peggy, tell her that whenever Jasmine calls, you'll let her in, and take yourself for a walk to leave them together.'

'Eeh, lass, that cost you sommat to say. By, I've allus admired you, Tilly, but you just went up even higher in me estimation.'

'Ha, don't put me on too high a pedestal, as it's a long way to fall from the top.'

They both laughed at this, and Peggy opened her arms to Tilly. Tilly went into them. She'd never thought she would get this close to Peggy Gilly. She'd known her ma more as she'd helped her often, especially when she put her dislocated shoulder back in its socket. But now she found that quiet Peggy was not what she'd always seemed and their friendship was deepening as they both loved and cared about Beth.

Coming out of the hug, Peggy asked, 'What do you reckon to what she said, Tilly? She gives me the creeps.'

'I'm trying to ignore it, but I knaw from old that there's some truth in what they say they see, though we'll not tell Babs that. It's why I came out: I was going to challenge her to tell me more.'

'Aye. Well, as you say, I'll not stop her coming in next time, and I'll try to find out. I'll make out as I believe the mumbo-jumbo she spouts.'

Back in the living room, they found Beth and Babs holding hands. Beth had wheeled herself to the side of the sofa where Babs now sat. They both looked concerned. Tilly asked, 'Tell me, me lasses, are you for believing what Jasmine says?'

Both nodded.

'Have you proof that she can tell when sommat's going to happen?'

'Aye, we do, Ma, she did it all the time.' Babs looked fearful. 'She knew exactly what weather we would have, if any of us were going to ail, if there was going to be a disaster ... everything!'

'Yes, after you'd gone, Babs, she knew that you were in trouble, and one night she was in agony, and she said it was because you were, but she wouldn't say what was wrong. Now you have told us about Mario, I think I can put it to that time.'

'So, now you fear that there really is sommat that will happen to you and Art, Babs. Eeh, me little love, please don't worry. We'll keep you safe. Me and Tommy. I promise.'

'I knaw you will, Ma. Eeh, we're all being daft. Where's that pot of tea you promised us, Peggy?'

With this the atmosphere lightened, but Tilly knew that both her girls were worried. She was herself, but as much as she sought answers, none came, as she couldn't think of anything that could harm her Babs and little Art.

'Well, me lasses, I'll leave you together for a while and pop along to the shop. I've to see if Molly is all right. I'm worried about her lately. Her nerves are on edge with trying to keep Mary going, and worrying about Brian in the thick of the fighting.'

The wind hadn't let up, but it didn't bother Tilly as she walked along the promenade. Nor did it seem to bother those who'd come for the early spring break as there were many visitors strolling along as if they hadn't a care in the world.

The stalls were all open, and traders shouted out their usual encouragement to the punters to come and spend their money. Stopping by Ida's stall, she asked after Mary. Ida's two daughters, Vera and Mary, had married Molly's sons Gerry and Brian.

'Eeh, she's so in the doldrums, I don't knaw what to do for her, Tilly.'

'Aye, poor lass. Has she got little Gerry today?'

83

'Aye, she has him when Molly's at work, but you knaw, she's not really capable. I send our Vera home a dozen times during the day to check on her. But Molly reckons as it's the best thing for her to have Gerry.'

'I think so an' all. It gives her some responsibility. She'd never hurt him, she thinks the world of him, so I would leave her be and let her get on with it if I were you.'

'Easier said than done. I can't wait for the warmer weather when she can bring him here with her and I can keep an eye on the pair of them.'

This worried Tilly and she made her mind up to talk to Molly about it.

The organ grinder started up at that moment, and Tilly was transported to a world she loved – Blackpool's world of music and fun. With the sound, the stallholders seemed to come to life and all shouted louder, offering all manner of prizes for knocking a coconut off a stand with a bag stuffed with pebbles or getting a ping-pong ball into a bowl to win a goldfish.

With this awareness came the sound of the sea crashing onto the sand and the smell of fish and chips. Suddenly she felt hungry for her favourite food, and although she felt a little guilty as Babs and Beth hadn't got any, she went to the stall and bought two portions of chips.

'Want any fish, love? It's freshly caught this morning.'

'Aye, go on then. Put one on as me and Molly will eat that between us. Eeh, Fred, your fish are more like whales.'

'Aye, them Fleetwood boats get the best catch. They brought this in this morning and got it to me by nine. Lovely it is.'

Fred's belly was proof that he knew what he was talking about. He always tasted his own wares.

Clutching the hot parcels of her fish and chips wrapped in newspaper, Tilly put her head down as the wind got stronger.

'By, it's enough to blow you to kingdom come, Molly, lass.' Tilly had run into the shop as soon as she'd reached it and stood holding the door closed behind her.

'Aye, don't let it in here, lass. It's finding all the inlets as it is, I'm frozen stiff.'

'Well, I've sommat to warm you. Shall I put the catch on the door and then we'll have these, eh?'

As they ate their chips, Tilly broached the subject of Mary.

'I knaw, lass. I do all I can but I'm grieving an' all, and can't talk to her about Gerry, it breaks me heart. I just don't knaw what to do.'

'Look, lass, I've been thinking a lot lately. Me and you, we don't need to be here as much as we are. We're well established now, and I have put a big burden on you lately with me having more time at home since Tommy's injury . . .'

'Eeh, Tilly, every time you mention it, I go cold. I want to work longer hours to give you the time with him. It makes me feel better about it all being my fault – like I'm paying back for what I caused.'

'Molly, you can't say sorry for ever, and we don't want you to. It happened and that's that. Besides, I've told you a dozen times that we don't put blame on your shoulders. No driver – even good ones, which me and you are not – could have avoided what happened. There was a patch of black ice that none of us had seen, so when you braked you went into a slide, there was nothing you could have done. Look, I have a plan.'

'Oh? Better stand by me bed, then, as your ideas usually mean more work.'

'Not this time. Well, not after the initial setting up. What I'm thinking is, why don't we get Mary here and teach her the basket making, or your work, making the cushions and such, eh? I knaw as she could work with her ma, Ivy, on her stall, but that's being out in all weathers, and her sister Vera seems to like doing that more than Mary. Then Mary will be with Beth, who loves to be here making baskets. And maybe Babs, who's talked about having a job at the shop. They can have their babbies here an' all – there's plenty of room upstairs. We can make the bedroom, which we've never changed, into a nurs-ery, and they can take turns working or looking after the young ones. But as the bedroom is only next door to the workshop, all the mams are on hand if their little 'uns need them.' Warming to her theme, Tilly went on to explain the benefits. 'We can go down to working here just one or two days a week and can look after the babbies on some of the days we're off. And on the days as Gertie's not here to mind the shop, then the girls can take it in turns to do that. What do you reckon, eh?'

'By, Tilly, when did you come up with all that?'

'I've been mulling it over for a long time. Well, to tell the truth, I've had a lot of symptoms of the "change" that women are allus on about, and ain't felt meself.' As she said this the dreaded heat that crept up from her belly seeped over her and beads of sweat trickled down her back and stood out on her forehead.

'Eeh, Tilly, lass, that were on cue.' They both laughed at this. 'But I knaw what you're going through, I've been suffering a while, but for me it's been mostly at night. I didn't like to say owt, but well, I knew you might not be long in joining me as you're the right age for the change now. I didn't want you worrying, though.'

'You should have, you daft apeth. Eeh, give me sommat to fan meself. It seems to happen more when I'm eating me meal, and I tell you, me monthlies are all over the place. Gave me a scare they did, when I missed a couple.'

'You should go to sleep at night instead of rocking your Tommy then you wouldn't have that worry. Poor bloke, he'll be worn out.'

They went into a fit of giggling again at this. 'Eeh, Molly, I love you. You're me best mate, and you allus make me laugh . . . but then laughing makes me sweat more. Eeh, it gets me down some.'

'Don't let it, lass. It's just another stage of life. Fight back like you allus do with everything else that comes along. It'll be wrinkles and grey hair next, so you'll not be able to sit back on your laurels. I tell you, we've a battle on from now on to keep ourselves attractive, but there's one consolation: our menfolk can't see as well as they used to. Will has to wear glasses now for close work, so they'll not notice.'

Their laughter rang out and they ended up in each other's arms having a hug. For Tilly, this moment with Molly had lifted her, as she'd felt lower than she'd wanted to admit with the encounter with Jasmine playing on her mind.

'You knaw, Tilly, if we take on your idea and the girls are all for it, I'll miss not seeing you as often. You're like a shining light in the darkness for me.'

'Aye, and you are for me an' all. I can talk about owt with you. I tell you what would be good, Molly. What if we meet up once a week on our day off? We can shop – eeh, we've got the money now, and naw time to spend it – and you knaw what? I'd love to go into Manchester on the train one day and have a look around the shops there. And we can have our lunch out like the posh women do an' all.'

'Lunch? By that is posh. I allus call it me dinner and me big meal when I go home at night is me tea.'

'Aye, and that's what it is an' all, but we're ladies of means now, so we can lunch.' With this, Tilly stood and did an exaggerated walk. 'I'm Madame Tilly, of Tilly and Molly's Emporium, you knaw.'

'Aye, with hot sweats an' all. I tell you, Tilly, them ladies as have lunch don't sweat. They perspire!'

This had them collapsing in yet another heap of giggles that brought tears to their eyes, and for Tilly dispelled the last of the niggly worry that had embedded itself inside her. With Molly by her side she could cope with anything.

EIGHT

Beth

With taking Jasmine's potions regularly, Beth had felt much better over the last few weeks and so the position in the shop that Ma was telling her about really appealed to her.

Whenever she worked with cane and wicker, she found she could lose herself for a time, so now seemed the right moment to tell of an idea that had occurred to her recently. 'Ma, that all sounds wonderful, but what do you think to me helping in the meantime here at home? I could make some of the smaller items. I need something to occupy myself and I love weaving. I find it soothing.'

'I knaw what you mean, lass. And aye, I reckon that would really help you, and me and Molly an' all. You could make the sewing baskets as they are our best sellers. By, lass, you're like me in how you love the basket work.'

'You're going to miss it, Ma. Are you sure you want to do this? I know you'll be in the shop a couple of days a week, but well ...'

'I'm sure. Really sure. I've worked hard since being a lass, and I'm ready to ease up a bit. I'll still enjoy making the bigger commissioned pieces. I love making them, lass. They need planning and designing and they challenge me to come up with different techniques. And to knaw as the piece is an exclusive excites me. I allus put me initials on them an' all, so in years to come, the ancestors of the posh folk who buy them will look at them and wonder who T.O. is. Tilly O'Flynn, basket maker. Eeh, it's a long way from when I trudged the streets with me wares.'

'I remember that time, Ma, and now I am back I remember more and more. Little snippets keep coming to me. Like when I saw Aunt Florrie again. I was reminded of the house where she was a maid and how kind she was to us. Oh, I can't wait for Sunday when we'll all be together. I think it's a lovely idea of yours to all go back to the farm after the christenings. I'm looking forward to seeing Aunt Florrie again and meeting her husband Reggie. Then their son, Phil, will be there. Oh, I know he is always at the farm carrying out his work, but to socialise with him, and Cliff and his dad and the lad Cliff brings to the farm to help out . . . I'm so glad that you asked them.'

'Aye, I don't knaw where we would have been without Cliff and young Jack since the accident. Phil's took it on himself to be the boss, you knaw. Ha, it makes us smile to hear him dishing out the day's chores. And to see him teaching young Jack is a treat. He has sommat special about him does Phil.'

'He does. I think Eliza keeps him in check, though. They're like an old married couple them two, and them not much more than bairns.'

'Yes, you can see the love between them. Let's just hope this war is over before Phil is old enough to go.'

'I knaw. I dread them raising the age of conscription. It's already forty-one. Tommy just missed it.'

'They won't take farmers, Ma. They're exempt – well, the older ones are. But even if he volunteers, Tommy wouldn't get through. Babs did her best with his leg but, well, it will trouble him in the future. He needed an operation really. Babs and I were surprised when the doctor didn't make us take him to the hospital.'

'Eeh, why didn't you say, lass?'

'I – I . . . well, look, Ma, you have to understand, it wasn't our place to. We've been schooled to leave such decisions to the doctors, and wouldn't dare question their superior knowledge. If a complaint went to the medical board about us, we could never nurse again. I wasn't thinking of me, as I'll never be able to, but Babs, she might need to in the future.'

'Eeh, Beth, that's hard to take in. It's as if you're saying your futures were more important than Tommy's well-being.'

'No! Oh, don't think that. I'm sorry, I didn't explain it very well. But to go above a doctor is not something that we, as nurses, can do. Besides, us thinking an op would help doesn't make it so. The doctor is far more qualified than we are and he did a thorough examination. We have to accept that he was right in his judgement. We so often find that to be the case.'

By the look on her ma's face, Beth knew she had to say more. 'Ma, I can see that you're still struggling with this. I wish I hadn't said anything. Tommy will be fine. He will just have a slight limp, maybe, but I've been thinking. He could do with some structured exercises. I could help him with that and so could Babs. We'll talk to him about it on Sunday. I want to help him all I can. I have seen lads with far worse injuries and they improved massively with intensive exercise.'

To Beth's relief Tilly brightened. 'Really? Awe, lass, if anyone can help me Tommy, you two can. I'm proud of what you and Babs did when nursing in France; you're heroes in my eyes. And with how you're carrying on with your life, Beth, despite everything.'

'You all help me with that, Ma.'

Her ma's smile widened, and then, as if making her mind up to accept Beth's explanation, she changed the subject. 'Being all together helps us all. By, it'll be lovely to have a celebration on Sunday. Sommat to combat all this doom and gloom. Aye, and it'll be lovely for you to see Henry's ma and his sister Janine and her young man an' all, Beth. Though I'm glad they didn't take up me offer of staying at the farm with us. I think they're really nice, seeing as they're posh folk, but I'd be on pins if they were in me house with just me, Tommy and Babs as I'd not knaw how to go on.'

'Ma, you are daft. Of course you would. They love you, and love the relaxed atmosphere of the farm, but they just didn't want to put you out, especially as Tommy is still struggling, and that's why they booked into the Blackpool Hotel. Besides, you've enough on your plate, just look at the guest list – Aunt Molly and her Will, and Mary and Vera, and Ivy. And Aunt Florrie and Reggie. Then me and Peggy, and Babs and Eliza as well as my in-laws. Oh, and that's besides those we've already mentioned.'

'You missed out my shop assistant, Gertie, and her bloke, Alf.'

'Oh, Ma, how are you going to manage?'

'It's all in hand. Eliza's on with making the cakes, I've tins of them stacked in me pantry. And you'll never guess, but Ma Perkins has offered to let her bake a special christening cake in the oven in the shop! Eeh, I reckon as our Eliza can charm a snake as naw one has ever got through to Ma Perkins like she has. The old girl thinks the world of her.'

'I'm not surprised. Eliza's so lovely. A credit to you and Tommy.'

For a moment Ma looked downcast and Beth instinctively knew that this remark had brought home how Ma hadn't been able to have a hand in shaping Babs and herself.

'Ma, I'd love a hug.'

With this, Ma came over to her with her arms out. Going into them, Beth knew all the love she needed in the world was in the hug.

'Ma, help me to stand, then hold me under me arms with your arms around me. I want to hug you properly.'

In no time, Beth was encased in her ma's arms, making her feel safe and loved.

'Right, sit down now, lass. We don't want to tire you and I'm to wipe me face, it's wet with me tears. Eeh, I'm blessed. Three lovely daughters, and two beautiful little grandsons.'

'Ma, you shivered then as if someone had trodden on your grave.'

'I knaw. It's this feeling I've had since Jasmine visited that day.'

'I know it is upsetting, but Ma, though Jasmine can see into the future – and that has been proven many times – I have also often known her to say things just to get her own way. She wants Babs back and so came up with something that she thought would make Babs seek her help and protection.

93

Nothing will happen to little Art.' Though she said this, Beth still feared Jasmine's words. Suddenly she felt the need to convince her ma of her love. 'Don't let thoughts of Jasmine spoil us having our first proper cuddle. Oh, Ma, I do love you. You know that, don't you? And you are more important to me than anyone after Henry and Benny.'

'Eeh, I reckon as you're right. And I'm happy to take third place after them two lovely lads, me little Beth.'

Beth felt better as her ma giggled at her own words. 'Oh, Ma, you are funny.'

'Laughter's the best thing for us all. And I've done a lot of that since having you and Babs back in me life.'

'I'm glad, Ma, as we are so happy to be back.'

Ma held her hand and squeezed it and Beth felt a love surge through her for her wonderful, strong mother. Changing the subject, she asked, 'You've remembered that I'm going back with Philomena and Janine to Maidstone after the christening, haven't you, Ma?'

'Aye, I have and it'll do you good. And you said as they're going to take you to visit yours and Henry's home in Margate an' all. That'll be lovely for you. But, well, you will come back, won't you?'

'Of course I will. I'm here till the end of the war, when Henry comes home. Then you know that I will have to live in Margate where his work is, but we'll visit often, and you can come and stay as Henry talks of buying a bigger house. He says it will be big enough for all my family to come and visit and that he can't wait. Not sure if he meant he can't wait for us to have a home, or for you all to come and visit, as I know he loves you all as if he's known you forever.'

'And we love him an' all, lass. You got a good 'un there. Well, I've to get off now. I'll see you on Sunday at the church.'

The house seemed quiet without her ma. The day that Babs had left to go back home had been a sad day and had plunged Beth's spirits low. She needed company. Oh, Peggy was lovely, but when someone different came to visit, or she went to the farm or to the shop, it lifted her and made her feel that she could cope.

Sunday was a bitterly cold day, heralding April as it was the first of the month and Palm Sunday, just a week before Easter day. Beth was excited on two counts – the christening this morning and then, after that, the trip to Maidstone with her in-laws. She only felt sad that Henry wouldn't be here and at not being able to have Jasmine and Roman with her as Benny was baptised, but there was something planned for them, as she'd promised that when she returned from Maidstone they would all go to church together, which had led them to arrange a real gypsy celebration for afterwards.

St John's church wasn't decorated with flowers as they would have liked when they arrived for the service, as it was still Lent, but the crosses made of dried palm leaves that were strewn about gave a little light touch.

The babies looked lovely in their gowns. Benny's, a delicately stitched white lace gown made by Jasmine, was probably a little overstated, with the pearl beads that were sewn onto the bodice and around the hem, but Art's was just as fetching with the fine smocking of the bodice and long skirt topped with an intricately crocheted lace, which Molly had made.

Janine and Peggy stood as godparents for Benny and Eliza and Molly for Art, and the babies were well behaved, though Peggy had to take Benny from Janine as he made his usual protest at anything different happening to him and wailed loudly when the priest poured the water over his head.

It was good to see Tommy walking with just the aid of a stick. Beth hadn't seen him accomplish this before as mostly he'd been in the second wheelchair that had belonged to Ivan and was kept at the farm for her use.

Back at the farm, everything was lovely. Ma had the huge dining table laden with food – sandwiches and Eliza's amazing cakes, with the centrepiece being the christening cake, iced in white with two cots adorning it, linked by a blue bow. The loveliest cake that Beth had ever seen. She and Babs hugged Eliza and thanked her by giving her a present of a silver locket that they had bought between them.

Beth was sitting in an armchair in the Sunday best room, which seemed crowded with people all laughing and chattering. Tommy came up to her, leaning heavily on his stick, but managing to carry Art in his free arm. Smiling at him, she told him, 'I have to thank you, Tommy, it was so good of you to arrange for the lads to give the yard a real clean-up. I didn't smell a cow dung or see a bit of mud in sight as we crossed it.'

'Well, me wee lass, we've two little kings to honour today, so we have, and to tell the truth, I couldn't see your ma-in-law, the lovely Philomena, wading through the muck as usually graces me farmyard.'

'By, it's all right for your wife then, Tommy O'Flynn?'

Neither had seen Ma approach. Tommy put his head back and laughed. 'Well, isn't it that you're used to the muck, Tilly, me wee love?'

As Tommy and Ma moved away to talk to others, Peggy, who sat on the arm of Beth's chair, leant forward. 'By, Beth, you look lovely. As I said when I helped you to dress, I'll give that Jasmine that much, she can sew.'

Beth smiled at Peggy. 'And so do you.' Though she said this, and Peggy did look smart, she always thought that Peggy preferred to dress in a dowdy way. Her brown costume, with its straight skirt, wasn't improved by the fact that she had teamed it with a brown silk blouse, and her pointed hat didn't help as it seemed to follow the line of her nose and accentuate how thin and pointed that was. Her own outfit had been made for her from a drawing she'd given to Jasmine. A rich cream flared velvet jacket topped a skirt in the same material, which also had a slight flare to it as it flowed to her ankles. To bring the outfit alive, Babs had found a lovely silk blouse for her. In a burnt orange, with a ruffled effect from the buttoned-up neckline to the waist, it was comfortable, and yet showed off Beth's slim and curvy figure and enhanced her raven hair.

She looked over at Babs and had a warm feeling as she saw her laughing with Janine. The two got on so well. Janine's husband joined them and, not for the first time, Beth wondered why he hadn't gone to war. Was there one rule for the very rich and another for everyone else? This thought made her feel a little peeved at Gareth and Janine for their lack of war effort, something that she hadn't felt before. She made up her mind to tackle them about it.

As if sensing Beth was thinking about her, Janine turned her head and looked at her. Her beautiful large cream-coloured hat shaded her face for a moment, leaving Beth unable to read her expression. As Babs left them to go to talk to Cliff, Janine walked towards Beth, a fusion of a deep purple long flowing frock, long cream-coloured gloves and matching short fur jacket. She smiled. 'Beth, you look lovely. I feel overdressed.'

Peggy got up, greeted Janine and then excused herself and left them alone.

Beth looked up at Janine and told her, 'No, not at all, you look beautiful.'

'You have a funny expression on your face. Is something wrong? I mean, apart from the obvious awful absence of our darling Henry?'

'Can I ask you something, Janine?'

'Of course, anything. What is it, darling?'

'Well, I just wondered what if anything you and Gareth are doing for the war effort?' Having said it, Beth immediately regretted it. 'I – I mean, it's none of my business, of course, but, well, with conscription and everything . . .'

'No, I understand, we get asked that a lot. As far as Gareth's concerned, I cannot tell you, except to say he does go away a lot. Other than that it is top secret. But I can assure you it is vital to the war and why we got married very suddenly and on our own. Me? Well, I did look into being a VAD, but they don't take married women, so, as you will find out when you come down, Mama and I have organised a lot of other women into a sort of help group. We do all sorts, from knitting socks to send to the soldiers to raising money for those who come home wounded. And I have other news too. I'm pregnant! So, other than what I am doing, I wouldn't be able to do anything else.'

None of this was said in anything other than a matter-of-fact, gentle voice, but Beth felt terrible and wondered at herself for even asking Janine such a question. 'I'm sorry, Janine, forgive me, I didn't mean . . . Well, you know how it is with all these conscientious objectors; they just seem like cowards somehow.'

'Oh, Beth, they're not. I know some who help us and they are just as brave as anyone else and would go to the front line to help the wounded if they could, but they have a right to their religious beliefs or their own moral code about not killing another human being.'

'Oh? They're portrayed as cowards, so I thought—'

'I know and they suffer a lot because of that image. Anyway, enough talk about the war, except to say I was so pleased to hear that Henry is working in a safe environment now, and on that front, I have news that I can share, but it is no good asking me questions about it as I have no idea about the reasons behind it. Anyway, Gareth is going to Paris in a few weeks' time, so when you are with us, I thought I'd take you shopping for him. Gareth said he can get something small into his pocket that no one would question, so we'll have to be careful what we choose, but I thought it would cheer Henry no end to get a gift from you.'

'Oh, Janine, that would be wonderful! And congratulations on expecting a baby, that's lovely news. I want to hug you. I feel blessed having a lovely sister-in-law like you, and please forget that I mentioned anything.'

'That's just it, we are sisters now, Beth, and you can say anything you like to me. I'm glad to get a chance to explain to you. I couldn't write about it as it would seem that I was bragging about what is essentially charity work and, of course, I can't say anything about Gareth. But I understand. I asked the same of the young man over there who Babs is with. Then wished that I hadn't. So, we all think the same way. Maybe you could let all of your family and friends know about us, but in a subtle way. I want everyone to know that we are both very much involved in important efforts towards the cause.'

'I will. Not that anyone has said anything at all about it, so don't worry. Just relax and enjoy yourself.'

'I am. I'm having a lovely time, Beth. I love your sister and your mother. I could listen to their lovely accent all day.'

'I can never get over how accepting you all are. I used to worry that you would think of them as common.'

'No! The salt of the earth, more like. Oh, you haven't got a drink, has everyone forgotten you?'

'No, I didn't want one at first, but now I would love a sherry, please.'

'I'll see to it.'

As soon as she left Beth's side, Peggy returned to perch on the arm of her chair again. 'Are you all right, lass?'

'I am, Peggy. I feel so lucky to have such a wonderful family, and to see everyone enjoying themselves.' Beth looked over to where her ma was chatting with Molly and Gertie as she said this and thought they were probably talking about the shop. For all Ma and Molly were saying they wanted to shorten their hours at the shop, she wondered if they really did. They'd built their business up from nothing and it was a huge part of their lives. Ma looked lovely in a flowing navy skirt, white blouse and hip-length, swirling rose-coloured jacket.

Tommy came over with the drink Janine had promised. 'Isn't this for being a wonderful day? Here you are, a sherry for you to enjoy. I have been for checking on Benny – not that your Peggy is not doing that every five minutes,' he winked at Peggy. 'And he is still sleeping soundly. I think the ceremony was for tiring him out, and here is me longing to hold him.'

'You will before long, I'm sure . . . Tommy, I never said, but you have been so lovely in how you have accepted me and Babs, and made us feel this is our home. Thank you.'

'Is it thank Tommy day today then? No one was for telling me that!' They giggled, but then Tommy became serious. 'Beth, it is that I love you both as if you were me own. Well, I have lived with you since I met your ma. For hasn't she been like a person torn in half for years? It was for being as if someone had ripped her soul in two. But it's good to see that the half of her that was raw, and hurting her every waking hour, is now mended.'

A pang of guilt entered Beth. Hadn't she rubbed salt into that wound? 'I – I'm so sorry, Tommy. I shouldn't . . . Oh God, I'm in such a quandary about it all.'

'I understand. It is that we all have a pull on our emotions and have to choose. Haven't I been for being torn about being here and not being in me beloved Ireland, where I have land as far as the eye can see? But for your ma's safety, I had to leave rather than fight for what is rightfully mine. It breaks me heart to think of the farm that belonged to me great-grand-father and his son, right through to me pappy, then me brother, and then me, going to rack and ruin, or used for the purpose of them as would cause trouble with the north, but it is a sacrifice I had to make.'

Beth couldn't answer this, except to say how sorry she was. She knew Tommy was hinting that she should give up Jasmine and Roman, and for the first time, she felt herself agreeing, for the terrible hurt Tommy had spoken of that her ma had suffered had ultimately been down to them.

Tommy bent and patted her hand. 'Well, me wee lass. I've to do what your ma told me and circulate, as much as me leg will let me. Oh, and on that, it is grateful that I am that you and Babs are planning to help me to improve even more. I think I'll go and chat to that young Gareth, and on me way I'll rescue your ma and tell her as you would like to be having a word with her.'

'Thank you, Tommy, I'd love to have her over here with me, but Tommy, a little word about Gareth. He is doing his bit for the war.' She told him what Janine had said.

'Well, it's glad I am to hear it, as I did wonder and thought to broach the subject. The young man comes over as having the world at his feet and being above the suffering that's going on, when all the time he's probably involved in vital work that's more dangerous than those on the front line are facing.'

'Well, I don't know about that, but it is good to know he is doing something. I was worried about it.'

As she waited for her ma to come over, Beth thought what a lovely atmosphere there was to this occasion of mixed classes of people. Laughter rang out from Philomena, her mother-in-law, who was now in conversation with Peggy, who'd moved from Beth's side when she and Tommy had begun to talk about Ma. Beth couldn't imagine what the two women found in common, but it was lovely to see. As she watched she saw Tommy join them and within seconds their laughter increased. She loved Tommy and would think hard about what he had said about making sacrifices. The problem was twofold now as Jasmine and Roman adored Benny as if he was their grandson, which to them he was.

Sighing, she put it all out of her mind as her ma came up to her and gave her a hug.

'I do love you, Ma, so very much.'

Her ma stood up straight and looked down on her. 'Awe, Beth, don't torture yourself. You've enough to put up with without adding me an' all. I'm your ma, and'll love you naw matter what. So stop worrying, lass.'

At that moment, Beth realised what a wonderful, strong person her ma really was, and her guilt deepened.

'Hey, naw tears, not today. I forbid it.'

Beth swallowed hard. The conflict inside her was such that she wanted to scream out against it. Janine saved the day. Seeing something was wrong, she glided over. 'Ahh, Beth, you've got your sherry then? Well, chin-chin.'

Ma looked astonished at this. Her expression made Beth smile and her mood lightened. 'Up here we say "cheers",' she told Janine.

'Oh, yes, I've heard that. Well, cheers both, and thank you so much for this lovely occasion. Oh, and the food. It looks so yummy, just staring at it makes my tummy rumble. The cakes! They look out of this world.'

'Aye, and they'll taste that an' all. Me Eliza made them. She's an apprenticed baker, you knaw.'

Ma said this with such pride that another pang seared Beth. Eliza was the daughter that she and Babs couldn't be, but should have been. The thought came to her that all of that was stolen from them, and a feeling took root in her that she'd like to slap Jasmine and Roman for the damage they did. The feeling shocked her.

'Darling, what is it? You trembled. Eeh, me little love, what is it?'

'Oh, Ma.'

'Beth! Oh dear, what is the matter?' Janine knelt down beside her. 'Dearest Beth, I know your pain, I feel it every time Gareth has to leave me.'

'I – I'll be all right. I . . . I've just realised that I've done something terrible. Forgive me, Ma. Forgive me.'

Ma bent over and held her. 'Hush, me little darling. Don't upset yourself. You've done naw wrong; others have done wrong by you. I don't blame you for owt, me darling, all can be put right. Forget it for now and we'll talk later, eh?' Straightening, she asked Janine, 'Janine, love, can you start to laugh to cover up for Beth? We don't want her embarrassed.'

Janine, ever the one to love attention, laughed a lovely laugh. Ma stood and clinked her glass on Janine's and laughed with her. A surge of love shot through Beth for her brave ma, but with it came a surge of hate for Jasmine and Roman. The feeling was so alien to her that for a moment it left her bereft, but then it took root in her and her thoughts formulated into how she could free herself from their clutches as now, she couldn't believe that she'd ever loved them or put them before her beloved ma.

NINE

Babs

Babs laughed out loud at Cliff. He could be so funny. His tell‐ing of how Jack, the boy who helped on the farm, had fallen into a bucket of pig swill that was too heavy for him to carry had brought tears to her eyes.

'Awe, you're allus laughing at me, Cliff,' Jack said as he munched on his second iced bun.

Cliff ruffled Jack's hair. 'Eeh, lad, and you're allus stuffing your face. Go easy on them cakes, then there might just be some left to take home with you as Eliza said you could.'

Jack looked embarrassed, so Babs changed the subject. 'How is your ma, Jack?'

'She's grand, missus. She says as we've never had it so good now that you and your ma visit and bring us food and such like, then there's what I tip up. That pays the rent.' Jack looked so proud of himself as he said this.

'I'm glad to hear it. But you let me knaw if you need owt else and we'll see what we can do.'

'Ta, missus.'

It felt funny to Babs to be addressed as missus, but though she'd told Jack to call her by her name, he didn't seem comfortable doing so.

Since Christmas, when Cliff had first told them about Jack's family, she and her ma had visited them a couple of times and taken most of Ivan's things to them. The clothes were too big, as they were only able to give them what Ivan had when he was older, the others being far too small. But Molly was on with altering what she could to fit them.

They'd discovered that Rita Rawcliffe was a widow and only managed to keep going by begging. She'd been given notice on her house and was preparing to go into the poorhouse. Ma, knowing what her circumstances felt like, had paid her back rent for her, and made sure Jack took enough home to cover it for the future. This was almost as much as Phil earned, but Tommy had spoken to Phil about it and he'd understood. Ma also sent Jack off each visit with plenty of fresh food. Now she was thinking of opening up the house that Aunt Liz had left her. She'd never done anything with it, other than make sure it was maintained as she'd not wanted to sell it as that seemed disloyal to Aunt Liz. Like Molly, Liz hadn't been a real aunt, but Ma's long-term friend, who'd had a tragic life. Babs could just remember her, and some of her young 'uns.

Ma had the idea to make Liz's house into a refuge for anyone threatened with the poorhouse. It was big enough for two families, and she intended housing those who weren't coping, then helping them to cope and to get back on their feet before they would move on to rented property again and another family could be helped. Babs had heard her ma being

106

called an angel, and though she'd always known this herself, this plan confirmed to her that Ma really was a true angel, kind and forgiving.

Thinking this, she looked over to where Beth was sat. Ma was forgiving of Beth, and Babs just wished that she could be too.

'Penny for them?'

'Oh, sorry, Cliff. I was deep in thought then. Actually, I would like to share what's going on in me head with someone. But I don't knaw if now is the right moment.'

'Well, I'm a good listener and I've been meaning to ask you if you'd like to go for a drive sometime. Up into the Bowland hills? Give you a break. I love it up there, and maybe take a picnic?'

'Eeh, that'd be lovely, Cliff. I would. Just to get away for a bit and do sommat different. But I don't knaw as we can plan a picnic, there's still snow on the high grounds and more threatened in the near future.'

'We can eat in the van while we look out at the view. It's beautiful up there, and even more so when the trees are covered in frost, the hedges are dripping with icicles and there are snowcaps on the hills. And me da's got a little primus stove, so we can take everything with us to make a hot cuppa to warm us.'

The picture that Cliff had painted made her long to be there at this very minute. Somewhere to find peace from inner turmoil.

Cliff cut into her thoughts. 'By, I don't hear naw objections now ... Well, how about Sunday, then? I've to go to early mass, then come here to help Phil with the milking, but after that I'm done for the day. I won't change before I get here as I can wear me milking coat over me smart wear so I won't be in me scruffs.'

Babs laughed out loud at this. 'Well, I wouldn't go with you if you were in your scruffs, that's for sure! Aye, all right then. Eeh, an outing, it'll be grand.'

Tommy came over to them then. It seemed he'd really found his legs today as Babs had seen him circulating and chatting to everyone, and though she'd watched him lean heavily on his stick, he didn't seem to have had the need to sit down. Maybe at last he was on the mend.

'Well, it is that you two sound as if you're having a grand time. I'm glad to see it.'

Babs felt herself flush at this. It seemed that Tommy was talking to them as if they were a couple, when nothing of that nature had entered her head. Nor Cliff's as far as she knew. They were just very good friends. And a friend was what she needed more than anything.

As Cliff told him what they had planned, Tommy nodded in a knowing way, and smiled at Babs, increasing her embarrassment. Deciding not to protest, as she knew this could make things worse, she turned the conversation in a different direction. 'Is Beth all right, Tommy?'

'That's why I came over. It is that she seems to be upset. Janine is helping her, but I thought you were the best to do that.'

Despite being cross with Beth, this made her want to go to her. Without asking what was wrong, she left Cliff's side, crossed the room and made her way to Beth, having to excuse herself to those she passed, saying that she would return to talk to them in a moment.

Reaching Beth's side, Beth smiled up at her but the smile didn't reach her eyes and in them, Babs saw an appeal for help. 'Eeh, Beth, what's wrong, lass? Is there owt I can do?'

'She's a little upset, Babs.' Janine had leant forward and whispered this. 'Maybe if we could get her out of the room on some pretext, just to give her time to compose herself?'

'Aye, I'll sort sommat. I'll go and get your chair, Beth. No one'll think owt of it, they'll just think that you need to go to the loo. I won't be a mo.'

Beth still hadn't spoken and Babs knew that if she did, she would cry, so she didn't push her, she just went over to Peggy and quietly told her that she would see to Beth. She didn't want Peggy fussing if she saw anything happening with Beth that she wasn't party to.

With minimum fuss, Beth was soon sat with Babs in the quiet of Ivan's old room. 'Beth, what's wrong, lass? Is it just missing Henry, or has owt else happened?'

'I – I ... Oh, Babs, I'm sorry. I'm so sorry. I've caused so much pain! I didn't mean to, I just didn't see what I was doing.'

This shocked and pleased Babs and the hug she and Beth went into was the best hug they'd had since that very first one that had reunited them. 'It'll all be all right now, Beth. Ma'll knaw the complete happiness she's allus wanted, and me and you'll be as close as we were when we were young 'uns. Everything'll be grand without those evil monsters in our lives. Aye, and to see them justly punished would be a bonus, but I doubt they will be – they'll go to ground like the snakes that they are.'

They hugged again. 'I love you, me Beth. I love you more than I can tell you.'

'And I love you, Babs. I've missed you so much. Well, I know we haven't not seen each other, but there's been this feeling between us that I had created but didn't know how to surmount, but that will go now. I promise, Babs. I'll rid myself of Jasmine and Roman.'

'Not on your own you won't, Beth. Let Ma and me help. You arrange for them to come to yours and we'll be there to tell them they are not wanted ... Naw, we'll do more than that. It just occurred to me, Beth, that we could have the coppers waiting in your house to grab them when they arrive. By, it would be good to see them go to jail.'

'No, Babs, you've got to let me do this my way. I ... well, I don't want revenge on them, I just want to threaten them with the police. That will be enough to make them disappear, but I'll feel better knowing they are free than I would if I had to think of them in jail.'

'They should suffer, Beth.'

'Oh, they will. I promise you. They genuinely loved us as if we were their own, Babs. Delusional – I can see that now – and wicked, but when you left, they were heart-broken and suffered every day from your loss. Losing me as well will be torture to them. I think that is punishment enough.'

'But what if they don't accept it and keep bothering you? They might wear you down, and I'm telling you, Beth, that would hurt more. If you went back into their fold after letting me and Ma – especially Ma – think that you have given them up and can see how wrong they were to do what they did, it would break her. It would be like saying that you knaw they did wrong but you don't care.'

110

'That won't happen, Babs. I intend to tell them that I will go to the police. And I won't break. I feel only hate for them both now. They will see that I mean it and just the mention of the police will have them disappearing into the night. They won't dare contact me again.'

Babs didn't feel so sure of this, but she could see that Beth was determined. This was a side that Beth didn't show often, but when she did, it was time to take heed, as it was almost impossible to change her mind. Besides, Babs knew this wasn't the occasion to have a blazing row with her sister. Especially not now they had made up. 'All right, Beth. If you're sure. Eeh, I can't tell you how happy you've made me. Come on, let's go and find a glass of sherry and celebrate, as I don't knaw about you, but I'll soon have to be feeding Art – I can feel me milk coming in. By, it's grand to be feeding your young 'un, but it makes you feel like your akin to the cows in the dairy, being milked.'

Beth burst out laughing. 'Oh, Babs, I know just what you mean. And the fear of the wet patch appearing through your blouse . . . Oh, who'd be a nursing mother, eh?'

They looked at each other, then together they nodded and said in chorus, 'We would!' Their giggles at this brought tears to their eyes and bonded them as sisters once more.

'Well, let's get on with it. I'll go and ask Ma and Peggy to bring the boys in to us. We can sit in here and see to them. I have a basket – made by Ma, of course.' They giggled again. 'Everything we need is in it.'

'Oh, I'll not take one of Art's nappies, thanks, Babs, I brought me own in my own "made by Ma basket".' This set them off laughing again, and it felt to Babs that all hurts had been erased and that nothing could spoil their lives again.

But as she left the room, she shuddered as the thought of Jasmine's prediction came to her. Shaking the feeling off, she almost ran through the kitchen to the Sunday best room and found Ma and Peggy. Neither took any persuasion, but were ready to help and to fuss over the babies and Babs and Beth at a second's notice.

Everyone coo-ed and ahhed over the boys. Art took it well, smiling and gurgling, but Benny must have suddenly realised he was hungry as he yelled in a way that said, 'Get me to my mother, and now!'

Babs took him from Peggy and stroked his head. 'There, me little one, don't be impatient now. Everything comes to he as waits, you knaw.'

Benny stopped crying and looked up at her. His look filled her with love for him, something that had been an instant feeling when he was born, but had become a stranger to her as she'd been estranged from his ma. 'Aunty loves you, little man. Aye, and I'll allus be here for you, no matter what.' She tweaked his nose. 'Though, there'll be naw messing with me, naw running to me when you've been a bad 'un, as I'll skelp your lugs for you. You've to be a special boy. One as takes care of your ma.'

Benny looked quizzically at her, as he always did. It was as if he wasn't sure for a moment. She wondered if Art felt the same when Beth held him. It must be confusing to see another woman looking exactly like your own mum. But this look was different and it seemed to Babs that Benny understood but was questioning her. 'Well, I might let you get away with a bit more than your ma and da will, but only a bit.'

Benny smiled then. 'By, lad's got an old head on him, did you see that? He's just wrapped me around his little finger without being able to say a word.' Ma and Peggy laughed at this, and Benny gurgled, then turned his head towards her breast and opened his mouth in the way that babies do to all women. But though she knew that this was all it was, something in Babs made her hold Benny a little tighter to her. And she thought, *You can allus turn to me, allus, me little Benny. I love you, lad. I love you like you were me own.* The thought brought a little enlightenment on what Jasmine had felt for her and Beth, but with it came a gladness that the pain Jasmine would experience really would be very deep.

As they reached the door to the bedroom, she turned to her Ma. 'Ma, there's news that'll make your day.'

'Eeh, lass, I hope it's what I think it is. Is Beth all right?'

'She is, more than all right, but what she's going to do, we have to let her do in her own way.' As she said this, Babs wished with all her heart that Beth would do the sensible thing and have Jasmine and Roman dealt with by the law. She didn't trust them. And she didn't believe that they would just disappear into the night. Oh, they would initially, but they would hatch some plan, she was sure of it.

As they fed their babies, she and Beth chatted in the way they had always been used to: easy, companionable chat with an understanding of each other that no one else could have. They giggled at their sons' antics and compared motherly notes on their boys. It was a time that Babs knew she would cherish forever. 'Beth, let's spend a lot more time together, eh? Just you, me and our boys. That'd be grand.'

'Well, with Ma's plans to set us to work in the shop, we'll have no choice.'

'I knaw, but I'm not sure that's what I want to do. I knaw as you'll be in your element, but I'd hoped to return to nursing, maybe in Blackpool Victoria Hospital, or as a district nurse. I were thinking of finding someone like your Peggy to care for Art for me. Not that I want to leave him, but I need sommat to occupy me every minute.'

'Really? Well, Babs, I never thought. I mean, well, of course I loved nursing when I did it, but I don't think it was my true calling. It was more the fact that I wanted to be like a nurse who once looked after me when I was hospitalised for a long period of time. But I know now that my real vocation is following in Ma's footsteps.'

'Nursing is mine. I were sort of led into it when I landed in the convent, but I've allus known since that it's me true course in life – well, until I met me Rupert. Then I thought I'd be a wife and mother.'

'I know. Look, Babs, don't be led into something you don't really want to do. Talk to Ma, tell her how you feel. You'll be stifled in the shop. And I know she will understand. I think she's only creating these jobs for us as her natural heirs, and because of her need to step back a bit from the business, but she hasn't set her heart on it. Besides, if Mary agrees to it and takes to Molly's work, making cushions and lining baskets, we'll be fine with Gertie looking after the shop floor.'

'Eeh, it's good to have you to talk to. And you're right. If I want to return to work, and I think I will, then it's best that I'm not led into owt as isn't me choosing.'

Art let go of her nipple at that moment; he'd not been suckling for a few minutes but instead half dozing. Now his head flopped back and his milk-stained, cherub lips parted as he fell into a lazy sleep. Trapped wind made his lips form a lovely smile. 'Eeh, me little lad, I love the bones of you, even though you are a lazy little monkey. Come on now, let's get a big burp from you.' Patting his back did the trick. Babs was rewarded with the sound of wind being released from both ends. 'There you go, me little darling. Now you can sleep.'

'You talk to him as if he understands you, Babs.'

'He does. Talking to your babby makes them into a real person and gets you treating them like one instead of constantly cooing over them. You should try it. Then you will soon build up a relationship with your Benny and find the real little person that he is.'

For some reason that Babs couldn't fathom, motherhood didn't come easy to Beth. Maybe it was because she was so totally looked after herself that she left a lot of Benny's care to others. 'You need to really bond with your lad, Beth. Make all the decisions for him, and not let others take charge of his life. There's none better than a ma for a babby.'

'I know. It's not that I don't want to but, well, everyone, except you, doesn't seem to think me capable. They all seem to think they know better than me where Benny's concerned.'

'That's women for you. They're all mother hens, and when they're too old to have their own, they start interfering with ours. Stand up for yourself – and if not for you, for Benny. He'll soon settle down once he knaws he has your full attention.'

Beth looked down at her son and Babs felt good as she heard Beth talk to Benny for the first time as if he was a person.

'Well, what do you think of that, Benny, eh? Are you and me going to let the world know that I'm your ma and you're my number one son?'

Benny looked up at Beth, his eyes full of love and the trust that only a baby can show. Babs's eyes filled with tears as Beth said, 'My darling little boy, I do love you so very much,' and Benny's little hand broke free of his shawl and reached up to her. Beth took his hand and kissed it. 'It's me and you against the mother hens, son. We'll let them know that we know best, won't we?'

As Beth looked up at Babs, she said, 'I feel differently already about being a mother. I feel in the last few seconds like I really became one. But I think I'll have a fight on my hands with Peggy and Ma. They want to do everything for me, and Benny. But, Babs, I'm going to do as you say and gently take the reins from them. It's me and Benny from now on who decide what's what. And we'll start by getting your wind up, little man. No passing you to someone else, your ma's with you now.' When she sat Benny up, he gave an appreciative burp then closed his eyes, content with his world. Beth held him to her. Her head rested on his, and it was a sight that spilled Babs's brimming tears.

It felt to her that everything had come right on this lovely christening day – well, with her and Beth, and for Ma, with Beth determined now to rid herself of Jasmine and Roman. Nothing could put everything right in her world for her, but she had a lot to be thankful for, and that's all she could wish for.

TEN

Tilly

'Ooh, ta, Tilly. I'm ready for sommat to eat and they smell good . . . Eeh, naw, it's that bloke again.'

'What bloke, Molly?' Tilly closed the shop door with her bottom as she juggled hot tatties in her hands.

She and Molly were working at the shop today – herself upstairs, making a wicker chair to add to her stock as these were a huge seller during the summer when the rich flocked to Blackpool for health benefits, and Molly minding the shop as she hand-sewed the linings she'd made into sewing baskets.

Bewildered by what Molly had said, Tilly looked out of the window. She'd only been gone for a few minutes, so couldn't think who could have upset Molly in such a short time. The tattie man had his brazier set up across the road from the shop and the griddled tatties, with their burnt-to-a-crisp skin and delicious fluffy insides, were Tilly's second favourite after fish and chips.

'There, look. He's just walked that way past the window and now he's walking back again; he's done that twice now.

And each time he peers in and looks at me and around the shop as if he's looking for someone.'

Tilly felt a fear zing through her. She couldn't have said why, but she turned and snapped the lock into place.

The gentleman Molly pointed out wore fine clothes which Tilly likened to those that her solicitor dressed in. As she looked at him, he stopped and stared at her and then made as if to open the door. A shiver ran up Tilly's spine as she reached for the sign and turned it to closed.

This didn't deter him. His sharp rap on the door and his intent look made Tilly jump back.

'Do you knaw him, Tilly?'

'Naw, but I don't like the look of him.'

'You go in the back, lass. I'll deal with him.'

Tilly hurried into the kitchen. She stood just inside, behind the door, straining her ear to hear what was said.

'I'm looking for Mrs Rupert Bartrum. I have information that her mother, Mrs Matilda O'Flynn, owns this shop and I believe, from the description that I have been given, that Mrs O'Flynn has just entered this premises. May I speak with her, please?'

'She's not available at the moment. And nor is her daughter.'

'Then I will wait. What time do you reopen the shop?'

'It can be anytime, or naw time, we please ourselves.'

'Well, will you please enquire of Mrs Bartrum's mother when she can give me a few minutes of her time, or maybe you can tell me where I can find Mrs Bartrum herself?'

Tilly felt cornered. Whatever this was it wasn't going to go away. Folk like this gentleman had means of getting what they wanted. Feeling sick with nerves, she came out to face him. 'What do you want with me, sir?'

'It is your daughter I want to speak to. Can you tell me where I will find her?'

'Not until you tell me what you want with me Babs, naw.'

'I represent the Earl of Westholme. Your daughter married his late son. The earl wishes to have contact with his son's child, who is his sole heir.'

'Why? He disowned his son as I understood it. Said that he'd married beneath him.'

'As he did, of course.'

This incensed Tilly. 'We're as good as the next one, mister. Don't come here insulting us and then expect favours. Get out of me shop and tell Earl whats-his-name to leave me family alone. He's naw rights over me grandson.'

'I think you will find that he has every right. I am author-ised to take the child to him. The earl has sought custody of the child and been granted it. The child will reside with him and be brought up by him and him alone.'

'What! Naw, naw ... he can't. Naw one can take a child from his ma. Naw. Get out! Get out!'

'Screaming at me won't make any difference. This decision is one taken by a court of law. Now, where is your daughter and the child? I have a nurse with me who will care for him on the journey.'

'Just get out!' Tilly lifted her fists and the man cowered.

'Tilly! Tilly, lass, naw.' With this Molly grabbed her and clung on to her. Tilly felt a sense of despair overwhelm her. Something told her this was a force she couldn't fight. What these monied folk wanted, they got. *Oh, me poor Babs! Naw, don't let this happen. Dear God, don't let this happen to me Babs.*

'Are you going to tell me where I can find your daughter, or do I have to get the police? I have legal rights as the earl's solicitor and representative to do so. You cannot fight this. It is an order of the court.'

Tilly, who hadn't yet removed her coat, did up the buttons she'd undone. Defeated, she walked past the man feeling as though the last few minutes had aged her. 'Aye, I'll take you to her. You've naw need to get the police. But let me go in and prepare her. Don't, please, barge in and just take her babby.'

'I want this to go as smoothly and painlessly as it possibly can. We all do.'

'Tilly, awe, Tilly lass. Oh God. I don't knaw what to do. This can't happen, it can't.'

'I knaw, Molly. I – I, eeh, Molly, lass.'

'What about your solicitor? Won't he help? Surely you have rights. Don't take him to Babs, Tilly, don't. This'll break her.'

At this, Tilly felt a wave of hope, 'Me friend's right. I do have rights, and I have a solicitor an' all. I'll take you to him first. He'll tell you as you can't do this and send you back to this earl, who I understand didn't care much for his son. We weren't given a chance to fight this. Well, now we are going to. We'll fight it all the way.'

'You'll only be delaying the inevitable. It's all a waste of time. I'd advise that you let the law take its due process and allow us to take the child to its rightful family. Your daughter will soon get over it. You people breed like rabbits, she'll soon have others and forget this one.'

'How dare you! I – I'll—'

'What you will do is stop wasting my time and take me to your daughter, NOW!'

Tilly jumped back from the nasty threat in the man's voice and his demeanour as his voice shook with anger.

A large man, he came over as intimidating and thuggish, despite being posh. His eyes were dark and held no compassion, only contempt. He made her feel as though she was a bit of dirt that he didn't want to deal with. But though she was scared of him, she determined not to crumble. Standing straight with her head high, she told him in a strong voice, 'Naw. The only place I'll take you is to me solicitor. That's where I'm going, and you can follow me or not. It's up to you.'

Striding past the man, she went out, got into her van, which she'd parked outside the shop, and slammed the door. For all her worth she wanted to just take off and leave him, but she waited. Watched him come out of the shop and make for a car parked on the other side of the road. Once he was in it, she shot off with a vague notion of losing him. That didn't happen. His car was far superior to her van and he was behind her all the way.

They hadn't far to go. Mr Fellows had moved to a new office in Abingdon Street. As she headed towards North Shore, Tilly's trembling increased. Part of her wanted to lead the man a merry dance, but something told her that would be a hopeless quest, so she turned into Talbot Road and took the direct route to Mr Fellows' office, praying for all she was worth. *Oh God, please, please don't let this happen. I can't bear me Babs going through what I went through. I beg of you. If you never do owt else for me, do this for me, please.*

★　　★　　★

Her heart sank at the worried expression on Mr Fellows' face as he scrutinised the documents handed to him by the gentleman, who had introduced himself as Mr Renshaw, of Renshaw, Renshaw and Burrows, Solicitors of the county of Kent.

When Mr Fellows looked up, Tilly knew before he spoke that what he was about to say would change everything for them all and, in particular, her beloved Babs. His head shook. 'I'm sorry, Matilda. I'm very sorry, but these papers are in order and do state that your grandchild, Rupert Mario Arthur, is now the legal ward of the Earl of Westholme.'

'But how can that be? How can it be right that these folk have done this without me Babs having a say?'

It was Renshaw who answered. 'The Earl of Westholme has every right to do as he pleases.'

A noise came from Tilly that she wasn't conscious of making. It signified her complete and utter helplessness to fight against a force that was unstoppable. 'But it's cruel. Cruel. Me Babs has already lost her husband and is grieving for him. She's a very brave lass, who worked on a hospital train nursing our soldiers. She went through a terrible explosion and though she knew her Rupert was dead, she carried on and nursed those who had survived. Please, please, Mr Fellows, there must be sommat you can do! Will she never see her babby again?'

Mr Fellows was very quiet for a moment. A caring man who'd helped Tilly over the years in many ways that fell outside of his remit as her solicitor, she could see that he had been devastated by the horror of this latest tragedy to hit her and her family.

Renshaw stood up, his manner one of utter contempt as he leant over Mr Fellows' desk. 'All of this is a waste of my time and yours, Fellows. Well, maybe not yours, you, being a back-street solicitor in a bloody awful northern town, but mine definitely. I demand that you instruct your client – the likes of which would never find her way onto my client list – to arrange to hand over the Earl of Westholme's grandson immediately!'

The scraping of Mr Fellows' chair on the linoleum covering his office floor made Mr Renshaw step back. Mr Fellows, as tall as Renshaw, looked imposing as he displayed an air of command. 'I beg your pardon. Take those insults back. How dare you come here and make such insinuations that cast a doubt over my credentials, and my client's rights and standing? I will take this to the Law Society.'

Mr Renshaw coughed. 'I apologise. But nevertheless, you do know that I am within my lawful rights and that you should be instructing your client to abide by my lawful claim to take the child.'

'I will do that, but I want your full details and those of the earl. I am filing for an order that my client can have regular contact with her child and a say in his future well-being.'

'Puh! I wish you good luck, but don't hold out much for your chances. The earl is a force to be reckoned with, and he'll not have that happen. You have a fight on your hands, my learned friend.'

'I enjoy a legal fight more than anything in this world, and I enjoy winning, which I shall.' Turning to Tilly, Mr Fellows softened his expression. 'I'm sorry, Matilda. For now, your grandson has to be handed over, but I assure you, I will fight every step of the way so that you and she can have a right to see the child. There are very good grounds for such a claim and though it will take time, I can see no reason why we shouldn't win. For now, it is going to take a great deal of courage on your daughter's behalf to comply with this order and it will be a huge toll on her. But knowing you like I do, I am certain that you will help her through this.'

Tilly felt defeated. The one person in all the world whose word she would take on matters to do with the law was allowing this to happen. 'Naw, naw. Please, please.'

'Matilda, don't give this abominable man the satisfaction of seeing you beg. Hold your head up high and help your daughter through this. I'm so very sorry. Of all the people who shouldn't have bad things happen to them, you least deserve this. My heart goes out to you. You have suffered enough. But I am helpless to do more than what I have promised to do.'

Tilly looked into Mr Fellows' kind face and knew the fight was lost. That all her beloved Babs would ever have in the future was a few hours here and there with her son – and only if Mr Fellows won her the right to it.

Her heart was full of pain as she stood. 'Mr Fellows, can you at least make him wait while I go and prepare me Babs? There has to be time given to me for that.'

'Mr Renshaw?'

'No. I want to get out of this place before dark. I have a long journey to undertake. I cannot sanction a wait as I cannot think of staying around here a moment longer than I have to. I want the child given over to me and the nurse I have with me. I will follow this woman to her daughter's now.'

'This woman? Did you not even bother to ask her name? This woman! She is Mrs Matilda O'Flynn and from now on you will treat her with respect. Matilda, do you want me to come with you to keep this excuse of a solicitor in check?'

Tilly nodded. 'But stay in your cars. This is going to be an almighty blow to me daughter, and I don't knaw how she will cope with it.'

'We will. There will be nothing unlawful, such as snatching the baby, while I am around. I could get Mr Renshaw struck off for that, and he knows it. Now, give me a moment to have a word with my secretary so that she can rearrange my appointments.'

When they reached the farm, Tilly jumped out of her van, and as she did, a thought came to her that she wished that the yard was still as clean as it had been three weeks ago, but then thinking of the happiness of the day of the christening increased her pain. She screamed at the top of her voice for Tommy. He came hobbling out from the cowshed, moving much quicker now that he was being helped by Beth and Babs to carry out specific exercises. 'Tilly, me lovely, what is it that's happened?'

'Oh, Tommy.'

'Who is it that you have with you? Oh, me little Tilly, what's going on?'

'They've come for little Art. Oh, Tommy, help me, help me.'

'Ma?' A shocked Babs stood on the steps of the farmhouse. 'Naw, Ma. Why, why? They can't. They can't take me babby.'

Babs's body shook, her eyes stared out from their sockets.

'Oh, Babs, me Babs. I – I tried to stop it, I did.'

'NAW!'

Babs ran inside. Tilly and Tommy followed her. Babs had run upstairs. Following her, they found her with her back to Art's cot facing them. Her look was akin to that of some of the mad women that Tilly had known in the asylum.

'Babs, me Babs. There's nowt we can do today. But Mr Fellows is going to fight this.'

Through her sobs, Babs asked, 'Who are they, Ma? Why can they take me babby? Ma, naw. Don't let it happen.'

'One is my solicitor, Mr Fellows. The other . . . Oh, Babs, he is solicitor to the Earl of Westholme.'

Babs gasped. Her head shook from side to side. Her protest came out as a whisper. 'Naw. Not Rupert's father. He can't do this, can he, Ma?'

'I'm so sorry, me Babs. I'm so sorry. There's nowt we can do. It's been passed by the courts that the earl is to be the guardian of Art as he is his sole heir.'

'But there's a cousin. Rupert told me that he'd given up his right to inherit the title and his cousin would take his place.'

'I knaw nowt of that, Babs. I only knaw as Mr Fellows, me solicitor, has said that for now we have to let Art go. But there is hope. He is going to fight for the right for you to see Art on visits. For us all to see him. I tried, me Babs, I tried.'

With this, Tilly broke. Tommy held her. He didn't speak, but then, what could he or anyone say?

A defeated Babs turned and lifted her child. Her tears soaked her face. Tilly thought that she was going to hand the babby over, but she suddenly dashed by them and ran down the stairs.

★   ★   ★

Babs felt her world splitting in two. She had to get away from here, take her Art and run. Reaching the door, she stopped. The cars in the yard looked like monsters. Turning, she ran through the house. Ma and Tommy were coming down the stairs; they called to her, but she didn't answer. They were the enemy; they were allowing this terrible thing to happen to her and her beloved Art.

At the front door, she fumbled to get the key off the hook. At last she had the door open.

'Babs, Babs, naw, don't do it.'

Ignoring her ma's pleas, she ran down the drive and onto the road. There she turned away from the direction that would take her to Blackpool.

Hearing the sound of a car, she begged out loud, 'Naw, Naw, don't let this happen. Please don't let this happen. Me babby, me babby.'

Suddenly, she felt her body hurtling towards the ground. Twisting so that Art was safe, she landed near to the kerb. Her head smashed on its edge and she knew no more.

When she came around, she was in a hospital bed. For a moment, she didn't know why, but then memory hit her, and she wailed out against it.

'Hello, Barbara. You're all right, lass.'

Opening her eyes again, she looked into the kindly eyes of a nurse. 'Me babby. Where's Art? Where's me babby?'

'Don't worry yourself. I'm sure he's being looked after. Eeh, you've a rook of folk waiting for you to come round. You had a fall and knocked yourself out. You'll be all right, but you need to stay with us a couple of days to make sure.

I should think that Sister will let you have a visit from your child.'

'Have they taken him? Is me ma here? Please don't say that me little Art's gone. Please.'

'Eeh, I think as you're still a little confused, Barbara. Try to rest. I'll see if Sister will get the doctor to you to help you to relax.'

'Naw, I want me ma. I must see me ma, please, Nurse. I must see me ma.'

'All right. If that'll settle you. But if you get any more upset, then I'll have to get the doctor to you.'

When her ma came through the door to the ward, Babs knew. Never had she seen her ma look in the state she was. Her lovely raven-coloured hair hung in strands of fallen curls. Her face, tear-stained and drawn, had aged.

'Me Babs, me lovely Babs.'

'Ma?'

'I'm sorry.' Ma's head shook from side to side. 'I don't knaw what to say, me heart's bleeding for you. Oh, Babs.'

'Naw, don't let it be the truth, Ma.'

Her ma got onto the bed and lay beside her, taking her in her arms. Babs clung on to her as she let in the enormity of what had happened. Her worst fear had been realised. Her babby, her precious little Art, was gone.

ELEVEN

Beth

Frustration made Beth thump the arms of her basket chair. She'd dropped the basket she'd been working on and couldn't reach it when she bent over. She'd tried to concentrate on her work for her ma and blot out all the horror of what Babs was going through and the thought of maybe never seeing her darling nephew Art again, but her efforts just made her more and more upset with her own limitations. *Oh why, why did this happen to me? What use am I to anyone? I'm just a nuisance that has to be helped to do the simplest task.*

She knew it wasn't the basket falling that was really making her feel so at odds with being incapacitated but her inability to be of help to Babs and the pain of having Babs at odds with her again, not to mention the upcoming showdown with Jasmine who was due to visit.

Jasmine would be full of the christening celebrations that the gypsies were planning, and what Beth had to tell her would break her heart, but then she deserved that, didn't she?

Beth had analysed and analysed her dependence on Jasmine and Roman over the time that she had spent with Henry's family. A quiet but lovely time that had helped her with her decision as she found Philomena and Janine so easy to talk to.

They'd expressed their agreement with what she was doing, and had reinforced her determination to rid herself of Jasmine and all the gypsies. And the nice thing had been that their motive wasn't from any prejudices that they had against those considered of a lesser standing than themselves, as Henry's family didn't have any such notions, but because of the wrong that Jasmine and Roman had done and the hurt they could see had been caused to her ma.

Added to this, the terrible, horrific taking of their little nephew: seeing Babs's distress, not to mention her own at being wrenched from little Art, had cemented in her the devastation the kidnap of herself and Babs would have caused her ma. But still she had delayed this moment since returning home, something which she could only put down to her own weakness. It was something that had got Babs's back up and made her cross and distant again, but though she'd tried again to make the break, she'd failed and at the last minute had told Peggy to tell Jasmine that she was at the shop on the first visit Jasmine made and on the second that she was at her ma's.

But today, the cowardness had to stop. Babs needed her. She knew there would be no getting back to the lovely relationship they'd rekindled on the day of the christening while she hadn't carried through her promise to rid herself of Jasmine and Roman. Today, she was determined to do that.

The door to the kitchen opened and Peggy came into the living room. 'Eeh, lass, what's to do? Why didn't you call me?' Peggy bent over and picked up the basket.

'Put it on the table, please, Peggy. I can't work. My mind's not on the task. Oh, Peggy, everything's gone wrong and I don't know how to put it right.'

'Well, I'd say as you're making a good start by facing up to Jasmine, and not before time. For your poor Babs, there's not much any of us can do, but you will at least help her by getting them gypsies out of your life. It's all she wants of you. She is torn in her loyalties to you and her ma. She can see you are hurting your ma, and doesn't feel she can collude with that by being on good terms with you. So, what you are going to do today will be a massive step in the right direction for you, lass, and for Babs. It's a crying shame, her losing her little lad . . . Eeh, it beggars belief the troubles that hit your ma, you and Babs, and yet, you are three of the loveliest women I knaw.'

'Thank you, Peggy. I found a gem in you. But you know, all of the things that happen in life are triggered by circumstances. Everything would have been all right for us if Da hadn't been killed at such a young age. Ma tried to keep us together. I was only young, but I remember her struggle and I think she would have succeeded in caring for us, but for the gypsies. I hate them with a vengeance now. Oh, Peggy, how could I have been so blind to what they did? How could I have been so taken in by them? I should have left them when Babs did. Why didn't I?'

'Naw, I reckon you did right to stay then. I don't knaw it all, but I have gathered that bad things happened to Babs as a result of her trying to get back to your ma. But maybe you

131

should have made the break when you became independent . . . Oh, I don't knaw, lass. Life's full of maybes and should haves. We none of us are given a glimpse into the future. They were all you had, and I'll give them their due, they did right by you, making sure you were educated and supporting you to become a nurse. That must have cost them a pretty penny, I reckon. And went against their whole way of life, so wasn't sommat they understood. Eeh, hark at me, I sound as though I'm defending them when I reckon what they did was vile.'

The door knocker rattling made them both jump.

'I'll let her in, lass, then seem like I'm busying meself in the kitchen, but in truth I'll be listening at the door, and if she cuts up rough, I'll be through with me frying pan and'll sort her out, I'll tell you.'

Beth's heart sank. She hoped with all her heart that this confrontation wouldn't come to Jasmine having to be physically removed from the house.

When Jasmine entered the living room, Beth could see that she knew something wasn't right.

'Beth. Oh, Beth, it is good to see you. I have been so very worried. I know that it is that something is wrong with both you and Babs. What is it? Tell me.'

In the silence that followed Beth registered the kitchen door closing behind Peggy. The click it made grated on her fraught nerves. Taking a deep breath, she looked directly into Jasmine's dark eyes. 'I do not want to see you ever again, Jasmine.'

Jasmine's gasp filled the room. So pain-filled was it that it almost undid Beth's resolve.

'But, why? No, don't do this, my Beth, we will always be by your side. When you move to Kent—'

'No! You did a wicked thing, Jasmine. You stole me from my ma. You caused so much to happen in our lives.'

'But this isn't true! Your ma didn't want you, she—'

'Stop it! Stop telling me those lies. You stole us – kidnapped me and Babs. You ruined our lives and that of our ma. I hate you! How I could have loved you and hurt my ma by sticking by you, I just don't know. Please leave, get out of my life, Jasmine.'

'I cannot do that, little one. It is that my heart will break. You are my child, my life, everything. Nothing has any meaning without you.'

Beth could feel herself weakening but knew she had to do this. 'If you don't, I will go to Ma's solicitor and he will go to the police. Your crime will be punished by the law then. I need you out of my life. You're nothing to me, nothing but a hateful memory.' Beth's body trembled, but she felt empowered. She knew that what she was doing was the right thing. That Jasmine's pain at her action was deserved. She shouldn't be allowed to have peace of mind ever again.

'No. No!' Though this was a plea, Jasmine's face suddenly changed. A fear zinged through Beth as she saw an expression she'd never seen before. The spite that showed made Jasmine look ugly. 'I will never, ever be out of your life! Always you will look over your shoulder and know that I am there, waiting. I curse you and Babs – Babs more than anyone – and my curse is already taking effect on her life as once more, her rejection of me is resulting in great pain for her. But now you too will know this pain! My curse that has been on your ma and Babs is now on you!'

'Get out! Eeh, I've never heard the like. Get out of Beth's house and out of her life.' True to what she'd said she would do, Peggy burst through the kitchen door brandishing a frying pan. The absurdity of this made Beth want to giggle, and she would have but for the fear that clutched her. Part of her believed in Jasmine's powers and the thought of her curse terrified her.

Jasmine looked at Peggy with the same evil expression, but Peggy was having none of it. 'By, don't you start with that cursing on me, lady, or I'll knock you to kingdom come. Now get out of here and don't come back. You're evil. EVIL!'

Jasmine cowered from the raised pan. She turned to leave, but as she reached the door, she spat out the words, 'Evil does as evil is, and my powers are against you. All of you. You are doomed. Doomed!'

As she disappeared through the door, Beth gave way to the sobs that had threatened her. Never had she experienced a feeling like the one that took her. Grief? Yes, she had to admit that she did feel grief at the loss of a huge part of her life. But she was also filled with dread as to what Jasmine could bring down on them. But despite this she had no remorse at ridding herself of Jasmine, only that it had taken her so long to do so, and how much pain she'd caused by not doing it before.

'Eeh, me lass.' Peggy dropped her pan and came to Beth. Beth felt herself being held in loving arms and realised in that moment how much Peggy thought of her, and her love for this woman filled her. She clung on to Peggy as if doing so would save her from falling into the deep pit of misery that seemed to be clawing at her.

So much was not as it should be – her Henry, her beloved husband was not by her side, her lovely sister Babs was suffering deeply from the loss of her husband and now her son, Ma was so tired, and trying to be all things to all of them, and unable to cope with not being able to be. Tommy was yearning to be farming the land of his ancestors in his beloved Ireland. *And me, stuck in this chair, a liability to them all! Oh God, why? Why?*

'Lass, why don't you do as your ma asks and move in with them? There's nowt pulling you from them now. By, you were a brave lass to make the break with that lot. I were proud of you.'

'I want to do that, I do, I want to be with Babs to help her, but what about you, Peggy? And Ma's shop? She wants me to work in it to give her more time off, and it is something that I want to do, but I wouldn't be able to get from Marton easily.'

'Aye, I can see that, but you've naw worries over me. I can go back to me cottage as I've kept on. Or I can take up your ma's offer and be a live-in nurse and general help to you as I am now.'

'Oh, that's what I'd like, Peggy. I'd be such a burden to Ma. And you know how to handle me. But there's still the question of getting to the shop, because somehow I must lighten Ma's load.'

'Well, I'm sure that could be got around. But I don't feel safe here anymore. By, that one fair put the wind up me, she did. Do you reckon as her curses can come true?'

In her heart, Beth knew that she did believe they could. She didn't want to, but she'd seen so much of what Jasmine and the other gypsies had done and had known their predictions to come true so many times. With her saying that she had cursed Babs before this, all that had happened to Babs seemed proof of that.

'Beth?'

Beth heard the fear in Peggy's voice. 'Don't worry, Peggy. I have known bad things to happen when the gypsies wished it on someone, but I am sure they were coincidences and them only stating the obvious. She says that she cursed Babs. Well, predicting that bad things would happen to Babs when she left at such a young age to traipse across the country alone and without protection was something anyone could have done. And what has happened to Babs now isn't Jasmine's doing, it was the war throwing everyone together no matter what your class, and taking lives as if they are nothing. Babs would never have met an heir to an earldom if it wasn't for the war, let alone fell in love with him and married him. Jasmine didn't do that. She's only playing on it. Let's forget her and decide what it is that we are going to do.'

'I could learn to drive; your ma did. And I could buy meself a motor – I've enough saved. Aye, and thinking about it, being able to get around will mean I can take up some of the work I used to do – delivering the babbies around here and tending to the sick. After all, you'll not need me so much, and it'll get me from under your ma's feet when you're at the shop. Aye, that'd work out nicely. What do you think, eh?'

'Yes, Peggy. Let's do it. I can help with the purchase of the car. Oh, I wish that I could learn to drive, but they all have foot pedals.' Once again, Beth felt the pity and frustration of her condition. Life seemed so unfair. But she had the chance to do something to help the situation as it was, as surely she could be a help to Babs by being with her.

The move into what Beth knew was her real home didn't resolve everything as she had hoped. Babs was in a terrible

136

state and no matter what Beth tried to do to help her, nothing worked.

Over the last week she'd woken twice to see Babs getting a bottle of gin from the bottom of their wardrobe.

Beth hadn't told her ma, hoping that this phase would pass and half thinking that if it helped Babs to sleep, maybe it wouldn't do any harm. But Babs was like a demented woman today, as she ran around screaming and hitting the walls as if they imprisoned her.

'Oh, Ma, Ma. What can we do for her?'

'Very little, lass. I knaw the pain she's in. Poor Babs has lost so much.' They sat at the kitchen table. Babs had now locked herself into the bedroom which Beth and she shared.

'It's being able to imagine your pain, now that I have Benny, that made me realise what you went through Ma. I—'

'Naw more apologies, Beth. You can't spend the rest of your life regretting. You did what you thought was right, and now you've mended it. Let that be an end to it, lass. If you let things haunt you, they can drag you down, and there's naw need. I have you back now and that's all I ask for.'

Stretching across the table, Beth took her ma's hand. They didn't speak for a moment.

The door opened and Peggy came through. 'Eeh, what's to do? I could hear the noise. I would have come straight in, but that flipping goat decided he'd have me skirt for a snack. Just look what he's done.'

Beth could have hugged Peggy; she always seemed to make every situation normal. Never mind that Babs was raging behind a closed door, the goat had dared to eat her skirt!

'Come and sit down and take the weight off your feet, Peggy. You tire me out with constantly being on with sommat or other.'

'I'm sorry, lass, I just don't want to add to your burden, but try to take away from it if I can.'

'You couldn't add owt, only lighten what I have on me plate, lass. It's good to have you here. But, eeh, what we're to do for me poor Babs I don't knaw.'

'Ma, there's something I haven't told you.' Beth told them both about the gin.

'Naw. By, that's what I did, and it didn't help. Not really. It did while I was drinking it, but it led to consequences. She must have got it from the cellar. Peggy, love, will you go into the cellar and empty what's left of the drinks we had in for the christening down the drain?'

Peggy scurried away, eager as ever to please. Beth hoped that she would soon settle and feel that she was part of the family. She hated her thinking that she might be in the way.

When she came back, she told them that there were only two bottles of gin and two of sherry.

'It seemed a shame to waste it, but I knaw what you mean, that stuff does get hold of folk. I've seen decent women take it to bring on their labour and end up hooked on it.'

'By, how did Babs manage to hide that from me? I was sure there were at least four to five bottles of gin.'

Babs's wailing had stopped while they'd been talking. Beth so wanted to go to her, and felt again the frustration of not being able to simply get up and do just that. 'Peggy, will you help me into my bath chair, please.'

'Aye, of course.'

'I'll go to Babs. You stay there, lass.'

'No, Ma. I want to come. I know it takes me longer, but that doesn't mean that I can't do what I want to.'

'Awe, me lass. It's my turn to say sorry now. I had to learn that lesson with Ivan, but it was a gradual process as me and him made sommat new to help him achieve what he wanted to do. With you, I want to do everything for you.'

'I've noticed that, Tilly. But it will take you a bit of time to get used to Beth's independence. I knaw it did me. When I arrived, I had this idea of sorting her out my way, and that meant doing everything for her, but she soon put me right, I can tell you.'

Peggy had Beth in the bath chair by the time she'd said all this. 'There you go, lass. Now, do as you have to do. I'll leave you both to it and get these veggies stored away.'

Tilly got to the bedroom door first. Knocking on it she called out, 'Babs? Babs, love, it's Ma.'

'I knaw, Ma. Oh, Ma, help me.'

'Open the door, lass, and let me hug you.'

The lock clicked. 'Eeh, me Babs.'

Watching Ma and Babs in a hug, and hearing them sob, set Beth off. Her heart was breaking for them both. Ma with her pain of yesteryear, and Babs in agony over her loss.

Reaching out her hand, she touched Babs's arm. Babs didn't come out of the hug with Ma but reached her hand towards Beth. This was a breakthrough, as Babs had been cold and stiff towards them all.

Ma patted Babs's back. 'Come on, lass. We'll get Peggy to make us a nice cuppa and sit out in the garden, eh? It's a warm day.'

Babs allowed herself to be guided towards the kitchen by Ma.

'Kettle's on, me loves. You go on out, I'll be with you in a mo.'

'Was that sixth sense?'

'No, Ma, Peggy has very acute hearing, especially where someone might need help – well, either that, or she listens at doors.'

'Ha! I suspect it's the last, but in a nice way, ready to give aid if she hears it's needed.'

Beth agreed with this, as always Peggy was there with a helping hand, and that hand usually contained a pot of tea.

The sun bathed the farmyard in the light and warmth of a mid-June day. Tommy could be seen hovering at the end of the barn as if he didn't want to intrude, but no doubt he'd heard the noise and couldn't get on with what he needed to. He waved to them and they all waved back. It was good to see him now able to work alongside Phil, Cliff and Jack.

'By, me Tommy's that upset, bless him. He has loved you girls, through me telling him of you and the sadness he felt for you both and for me over the years. He often vowed to find you but didn't knaw where to start. Now he has you, it's as if you are his own daughters.'

'And we love him, Ma. It was a bit scary at first to know that you'd married again, but you couldn't have picked anyone better than Tommy to take Da's place.'

'By, Beth, Tommy hasn't done that. Your da will allus be in me heart. As will Jeremiah. They have their own place inside me.'

140

'One day, I'd like to learn more about Jeremiah, Ma. I feel I'd like to hear about a good gypsy, as he sounds as though he was.'

'He was, and there are many good ones, Beth, never forget that. I met the same measure of good and bad that I meet in our communities; they just live their lives in a different way. Now, are you comfortable, Babs?'

Babs nodded, unable to speak for rebound sobs shaking her body. Her face was all swollen and red, blotchy patches marked her cheeks. She looked a picture of misery. Suddenly, as she caught sight of Benny's pram standing under the huge lilac tree, her face changed. She looked from it to Beth.

Beth recoiled against the hate she saw in her beloved twin's face.

'Everything allus turns out right for you, Beth. Aye, you were injured, but that led you to land a man with naw complications, with a family who accepted you and would never steal your babby from you. Why? Why is it that you allus come out of every situation with a smile on your face and hope for your future, eh?'

'I – I don't know, I—'

'Aye, and your fancy way of talking, leaving your roots behind is all part of it.'

'No . . .'

'Babs, don't do this. Don't turn on them as love you and wouldn't do you any harm, lass.'

'But does she, Ma? Everything is on her terms. Look after Beth, Babs. Watch out for her. Don't upset her, you knaw how she can be. Well, she does a very good job of looking after herself. It suited her to be with Jasmine and Roman and to

twist them around her finger so that she got a good education. She wouldn't come with me to find you, Ma. Oh, naw.
She were cosy and that did her. Tell her, Beth. Tell Ma how
you didn't want to leave the love of them gypsies to find your
own ma.'

Beth was aghast. She couldn't speak. How could this
happen? That Babs should turn on her again, but this time
with such vitriol? Her heart sank, as she knew that some of
what Babs had said was the truth. She looked up at her ma
and in her face she saw a question. *Oh, Ma, don't lose faith in
me, don't!*

TWELVE

Babs

The night hours were the worst. Lying awake, listening for Art's cry, in agony as the milk meant to feed him had no release and swelled her breasts till she felt they would burst.

Getting out of bed, Babs looked over at Beth sleeping like a baby. How she could do that when there was such turmoil going on around her always amazed Babs.

The feeling of being at odds with the world and herself ground into Babs. Beth had never supported her; always it was the other way around. And even now, when Babs most needed her, she was only here because of her own needs, having at last decided that having Jasmine and Roman in her life no longer suited her. Babs wondered why this was. Oh, she said it was because she'd suddenly seen the hurt that she'd caused and realised what Jasmine and Roman had truly done. Well, it had taken her a bloody long time and was done at her own convenience. More likely it was because she saw that they were not useful to her anymore, and just an embarrassment. Beth didn't do anything unless it suited her to do it.

Walking towards the window, Babs looked up at the moon with its seemingly mocking face, and wanted to scream out loud against her pain – physical and mental.

Beth gave a small snore, bringing Babs's attention to her once more. How often in the past she'd given and received comfort by snuggling up to her sister, and yet now, she only felt resentment towards her that bordered on hate. This compounded the loneliness that engulfed her as she didn't feel she could reach out to Ma either. Not because she felt at odds with Ma, but because Ma's own pain became raw and she never wanted to hurt her.

A longing came over her to seek the oblivion that Ma's gin gave her. With this being a guilty secret, she crept quietly out of the room so as not to disturb Beth. Having always been a strong person, this need shamed her, but she couldn't cope on her own any longer.

Taking an oil lamp from the shelf in the kitchen, she lit it and went towards the cellar with a feeling growing inside her that she would soon be able to blot out the hurt and that this justified her actions.

Finding the flagons of sherry empty and no gin bottles in sight, a sense of panic washed over her. How was she to cope now? Why was there no drink left? Beth! That must be it. Beth knew and had told Ma. The feeling of desolation that took her jagged at her heart. She hadn't wanted to find proof of her sister's cunning ways working against her. She hadn't wanted to believe the thoughts that she was having about Beth. But this was the sort of sneaky action that Beth took. Why? *Why didn't she just speak to me about it? Why shame me to Ma behind me back? Why make Ma treat me like a child by taking away what I need, instead of talking to me? God, do they all think I'm a drunk or something?*

Loneliness crowded in on her. She had to get away from here, where decisions were being made for her, where memories of little Art were everywhere: his tiny clothes, his empty cot – even the smell of him hung in the air. Not that she ever wanted to forget him, but she didn't need these reminders rubbing her raw pain every minute of the day.

Sitting down on the cold cellar steps, weariness took her. Where would she go? How would she keep herself? Back to nursing? Was that the answer? Would putting herself back into the hell of other people's pain help her own?

Suddenly, she knew that it would and that's what she'd do if what she dreaded happening happened – if the solicitor lost the case to get her the right to see Art.

With this thought, she no longer needed the gin. Some of her strength came back into her. She had a means of escaping, of doing something to help others and, in so doing, help herself. The new plan didn't relieve her loneliness – if anything, it compounded it – and still she saw that as Beth's fault. Beth had let her down in so many ways. Being away from her wouldn't be painful this time, but a relief.

Getting up, she made her way to the bathroom. She had to get the milk from her breasts and bind herself to try to prevent it coming in again. She had to try to accept that Art was gone. How, she did not know. It was easier to bear little Mario's passing than having Art torn from her. Not that she loved Mario less, but he couldn't stay with her, he needed to go to heaven, and she knew he was happy and would always rest in her heart. But her second son was probably in the arms of a wet nurse at this very moment suckling a stranger's milk when hers – the milk he should be suckling – went to waste. *Art, Art, me darling son . . . Rupert, Rupert, wherever you are, help me, Rupert. Oh, me Rupert, I need you.*

Clinging on to the sink, Babs knew that the strength that had come to her in the cellar was ebbing away. She couldn't let it. A barrier had begun to form against the pain, and she needed that. Putting her attention to relieving her breasts of their load, she felt some of her physical pain lessen. In her ma's linen cupboard in the corner of the bathroom she found a cot sheet. For a moment she held it to her face hoping to smell her little Art on it, but it only smelt of cleanliness and the fresh air it had dried in after it had been washed.

Making a band with it, she wrapped it tightly around her breasts, flattening them to her, then reached for a pin out of the Toby jug that stood on the windowsill and held all manner of odd pins, hair clips and rolled-up ribbon. As it always did, the sight of the jug took her back to being in the gypsy caravan and an anger reeled up inside her against Jasmine and Roman. They were responsible for so much that had happened to her. But she didn't give them much time in her thoughts, she needed to keep herself from going down that road.

Feeling more comfortable, but unable to dispel her emotional pain, she couldn't get away from the idea that she needed a drink to help her. As much as she tried to convince herself of her growing strength, it didn't work.

It had been a week ago that she'd woken and the thought had first come to her that she should seek the feeling that alcohol had given her at Christmas, when they had all been in a party mood. Although she hadn't done so, the feeling had made her want to dance in the way that the gypsies did – with wonderful abandonment, twirling and stamping her feet and skipping and bending as she swirled her body. To feel her hair loose down her back, swishing over her face and then back down to brush her neck – a glorious feeling of freedom.

That same feeling didn't come to her when she'd crept down to the cellar and taken a good gulp, but she had felt her pain become less intense and had fallen into the blessed relief of sleep.

It came to her then that there might be some sherry left in the dresser.

Encouraged by this, Babs went into the Sunday best room and hoped against hope that she was right.

She was. And it was with a growing anticipation that Babs put the oil lamp down on one of the occasional tables and reached for the bottle, uncorked it and poured herself a large measure.

Sitting in one of the huge armchairs, she relaxed back. The effect of the drink and the hush of the still night began to soothe her and clear her mind so that she could think. But she wouldn't let it visit places that hurt, only to try to map out a future for herself. She didn't believe that her future lay here with Beth constantly undermining her, or with all the memories that relentlessly prodded her. And she couldn't let herself believe that she would ever see Art again. That would be setting up more pain for the future. No. She must do what had come to her a few moments ago in the cellar – tomorrow, she would contact the Red Cross. Everything would be all right tomorrow. She just needed to leave everything behind tonight.

Gulping down the glass of sherry, she poured another.

★   ★   ★

'Eeh, lass, lass.'

The voice sounded a long way off, but she knew it was her ma, her lovely ma.

A pain zinged through her head as she tried to lift it. 'Ma?'

'I'm here, me darling. Oh, Babs.'

Opening her eyes, Babs saw her ma bend and pick up a bottle. For a moment, she couldn't think why, but then memory slapped her and she sat up as shame washed over her. 'I – I was in pain, Ma. I wanted the pain to go.'

'Not this way, lass. Not this way. I knaw the perils of this path. Oh, me Babs, I knaw your pain, I do. And I'm at a loss as to how to help you, but if I could stop you going down the road of drowning your sorrows in the drink, I would.'

'I knaw, Ma. I knaw what happened to you, but you had naw one. I've got you. I'll be all right. It's just till I can cope.'

'Naw, lass. This won't help you to cope. It can only lead to more pain being piled on top of what you're already suffering. In the end, I had to face the pain head on. I had to fight me way out of the misery and build a new life. Eeh, I'm not saying as that life didn't include you and Beth, it did, you were allus with me, and the rawness of my heart never healed, but I coped. I found happiness to run alongside the hurt. You can do that, I promise you.'

'I'm going to try, Ma. I'm going back to nursing.'

'What? Oh, I . . . Well, me little Babs, if that'll help. But me heart wants me to go on me knees and beg you not to. But I won't. It's not me place to. I've to support you in whatever you want to do, Babs, but you will wait until we find out if you have the right to see little Art, won't you?'

'Naw, Ma. I'll not win that, and you and Mr Fellows knaw that. There's so much in me past against me, and the earl will dig it all up. He won't want me in Art's life. All I can hope for is what you hoped for: that when he's older and can make his own mind up, he'll find me and want to be with me. Or, as I'll allus knaw where he is, which is different to what you had to put up with, I can one day approach him and tell him how much I love him and how he was stolen from me.'

'Eeh, me Babs. Let me hug you, me darling girl.'

Going into her ma's arms, Babs tried to dispel the sinking feeling of knowing that her ma couldn't deny her fears and that Ma knew it was hopeless, just as she did.

'Ma, maybe you hadn't ought to waste the money on the solicitor.'

'Naw, love, I must. Even if we lose, I want Arty to knaw that we tried. What will he think if we can't tell him that?'

'Eeh, Ma, I never thought of that. Aye, we must fight. But I have to get away, I have to do sommat, and, Ma, I wouldn't be happy in your shop. I'm sorry, I knaw as your plans are to hand it over to me and Beth, but it wouldn't work, Ma. I couldn't work with Beth, I need to be away from her.'

'Naw, naw, don't say that, Babs, don't. It cuts me in two.'

'I don't mean to sever all links, but we thrive better apart. I knaw it shouldn't be like that, but I feel that Beth needs a lot more than me in having your attention and that she discredits me. I knaw you don't like to think it, Ma, but Beth does what suits Beth, and she has a hard core that you'll never recognise as she's allus been the weak one in your eyes. Well, she's weak in body now, but not in spirit. Look how she clung on to Jasmine and Roman, hurting you and me, and not caring about that.'

Ma was quiet for a moment. Babs saw many emotions cross her face and felt sorry that she'd provoked them. Jumping up made her head pound, but she went into her ma's arms. 'Eeh, Ma, I'm sorry. I'm sorry to the heart of me, but I think that if apart, me and Beth will get on a lot better than we will living and working together. It's best for all that I go.'

Her ma clung on to her. The feeling of love her ma gave her nearly undid her resolve, but then another feeling took her and she had to leave her ma's arms and run for the bathroom.

As she opened the door, she saw the back of Beth's wheel-chair disappear into her bedroom and the thought came to her that those who listen hear no good of themselves.

In the bathroom Babs threw her heart up and felt so ill that she went down on her knees as her strength ebbed away.

'Oh, Babs . . . I'll get a bath ready for you. But please, please let this be the last time.'

'It will be, Ma, I promise you.'

And with saying this, Babs determined to make it true. She was stronger than this, wasn't she? She could find a way to cope, just as her ma had. But as another bout of vomiting took her, she wondered if she truly could.

Lying in the bath, she let her mind drift to Rupert. So often she'd blotted him out, unable to deal with thinking about him. But now, his smiling face came to her and she felt she could reach out and touch it.

'Is there sommat as you want, Babs?'

With this from her ma, she knew she'd lifted her arm and reached up. Her heart jolted, but she swallowed hard. She'd cried a lake of tears and had no more left inside her. 'Naw, Ma, just me imagination giving me Rupert. I didn't knaw as I reached up for him, I thought it was all in me thoughts.'

Ma was sat on the side of the bath. 'That's good, me little Babs, it means that you can be with him whenever you want to be now that you've let him come back to you. All you have to do is to close your eyes and he'll be there. I've allus done it with your da, and Ivan and your Aunt Liz. Oh, and many others ... Martha. Do you remember, Martha? It was her leaving me her house and some money that got me the shop.'

'I sort of have a memory of her every time you talk of her, and of Aunt Liz.'

'Aye, lovely Aunt Liz. Well, I'm on with me plans for her house an' all. I've spoken to Mr Fellows and he is going to get the plans sorted to make it into two dwellings – it's almost done anyway, as Liz and Dan had a little flat made for Dan's aunt. And I've made me own will to leave the house to you, Beth and Eliza, to do with it whatever you want.

'Eeh, Ma, that's good of you.'

'Me shop an' all, as I own the building now, and Molly is just a partner in the business run inside the building. Anyroad, that's all for the future, and it's nice for me to knaw that I have something to bequeath to you both. Now, I've to go and see if Beth's all right. And, Babs, try to look differently on how Beth is. It pains me to see you at odds with her.'

Babs didn't answer this. She'd never want to cause her ma hurt, and could see that she had. She'd make it up with Beth, and at least make it look that they were all right together. *Mind, I'll watch out for her. I just don't feel that I can trust her anymore. She's not my Beth. Not the Beth I knew when we were young 'uns.*

Ma had reached the door. 'By the way, Babs, I noticed the band you've made yourself. Has it helped?'

'Aye. Me milk didn't come in this morning.'

'Good. You'll be more comfortable now, but I'd keep wearing it for a couple of days, lass. How did you knaw about that method of stopping your milk flowing?'

'From me work in the convent, Ma. It was good work. The nuns in that convent were a different breed to the first lot whose care I were put in. They really were saints and they taught me a lot of things that helped the young mothers when their babbies were took away. You knaw, I often think of them all and could weep for them. They're all in the same situation as I am now.'

'It's a cruel world for us women at times, lass. We have to be strong, it's the only way.'

With this Ma closed the door behind her and Babs heard her go along the hallway towards Beth. Determined to undo the damage she'd done, Babs quickly washed and got out of the bath, wrapping a towel around her.

When she got to the bedroom door she stopped. 'I heard, Ma,' Beth was saying. 'She hates me, and it's breaking my heart. How did that happen?'

'Beth, Babs needs someone to lash out at, and it happens to be you. Be patient with her. The love she has for you will out, I promise. As a little girl, you were her world.'

'I was right up until she left. I relied on her. She was everything, and with her strength, I could get by. But when she left, I had to get stronger and cope on my own. I found ways of doing that. And looking back, Babs is right, I did use Jasmine and Roman to my own ends. What else could I do? Getting educated and becoming a nurse gave me my freedom, but then the war came, and we had no choices then. There was no time to look for her or you, Ma. But that doesn't mean I didn't care or want to try, I just did it all in a different way to what Babs chose.'

Understanding filtered into Babs. She opened the door and ran to Beth. 'Eeh, forgive me. Ma's right, I'm punishing you for all that's happened to me. Beth, I'm sorry, lass.'

'Oh, Babs, of course I forgive you. I love you. You're the other half of me.'

Beth held her to her. In Beth's arms Babs thought she would find the solace she was looking for, but voices inside her wouldn't still. She'd beat them. She would. For Ma's sake, she had to.

They sat in Mr Fellows' office two days later, Ma having made the appointment and begging Babs not to go until they had more news.

'I'm very sorry, but it isn't looking good. I have their objections here and they have looked into all of your past, Barbara. They say here that you went to prison suspected of murder. That though you were found innocent, you then went on to have a baby out of wedlock. That you were brought up by gypsies – which seems to me, with how they have worded this, is the hook they will use as their strong point. They will argue that to have spent most of your growing-up years with gypsies you may have their "mumbo-jumbo" ways, as it states here, and that they think for this reason you will be a bad influence on the earl's heir and could not possibly prepare him for his future role. That you seduced their son at his weakest moment while he was away from home and coping with the horror of war. And that, yes, being an honourable man, he would have married you to protect his son.'

'But all of that's not right. Well, some of it's the truth, but there's reasons behind it. But as far as me and Rupert were concerned, we fell in love.'

'Did you get pregnant before your marriage or after? Is there a possibility that Rupert married you because he knew he may have made you pregnant?'

Babs knew that it was a possibility that she was pregnant when they married, but she also knew that Rupert would have married her anyway; he loved her and she loved him. But how would it all look in the eyes of the court?

'Barbara?'

'It wasn't like that. It wasn't. We loved each other.'

'I know, and I believe you, but I also know what these lawyers are like. They'll tear you to pieces on the stand.'

Suddenly, what her ma had said came to Babs. 'I am willing to let them try. Me son has to knaw as I fought to keep him in me life.'

On a huge sigh, Mr Fellows said, 'Very well. But I have one more thing to tell you. And this is a measure of the nastiness and power you are up against. They have said that win or lose, they will file for their costs. I'm sorry, Barbara, but in my mind, you don't stand a chance. They are talking hundreds of pounds ... hundreds! And if you can't pay, you may be committed to a debtor's prison.'

A sense of defeat filled Babs. She couldn't win against such a force. She had to accept that. Bowing her head, she conceded. 'Aye, you're right, it's hopeless. I'll not let that happen as it'll be me ma and Tommy's money as I'd lose. I'll just have to get on with me life and get in touch with me lad when he's a man and hope he believes that I wanted to get him back but couldn't.'

'I can help you with that, Barbara. I can make up a file that will be delivered to him on his twenty-first birthday, or on the death of his grandparents if that is sooner, because then he will become the Earl of Westholme and will make his own decisions. I will put these papers in it so he can see what you were up against, and your circumstances at the time. Also, you can add to it over the years. Make it a treasure for him that tells him about his father, your work in the war and, well, any milestone in your life. Even include what has happened to you up to this point and stories about his grandmother Matilda and his aunts Elizabeth and Eliza. With your permission, they can add to it too. That way, he will know that you wanted to try to keep him, and the reasons why you couldn't.'

'Eeh, Mr Fellows, I knaw as Ma, Beth and Eliza would love that. Would you really do that for me?'

'I would. I've seen enough suffering in your family. I would help you all I can.'

'Ta ... ta, ever so much. Kindness such as you're showing me has been rare in me life.'

'I know, and in Matilda's too, and none of you deserve it to be so.'

Babs felt her Ma's hand come into hers. She looked into her lovely dark eyes and saw her strength. *I'll be like that. I'll grow strong and I'll make meself someone as me lad can be proud of.*

THIRTEEN

Babs

Back at the farm, Babs spotted Cliff standing near to the barn as if he was waiting for her. She'd avoided him since that awful day when Art had been taken, but seeing him now lifted her, and she knew that his simplistic way of looking at life's problems would be a salve to her.

Suddenly she longed to go on that picnic he'd asked her on. He was the only friend she felt she had since coming home. Oh, she had a lot of folk who loved her and cared about her, but that wasn't the same as a friendship with someone of your own age. Babs so missed Cathy who had worked as a nurse on the ambulance train with her and had been killed in the bombing of the train alongside Rupert. And Daisy, how often she thought of Daisy. She must write to her, but how did she put into words what had happened, when in the last letter she'd sent to Daisy and Sister Theresa – her mentor when she was in the convent with Daisy – she'd told them of Art's birth?

'Let's get in, lass.'

'I'll be in in a mo, Ma. I'm going to have a word with Cliff.'

'Aye, that's a good idea. Lad's been asking after you, and pestering me and Tommy to let him see you, but we knew you weren't ready.'

'Naw, but I am now. I, well ... I need someone to talk to who ain't involved – a friend.'

'I knaw what you mean, lass. Me friends have been me mainstay over the years. I don't knaw what I'd have done without them, though I've never known a fella to be just a friend. Be careful, lass, as the lad has feelings.'

Babs turned away from where Cliff stood. A feeling of disappointment took her. She linked in with her ma. 'I will come in after all, as I don't want owt like that, Ma.'

'Babs! Eeh, Babs. I just wanted a word.' How Cliff crossed the yard to get by her side so quickly she didn't know, but she flushed as she thought of her ma's words. 'I – I, well, I ain't up to having a word at the mo, Cliff. I'm sorry. I'll see you later, eh?'

'All right, lass. But you knaw, that offer of a ride up into the Bowland hills is still open to you. Just to take you away from all of this for a little while. Like I told you, up there it is a different world – peaceful, quiet. You don't even have to talk, if you don't want to. Or you can talk to God, as that's where I feel closest to him.'

Babs felt the peace he was speaking of, and wanted to experience it for real, but as for the God aspect, she was too angry at how He had let this happen to want to be close to Him. 'Ta, I will come. What time are you working till?'

'I've already spoken to Tommy about it and he has said that if you want to go, I can leave now.'

'Aye, I would. I'll not be a mo.'

Turning to her ma, Babs saw that she was smiling – not a knowing kind of smile, or one of satisfaction, just a kindly smile that allowed Babs to feel that what she wanted to do was fine by her.

When they went into the house, a small parcel caught Babs's eye. It stood on the kitchen table. For some reason she felt wary of it.

Peggy turned from whatever she was doing at the sink and greeted them. 'Eeh, I can see it ain't been good news for you. I'm sorry, me lass.' She nodded towards the parcel. 'That came for you. Happen it'll be sommat as'll help you. They say as good things come in small parcels.'

'Oh, I wonder what it is, Babs? Open it.'

'I will in a mo, Ma.'

Beth wheeled herself through the door and joined them in the kitchen. Her look was one of apprehension. 'Oh, Babs, it didn't go well then?'

Babs swallowed hard. 'Naw. It didn't go well.' She told of how the outcome would surely go against her and at what cost. 'But there's sommat good going to happen, ain't there, Ma?' With as much enthusiasm as she could muster, she told them about Mr Fellows' idea.

'Oh, that's a lovely thought, how nice of him. I would love to add to the box, Babs. And do you know? I think this will lead to us having Art back in the future.'

'Aye, I do an' all. A long way in the future, but it's our only hope.'

As she said this, Babs moved towards the table and picked up the parcel. She recognised Sister Theresa's handwriting. Her heart jolted. Instinct told her that this was a present for

Art. 'I'll not open it yet.' She put it back down as if it had burnt her. 'I'm to visit the lav as Cliff is waiting for me.'

With this, she almost ran towards the door that took her into the hall and through to the inside lav.

Her breath came in deep pants as she leant against the closed door. Slowing it and taking deep gulps of air, she quelled her panic. When she emerged a few minutes later, she felt in control.

Her ma, Peggy and Beth were still in the kitchen and looked as though they hadn't moved from the positions that she'd left them in. Picking up the parcel again, she said, 'Well, I'll see you all later.'

The air was warmer now as the sun had broken through, and this being June, the nights were drawn out a little so that dusk wasn't until seven or eight, giving them plenty of time.

She hadn't got across the yard before Cliff was by her side. 'Eeh, lass. Let's get going.'

They drove in silence. When they turned off the main road that led to Lancaster, they travelled along what was no more than a lane pitted with holes. The van jolted over them, leaving Babs having to hold on to stop herself sliding along the bench seat. She sat as far away from Cliff as she could, her Ma's words still worrying her.

As they climbed higher, Babs felt herself relax as the beauty of the Bowland hills unfolded before them. A magnificent vista of rugged landscape with a backdrop of hills that seemed to want to proclaim themselves as mountains as they reached towards the sky.

The sun danced in and out from behind the many fluffy clouds, making a pattern that reflected onto the greenest grass

Babs had ever seen. Clumps of fir trees stood like dark green pyramids, as the ever-widening stream at the side of the road mirrored their image, creating a wonderous sight.

Sheep grazed on the sides of the hills as if they had two legs shorter than the others – how they kept their balance, Babs didn't know. Then as she was watching them, one didn't and made her giggle as it toppled over, then righted itself and looked for all the world like a grumpy old man saying, 'Who pushed me?'

'By, that were a nice sound, Babs. What brought that on?'

'The sheep.' She told him of the antics of the hapless sheep she'd seen.

'Ha, they're daft as brushes. No doubt others will fall now, just because that one did.'

'Aye, I knaw. It were sheep that introduced us, if you remember?'

'Ha. They did an' all. I never thought as I'd meet a friend because of a load of daft sheep!'

Babs relaxed as Cliff said this.

'You are a friend to me, Cliff . . . You knaw as I don't want owt other than a friend, don't you?'

'I do, Babs, and that's all I want to be to you. I've never met anyone who I can talk to like I can you. And I want to help you, if there's owt anyone can do to help.'

'Awe, Cliff, ta. It's good to hear you say that. What you're doing today, and offering to just be me friend, is more than enough.'

'You can say owt to me, you knaw. It won't go further, and I won't try to offer advice as I ain't much good at that. Besides, everyone knaws what's best for you, or so they think. I reckon there's only you as knaws that – and God. So though you are cross with Him, try opening your heart to Him. Anyway, if nothing else, I hope this drive is helping you.'

'It is, Cliff. So much. I feel as though I can breathe. When I'm at home, someone is always by me side wanting to comfort me or, like you say, telling me what they think I should do. I knaw it's out of their love for me, but I feel stifled.'

'What do you want to do, Babs? 'Cause if there's owt I can do to help you do it, I will.'

She told him of her plans.

'Well, that will mean you'll need a few lifts to places. I can help with that, and if you get a position locally, I can teach you to drive so that you can take yourself.'

'Naw. I mean to go back to being a voluntary nurse in France. Not on the ambulance train again, I couldn't take that, but in a hospital or a field hospital. Somewhere that's so busy that I don't have time to think, and I can find solace in helping them as are worse off than me.'

'Well, you can allus find them. Thinking about it, I wonder who's the very worst off in all the world? If you can find any suffering more than you, Babs, they must be in a pretty poor state.'

Though it wasn't appropriate to, Babs giggled at this. It was just such a funny way of looking at things. 'Aye, well, I pity them, because I can't think of any worse pain than I'm in.'

The van slowed then. 'Here's where I stop to just be at peace with meself.'

Cliff pulled the van onto a wide recess just off the road as he said this. They were facing the stream, which was now more like a small river, and across from it was nothing but the clumps of pine trees and slanting hills. A still scene, that held a haunting beauty as if no one had ever trodden its earth and disturbed even a blade of grass. Dotted in the grass were buttercups and daisies, creating a patchy yellow and white carpet interspersed with touches of purple as the odd thistle made its presence known.

'It's beautiful.'

In the silence that followed, Babs became aware of the parcel which she'd lain on the seat next to her. Reaching for it, she turned it over in her hands.

'A present?'

'Aye. It'll be from an old friend. I hardly dare open it, for what it might contain.'

'Well, perhaps best not to, eh? It can wait till you're ready.'

It was this simple acceptance of her wishes that Babs loved about Cliff. She never felt any pressure from him, even though her ma had woken her to the possible feelings he may have for her. She knew that if he did have them, he'd never express them unless she prompted him to. She thought him an honourable man and a special one, and his deep faith added to that.

'Ta for bringing me up here, Cliff. I think I'll get out and walk a ways along the water. I might even paddle, the stream looks that inviting.'

Cliff didn't answer, nor protest when she opened the door and got out of the van. She felt no resistance from him, nor did he even ask to join her. The freedom of this warmed her to him further. He truly was the kind of friend that she needed.

As she walked towards where a farm entrance would take her across the stream, the sound of the rippling water travelling to wherever it was going over hundreds of glistening stones, Babs could feel herself welling up. It was the peace. It allowed feelings to come to the surface. By the time she got across the bridge and had climbed over a stile that brought her into the field near to the fir trees, her tears were tumbling down her face. Though she hadn't meant to cry, now that she was, she let her emotions have reign.

A sudden urge came to her to run and run, and never to stop. Taking off, she ran towards the trees. Once in the shadow of them, she collapsed on the floor and sobbed her heart out. It seemed to her that her whole body fragmented into dozens of pieces. Each piece held a sorrow so deep that she knew that once they had their release, she would be left a stronger person than she had been before.

That time came, but she didn't know how long it had taken. She only knew a peace of a different kind to settle in her. A peace that held the strength she'd prayed for. Nothing was mended. It never could be, not ever. Yes, one day she may get her lovely Art back, but she'd never get Rupert back, and that's what it would take to put her world right – to have both of them.

But she knew now that she would find a way to go forward. Though she was still clothed in utter misery and the clogged-up feeling that crying gave, in her heart she knew that she could carry on – that she had to.

When she rose, she walked towards the stream. There she took off her shoes and socks and, lifting her skirt a little, waded into the icy-cold water. Bending, she splashed her face and enjoyed the tingling it caused her cheeks. She felt cleansed by the action.

Looking towards the van, she saw that Cliff was watching her, but he hadn't attempted to come to her. She waved to him, motioning that he should join her. As he did, she dropped her skirt. The feel of it swirling around her ankles as the water danced with it made her want to swirl too, as the freedom of having made a decision took hold of her and lightened her.

'It looks too cold for me. I'm a coward when it comes to putting meself into such things as cold water.'

'Ha! It's fine when you've been in a few moments. Come on, don't be a babby.'

Cliff took off his boots and eased his socks off before rolling up the bottoms of his trousers. 'By, you're a mad woman and you're making me as daft as you are.'

Babs giggled. A tentative giggle that was akin to a sob. Cliff ignored the sound. 'Right, I'm coming in, and I might just duck you for making me do so!'

'Naw, naw, don't, Cliff. Me feet is all I can stand in this cold. If you put any more of me in, I'll never talk to you again!'

'In that case I won't.'

Coming up to her, he took hold of her hand. 'There's safety in clinging on to someone. Eeh, it's soothing on your feet once you brave it.'

'It is. And on your soul.'

'Aye. I hope it is, lass. I want nothing more than for you to be soothed and, aye, healed a little.'

Babs looked up to him, something she didn't do to many folk, being tall herself. 'You've helped me more than you can knaw, Cliff. This place'll allus hold my heart.'

As she said this, the tears flowed again.

'Eeh, lass, can I hold you? I mean ... like a friend would, nowt else.'

'I do need a hug, Cliff.'

With this she went into his open arms and snuggled into him. The hug was like no other she'd ever experienced. Yes, she felt his love for her, but it was a different love – a non-demanding love, a love that promised care and understanding.

'I hadn't thought I would cry again. Up there in the trees, I thought I'd drained meself of tears.'

'You could never do that, Babs. Not with the heartache you have. I reckon you will allus cry, but let it happen. Whenever you need to. Don't bottle it up under a false strength. There's strength in feeling sadness, as much as there is in a stiff upper lip. You're you. You've been hurt beyond measure, but when you're ready to talk, I do have a little hope for you.'

Pulling away from him, she looked quizzically at him. 'Hope?'

'Aye. Let's get out of this water and let the sun dry our feet, eh? And I've a big hanky in me pocket; you can wet it and soothe your swollen eyes with it.'

'Oh, Cliff. You're like me very best friend.'

'I am your friend, and want to be your best one. Oh, I knaw you can't share some things with me that you'd share with a girlfriend, but, well, look, I need a friend an' all. I have stuff that I need to talk about. And its stuff as I don't knaw whether you'll laugh at me, or think differently about me for, but somehow I don't think you will. I feel safe with you, Babs.'

This intrigued Babs but she felt that the time wasn't right to press Cliff into telling her what it was. Like her, he'd find his moment.

Once her eyes were soothed, Babs lay back on the grass and allowed the sun to warm her. Her time in the water had chilled more than her feet.

'Babs, I spoke to the nurse who came for Art.'

'What?' Babs sat up.

'Aye. She was sat in that bloke's posh car and I could hear you screaming, so I approached her and asked her what was going on. She were in tears. When she told me, I felt like coming in and bashing that fat-gutted bloke till he screamed for mercy. That nurse were distraught at the thought of taking your babby from you. She asked me to tell you sommat, but I haven't been able to get near to you, and today, well, I've been waiting for me moment.'

'What did she say? Please tell me, Cliff.'

'She said to tell you that if you wanted her to, she'd write to you now and again telling you how your babby were doing.'

'Really! Oh, Cliff, that's wonderful! What do I have to do?'

'She said to write to this address.' Cliff handed her a piece of paper with an address scribbled on it. 'She said it's the address of a woman who was once your husband's nanny.'

'I know of her! Oh, Cliff, this is amazing. Why didn't you tell Ma about it so that I knew before now?'

'Because they all seem to be controlling your life, and might have made the decision not to tell you. I wanted the decision to be yours as to whether you contact the nurse or not. But like I say, I haven't been able to get near to you, and when I've asked to see you, Tommy's told me that I've to wait a while, and your ma had a word with me an' all. I felt bad as she was almost saying that she thought I fancied you and that it wasn't appropriate for me to show such feelings at such a time.'

'Oh, Cliff, she didn't! Oh, I am sorry, lad. I'm mortified. But you knaw, they think they are doing the right thing. They think they have me best interests at heart.'

'Aye, I knaw. But I thought I would bide me time, then today, I just wanted you to do what you wanted to do. The time weren't right till now.'

Reaching out, Babs took Cliff's hand. 'Cliff, you're the kindest, most caring man I've had the pleasure to meet. Even me Rupert weren't as caring as you. He blotted his copybook good and proper when we first fell in love – he only went and asked me to be his mistress!'

'Eeh, I bet he got short shrift on that one! But I knaw as that's how these gentry go on. They marry to better their coffers, but keep the real love of their lives in clover, in a love nest, and live happily ever after. Well, not ever after as it is sinful to commit adultery.'

'I wish that everything was as simple as you see it, Cliff. They have hundreds of years of that culture, and don't see it as wrong. Well, Rupert did when I told him how I weren't for it!'

'I knaw. I don't judge them, but I do get angry when I see how feted they are at church. The priests almost lick their boots and yet they knaw they are sinning.'

'Well, they line the coffers of the church.'

'Aye. And it's all of that that puts me in a quandary. Look, I were going to tell you sommat, but I don't think I can yet. Can we come up here again, Babs? Soon? I mean, I want to be sure of a couple of things before I open me heart.'

Babs thought this strange, but her own heart was pounding so greatly with the wonderful news that she may have contact with her little Art that she didn't give Cliff's problems any more thought. 'Aye. But on the way home, you're to tell me word for word what the nurse said. I need to get me head around it, and to think how it's best to put it into action.'

Getting up, they went back to the van. Babs knew there was something troubling Cliff and felt a little guilty that her happiness was such that she didn't press him, but then, he had never pressed her, so probably wouldn't want her to force him to speak out. He'd tell her when he was ready.

Once in the van she tore open the parcel, eager now to see what it contained. A pair of knitted white bootees fell out. 'Oh, Cliff. Look.'

Cliff had tears glistening in his eyes as he looked at the bootees. 'Eeh, they're grand.'

'They are, and do you knaw what? Me little Art will wear them. I'll make sure of that. I'll get them to that nurse, naw one'll notice, and I'll ask her to keep them safe to give back to me when Art's grown out of them. Then I'll put them in his box.'

'His box?'

'Aye, I've so much to tell you, Cliff. And, Cliff, when you're ready, you can talk to me – at any time. What you've done for me today means the world to me. You're a true friend, Cliff, me very best friend.'

Cliff reached for her hand and squeezed it. As he did, he looked deep into her eyes. 'And I've a feeling that you're going to be mine, but that'll be determined when I tell you what I have to say.'

'Whatever it is, I'm here for you, Cliff.'

'Maybe I'll write it in a letter to you. Aye, happen as that will be best and then I don't have to see your face when you hear it.'

She thought she had an idea what it might be, as in her work Babs had come across all types of men, and this afternoon had shown her so much of Cliff's character. But she didn't want to prompt him, so she leant towards him and kissed his cheek and was rewarded with a smile that only by friendship – with no ties, no limitations, no expectations of her as a woman – could be given.

FOURTEEN

Tilly

Saying goodbye to Babs wrenched at Tilly's heart. To her mind, Babs wasn't ready. And though both Babs and Beth tried hard to cover it up, she knew there was an atmosphere between her lovely daughters.

There was an element of her that understood this. They'd taken different routes to get home – the one throwing caution to the wind, the other plotting until the time was right. And they'd experienced very different lives – Babs going through hell, pain and loss, and Beth having a stable, happy life. Even though she had suffered the massive trauma of becoming partially paralysed and was separated from her Henry, she had always been cared for and had people around her who loved her. And so, there was resentment to contend with, which she knew Babs fought, but in every situation that occurred saw Beth as the instigator.

Of her twins, Tilly worried much more over Babs. Memories of her own hell were mirrored in what was happening to Babs. And hadn't she herself turned to drink to blot it all out? Sighing, she knew that Babs had made a massive effort not to drink, but she also knew how strong the urge could be once you knew the release the drink gave you. The only hope was that the work Babs had chosen to lose herself in would help her to cope. Hadn't she found that was the only way when she had immersed herself in work to help ease the pain?

'I'm ready, Ma.'

'All right, Beth, I'll be through in a moment.' Tilly didn't move from where she'd been stood at the window in the living room. Outside, Cliff was going about his daily chores, and yet she'd not really registered what he was doing. The lad was heartbroken at Babs leaving. He'd fallen for her, but Babs had been unaware of his feelings. His nature hadn't allowed him to push himself forward, and Tilly was glad of that. Babs wasn't ready, but she hoped with all her heart that one day she would be. Tilly could think of none better for Babs than the lovely, gentle Cliff.

Mentally shaking herself – as she always did recently because she wasn't able to do anything without taking a moment to get herself into the person that each expected her to be – she went to turn away from the window, but two arms came around her waist, making her jump. She'd forgotten that Tommy hadn't yet gone out to begin his work. More and more of late he left the day-to-day grind of the farm to Phil and Cliff.

Cliff had turned out to be more useful than expected, as he could put his hand to anything, even tinkling with Tommy's beloved tractor and making it work when it seemed to be refusing to do so. And the best thing was that Cliff respected Phil's superior knowledge around the farm, and allowed him to be in charge, even though Phil was his junior. Phil adored him. This made for smooth-running and allowed Tommy not to worry when his leg pained him too much to help out.

'I wish it was that we had no cares, me little Tilly.'

'Eeh, that's families for you, Tommy, lad.'

Tilly leant back into Tommy. She was always grateful of his love for her and the deep understanding he had of her moods. He didn't have to ask what was wrong, he knew. 'Babs is for being like you, me Tilly – resilient. She will find a way to cope. You have to be at trusting that. Aye, she may falter along the way – who wouldn't with what it is that she has to contend with? But she'll win in the end, so she will.'

'Aye. You're right, Tommy. Well, I'd better get going. I can't put off the precarious ride into Blackpool much longer.'

'Is it that Peggy is no further forward with her driving skills then?'

'Naw, and I wonder if she'll ever master it. Me heart's in me mouth for the whole journey, but I just hope it clicks with her soon as it would be nice not to have to sit in with her, but to let her take Beth and Eliza into work on the days that I don't have to be there.'

'Is it that you are missing working?'

'Naw. I'm enjoying doing other things, and so is Molly. Though Mary's not as ready to take over from Molly as Beth is from me. Poor Mary, it is hard to lift her mood. But understandable. Anyroad, me and Molly are meeting up with Florrie once we have Beth and Mary settled in the work room of the shop. I asked Peggy to come an' all, as we could have taken little Benny and Mary's little Gerry with us, but naw, she's stopping at the shop with Beth and taking care of the boys there. Our old bedroom has made a lovely living room-come-nursery. It's very handy for Peggy to look after the boys in there and to be on hand to help Beth if she needs it. There's two cots and a sofa and chair, and all she needs to do her fussing over the babbies and Beth. She's quite happy and no longer talks of going out to do district nursing again.'

'Aye, you've got a good set-up, and it's good to see you having time to yourself, although it is that I'd like us to spend more time together, me little Tilly.'

'Oh? And what did you have in mind?' Tilly giggled up at her Tommy. With him she always felt like a young woman again. All cares, hot sweats and changes to her body left her and she felt beautiful and desired.

Tommy tapped her bottom. 'That which you have in your look, me lovely girl, as well as, oh, I don't know, maybe riding off into the sunset and forgetting everything for a wee while.'

Turning towards him, Tilly snuggled into him. 'Eeh, me Tommy. I knaw as I'm pulled this way and that, but you're me world. Without you, I'd not be able to get through it all. There'll come a time when we can do just that – maybe sail away and see some of the world. I loved it on the boat crossing over from Ireland and have often thought I'd like to sail away to exotic places.'

'Well, well, it is that I wasn't for knowing that and that I'm still learning about you, me Tilly. I'd like to be doing that meself, so I would, though what happened to the *Titanic* makes you think.'

'I knaw, it were a tragedy, but you have to think, Tommy, that for all the ships sailing the oceans before the war, there weren't many disasters. Once the war ends, I'd love to take off with you and leave all our cares behind.'

'It's a date, me little Tilly. But let us be at hoping that we have no cares then, that the world is at peace and so is our little family.'

Tilly smiled up at him. His lovely eyes held a twinkle she knew well and felt a response to until Eliza's voice broke the magic. 'Mammy, Mammy, hurry up, will you? If I'm late, Ma Perkins'll go spare!'

Tommy giggled, making Tilly burst out laughing. 'Eeh, they'll be naw sailing off into the sunset for a good while, Tommy O'Flynn, not while that one demands attention.'

'You're right, but she and Ma Perkins can wait a wee moment while I kiss me lovely Tilly.'

His kiss, as always, warmed Tilly to the heart of her. No matter what was happening in their world, they had each other and always would have.

The crashing of the gears grated on Tilly's nerves. Peggy still had no idea about driving, even though it had been three weeks since her daily practices had begun. And her steering left a lot to be desired as she over-steered if anything came towards her or tried to pass her, making Tilly worry that one day there would be an accident. Thank goodness there wasn't a lot of traffic for most of the journey, but when they hit Blackpool front, it was hair-raising. Tilly was determined to persist with her, though, so she could be relieved of her duty of taking everyone everywhere.

Suddenly, Tilly's thoughts became a reality as a car coming towards them seemed to spook Peggy and she swerved, as if making for the ditch. Tilly grabbed the wheel and righted the car but, always one to speak her mind, Eliza spoke up in an exasperated voice, 'Eeh, Peggy, I'm not saying as you won't master driving eventually, but Mammy, couldn't you teach me first? I'm good on the tractor and drove the van when I went with Phil to the market that day.'

'You have? Eeh, me lass, I never thought. You're—'

'So young? Aye, I knaw as that's how you look on me, but I'm not. I'm all grown, I have a job and I'm in love an' all.'

Tilly was shocked by this and didn't know whether to burst out laughing as she always felt like doing whenever Eliza was exasperated, or to take Eliza seriously, as she deserved her to. Beth saved the day. 'Oh, Eliza, I'm so happy to hear you say that. Poor Phil has been hankering after you for a long time now. When did this happen?'

'I've loved him forever, Beth, but he had to grow up first. Boys can be so babyish, they're not a bit like us womenfolk.'

Tilly did burst out laughing at this. But she quickly covered up so that Eliza wasn't offended. 'I knaw exactly what you mean, lass. And I'm glad to hear that Phil has at last grown up and is worthy of your love. There's not a nicer lad I would choose for you, but you're still, well . . .'

'Eeh, Ma, I'm not thinking of marrying him or owt. Not yet. I've me apprenticeship to finish and me own shop to establish. Besides, Phil's getting on me nerves lately. He's like two people, one minute all grown-up and talking of wanting to go to war and as if he could win it on his own, and wanting to do things with me that I won't let him, then the next sulking if he can't get his own way, and he gets excited about things like driving a flipping tractor!'

This undid Tilly, as it did Beth and Peggy. They all doubled over with their laughter. So much so that they were suddenly bumping up and down in a precarious way as Peggy lost control and drove onto the grass verge, then through a gate and over a ridged field that was making the van feel more like a boat on the rough waves of the sea.

'Peggy, Peggy, lass . . .' But Tilly could say no more as her sides were splitting.

It was Beth who sobered them all. 'Ma, help me, Ma!'

Turning, she saw Beth's bath chair was almost on its side with Eliza clinging on to it for dear life. Peggy, ever alert to anything being wrong with Beth, promptly slammed on the brakes. The van went on two wheels. Eliza screamed. The world toppled, but then righted itself as the van banged back down onto its four wheels again.

Turning to look anxiously into the back of the van, Tilly shouted, 'Beth, Eliza, are you all right, me lasses?' Only to have her worry turn to a laugh as Eliza replied, 'Aye, I am, though I feel like a jelly must feel when I wobble it on its plate.' And it was a relief to hear Beth giggle and say, 'A bit like Eliza's description, but all right, Ma. Are you both unhurt?'

'Aye, but . . . Eeh, Peggy, what's to do, lass?' Peggy was cling-ing on to the steering wheel staring ahead as if she could see a ghost.

'She's in shock, Ma. Peggy, Peggy, love, it's all right, no one's hurt. Turn and look at me, Peggy.'

Peggy turned. 'Eeh, me Beth, I thought I'd killed you. By, I'm sorry, lass, I'm sorry, but I've to tell you that I can't ever drive again. I can't.'

'Well, I'd say that was a good thing, Peggy. Not that I'm being unkind, but I reckon as you'll end up killing the whole world if you carry on.'

'Eliza! That's not a nice thing to say. Peggy hasn't hurt anyone.'

'Yet, Tilly. Naw, Eliza's right and we can allus rely on her to tell it how it is. Though I think we need to have a word with that Phil. Who does he think he is wanting to do things to her!'

This shocked Tilly. It was as if Peggy was taking over half-ownership of her family. Besides, she didn't like Eliza to be embarrassed in this way. She knew the way of it with lads and was confident that Eliza could keep Phil in check, but before she could say anything Eliza stood her own corner.

'You'll do naw such thing. A young man has his feelings, and my Phil knaws how to control himself most of the time. He says it's because I'm too beautiful and he loves me so much that he forgets himself now and again. I can handle that on me own, and in a kind way, and Phil listens to me. And if you're going to be like that about it, Peggy, I'll not tell you owt else.'

Tilly clamped her mouth together and prayed to God not to let her laugh at her lovely young daughter, who thought herself a woman, and was making a wonderful job of reaching that status. She knew that now wasn't the time to show amusement at, or to admonish one of Eliza's outbursts.

'Eeh, I'm sorry, lass. Of course you can look after yourself and your lovely Phil . . . I – I . . .' To the surprise of all of them, Peggy burst into tears.

Eliza was immediately remorseful. 'Eeh, Peggy, I didn't mean—'

177

'Naw. Naw, lass, it's all right, I – I had a bad experience once, and it ruined me life and makes me overreact. It was naw business of mine to speak out like that. It weren't me place, and I don't knaw where it came from.'

'Peggy, don't get upset.'

At this from Beth, Tilly took the sobbing Peggy in her arms. Suddenly the mystery of why Peggy, who was such a lovely woman, had never married became clear. Whatever had happened to her must have been so bad that it put her off men for life. Maybe one day Peggy would tell them, but for now she needed comfort and reassurance. This came from Eliza too. Ever the one with an old head on her shoulders, she'd got out of the van through the back door and was now opening the driver's door. 'Eeh, give me a cuddle, Peggy. Whatever happened to you, we all love you and'll allus be ready to look after you when you feel down, won't we, Ma?'

Tilly could only nod as she watched her beautiful daughter take the older woman into her arms and bring a smile back to her face. 'You're special to us, and can never not be in our business, Peggy. I'd have said the same to me ma if she'd have said she would have a word with Phil. And she would have, you knaw, if you hadn't said it first.'

Tilly felt affronted at this, as she'd had no intention of mentioning it, but she agreed for the sake of cheering Peggy. 'Aye, we older ones can put our foot in it at times. But Eliza can cope with that. Eeh, our Eliza, I wonder at times if you were born a babby or an old woman with the wisdom you have. Even when in me arms as a newborn you looked around as if to say, "Well, there's a lot that I can put right with this lot."'

This caused laughter again, and Peggy straightened. 'Well, I think there is, Eliza. For a start, you can get us out of this, lass. I'll sit in the back with Beth, and you take the wheel. My driving days are over, and I wish to God they'd never started!'

'Naw, I'll drive it . . .'

'Mammy, I'm in the driving seat now, so you stay where you are. And hold on to your hat!'

Tilly felt well and truly told. She didn't hold on to her hat but did cling on to the door handle with one hand and her seat with the other and closed her eyes.

As soon as the back door slammed the van went into motion as if gliding along – well as best it could over the mounds in the field. Finding herself relaxing, Tilly opened her eyes and was aghast at this nearly-woman daughter of hers as she expertly drove the van towards the road. 'Right, lass, you've proved your point. I'll take it from here. But we'll go into the council office when we reach Blackpool and I'll apply to buy you a licence. If they have no objections – after all, you're still only fifteen – then we will start your lessons. Not that you will need many, you handle the van better than I do.'

As Tilly took the wheel and drove them back onto the highway, she sighed. She hoped there weren't any obstacles put in their way by the council as with the problem of transport solved, she might be able to spend more time with her beloved Tommy.

Driving into Blackpool, Tilly became fully aware of the bond between Peggy and Beth as she glanced in the mirror and saw them holding hands. But she felt no jealousy at this. It was right what Eliza had said, Peggy was a part of their family, just as Molly and her brood were and Florrie and Reggie and Phil. Yes, she had to admit, especially Phil, who it seemed may one day become a full member when he married Eliza. This, she told herself, wasn't fanciful. She knew her Eliza and if she said she was in love with Phil, then she was, and that was that.

With the girls settled in their work places, Tilly visited the council office. The licensing authority were not helpful. They were worried about Eliza's age, and said Tilly was to try again when her daughter reached fifteen. This upset Tilly, as she had an inkling that if it was a lad she'd asked for, she might have got it. But she cheered when she was walking back along the promenade and saw a horse and cart go by, as it occurred to her that horses had long been available to buy again – their own had been taken for use by the army, and only their aged mares and stallions had been left behind. But lately she'd seen an increase in the number of horses pulling traps and carts on the roads, so she made her mind up to get Tommy to purchase one. Even Beth could learn to handle one if she had a special seat to be strapped in. And Eliza was already a skilled handler and had been since she was a young child.

With this settled, meaning that very soon future travelling arrangements for the girls and Peggy wouldn't all be down to her, Tilly let in the sounds and smell of the sea. Taking a deep breath, she hurried her steps. She was ready to spend the rest of the day with Molly and Florrie.

When at last they were all sat in Ashton Marine Park on a bench looking out across the lake, Tilly felt contented and blessed, despite the troubles her poor Babs had and missing her and little Art.

Her sides ached from telling Molly and Florrie about the morning's capers in the van. But now they were quiet, enjoying the peace of the beautiful lake, as the sun dappled on its surface, turning it into a sheet of daytime stars.

The lake was adorned with graceful swans gliding up and down in their faithful pairs, and the only disturbance to the peace was the busy quacking ducks as they parented their young. An adorable sight passed them by as what looked like a small army of ducklings were kept in check, the mother duck only happy when they were all in a line following exactly what she did.

'Eeh, lass, that was a big sigh.'

'I knaw, Florrie. Sorry. Just me thoughts, wishing the world was as simple a place for us as it is for them ducks.'

'What? You'd like to have your brood all fall into line when you quacked?'

Both Tilly and Molly laughed at this.

'Sommat like that. Anyroad, I'm ready for a cuppa, how about you two?'

As they stood, Tilly jumped as Florrie promptly sat back down again with a thud. 'Eeh, what's to do, lass?'

'Sorry. I have these funny turns. I go right dizzy if I stand up quickly.'

'Awe, another one on the change of life if you ask me.'

'Is that what it is, Molly? By, I thought I'd be young forever!'

'We all thought that, lass. But naw. We're heading for middle age and dried-up fannies.'

'Molly!'

But though she was shocked and sounded it, Tilly had to laugh. Molly was usually the practical one, not the lewd one.

Tilly knew she herself could be like that at times and enjoyed shocking her mates – but Molly?

Florrie gave it some normality by saying, 'Well, I'm not looking forward to that!'

'Ha! Well, girls, we have to face it, and like we said the last time the subject came up, it's good to have friends going through the same thing. Me and Tilly are in the same boat, lass. Are you getting hot flushes as if someone is filling you up with boiling water from your toes to your head?'

'Aye, I am. I'm having one now as it happens.' Florrie fanned herself with her hand.

'And wetting your knickers when you laugh?'

'Eeh, Molly.' Florrie looked even more flustered. 'I'd never have said, but I could do with a trip to the bathroom now.'

At this Molly opened her bag, and knowing what she was going to do, Tilly did the same. Both pulled out a clean pair of silk pantaloons and waved them at Florrie. Florrie bent over with her laughter. 'By, they look like flags to our old age! And, aye, I've a pair in me bag at the ready.'

'Naw. Not old age. Just another phase of our lives, lass. Join the Tilly and Molly Change of Life Club. We're allus having a laugh about it, ain't we, Tilly? And neither of us feel embarrassed. We have a drawer full of these at the ready in our workshop. And it's good to have a mate to talk to about it. There's nowt written about it and naw help for the symptoms. All we knaw is what's passed on by old wives' tales and some of them would scare the pants off you . . . Eeh, that's apt an' all.'

Again, they laughed, then Tilly pointed towards the little café, which they knew had an outside lav. 'That way, girls, and bags I go in first!'

When they were served their tea, and each having paid a visit and now feeling more comfortable, the conversation turned to families and it was then that Florrie dropped a bombshell. 'I'm afraid there's more to me funny turns than the change of life. It's me heart. Lady Clefton got her doctor out to me when I had one while serving her tea the other morning and he said as me heart goes out of rhythm every now and then. It sort of jumps a few beats or sommat. Anyroad, I'm to take it easy, and have to give up me job.'

'By, lass, naw!' Tilly felt as if someone had punched her. She and Florrie had been friends for a long time, much longer than she'd known Molly. And she'd been with her through thick and thin. They'd only lost touch for a short, dreadful time in Florrie's life. She couldn't bear for the lovely Florrie to be unwell.

'You're not to worry too much, Tilly, lass. It's just that I shouldn't exert meself.'

'Eeh, and we had you laughing that hard that it brought on that turn! You should have told us, Florrie.'

'Never stop me laughing, Molly, lass. Without that, what have any of us got? And you two are a tonic to me. Working in the house of a lady, where everything's prim and proper and run like clockwork, can get a bit boring. Even my Reggie's a quiet sort, as you knaw. Naw, when I see you two, it's as if I come alive. It's just that, well, I had to be truthful with you. I am experiencing all the things that you two are, and it's a relief, I can tell you, to talk to someone who understands. Reggie tries his best, but if I get hot at night, he throws the covers back and says it's like sleeping with a kettle!'

This lightened the moment, and Tilly knew that no matter what, they had to be as normal as they could be around Florrie, but still she worried deeply. She didn't want anything to happen to her dear friend.

Putting out her hands, she reached for one of Molly's and one of Florrie's. 'Eeh, I were feeling blessed as we sat by the lake, and that's not changed. I am blessed to have you both in me life. I can't bear to think of owt happening to either of you.'

They held hands, making a circle, and Tilly thought to herself that it was a circle of love, as she loved these two women with all her heart.

'Tilly, love, nowt's going to happen to me, I promise. But I did want to talk to you both. Well, you see, money's allus scarce. Not that we don't have a good living – we do, as Reggie can have the pick of the crop from the vegetable garden and of any of the animals before they go to market. The local butcher kills and joints it for us, and the meat is hung in our cold cellar. But, well, because of all of this and our free cottage, our wages have been a pittance, and you can't put a carrot in the bank for your old age.'

This made them both smile.

'What is it, Florrie? Do you need some money?'

'Naw, Tilly. I need a job. Now, I'm not talking of coming to the shop, but I'm a very good seamstress, even though I say it meself. By, you have to be all things, working in big houses as I've done all me life – well, apart from that time when …

Anyhow, what I'm asking is if you can give me some work at home? I've got a treadle machine.'

'By, of course we can, lass!' Molly beamed. 'Eeh, you're the answer to our prayers. Mary tries her best, but she's only at the stage of sewing a seam up as of yet and I want to be relieved of the more intricate stuff, like Tilly is, as Beth's basket-making is really coming along. We work like slaves on our two days in, Tilly making the specials and me trying to keep my stock levels up, so you could really help me with my load. What do you think, Tilly?'

'I think it's a grand idea. I could bring everything to you, Florrie.'

'And my Will can help with that an' all. He's got time on his hands since the saddlery cut back on staff. He spends a lot of his time making the oddments he makes out of leather to sell in our shop, but it don't keep him fully occupied. He'd love an extra job. He wouldn't want paying as I don't think we could run to a fifth wage; we have Gertie, Mary and Beth as it is, and with you, Florrie, that would be a full compliment.'

'Naw, but we could pay for his petrol, Molly.'

'Aye, we could, Tilly. That's it then. Done deal.'

Florrie had tears in her eyes. She clasped Tilly's hand tighter, and Tilly saw her do the same to Molly. 'By, I love you, lasses.'

Together, they said they loved her too, and to Tilly, the circle of love was confirmed, and it swelled her heart.

PART TWO

SEPARATE WAYS

1918–19

FIFTEEN

Babs

Sighing, Babs put down her pen. Adding to her story for her son brought the pain of losing him back to her, and she wondered, not for the first time, if she should have gone into such detail about her early life. But then, if Art knew everything about her, he could better judge if he wanted to have her in his life, and she'd have kept no secrets from him.

When it came to telling him about the wicked Cecil, she'd been very careful how she worded what happened, but by the time he was of an age to receive everything, he would be able to guess by the fact that the result had been her having his little half-brother out of wedlock.

Telling him about his father and their love for one another had been the easy part, even though, emotionally, it drained her. But overall, Babs found the experience of writing everything down helped her to find some peace.

Though doubts did trouble her – maybe she'd put too much of her feelings into words? She didn't know, and only time would tell. When each chapter was written, she sealed it in an envelope and held it to her heart, praying that her son would understand. Maybe the upbringing he would have would make him unable to, especially if he was fed terrible tales about her over the years, but ever since Mr Fellows had suggested this approach, she'd known it was the right, and only, course that was left for her to take.

And at last, she was getting on with her life just as her ma had done, knowing it was the only way. She was filling every waking hour with doing something. Learning was her main occupation and she studied whenever she wasn't on duty, and she found, as when striving for her qualification to become a nurse, that she was like a sponge, soaking up and retaining knowledge.

Her pride and joy was being able to speak almost fluent French. She'd picked up a lot of the language the last time she was here and by the time she had left had been able to order whatever she wanted in the cafés, and had been able to talk about their basic needs with any wounded French soldiers they had dealt with. That experience had greatly helped her in her quest to fully understand and to speak French. As had her lovely friend and fellow nursing sister, Pearl. An upper-class girl who had no side to her, she encouraged Babs all the way. Now, she loved conversing fully with any French patients to reassure them, and with the few French workers that they had helping at the hospital to explain instructions and talk about life in general, and found it a joy to be understood and chat with traders and anyone she came into contact with on her trips to town.

Whenever they were off together, or sometimes in their quarters – a Nissen hut where they shared a bedroom and had their own bathroom – she and Pearl would converse in French, with Pearl correcting or teaching her new words as they went along. Acquiring this skill gave Babs more confidence in herself which, despite all her achievements to date, she still lacked when it came to thinking of herself as being as good as those of a higher class. And she loved the shocked look she'd seen on many a wounded British officer's face when she'd chatted with a French officer in an adjoining bed.

Sitting back, Babs rubbed her eyes. The night was quiet. The gunfire and shelling that had been their constant companion over the last few months as the fighting had intensified around them was now a distant sound. The Allies, especially the Americans, were pushing back the Germans and the mood here in the tent hospital in Château-Thierry, two months after the battles had raged in the fields and woods around them, was lifting. Everyone was looking forward to the end of the war, which seemed likely now.

She listened for a few minutes to the hushed sounds of the only noise that filtered into this cornered-off section of the ward – that of the toing and froing of the other staff on duty and their whispered conversations, and, as she often did, she wondered what the young nurses thought of her as she'd avoided any chit-chat about family and 'back home', which they talked about all the time. Pearl was the only one she had any sort of conversation with, but she never intruded or asked Babs questions about her private life. *They probably have me down as being an old maid, which is what I have felt like these last months.*

She thought back over her time here. She knew she had shut herself down emotionally. Even Christmas hadn't meant much to her; it had come and gone without her feeling as though she was taking part. Though she had made sure that all of the patients had a happy time.

For herself, the highlight of that time had been a trip by train into Amiens, a beautiful medieval town, with the River Somme snaking through it, where she'd used her French to help her to buy perfume for her ma, Beth, Molly, Peggy and Eliza, and a scarf each for Tommy and Cliff. For Benny she'd bought a bonnet, and for her Art a little silver bracelet, which she'd sent to Rupert's old nanny, who she'd learnt was called Elsie.

This connection with Elsie and with Art's nurse, Annie, was a real solace to her. She'd asked that Annie put the bracelet on Art's wrist for a moment or two, and then to send it to Mr Fellows for his memory box, just as she had with the little booties from sister Theresa and Daisy.

With the bracelet she'd sent an embroidered hanky each for Elsie and Annie. Presents for home were taken to the Red Cross HQ in Paris and sent out from there.

For Mario and Rupert, she'd found a thick candle with a trail of roses worked into the wax. The candle she lit every night while she said her prayers, and chatted in her mind to her two little sons and Rupert. This brought her comfort.

Her ma had sent her a parcel filled with little treats – a tin of mince pies made by Eliza, which had kept remarkably fresh, a little basket for her hair pins made by Beth, with a lovely scented soap from Benny, a case for her pens made by Molly, and a tray for her dressing table made by Ma. This had fascinated her and made her wonder at her ma's creativity. The base was inlaid with glass, under which was a bouquet of pressed wild flowers – dog roses, poppies and heather on a background of white lace. The sides were woven in layers of dark brown and cream wicker, and underneath, hand painted in white, were her ma's initials and the words 'with love'. Babs treasured it, and all her gifts, which had included a little pot of hand cream from Tommy, which she knew her ma would have purchased for him, and a card and a pack of three lace hankies from Cliff.

In the card, and in his many letters, Cliff hadn't yet opened up to her. Instead he'd spoken of missing her, and of his life on the farm, which brought her home alive for her.

The basket from Beth meant a lot to her as inside she'd written a note of love. How she longed to feel that carefree and yet intense love that she had always had for Beth. Now, it was tainted with her suspicions and resentment.

'Sister?'

Sighing, Babs got up and went to see what she was wanted for.

The casualties coming to them were not nearly as many as they had been, and for a wartime hospital that had been a place of hell, it was now almost as organised and peacefully run as any conventional hospital back home.

'What is it, Nurse?'

'I don't feel happy about Ronald Merchant, Sister. The sergeant who had the operation earlier to remove the shrapnel from his head.'

A fully qualified nurse, of which there were few left as most had moved forward with the fighting, Rose Cheenham knew her stuff and if she was worried, then so was Babs.

'Well, let's take a look at him. Poor chap.'

This seemed to be a cue for Sergeant Merchant to begin shouting. His voice cracked the silence as he called out warnings to his fellow soldiers.

One of the other boys who'd come in with the sergeant sat up. 'What's wrong with Sarg, Sister? He's going to be all right, ain't he?'

'Aye, quieten down, lad. Nurse will bring you a drink in a moment. We'll soon settle your sergeant, don't worry.'

As they neared the bed, Nurse Cheenham whispered, 'He was calling out your name, Sister.'

This shocked Babs. She looked intently at the man's face. Something stirred in her memory – a young man who she'd tended to in the early days of the war. A cheeky youngster, who needed stitches in a bad gash he'd sustained on his leg. She remembered him because he was from Fleetwood, a small fishing town near to Blackpool. She smiled as she thought about how he'd said that he had fallen in love with her and thinking about her would keep him going.

'Poor man. I do remember him. I treated him at the beginning of the war. It's sad to think what his life has been like these past four years and now he's injured for the second time.'

Rose sighed and shook her head.

Often there was no need for words as gestures said it all.

The doctor had reported to them that the operation wasn't successful as he hadn't been able to get the shrapnel out. But then, Babs knew that though he'd done his best, the young doctor wasn't qualified to carry out brain surgery and had only managed to drain the build-up of fluid, hoping the reduced pressure would make the sergeant more comfortable.

'I'll see to him, Nurse. You go and settle the others down. I'd like to try to do what I can for him before I go off duty.' With saying this, tiredness seeped into Babs as it always did at the end of a shift, especially when that shift was a night-time one.

Though more often than not, she put herself on this duty as she found she could cope better managing on naps during the day than she could on wakeful nights, when she would feel all alone in the world as she tossed and turned and mourn all that she'd lost.

Sitting down next to Ronald, she decided to stay with him, as though he was calmer now, she had a sinking feeling inside her that he didn't have long. When he opened his eyes, he stared at her. 'Sister Babs?'

'Aye, that's me. Fancy you remembering me.'

'How could I forget the only Blackpool lass that I've met out here, eh?'

'Well, I haven't met anyone from Fleetwood since.'

'There's a few of us out here. Did they get me sorted, Sister?'

'Naw, I'm sorry, lad. It wasn't possible, but they've put you down for the next train out, so you'll soon be back in Blighty, where you'll get the treatment you need.'

Ronald lay back.

'Look, you'll be all right, I promise.' How often she'd lied like this.

'Aye. But I'm more concerned about me men. I should be with them. I need to be.'

'I knaw. And I understand. There's sommat about being out here that binds everyone as if they were family.'

Ronald closed his eyes. Babs took hold of his hand. 'Go home to Fleetwood, lad. You've done your bit. Get back to doing what you were born to do, going out on the trawlers bringing in the fish.'

'Eeh, I can almost smell it.'

'Aye, me an' all.'

'Sister Babs, I fell in love with you, you knaw. I've kept a picture of you in me head all this time. When you come home will you come to see me? I'd like to take you out. We could go along to the fairground and ride on the big wheel, in the town, and walk on the sand, and paddle in the sea.'

Babs ignored his declaration of love, but his description of where he'd like to take her made her long to be home. 'That sounds grand.'

Ronald clutched on to her hand. 'I mean it, lass . . . You're the one for me. I – I've dreamt of walking you along the prom, eating fish and chips . . . Can you smell them? . . . Eeh, lass, I've thought of how I – I'd stop . . . and get on me knee and ask you to marry me. In – in . . . me dream, you said yes.'

Her concern for him grew as he struggled to say this and as she saw his face draining of colour to now look like a mask made of wax. Realising that his death was near, she bent forward and whispered, 'It's a dream that we'll make come true, lad.'

Ronald smiled, then the smile dropped away as he went into an unconscious state that she knew he would never come out of. A few minutes later, he breathed his last breath on what sounded like a contented sigh.

Babs closed his half-open, non-seeing eyes, and bent down and kissed his cheek. The tears were running down her face when she straightened.

Wiping them away, Babs called for one of the VADs. 'Take care of him, Nurse. Another lovely lad gone to his maker.'

Suddenly, Babs felt crowded with grief and sorrow for how she imagined Ronald's family would suffer. For him to get through the war only to die just as it was coming to an end felt like a grave injustice.

She knew that if she didn't get out of this hospital soon, she would give vent to the strong urge that gripped her to just open her mouth and scream and scream.

Leaving Nurse Rose in charge, Babs decided she needed a break. Once outside in the cold, early-morning air, she took flight and ran and ran, her pain crowding her to an unbearable level.

As she ran past the hut where she and Pearl were billeted, Pearl came out and called to her, but she didn't stop.

Her barrier had cracked, her emotions were out of control. When she reached the open field and was out of sight, she flung herself to the ground and sobbed. *Why? Why? How am I to bear it all?*

'Babs. Babs!'

Pearl flopped down on the grass beside her, gasping for breath. 'What happened, Babs? Oh, can't you talk about what troubles you? You know, a trouble shared and all that.'

Between sobs, Babs told Pearl about Ronald.

Pearl held her close in a hug that reminded Babs of her ma. 'Babs, you helped him to die happy. You could do no more. Come on, old thing. Let's get you back. You need a good shower and bed.'

Babs felt better for the comfort. Her strength came back into her. 'Ta, Pearl. You're a good pal.'

'And you're a lovely person, Babs. Though a sad one, and I accept that whatever is on your mind is your own private business. Just know that I'm here for you if you ever do want to talk.'

Babs couldn't answer this but allowed Pearl to help her up. She felt so tired. So very tired. 'I need to sign off duty and hand over. I'll be back at the billet soon. Don't worry about me, Pearl, I'll be fine now.'

Sleep didn't come easy. Ronald's face kept appearing to her, as did the sights and sounds of Blackpool that he'd evoked in her. With them came the feeling of being unable to run her life in the way she was doing for much longer. *I need to get away from here – all the death and pain and misery. But where would I go? And what would I do? Because I can't see a time in the near future when I want to be with my family.*

But as she thought this, she knew it was Beth she couldn't be near. Not until the resentment she felt had healed. Nor could she be near to little Benny, though she loved him and missed him so much. She wouldn't be able to watch him go through the stages that Art would be going through; it would increase her pain to an unbearable level. *Oh God! I'm lost . . . lost and very alone.*

Pearl interrupted this thought that threatened to over-whelm her. 'Here you go, Babs, I've made you a cup of tea, and guess what? We had a delivery of a bag of sugar, so I've put some in for you. How are you feeling, old thing?'

'Yukky. Like running away, but I don't knaw where to go.' Suddenly, Babs knew that she needed to talk, and there was none better than Pearl to unload to. She trusted Pearl. A girl from a wealthy family, they were miles apart in their standing, and yet their job had brought them together and they'd formed a deep bond of friendship.

They sat crossed-legged on Babs's bed as Babs told Pearl how she'd lost Rupert and her friend Cath and most of her colleagues and, finally, what had happened to Art. She couldn't visit the rest of the horror that she'd been through, and didn't know how Pearl would take hearing all of that.

Pearl's big blue eyes opened wider as she listened to Babs's story. Pushing her fingers through her light-brown hair, which always wanted to flop over her face when not restricted by her headdress, her expression was one of shock. Tears dripped from her eyes, even though she didn't appear to be crying. 'Oh, Babs, that is one of the saddest stories I've ever heard. How can you bear so much and yet carry on? Your baby . . . oh God, how awful to be parted from him.'

'That's the worst part. Everything else has had an ending – a final outcome that I can't change, even though it all broke my heart. But not being able to be with, or to see my son, is an open sore that I can't heal.'

'There must be a way. Couldn't you move to the area where his grandfather lives, and then at least you would see your son occasionally? Maybe when he's walking with his nanny, perhaps?'

'I do have one small contact with him. Rupert's old nanny and the nurse taking care of Art. The nanny lives nearby to Art's grandfather's ancestral home. Rupert loved her so much, but his mother sacked her because she was northern with an accent like mine. It happened after Rupert began to pick up some of her sayings. He said it devastated him to lose her, but that he saw her in secret and he was still writing to her before he died. I could perhaps go and stay with her, then I would see Art. The nurse is a secret friend of hers and if she can do so without being seen, she very occasionally takes Art to see her.'

'That's an idea. You know nothing can happen unless you make it happen. She might have an idea of a local job you could take up, and as she loved Rupert so much, she might give you lodgings. Or . . . I've just had another idea. What if you trained to be a nanny?' With a little excited giggle, Pearl warmed to her theme. 'Your little Art is going to need a nanny soon. Children of the gentry usually have a nurse until they are about two or three, and then they have a nanny. I did and all my friends did too. I still love mine and we are in constant touch. What if you were ready to take up such a position when Art's grandparents advertise?'

'Eeh, Pearl.' A surge of hope shot through Babs. 'By, that'd be grand. I'd be able to bring up me own little son, and naw one would knaw. Not even him, until he's much older and I could tell him. By then, he might love me so much that he accepts me as his ma.'

'What you've just said throws up a problem, Babs. Well, not what you said – how you said it.'

'You mean me accent? Awe, Pearl, I'm doomed afore I start.'

'No, you're not. Look how quickly you learnt to speak French. You're better at it than me now, and I took exams and studied for years – too much theory and not enough practices – whereas you have learnt on the job, so to speak, and can converse in French better than anyone I know. You can soon learn to speak the King's English.'

'By, nowt phases you, lass. You're right, I can. Me sister did, and she speaks like you now. If she can, I can. Eeh, Pearl, lass, you've given me so much hope ... I mean, thank you, Pearl, you are top o!'

They both collapsed in giggles at this and Babs felt her world change from one of doom and gloom to one of hope and excitement, but then another problem presented itself. 'Eeh, but I've just thought. Though Rupert's family have never met me, their solicitor has. He'll recognise me and expose me. By, it's hopeless. I'm thwarted at every turn.' As she said this, Babs's heart dropped into her boots, such was the feeling of having these wonderful hopes dashed.

SIXTEEN

Beth

Beth put the finishing touches to the wicker chair – her first. Ma was amazed at her skills. 'Eeh, lass, it took me many years to get to the stage that you're at. You're very talented, me little darling.'

'Well, I have an advantage, Ma. I have you to teach me what you have taught yourself and all of this equipment to help me. I've you and Peggy and Molly taking care of me and Benny and Eliza and Tommy encouraging me. You had none of that, Ma. How you did what you did, I'll never know.'

'It weren't easy and were a rocky path that I travelled, especially once I took to drink. It's one that I'm glad that Babs stopped herself from travelling. Her latest letter sounded full of hope for her future. Though she didn't say what her plans were, just that she had some and was putting them into force.'

'Yes, she said the same to me. Intriguing, isn't it? But I'm happy for her. And for me. Oh, Ma, the war is coming to an end. My Henry will be home soon, I'm sure. I cannot wait.'

They were in the workshop where Beth loved to be, though she felt guilt at the effort it took to get her up there, with Peggy and Mary lifting her from one step to the other and then sitting her in another of Ivan's special chairs. She loved to think of Ivan working in this same room with Ma and Molly.

'Aye, it'll be grand, though what all of them soldiers will do when they return, I've naw idea. It'll put all the women out of work and they ain't going to like that. Well, lass, I'll get from under your feet. I've to pick up me grocery order, then our Eliza has an hour off to come and have a bun and a pot of tea with me.

'Anyroad, I'll just go and have a chat with Peggy, then I'll be off. See you later, me little Beth, and you, Mary.'

Her ma's hug warmed Beth's heart. How she would have got through these last eighteen months without her ma by her side, she didn't know. But the time was coming when it would all be over.

An excitement tingled through her as she thought of Henry. His last letter had spoken of how everyone he came into contact with was saying they thought that it would only be a matter of weeks now before they all came home.

She looked up from her work. The sky was grey today and she could hear the wind and the crashing waves. Autumn had truly crept up on them.

Babs popped into her mind, and she wondered how she really was. Her letters just brushed the surface of reality, telling nothing of her feelings, or of what life was really like. Just that she was well and the odd snippets from her experiences. What was it that was between them? Yes, she could understand how

Babs felt in the beginning, but now that her relationship with Jasmine and Roman was over all should be well. Sighing, she put it down to the same thing she always did: that during their separation they'd grown apart, and that if they had a chance to be together for any length of time, they would grow together again. Maybe Babs would come to stay with her and Henry when they moved into a larger home, which they would have to do now they had Benny.

On cue as he came into her head, Benny made his presence known by calling out. Peggy came through the door with him. When he saw her, his face lit up with a smile that replicated Henry's and when Peggy released him, he came toddling on unsteady feet towards her. Gerry followed on his heels; now heading for four years old, Gerry played the part of older brother to Benny. He had his hands out as if to catch him if he went to fall.

Mary's rarely heard giggle lightened Beth's mood even more, as though they had worked together for months now, she hadn't felt that she'd really got through to her. Only Gerry could do that, and as Beth looked at Mary's face light up as her son ran to her, she thought how terrible it must be for Mary never again to have her husband come home to her.

'Eeh, they're a pair, these two.' Peggy looked and sounded very flustered. 'They've given me a merry dance this morning. I need a break. I'll go down and put the kettle on, aye, and visit the lav while I'm there – not the best place to find peace, but at least they can't get at me there: Gerry with his constant questions and Benny into everything now he can get about.'

Beth looked at Mary. 'Oh dear.'

'That's what I thought an' all. I reckon they're getting too much for Peggy. I've been thinking of seeing if I can get Gerry into school as I don't want to give up me job. I'm dreading when you go, Beth.'

This surprised Beth as she hadn't thought she'd made any impact on Mary. 'I'm going to miss you too, Mary. But, oh, I can't wait.'

Mary was quiet for a moment, then let out a huge sigh. 'I don't knaw what it's going to be like when all the men come home. Especially when Brian does. I'm so happy for me sister, Vera, but I don't know how I'm going to cope. Me hubby Gerry and his brother Brian were inseparable at times. They didn't work together – Brian worked at the saddlery with his da – but me Gerry were big in the theatre productions: the stage settings and that kind of thing.'

'Yes, my ma told me all about him. I'm sorry for your loss, Mary. It must be so painful for you.'

'I don't knaw how to be most of the time. Me ma-in-law is suffering, and it's going to be hard for her when just one of her sons comes home, and I want to comfort her, but part of me is dragged down by her presence. I feel that I have to act the grieving widow all the time – oh, I don't mean as I ain't. Me heart's broken, but there has been some healing, some part of me that's beginning to find peace with Gerry's memory, and aye, if I'm truthful, I'm starting to want to live me life again. But that's going to be put right back when Brian comes home as he's going to expect a grieving sister-in-law an' all.'

This was a revelation to Beth. Here they were all thinking that Mary would never lift out of the doldrums when all the time she was longing to. 'Mary, you mustn't feel guilty about healing. It is a natural process, and I think that Molly will be glad to see it happen. She often speaks of how she wishes you would lift your spirits and not be so sad all the time.'

Little Gerry looked up at Mary. 'I don't want you to be sad, Ma.'

Mary smiled down at him. 'I'll try not to be, me lovely lad.' She looked across at Beth then. 'I must have been a misery to work with. I'm sorry, lass, and here's you coping with all you have to and yet keeping a smile on your face.'

'It's the only way to be, Mary, and I'm glad you're feeling better.'

The smile they gave each other faded in shock as Gerry screeched, 'Eeh, Ma, look at Benny.'

Turning, Beth saw Benny teetering at the top of the stairs. She froze, not daring to call out for fear of frightening him and him losing his step, and yet feeling so inadequate that she couldn't just get up and run to him. Holding her breath, she watched Mary stand Gerry down, silently warning him to keep quiet, then rise from her stool and creep towards Benny.

Beth's heart thumped in her chest, her mind screaming prayers as she knew that one more step and her son would disappear head-long down the stairs. Visons of him breaking his neck and dying held her in terror.

At last Mary reached him and grabbed him. The fright made Benny scream out. His body wriggled and his arms came out to her. When Mary brought him to her, he clung on to her, little trembles shaking his body.

'Naughty Benny. You shouldn't go near to the stairs. I've told you that before!'

This outburst from Gerry broke the tension and Beth wanted to laugh out loud with relief and because Gerry had sounded like a father speaking to his son.

Mary did give a nervous giggle but put her hand over her mouth to try to stop it happening. But when Benny put his arms out to Gerry in a gesture of asking for forgiveness, Beth had to smile as the two boys hugged and Gerry said, 'I have to have me eyes on you all the time!'

Her smile turned to a giggle at this. Looking over at Mary, they both burst out with laughter. Beth knew it was a reaction to the shock, but the laughter changed the atmosphere that had always hung over this room since she'd begun working next to Mary.

'By, lads as young as me little Gerry are taking on the father role. It seems to come natural to them, even though most have never known what it is like to have a da.'

'That's so sad. Oh, I hope the news comes soon that it's all over and all the men come home . . . Oh, I'm sorry, Mary.'

'Naw, lass. I hope that an' all. I knaw mine ain't and I've sort of got used to that, though me heart will break all over again when Brian gives me a hug, but I'll make meself happy for our Vera, and'll be hoping that Brian soon makes her pregnant an' all.'

Beth laughed again as this.

'Ha, I knaw, it's a funny wish, but I've allus felt guilty about having me little Gerry. I caught for him on me honeymoon, but Vera didn't get pregnant, and the men went away after that. I've allus thought that she's envious of me. There's been sommat between us, and I think it's that.'

'It's funny you should say that, but me and Babs used to be so close, and now we have a strained relationship. It hurts and I so want to make things right.'

'I knaw. Well, I reckon a babby for Vera would put her right, but what about your sister? Do you knaw what's on her mind?'

Beth told Mary about Jasmine and Roman. Part of her felt a sadness at how she never saw them anymore, but it was only a small part and she denied it the chance to take hold. 'But I've severed all ties with them now, and Babs knows that, so I'm at a loss. I think she has some twisted idea that I do everything to please others so that I get what I want, while everything goes wrong for her. But I see that as her making bad decisions. I mean, the time she went off, she was only thirteen, she had no idea where Blackpool was, or how to get there; it was bound to lead to trouble.'

'Eeh, lass. Maybe when she comes home, you'll find each other again and clear all the misunderstandings.'

Beth hoped so, as she had a sixth sense that Babs wasn't happy. How could she be with all that had happened to her? But more than that, she had a feeling that things were still not going well for her, even though her letter sounded as though it was. She made her mind up that she would write to Babs and tell her, as she always did, of her love for her, and to do what she'd thought earlier and ask her to come and stay with her and Henry.

Peggy came back then laden with a tray of tea. Beth made a face and shook her head at Mary, trying to convey to her not to say anything about the incident, but she was forestalled by Gerry, who they knew mimicked Peggy as he said, 'He's been at it again, Peggy. Nearly tumbled down the bloomin' stairs. It's like you say, you need eyes in the back of your head!'

The room filled with laughter, and Mary hugged her son to her. 'Eeh, lad, you're me shining light. And I love you, all the sugar in the world.'

Gerry looked bemused, but then, he probably hadn't seen a lot of sugar with all the shortages, and the saying used to mean a lot more to children than it does now.

When they all quietened down, and Peggy had taken the boys back into the nursery, Beth pondered some more on the situation between her and Babs and hoped with all her heart that Babs would be home soon. Yes, she knew she had to accept that throughout their lives they would go their separate ways. *But, oh, Babs, wherever you are when you are not by my side, my love for you will still be strong. Always.*

Ma bustling in, followed by Molly, interrupted her thoughts, as she looked up and greeted them. 'I thought you two were meant to be semi-retired. It strikes me that you're here or out on your trips together more than you are at home, Ma.'

'I knaw, lass, but there's a new plan and we wanted to discuss it with you. We figured the boys would be having their afternoon nap and so won't disturb us.'

'Oh? You never said owt, Molly.' Mary looked a little wary as she said this.

'Naw, I didn't, lass. Me and Tilly had to sort everything out first. You tell them, Tilly.'

'Right, well, it's to do with the distribution of the work.' Beth listened to her ma outlining Florrie's new role. She glanced at Mary, who was smiling as if this was the best news she'd ever heard.

Molly looked even more relieved than Mary as she asked her, 'You don't mind, lass?'

'Naw, Molly, I'm never going to be a seamstress, let's face it. I'm still struggling to keep a straight line on this blooming machine! The thing hates me, and me feet don't seem able to do a different rhythm to me hands, so treadling it while I guide the material is sommat I'll never master. But I do need a job and love coming to the shop.'

'We knaw, lass.' Ma took hold of Mary's shoulder and bent towards her. 'And our problems are not sorted by a long way, as Beth will soon be leaving us an' all, but there will still be plenty of hand sewing for you to do, and you're good at that. And Gracie has just told us that she can no longer do the hours in the shop that she's been doing due to her swollen legs, so how about you become the shop manager and you can do the hand stitching when the shop's quiet, eh?'

'Eeh, that'd suit me. I love being in the shop and meeting the folk who come in. I've a lot of ideas for displays an' all.'

Ma let out a deep sigh as she said, 'That's settled then, but what to do about a basket maker, I don't knaw. I can see me having to work full time again when you leave, Beth.'

'You should think about taking an apprentice on, Ma. I know it will take a little while to train someone up, but once you have, even if it's just to make the smaller items, you can step back a bit. And another thing, if Florrie can work from home, why can't you? Once I've gone you could easily turn that downstairs bedroom into a work room, then you would still be near to Tommy and only have to travel in a couple of days as you want to.'

'By, lass, that's a grand idea. Working from home, I mean. Not sure about the apprentice, though.'

'Why not? There must be a lot of young people wanting a job, and if not them, you said yourself that you wondered where all the returning soldiers would work. Well, I think like you say, the women will be turned out of the factories to make room for the men again, so there'll be a lot of them looking for work.'

'Does it have to be a woman?' Mary asked. 'I mean, well, there's a few wounded soldiers who could do the job. They won't be welcomed into the factories.'

Beth could see that this idea appealed to her ma and to Molly as they both looked at each other as if a light had been switched on. 'Eeh, Mary, you may not be any good on the treadle, but your head seems full of ideas. You're just what we need in the shop, lass. I reckon as that's a really good idea. There's a wounded soldier who sits outside the tower begging, poor lad. It's a crying shame as there's nowt for them when they come home. I'll go this minute and talk to him. He's only got one leg, but he's got both his arms, basket making'd suit him down to the ground.'

With this, Ma turned towards the stairs. Beth giggled, and Mary joined in with the giggle as she said, 'Eeh, Beth, there's going to be changes around here, lass, and not before time. And me just on with telling you that I were fed up with this sewing lark an' all.'

'Really, you said that, lass?'

'Aye, I did, Molly, and well . . .' Mary looked over at Beth. Beth nodded her encouragement. Mary took a deep breath, 'Well, I – I don't want to be the grieving widow any longer either, Molly. I mean . . . well, I'll allus love Gerry and never forget him, but I'm ready to live me life again . . . I – I'm sorry. I—'

'Naw, don't be. Eeh, Mary, lass, that's grand news. I think you've been in the doldrums for too long. You're only young, and me Gerry wouldn't want you to mope around for the rest of your life. Life is for living. We only get one chance to live it as it is, and we shouldn't waste it by mourning what we've lost – well, I mean, we shouldn't do that twenty-four hours a day.'

Mary stood up and went into Molly's arms. To Beth it was a lovely sight and she hoped it marked a turning point for Mary. Once more she thought of Babs and felt the pity of Babs not having a mother-in-law to turn to. *I'm so lucky with having Philomena and my lovely sister-in-law Janine. Poor Babs. Why? Why is it that everything turns out right for me, but not for you?* Yes, some of it was down to Babs's poor decision making, but not all. Nothing she could have decided would have caused the loss of Rupert, or of darling little Art. A pain cut into her heart then. She hadn't known little Art for long, but she loved him so much and missed him every waking hour.

SEVENTEEN

Babs

The hospital had gradually emptied and the proximity of the fighting had moved further and further away. As news of the Hindenburg Line having been broken and the Germans asking for an armistice had filtered through, life had begun to change drastically for Babs and her colleagues.

Now most of their time was taken up with decommissioning some of the tents used for wards and packing everything into the crates that had been delivered. Meticulous labelling was carried out to ensure that the medical supplies and tents were sent forward to where they were most needed.

For Babs and Pearl, with time on their hands, life would have been dull but for the fun they were having as Pearl tried to help Babs to speak without an accent.

With the mid-October weather having a biting chill to it, they were huddled in their billet with the lighted wood stove keeping them warm.

Darkness was falling and they were in their pyjamas sitting crossed-legged on cushions on the floor. Pearl was beginning to get exasperated with Babs. 'You've got to stop saying what sounds like elongated "E"s, Babs. You must unlearn that, because even when you form a perfect sentence you fall into that trap. That and prefixing sentences with "by" too. It's as if you can't begin to speak without using these to lead you into what you want to say.'

'I knaw ... whoops! ... *know*, but none of it is coming easy to me. Especially as I have to speak in my natural dialect with the rest of the staff, so that I don't raise their curiosity. I don't want a lot of questions that I can't answer.'

'I know, it's difficult for you, old thing, but think of it as two languages, like you do with French. When you need to speak French, you do, and that's that. So, when you need to speak the King's English to me, you do, and the same for when you need your northern accent with the staff. It's as simple as that.'

Babs didn't think it simple at all. And the comparison didn't help. But she was determined to make a success of this, as still she saw it as the only hope she had, even though problems by the dozen had presented themselves to her.

Sighing, she again spoke of her worries. 'But, Pearl, even if I do master it, we still haven't come up with a way that I can get away with trying for the position of nanny when I might be recognised. My voice might throw that horrid solicitor off, but my appearance won't.'

'Then we'll have to change your appearance. Look, I've been thinking. Would you consider coming home with me for a time? We have plenty of room and I would love you to. I'm beginning to see the reality of the change in our lives that is looming, and I hate the thought of not having you by my side.'

'Eeh, Pearl, lass … Oh, bugger! I mean … Really? You would really consider taking me to your home?'

'Aye, I would an' all, lass.'

They collapsed in laughter, as they always did when Pearl mimicked Babs. 'You know, Babs, I think it would be easier for me to learn to speak like you than for you to speak like me!'

'Aye, I think you're right.'

'Look, don't be despondent. I mean it when I say I was astounded, and still am, at how you have mastered French. I have never known anyone pick it up so quickly, so you can master this. And if you will come and stay at my home for a few months, I can have you word perfect. Not only that, we can work on your story, too – you know, who you are going to present yourself as, as well as your disguise. Oh, Babs, it will be such fun. I have had such a lot of thoughts on the subject. For instance, my brother and my sister are both married, and both live on Daddy's estate. Both have children, and the children have nannies. So, I can get you some training too. What do you think?'

'But won't your folk think me deceitful? I mean, as they see me gradually changing, won't they want to know why, and even if we tell them about Art, won't they want me to follow the legal channels?'

On a huge sigh, Pearl conceded. 'You're right, and that sentence was spoken so well too. See, you can do it. Anyway, yes, you have a point. Daddy may even know this Lord Barnham – bound to, in fact – so won't like what we're planning at all. Bother!'

'What if I lodged nearby? They needn't even meet me.'

'That's it! As you know, my home is on the outskirts of Brighton, and there is loads of accommodation there. Though for a lady on her own it might be difficult. Oh, why is that so? Why can't we be seen as responsible in the wider world as we are when needed, like now? So much is put in our hands at the moment, but you see, as soon as we return home we'll be looked upon as not able to take any decisions or have a sensible thought of our own!'

Babs nodded her agreement, not wanting to comment as getting Pearl talking about the rights of women meant they would be up half the night. Not that she didn't agree wholeheartedly with all of Pearl's ideals, but tonight she was tired and weighted down with a hope that seemed dashed.

'Look, don't get downhearted, old thing. I will come up with something. I promise.'

Babs had no doubt about this. Pearl was always full of ideas. And some of them really good ones too.

'Let's talk about what we are going to do on Saturday. We're both off. Let's go out somewhere. That would be wonderful. Just to get away from seeing our lives as we've known them being packed into wooden boxes. Oh, do say yes, Babs.'

'Eeh, that sounds good, but where to?'

'Well, there's Chézy-sur-Marne and I happen to know that some of the American officers are still camped there; we might meet some. But in any case, officers from many regiments take their rest days there as it is so relaxing along the banks of the Dolloir, so that might be interesting.'

'Oh, Pearl, I'm not up for a manhunting trip, thank you very much. Besides, what about transport? It's not an easy place to get to.'

'One of the ambulance drivers has promised that I can borrow his motorbike when I want to.'

'What? Can you ride a motorbike?'

'Yes, I can. It's been a while, but my brother has one – a monster of a machine – and I ride that all over our estate at home.'

These mentions of 'our estate' always illustrated to Babs the wideness of the gap between her and Pearl's standing in life. But she had no side to her and was a good friend, and good company too.

'Aye, all right then. I'll come. I've never been on a motor-bike so that'll be sommat – something, I mean. And I'll allow you to chat up men, but please don't be involving me.'

'I promise.'

Babs felt surprisingly refreshed after only four hours' sleep. She'd woken with a feeling of anticipation at the coming trip, and had slipped into the shower, which soon had her fully awake as the water was cold, as usual. But the sun was shining through the small window and this warmed her, even though she knew from her view that the air would have that autumn feel that had painted the world red and gold.

Dressing wasn't a problem as she hadn't many clothes to choose from. Like all the girls, she had a few practical, comfort-able clothes and a couple of outfits that suited going on an outing on rest days. Babs chose a frock with a flared skirt that had a high neck and reached to her ankles. The material was cotton, in a pretty lemon colour. It was a plain dress, but for all that, it looked fetching. It didn't provide any warmth, though, so she teamed it with a navy hip-length cardigan that had been knitted by Daisy when she was preparing to leave the convent – a time that seemed a million years ago. Donning her heavy-duty uniform coat in navy, and tying the belt, and then plonking her velvet cloche hat on her head, she allowed the excitement of the coming trip to take hold of her.

It was an afterthought to grab her blue silk scarf to tie her hat on with as she remembered their mode of transport.

The journey was traumatic. Pearl didn't seem able to handle the bike at all, and Babs was glad to at last arrive in Chézy-sur-Marne and alight on wobbly legs.

'Pearl Jenson, you liar! You've naw more idea of riding a motorbike than I have, and I'd never seen one till I came to France!'

Pearl laughed. 'We're here, aren't we? And all in one piece, so forget it and let's enjoy ourselves.'

How they were to do that in what looked like a ghost town, Babs didn't know. She felt more like throwing up than anything else. She looked around at the many-coloured houses, all tall with peeling paint and firmly closed shutters.

'Come on, there's a café on the corner, we're bound to find some life there.'

The life they found was a relaxed group of American officers who all stood up as they entered. One spoke to Babs in French.

Almost saying, 'Eeh,' a look from Pearl stopped her. 'Oh, I thought that you were American, so why're you talking to me in French?'

He burst out laughing. A lovely sound. 'Sorry, I thought you were French. I'm Captain Rugely, Canadian army officer – French-Canadian, from Quebec. And you are?'

'Babs. Babs Barnham.'

'Pleased to meet you, Babs. I'm Marceau, known as Marc by my fellow officers and friends, whom I would very much like to count you amongst.'

Babs felt herself blush. He seemed very self-assured.

Marc put his head back and laughed. 'Well, I wasn't expecting that reaction. Sorry. Been too long in men's company. I'm forgetting not to be so forward in the presence of a lady.'

Babs laughed with him, as she secretly enjoyed being called a lady. The title had her holding her head high and gave her an inkling that she could pull off pretending to be something that she wasn't.

'Would you join me in a cup of coffee, ma'am?'

Looking around to see that Pearl was happily giggling away with a crowd around her, Babs nodded. 'I'd like that.'

Ordering the coffee, Marc asked, 'Will you be warm enough to sit outside? I'm finding it stuffy in here.'

Babs nodded.

Outside the sun was still shining, though not giving off a lot of warmth, but she didn't care as she sat down, glad to rest her still shaking legs. She'd chosen the seat that was against the wall of the building, and was surprised when Marc moved the wooden table and brought a chair to sit next to her. 'Good choice, we'll have the sun beaming down on us and yet be shielded from the wind.'

When their coffee arrived and Babs thanked the waiter in French and then answered him when he asked if she took milk, Marc looked at her in surprise. 'So, you do speak French! Or have you just learnt how to get what you need?'

'*Non, monsieur, je peux parler français.*'

'Gee, that's amazing! I mean, I know many English ladies study the language. Well, I would very much like to *parler français. La langue me rappelle la maison.*'

Babs thought this lovely, that she could help someone to be reminded of their home. She turned her head and looked at Marc, registering for the first time how handsome he was. Taller than her, he had clear-cut features and twinkling brown eyes. His hair was fair and cut regimentally short, but what was left on the top flopped over his forehead, giving him an appealing, impish look. His mouth seemed permanently fixed in a smile and this produced dimples in each of his cheeks. She liked him, and felt that in him she'd met another friend.

This thought brought Cliff to mind and she felt a little pang of guilt. She was meant to be a friend of Cliff's and yet she wrote silly, light letters to him, avoiding what he wanted to tell her. That wasn't how friends were. She should have prompted him. Made him feel that she would listen and wouldn't judge. For she had a strong feeling that what he had to say would be shocking.

'So, do I cut muster, ma'am?'

'Oh . . . I – I'm sorry. I didn't mean to stare. I was thinking of a friend at home. You reminded me of him . . . well, not to look at, but well, just how you are – treating me as a person, not an object for . . . Oh dear, I'm tying myself in knots.'

Although embarrassed, Babs did have the fleeting thought of how easily the King's English was flowing from her. She supposed it was because she was so relaxed with Marc.

'Glad to be of service, ma'am.'

Babs giggled. 'Stop all this "ma'am" business, it embarrasses me.'

'Would mademoiselle suit better?'

'No. I'm a married lady – well, a widow – so that isn't the correct term. But anyway, even if speaking in French, I like to be called by my name.' Mentioning her status – and so easily – surprised Babs. She didn't normally tell anyone she was a widow. There was something about Marc that made her feel she could tell him anything.

'I feel there is a story there, and a very sad one, but I won't ask you to tell me about it. Just to say that I am sorry, Babs. And that I raise my coffee to the fine gentleman your husband must have been. Not only to win fair lady, but my guess is that he lost his life to this rotten war.'

Without feeling the usual urge to shut down and crawl into a corner to weep at the mention of Rupert, Babs lifted her cup. 'Yes, he was. A fine gentleman, who I loved dearly and am very proud to hold the memory of. To my Rupert.'

Marc smiled as he clinked her cup with his. His not forcing questions on her reminded her once more of Cliff. He always allowed her to say just as much as she wanted to. She made her mind up in that instant that as soon as she got back to camp she would write to Cliff.

Leaning back against the wall, Babs let her eyes fall on the peaceful scene of the river, which was only yards away from them. It babbled through the centre of this small town and she found the sound it made soothing. Marc didn't disturb the calm by talking, which surprised her as most Americans she'd met were always talking. Oh, she knew he wasn't American as such but, well, American or Canadian, they all seemed the same to her.

Pearl was the one to shatter the companionable silence between her and Marc as she came out of the café. 'Are you all right, old thing? I've only just noticed that you were missing.'

Babs laughed. 'I'm not surprised, you were lapping up the attention you were receiving.'

Pearl giggled as she sat on one of the empty chairs. 'Eeh, it were grand!'

To the bemusement of Marc, this set them off giggling till tears ran down their faces.

'Sorry, I couldn't resist. Ha! I've decided I love your phrases and will miss them.'

'Well, think of it as another language and we can converse in it whenever we want to.'

This had the effect of setting them off again.

'Ladies, am I missing something here?'

Feeling so comfortable with Marc, Babs shared the joke. Telling him that to get a job of the same standing as the one she had in the war, she would need to give a different impression from the one her native northern accent gave and how Pearl had been teaching her.

'If I live to be a hundred, I'll never understand the English class system. In my country, everyone is equal, from a farmhand to a landowner. When this is over, Babs, why don't you visit me? You can be who you are over there.'

'Maybe I will sometime in the future, thank you.'

Marc had looked deep into her eyes as he'd asked her and now, she found that she couldn't look away.

'*Tu es très belle, Babs.*'

He thinks me beautiful! A small tingle set up in Babs's stomach and she knew this showed in her eyes. But then embarrassment took her as she remembered that Pearl was watching. She turned away to find that the seat Pearl had occupied was empty. This increased her embarrassment as Pearl must have heard and made herself scarce, thinking she was intruding. 'I – I have to go.' Standing, she bumped into the table, hurting her thigh. Her wince had Marc standing and catching hold of her hand. The feel of his hand in hers deepened her confusion.

'Babs, don't run. It's all right to live your life.'

'No, I – I'm sorry . . . I'm not ready. Let go of me. I have to go.'

Marc immediately dropped her hand. '*Pardon* . . . I didn't mean . . .'

'No, it's all right. I just need you to be my friend.'

As she hurried away, Marc called after her, '*Je serais toujours ton ami.*'

And somehow, she knew that what he said was true – he would always be her friend.

When she got inside the café, Marc wasn't far behind her. Pearl looked at her with concern in her expression. Babs shook her head, hoping to convey to Pearl not to question her.

Marc pulled out a chair for her, but she just wanted to go back to the hospital. 'I think we should get back, Pearl. We've left a lot on Rose's shoulders.'

Pearl didn't question her. She would know, as Babs did, that Rose Cheenham was more than capable and would cope well with seeing the shipment of crates loaded onto the train that was expected today, and making sure that all paperwork was in place for it.

They left in a flurry of goodbyes and wishes of good luck and had their hats tied on and were about to mount the bike when Marc came running out. 'Babs! Babs!'

'Do you want me to just drive away, Babs?'

This made Babs realise that she'd made it look as if Marc had insulted her, when the truth was far from it. Feeling more composed, she asked Pearl to wait a moment. Going towards Marc, she told him, 'I'm sorry for how I behaved. I – I, well, I'm still grieving, and I was afraid of the effect you were having on me.'

'You felt it too? Oh, Babs! Look, I understand, but at least let me write to you. We can be friends, I would never push you into anything else – not that I could as soon I will be thousands of miles away.'

With this realisation a dull ache took its place in Babs's heart. She wouldn't let the reason in, but knew that all she could do was agree to them writing to each other. One day, maybe things would be different. But for now she had to keep focused on how she could be with her little Art. 'Yes, I would like us to keep in touch.'

'Let me write down your address.'

'Better that you write yours down for me as I don't know where I will be after the war. Once it is over, I will write to you and let you know my address.'

Taking the slip of paper, Babs wondered at the sense in this. Marc would, like he said, be thousands of miles from her when he returned home, but somehow, she couldn't just let him go.

EIGHTEEN

Tilly

Christmas was only a few weeks away and Tilly was facing up to not having all her family around her once more, only this time it was Beth who would be missing, though it wasn't certain that Babs would make it back in time.

It had been a shock to her when Beth had said that she wanted to go to her home in Margate and, with the help of her in-laws, begin to look for a home to buy for when Henry returned.

Thinking of this triggered a sigh. When the armistice was announced for the eleventh of the eleventh the happiness that had abounded had included the thought that all those serving abroad would be home for Christmas. That wasn't proving to be the case. Hardly any were and the women of Blackpool were even more upset than they had been for the last four or so years.

And now, the number of cases of flu breaking out was alarming.

Driving into Blackpool, Tilly wondered if she was wise to keep the shop open. Trade was almost non-existent as everyone tried to avoid public places and visitors to the resort were few. She worried, too, about Eliza going into work. This morning as she'd watched her skilfully manoeuvre the horse and trap out of the farm gates, she prayed hard to God to keep her and all her family and friends safe.

The folk walking along the promenade were a chilling sight with half of their faces covered with masks. Tilly shuddered. Blackpool didn't look like Blackpool anymore. Many stalls were closed and she thought about their owners, hoping they were all well. Especially Ivy and her girls. With this in her mind she wondered if she would find Mary in work, or Alec. But then, Alec would be as he slept there now. They'd had a bed put into the nursery once more as with Peggy gone little Gerry was more often than not with Molly, though he was a good little boy and Mary could manage him with the help of Alec.

When she'd been to see the young lad sitting outside the tower begging for help, she'd found out that he was called Alec, and wasn't from Blackpool, but London. He'd been recovering in a house that had been converted into a hospital in Station Road, South Shore. Having been an orphan and in the poorhouse when war broke out, he had nowhere to go back to and liked the people of Blackpool.

He'd thought that on his discharge he'd find some work on one of the stalls, and lodgings, but he hadn't been lucky. She'd passed him a few times sitting outside the tower with a crumpled old hat in front of him and holding a carboard box lid with the words 'Need work' written on it. His situation had tugged at her heart. She'd never passed him without giving him what change she had on her and getting him some fish and chips or a hot tatty. He'd been her natural choice to replace Beth.

And what a choice it was proving to be. Alec had mastered the basics of basket making in no time, and was now producing some of the more intricate designs. She'd found that he had an advantage in his upper body strength as bending the canes and weaving the wicker posed him no problems, whereas for herself, even after all the years she'd been making basketware, the operation was back-breaking at times.

When she reached the shop and parked her car, Tilly fixed her own mask in place before she crossed the road. Children's voices drifted up to her. She looked down onto the beach and was amazed to see about six little girls dancing in a ring. She wanted to call out to them to go home and stay indoors. But then, these were kids that looked strong and the fresh sea air was good for them. Their chorus made her smile, and yet there was a sad truth in the words they sang.

'I had a little bird
Its name was Enza
I opened the window,
And in-flu-enza.'

As horrible as the sentiment was, Tilly felt lifted to see such resilience and, yes, defiance in the face of the dreaded flu virus.

'It's only me!' The shop bell resounded in the silence of the empty shop, as did Tilly's words. A worried frown creased her brow and her body broke out in one of her dreaded sweats as fear of the uncanny quiet settled in her.

Mopping her brow with her hanky, she ran to the back of the shop and grabbed the handle of the door leading to the work room upstairs. Once through she shouted, 'Mary, Alec! Where are you?'

Alec's voice, strong but full of worry, came back to her. 'We're up 'ere, Tilly, 'urry.'

Tilly's heart was in her mouth as she took the stairs two at a time. 'What's wrong? Oh, Mary, naw, lass. Whatever's the matter?'

Though she asked this, Tilly had guessed but didn't want to acknowledge her suspicions. On seeing the pallor of Mary's face and her shivering body Tilly knew with certainty what ailed Mary. She was lying on the floor. Alec was sitting on his footstool beside her – how he'd got down there, Tilly didn't know. Surrounding them both was a broken mess of all the makings of what was once a tray of tea. The lass was meant to be looking after the shop floor, but had obviously tried to look after Alec at the same time.

'Alec, where's your mask? And where's Mary's? Oh, why haven't you got them on?' As Tilly asked this her own mask was slipping in the sweat that was dripping from her face. Adjusting it, she knelt down beside Mary. 'Eeh, lass, naw, not you, I can't bear it. Where's Gerry?'

Alec answered. 'Molly 'as 'im today, Tilly. Mary was all right earlier, then she brought me a tray up and just fainted at me feet.'

His hand stroked Mary's hair from her forehead. 'You're going to be all right, Mary, love. I won't let anything 'appen to yer.'

In his gentle words and his look, Tilly saw the love he had for Mary and her worry increased. The lad had enough on his plate without seeing the woman he loved near to death. But she couldn't give this thought all her attention as her heart-ache was compounded by the moan that came from Mary.

'We need to get her onto your bed, Alec. I'll nip down and close the shop, lad. I'll see if there's someone outside who can run to fetch the doctor, though they're saying that he won't attend if he thinks it's flu. Not that he's much use as he's that full of drink these days that he don't knaw what he's diagnosing. When I come back, we'll sort a way of moving Mary off the floor.' Looking down at Mary, Tilly told her, 'Hang on, lass. Hang on.'

No one would answer her desperate pleas. All hurried by, keeping their faces turned away. Fear reigned on the streets, but she understood it as her own fear was making her body tremble.

When she returned, Alec told her of a method he'd seen used in the hospital. 'Get me a sheet, Tilly, and lay it out on the floor. We can roll Mary onto it and, 'olding a corner each, drag 'er to the sofa. Once there, we can lift 'er using the sheet as a 'oist.'

Doing as he said, Tilly found the method worked well. Though by the time they had Mary safely wrapped up and lying on the bed, Tilly felt like collapsing in a heap.

'Are yer all right, Tilly? You're not sickening for this virus, are yer?'

'Naw, lad. This sweating is a regular occurrence for me; just ignore it and let's see what we can do for Mary. But, lad, get a mask on. I implore you, please try to keep yourself safe.'

'I don't think they make much difference meself, Tilly. I think they make you hot and that gives a nice damp atmosphere for the virus to grow in. I'll take me chances.'

Although this sounded good sense, Tilly didn't want to take her own off. 'Look, I gave you both one of those that Beth sent me in one of her letters. She told me that they think the virus is spread by the droplets released when an infected person sneezes. With a mask on they're less likely to get into your mouth or nose. And they help in stopping you from touching those areas an' all. Beth said to wash your hands as many times as you can. She also said that I've to wash everything that I come into contact with that an infected person may have touched. But her advice on what to do if anyone came down with it was just to keep them drinking, keep them cool if they have a temperature and try to make sure they get oxygen. It's this last that we need the doctor for.'

'I'll bathe Mary, if you can get me a bowl of water, Tilly. And I'll put me mask on. I 'ave it in me pocket.'

Alec had no sooner said this and was fixing his mask when Mary sneezed. The action caused blood to come pouring from her nose. Tilly felt her spirits drop. She couldn't see them saving Mary and that was breaking her heart. 'Right, lad. I'll sort out a bowl of water for you and then I'll go and fetch that blooming doctor meself. I'll go in the van, so if he won't come, I can at least buy an oxygen cylinder from him, and get him to show me how to use it. Though how I'll get it into me van or up here, I've naw idea. I can't ask anyone for help, but happen sommat'll occur.'

As it worked out, there were some workmen outside the doctor's house, and though all in their fifties, they were strong and soon had the oxygen cylinder – the doctor's last – and all the bits needed for it in the back of the van. The doctor told her that he'd ordered in several cylinders for his patients, but

Tilly guessed he meant his richer ones. And she knew he must be making a lot of money as she was shocked at him asking all of three pounds for it – more than a man could earn in a month! But she didn't baulk at giving him a promissory note by way of payment.

The workmen didn't ask questions, probably didn't want to know, but one of them volunteered to come back with her and to help her to unload the cylinder for her after asking how she was going to manage.

He did more than that. Despite the dangers, when Tilly told him about Mary and how Alec wasn't strong enough to help, he took it on himself to carry the oxygen up the stairs for her.

'You can leave it there, I can manage it from here, and Mister . . .'

'Charlie, me name's Charlie.'

'Well, ta very much, Charlie. I were just going to say as there's a kitchen to your left when you reach the bottom of the stairs, so pop in there and scrub your hands.' She told him what instructions Beth had given her and why he should obey them.

'Righto, missus, I'll do that. If anyone knaws owt about this horror that's afflicting folk, our nurses should. We owe them a debt. And I hope as young lass gets well. Will you drop by sometime and let us knaw?'

'Aye. I will.' As he left, Tilly thought, *And there goes a true Blackpudlian*. Caring about others, kindly, and giving of his time to help anyone in need. Not for the first time, she thought that she'd never want to live anywhere else in the world than right here in her beloved Blackpool.

Alec came hobbling through the door. The lad managed well with his false leg and a stick. 'I'll 'elp yer get that in to Mary, Tilly. She needs it, she's struggling to breathe. I didn't think it'd take 'old as quick as this.'

One look at Mary's blue-grey sunken face, and seeing the struggle she was having as she tried to gasp for breath, intensified the deep fear that Tilly held inside her. 'I'll go for her ma, lad. And I'll let Molly know as she'll have little Gerry, and will be wondering why no one has come for him. Can you manage to take care of Mary, lad?'

'I can.'

'I'll be as quick as I can, but lad, promise me you'll keep that mask on, eh?'

Alec's haggard-looking eyes turned to her over the top of the mask and Tilly saw a tear seep out of the corner of one of them. She'd known a good while that the lad had a liking for Mary and had thought that Mary was so easy and happy in his company, now she wondered if they knew they were in love.

Inside she cried out at the injustice of this, if it was so. Mary and Alec deserved to find happiness. It was so unfair to think that they probably hadn't recognised their love for one another. Though she suspected that if Alec hadn't known it before, it was almost certain that he did now.

When she got to Ivy's house, she was shocked to find Polly Hanson, the district nurse, in attendance. It was she who answered the door – a mask covering all but her eyes. 'Don't come in, lass. They've all been brought down with the flu.'

'Awe, naw. Are they badly?'

'Ivy'll make a recovery, but then your age group seem to be able to ward it off better than the young ones. I'm not sure about Vera, though, she's really poorly, poor lass, and her expecting her man home any day. I hope he gets here in time.'

Tilly gasped with the shock of this. 'Oh, naw. Naw, this can't be happening. I came to tell them that Mary's been took with it and that she's not well at all. Dear God, as if we've not suffered enough.'

'I've never known owt like it. I'm rushed off me feet. I haven't slept in days. I were going to call on you to see if Peggy could give me a hand.'

'Eeh, Polly, Peggy's gone with Beth.' She told Polly where Beth and Peggy had gone to. 'Though I don't knaw how long Peggy will stay as I can't see her settling. She's like us – a Blackpool lass through and through.'

'Eeh, what will your Beth do without her?'

'I don't knaw. Get a replacement, I suppose. Anyroad, lass, I'm keeping you from your work. Will you let Ivy knaw about Mary? And if you do find a minute, will you come to the shop to check on her?' Tilly told the nurse what she'd done so far for Mary.

'Well, I can't do any more than that, Tilly. Lass is lucky. I just wish Vera could have some oxygen, but many who need it can't have it. They can't afford it for one thing, and there just ain't enough to go around for another. The hospitals are full to bursting an' all. It's like we're all doomed.'

'Eeh, don't say that. Keep on keeping on. It's all we can do. Look, let me in and between us we'll get Vera into me van. I'll take her to the shop to be with Mary. They can share the oxygen.'

'That might help. Aye, I can't see as we can do any more harm to her by taking her out. And bringing Mary here isn't

233

a good idea, I'm shocked at how cramped they are. Ivy seems to use most of her house as a warehouse. There's stock every-where and it ain't just items that she sells, so I reckon she's taking rent to store others' stock as well.'

That didn't surprise Tilly. Ivy was into all sorts, and was known as the local money lender too.

As she drove back with Vera wrapped up and laying in the back, Tilly renewed her prayers. But most of them were an angry tirade as she laid into God for sending more on top of what they'd been contending with for the past five years. *Look, God, you have to take some of the blame, but all I'm asking you is to please take care of me family and make Mary, Vera and Ivy better.*

Tilly wanted to call in on Molly to tell her what was happening and just be hugged and reassured by her, but she knew she mustn't. She did pull up and write a quick note which she posted through Molly's door and was back in the van in no time. She had to get Vera into the warmth, and by now, she felt her own clothes and everything about her must be heaving with the germs that spread the flu.

She made her mind up that once she had everyone settled, she'd scrub the shop from top to bottom, and then give herself a good wash-down. She'd put one of the wraparound pinnies on to cover herself. And there was always a cardigan or two hanging on the back of the kitchen door, and of course she always kept spare knickers in her bag. When she'd finished, she'd put her clothes into the stove that they always kept lit at the back of the shop during the winter months. She was sure that only burning them would rid them of any danger they posed of spreading this terrible flu.

And she would stay the night too, not only because Mary and Vera needed her, but she wasn't going to run the risk of taking the germs back to her home.

As always, she knew that Eliza would call in before she left for home. Tilly wouldn't let her in, but would shout to her through the door and get her to gather a few provisions for them and leave them on the doorstep.

When she reached the shop and let herself in, Tilly ran to the bottom of the stairs calling for Alec. As soon as she saw him, she shouted, 'Come down, hurry as fast as you can, lad. I need you to help me. Bring a sheet, as we'll need it.'

Having Alec's help wasn't much use as the lad could only hold part of the sheet that Vera lay on with one arm. Somehow, they managed to get her up the stairs. Alec showed his amazing upper-body strength as he went first, and holding on to the stair-rail with one hand, he tugged Vera up with the other. Tilly did all she could to stop the poor girl slipping out.

At the top, Tilly had to have a breather as she gasped for air and sweat ran off her face. How she'd done what she did, she didn't know, and even less how Alec had.

But when they renewed their efforts and got Vera onto the bed, Tilly was surprised to see that Mary, though deathly pale and looking near to death, was peaceful. The hollow sound of the oxygen pump was somehow soothing, as was watching the bag go in and out as it gave life-saving air to Mary. Alec slumped in the armchair next to the bed, and stared down at Mary. His body was shaking.

Tilly had no words of comfort to give him as she wondered if his mind was full of the same tales that hers was, of the calm before the storm. She closed her eyes and prayed once more for this to be a recovery and not what she dreaded. 'Aye, and listen to me this time.'

'Uh? Sorry, Tilly, did you speak?'

'Not to you, lad, to God. I've been falling out with Him all day.'

'I never fell in with 'im. I don't believe 'e exists. At least, not for the poor and needy 'e don't. If there is a God, then to my way of thinking, 'e's a toff and only looks after them as 'ave a pot full already.'

'Aye, it does feel like that sometimes, I have to agree. But I believe in us making our own good fortune. Though I like to think of Him being there supporting us and it's a comfort to talk to him – especially as he doesn't chat back!'

'Not like your Eliza, you mean! She's a card if ever I 'eard one. She'll be 'ere soon as she often calls before she goes 'ome. She 'as me and Mary in stitches at times.'

'Aye, I knaw. Well, turn your eyes away as I'm to make Vera comfortable, and then if her breathing worsens, we'll give her the oxygen for a while, but at the moment, she doesn't seem as bad as Mary. Then I'll go down and start the cleaning that I've a mind to do, and get meself cleaned up. When I've done that, you can get yourself a good wash an' all. I brought the last lot of the washing that I did for you, so get changed and we'll burn what you have on, along with mine and what you've taken off Mary.'

Alec blushed. 'I – I only wanted to swill her down and make her comfortable.'

'Aye, I knaw, lad. I weren't accusing you of owt. I knaw as Mary's safe in your hands. It had to be done, and you did it. It's as simple as that. Better someone who loves her than anyone else in the world.'

'You know?'

'Aye, I guessed. And I hope as Mary feels the same for you. But we've to get her through this lot before we can ask her, and that means we've a long night ahead of us with the both of them to care for. And, Alec, you may not believe in God, but he's your best hope at the moment, so if I were you, I'd make his acquaintance and say some prayers. He'll probably listen to you, seeing as you'll be a convert. He loves a convert, does God.'

Alec smiled. The lad had a lovely smile. It made his care-worn face look different. Handsome, she'd say, with a bit of a rakish charm about it. But then, she'd always found Londoners to have a way with them – an openness that got under your skin, and made you like them, yet she knew they were often wise boys. Alec wasn't like that. He was a quiet lad. A thinker. A lot like Cliff, really.

Thinking of Cliff, Tilly remembered the letter she had in her coat pocket. It was from Babs and had only arrived as she'd been leaving home. She'd read it when all was settled.

It was midnight before she had time to open the letter. And it was then that her tears flowed. Babs was full of her news, but the only bit that Tilly really took in was that she wasn't coming home to live. She would visit, when she finally reached England. And then there was the only bright thing in the letter – she really hoped she would be home for Christmas, but soon after she was going to live with a friend.

Be happy for me, Ma. My news is good. But I can't tell you of it all yet as there's still some things that need finalising.

Tilly looked at the date that the letter was sent. November 13th. So, Babs could be travelling at this very moment. She didn't like to think of the danger that Babs might be in from the flu virus, as the whole world was caught in its grip. All she could do was to hope that Babs would keep safe and that she would soon be here.

By the time daylight came, Tilly was exhausted. She'd lain on the sofa and had fallen asleep intermittently, but for a lot of the time she and Alec had emptied bowls of sick and cleaned both girls up umpteen times. Now, Mary seemed a little better; she'd kept some water down, and the aspirin they'd given her, and her breathing was easier. She hadn't needed the oxygen again after they had given it to Vera. Vera looked a little better too. But both were still desperately ill.

Alec was sitting in the chair, as he had been most of the night. His eyes were weary and bloodshot. His hand held on to Mary's. 'Eeh, lad, get some rest. I'll be awake now. I'll watch the girls. Lie down on them cushions for a bit.'

'I can't, Tilly. I want Mary to know that I'm 'ere for 'er. I feel that she is clinging on to me and if I let go, so will she.'

Tilly left him, knowing that she would never persuade him, and went down to make yet another pot of tea. As she went, she felt a weakness take her legs. *Naw! Naw! Don't let me have caught it. Dear God, naw.*

NINETEEN

Tilly

Days passed with Tilly not knowing how she was functioning. But somehow, she managed to. Mary was on the mend, but Vera was still caught in the throes of the virus. And now Alec lay on the bed, his body streaming with sweat, and his hacking cough resounding around the room.

As it had, midday and evening, the doorbell on the outside of the shop rang out. Tilly knew it would be Eliza. She'd been calling twice a day and Tilly spoke to her through the open, upstairs window. Ma Perkins was in hospital, and Eliza was opening the shop, baking bread only, and then leaving it outside in baskets for folk to collect.

'Mammy, are you all right?'

'Aye, I am, me lass. Are you? And is Tommy? And Cliff and Jack . . . ? Is there any news of Jack's family?'

'Naw. Jack's stayed at ours. Pappy thought it better than having him going back and forth bringing whatever germs he picks up with him. Cliff still comes and goes, as does Phil, but they both have a good wash and put on clean overalls as soon as they arrive. I don't go near any of them until I've had a wash-down and changed. And I'm boiling all me work clothes every night. Oh, and everyone's wearing their masks. Pappy's fine. No one at the farm has any signs of the flu yet. What's happening in there?'

Tilly gave her an update. 'Keep doing what you're doing, lass. But, eeh, I wish you would just stay at the farm.'

'I can't, Mammy. How would folk get their bread? Not all can bake it, you knaw. But, eeh, Mammy, some cheeky beggars are taking the bread and not leaving the money for it. Ma Perkins'll go spare when she's well.'

'Awe, lass. You have to understand, most can't go to work, or to the post office to collect their army allowance from their fellas, so you can't blame them. Ma Perkins will have to find some kindness and forgiveness in her heart.'

'That's if she lives, Mammy. I don't knaw what I'd do if she don't.'

Tilly heard a sob in Eliza's voice, which shocked her. She'd thought that as kind as Eliza was, some part of her would be glad to be out of Ma Perkins' clutches for a while, but then, she sometimes seemed very fond of the old girl. 'Happen she'll pull through, lass. A lot are.'

'Aye, but not the elderly, nor us young 'uns if we get it. Will Mary and Vera die?'

'Naw, not if I can help it, they won't. Did you get me some more aspirin, lass?'

'Not as many as you asked for. I could only get ten.'

'Awe, naw. I think Alec is coming down with it now. I needed more. Still, post what you have through the letter box.'

'I wish I could post me through the letter box. I so want to hug you, Mammy.'

'I knaw, lass. It's just you and me now, with Babs and Beth gone, but I'll be home soon. I promise. Then we'll get Christmas planned and sorted, eh?'

'Aye. Oh, I nearly forgot. I saw Aunt Molly. She said to tell you that she's had a bout of the flu, but it didn't get hold of her proper, and Gerry and Uncle Will are all right an' all.'

'Thank God. Let's hope we've seen the worst. There's nowt much as hangs around Blackpool for long. The sea air soon sends it packing. We'll soon be back on top. Nowt can keep us Sandgronians down for long, lass.'

Amidst kisses blown, as Eliza walked backwards towards her horse and trap, they said their goodbyes. When Tilly closed the window, she sat down at the workbench that she'd occupied for years, followed by Beth for a short time, and which was now Alec's seat. She felt her tears pricking the back of her eyes. Life had been disrupted of late and she missed her Tommy and Beth and Babs, and holding her Eliza. She daren't think further than that as the tears threatened to spill over. She mentally shook herself. *Eeh, I've not to let meself get into the doldrums. But by, I feel poorly.*

It was another three days before Tilly began to feel a little better. How the other three had survived she didn't know as the bout she'd had hadn't been anywhere near what they had been through, but she'd never felt so ill in all her life. As she looked at them now sitting around the workbench eating a bowl of soup, she thanked God that they had.

Not that they weren't ravished by the effects. Mary and Vera were half the size they had been and their cheeks were hollow, their eyes sunken into dark sockets, and their hair matted to their heads. Alec was even worse as he was still in the throes of having a nasty chesty cough.

Molly had called and left the soup in the shop, along with clean clothes for the girls. Tilly had been down and heated the soup on the small stove they had in the kitchen.

She was now eagerly awaiting the sound of the shop bell as Molly had shouted up that she was coming back and needed to talk to her. When the clanging resounded, Tilly was surprised at the energy she felt as she ran down the steps.

Opening the door, Tilly stood just inside the small hallway at the bottom of the stairs. 'Eeh, Molly, it's good to see you.'

'And you, Tilly – that is, what we can see of each other with our faces covered. How're you doing, lass?'

'It's been hell. But I think we're all coming out the other side now and we'll all survive. You said you needed to talk to me?'

'Aye, and it's not good news. We lost Ivy this morning.'

'Naw! But … I – I thought … Polly said she was on the mend!'

'I knaw. But she suddenly took badly again. Polly did all she could, as she allus does. The bloody doctor wouldn't come out. He's getting worse. Used to take pots of jam and the like in payment, but now he just wants cash … or whiskey.'

'He's a disgrace. But surely Ivy could have paid?'

'Could have, but wouldn't. Polly said she refused to give that old drunk a penny of her hard-earned money so that he could pee it down the drain. She said she trusted Polly and that was that. I don't think anyone could have saved her. Polly said she thinks that her heart failed her.'

'Oh, Molly, she brought them girls up on her own since they were little. She put me to shame. How are we going to tell the girls?'

'Eeh, lass, I don't knaw. But don't go down that road. Her man were a well-to-do businessman. When he died he left her with plenty. She didn't have the trouble that you told me you had, with naw money and being put out of your house. You did what you could, but forces worked against you. Anyroad, lass, I'm sorry to say as Ivy's death ain't all the news that I have. Ma Perkins has gone an' all.'

'Eeh, I'm sorry to hear that, but I were expecting it. Our Eliza will be devastated. She were fond of the old girl as much as you could be of someone so cantankerous as Ma Perkins was. Well, that means that I have to go home now, but what will happen with the girls and Alec?'

'I'll take the girls with me. I've got room for them and little Gerry. And Will and me'll help them to get everything sorted, or sort it for them.'

'And I'll take Alec home then. I don't want to as he's still poorly, but I can't leave Eliza to face her loss on her own. I can take every precaution so that he doesn't come into contact with anyone. Eeh, Molly, lass, I could do with one of your hugs.'

'Come here. I need a hug an' all.'

In Molly's arms, held by someone who loved her Tilly's tears flowed freely.

'Let it all out, lass. By, you've been a hero. I don't knaw how you've done it, and not being well yourself an' all.'

Drying her tears, Tilly looked into Molly's beloved face. 'It was a case of needs must.'

'Well, I think you are the most wonderful person, and the name as you were allus called by – an angel – still counts, as that's what you are.'

'Naw. Don't be daft.'

'Look, lass. I'd like to be the one as tells Mary and Vera. They're more than daughters-in-law to me. I look on them as me daughters.'

'Aye, I think that's the right way to go about it. But, lass, there's sommat as you should knaw. It wouldn't normally be me place to tell you, but I wouldn't want you to have the shock of finding out without me warning you.'

Molly looked taken aback. 'What?'

'Well, Mary . . . She . . . Eeh, it had to happen sometime, but well, Mary's in love with Alec.'

'Well, that's the best news that I've heard for many a day! By, when did that happen? You haven't been keeping it from me, have you?'

'Naw. I'm not even sure that Mary knaws it yet.'

'Ha! But Tilly O'Flynn does. You're a card, but I believe you. Mary is probably well aware but afraid to show it in case I find out. Well, I'll have to put her right on that as I would like nowt better than to see her happy again. She can't grieve for our Gerry forever. It's time she tucked him into a special place in her heart and lived again – especially now. Poor lass has been through the mill and has more to face.'

'Oh, Molly, I love you.'

They were in each other's arms again. 'And I love you, Tilly. I've been that afraid these last days thinking I might lose you.'

Tilly heard Molly's sob, but just held her closer. 'Come on then, let's go upstairs, Molly. Eeh, I'm dreading this. I can't believe it. Ivy were a canny lass, and could win most battles she took on, but she met her match this time, poor thing. I'm going to miss her.'

If Mary wasn't sure of her love for Alec, it dawned on her now, as her reaction was to turn to him in her moment of heartache. Alec enclosed her in his arms, and though it wasn't the moment, Tilly thought she saw joy light up his red and sore eyes. Through his mask he planted kisses into her hair. Molly clung on to Vera. Tilly hugged herself as the need for her own family threatened to overwhelm her.

Tilly honked her horn as she drove through the gate to the farm and hung her head out of the window. This being a Sunday, Eliza was at home and she and Tommy came running out of the house. At the same time, Cliff and Phil appeared from the cowshed. They would have finished milking and, as the cattle had to stay inside when it was iced over, they would have been seeing that there was plenty of food and water for them.

'Don't come near to me yet,' Tilly shouted. 'I've to get Alec out and to make sure as I'm cleaned down.'

'Oh, Ma, Ma. Are you staying? What's to do? Are you better, Alec?'

Alec managed a little wave to Eliza, but Tilly could see that parting with Mary and the struggle he had had to get into the van, had sapped what strength he'd had. 'Naw, he's not well still, Eliza, me little lass. I need to help him inside as soon as I can. Will you light the fire in me work room, Tommy? And Eliza, will you put some bedding in there for me? I've to make the bed up for Alec. He'll be staying till he's well.'

'Me little Tilly, it's good to be seeing you, me lass.' Tommy had tears in his eyes. This nearly undid Tilly, she so wanted to be in his arms.

'Eeh, Tommy, lad, I've missed you.' Checking that Eliza was out of earshot as she ran to do what was asked of her, she beckoned Tommy a little closer. 'It's Eliza who's going to need you, me Tommy. Ma Perkins . . .'

'No! I am sorry. Me poor wee Eliza. Well, I'm for thinking the old girl put up as good a fight as she could, but it is that she was a good age.'

'Aye, but that's not all of me news.' She told him about Ivy. Tommy shook his head, too shocked by this to say anything. Even though he hadn't known Ivy very well and had only seen her a couple of times, he would feel deep sadness for the girls.

Cliff stepped forward. 'It's good to see you, Tilly. Though you're not looking so well.' Then to Tommy, he said, 'I'll light the fire. And then I'll come back and help Tilly with Alec.'

'Naw, you mustn't do that. Just light the fire, ta, Cliff. And, Tommy, if you can get the wheelchair that Beth didn't take, then Alec will manage in that. His arms are strong, ain't they, lad?'

Alec just nodded. She knew he hadn't the strength to do more and knew too that he would need pushing in the wheelchair. But she'd pulled the van near to the path that Tommy had laid many years ago for Ivan's use.

Not allowing herself to think about Ivan at the moment, Tilly's worry increased as she saw that Alec was shivering, and yet beads of sweat had formed on his forehead.

'Is there owt as I can do, Aunt Tilly?'

'Eeh, Phil, Eliza's going to need you. I'm glad as you're still here. How's your ma?' Amidst all she'd had to contend with, Tilly had thought often about Florrie and prayed that she didn't get this terrible virus. 'And is your da all right?'

'Aye, they're all right. The flu hasn't reached Lord Clefton's estate yet. Mind, he takes every precaution. All deliveries have to be left at the gate, and naw one can collect them without wearing gloves. And we all have to change our shoes at the gate and keep our masks on at all times.'

'That's good. Well, I need you to put your mask on now, and you, Tommy, and tell Eliza and Cliff too an' all.'

'So, it is that we're all to look as funny as you again, me Tilly?' Tommy laughed. 'We were for wearing them at first, but haven't done so for a few days.'

Tilly tutted, but the sound of Tommy's chuckling was so good for her to hear, she wanted to jump out and run to him.

'Aye, me and Alec aren't going to look like fools on our own. Now away with you, Tommy O'Flynn, you've already got away with one of the jobs I gave you, so get on and get that wheelchair out here.'

Tommy went away laughing louder than before. Tilly felt glad she was home. She'd cope better here. But what the next few days and weeks would bring, she dreaded to think. Christmas now seemed unimportant as the world was fighting a terrible force that was being reported as capable of killing almost as many as the war had.

Once Tilly had settled Alec down, and was satisfied that she'd done everything she could to make sure she wasn't going to be a danger to anyone, she wearily went through to the kitchen.

Tommy stood by the table with his arms open. Going into them, Tilly wanted to weep her heart out, but she gained strength from Tommy. When she came out of his arms, she took the waiting Eliza into hers. 'Eliza, lass. I've naw easy way of telling you, but, well, Ma Perkins . . .'

Eliza shot from her arms. 'Naw, Mammy. Naw, she ain't gone, has she?'

'Aye, she has, lass. And after a life's work well done, we should wish her peace.'

Eliza just stood still. Her eyes stared out of their sockets. Tilly could see that apart from her grief and shock, Eliza had a look of someone who didn't know what to do. 'You're to be the brave girl that I knaw you are, me Eliza. You're to carry on running Ma Perkins' shop until any family she has, or her solicitor, sorts sommat out. Ma Perkins would expect that of you and trust you to do it for her. We'll sort your future out when the time comes, so you're not to worry on that score . . . Come here, me little lass.'

Tilly could feel Eliza trembling, but so far she hadn't shed a tear. 'I've other news, Eliza.'

On hearing about Ivy, Eliza did cry. 'Eeh, Ma, poor Mary and Vera. And Mary can't be with Alec either. We should fetch her here, Ma.'

'You knew about them?'

'Aye, I knew how they felt for each other. I teased them unmercifully, but they just laughed. I think as Mary were afraid what everyone'd think.'

'Well, she needn't be any longer. We all knaw as she has her Gerry in her heart, and will allus have him in little Gerry, as he looks just like his da. But we all want her to be happy. But as for bringing her here, it's better that she is with Molly and Vera; they need each other at the moment. The poor girls were devastated at losing their ma, and there's a lot for them to do. There allus is when there's been a death.'

'By, Ma, we've a lot on our plate. I remember the day me and Ivan ran Ivy's stall for her when she wanted to be involved in buying the wedding stuff for Vera and Mary. We were all so happy then. Me and Ivan . . . we . . . had such fun, eeh, Ma . . . Ma.'

Tilly held Eliza to her, her own heart breaking for her youngest daughter, who had shouldered so much and was yet to learn that Babs, the sister she loved most, was hoping to come home for Christmas, but would never live with them again.

Making her mind up that she would shelve the latter, she rocked Eliza, trying to soothe her pain.

After a moment, Eliza stopped sobbing. Tommy had come over and was holding them both. 'Me wee Eliza. I'm sorry for your loss, and for all of us. But it is that we have the O'Flynn spirit, and we'll get through, so we will.'

'I knaw, Pappy. Ivan'll help me, he allus does. And Phil. I don't knaw what I'd do without Phil, and I'm that glad the war ended before he had to go. I think I'll go and find him.'

Tilly and Tommy let her go. They stood and watched through the window as she crossed the yard. Phil, who'd finished his chores and was ready to go home, as he did on a Sunday afternoon, was sitting on the fence to the bottom field. He jumped down as Eliza approached and ran towards her. Eliza ran into his arms.

Tilly and Tommy looked at each other and smiled. Then Tommy took hold of Tilly and held her. 'Me Tilly, I've missed you. Never go away again, lass.'

'I won't. Oh, Tommy. Me heart's heavy as I have sommat else that I haven't told Eliza of. I had a letter from Babs. She's not coming home to live.'

'Now, you shouldn't be fretting yourself over that, me little Tilly. It is that we should expect this of Babs, as we did of Beth. And one day, it will be that Eliza, too, flies from our nest, but it is how life is. Babs has to make her way in the world, and I am not for doubting that she will visit often.'

'I know, I'm being daft. I just don't seem able to cope with owt. I feel so unwell. I've not got the flu symptoms now, but it's left me feeling as though all me stuffing's gone from me body.'

'Well, you're to take it easy now, me little Tilly. You'll recover, but it is that it will take time. We'll all muck in together, as it is that we have been doing. I tell you, it is a surprise that you're in for. Cliff is the best of cooks! And even Eliza is for giving him praise for his efforts. So, he can carry on with doing that as there's little else to do on the farm in this weather apart from seeing to the animals. Phil has been for taking on most of that duty. As for the cleaning, well, I've proven meself a dab hand with a mop, so I have, and Eliza has been for making the beds before she takes herself off to work, then putting the copper on for the washing when she comes home. So, you see it is that you have nothing to worry about.'

'Eeh, lad. You don't need me then?'

'Oh, but we do. *I* do, me little Tilly. Me arms have ached to hold you, and it is that me bed has been a cold, empty place without you.'

'Ha, I thought it wouldn't be long before you mentioned your needs, Tommy O'Flynn.'

'So, you're not for thinking the same then, me little Tilly? Now, none of your tales, I can see in your eyes that you are for wanting me too.'

'Eeh, Tommy lad, I do. Though with me lack of energy, I don't knaw as you'll find me the same lass as I was.'

'Just to hold you and be feeling your body next to mine is enough for now.' With this, Tommy's lips found hers and her heart soared.

TWENTY

Beth

Though missing her ma, Tommy and Eliza, Beth was happier than she'd been in a long time. She'd found a house that she thought Henry would love, on Albert Terrace, facing the sea. It was four storeys high, giving them five bedrooms and two bathrooms, one downstairs that didn't have a toilet as that facility was in the backyard, but the one upstairs did.

She'd relied on Janine to tell her how the upstairs was, and was pleased to hear that all the rooms were tastefully decorated and nicely furnished. The previous owners had only used the house for a holiday home.

But what really pleased her was the layout of the downstairs. This she was able to explore, and she found herself planning how the rooms would be hers and Henry's main living and sleeping quarters. A water closet would be installed in the bathroom – there was plenty of room for one – and the large sitting room on the left of the back of the house, opposite the kitchen, would be their bedroom. There was a long passageway that led from the front door to the back of the house which cut the house in two, so this meant that the front room on the left of the house could be their best room, the one on the right their everyday sitting room, and the smaller room behind this the dining room, leading directly into the kitchen, which had two entrances as there was one leading off from the hall. 'It's perfect, Janine. Ooh, I'm so glad that we found it. Henry will love it, I'm sure.'

'Yes, I know he will. There's one of the bedrooms upstairs that's perfect for an office for him. It overlooks the sea.'

'I must secure it with a deposit. Will you help me to do that? I will need you to take me to the bank and to Henry's solicitors.'

'Of course I will, darling. The agent is waiting in the front room for your decision. We'll go and tell him now. Then we'll have to get back as poor Peggy will be pulling her hair out with Benny and my little Emma to take care of. You're going to have to get a nanny, you know that, don't you? Peggy is more patient with adults than she is with children.'

'Oh, you noticed? I know. She soon gets flustered.'

'I can help you with finding a nanny. And the bedroom in the attic would be a perfect place for her to live – it's huge; you can fit it out like a sitting room-come-bedroom so she isn't under your feet, and the other attic room could be a nursery. I mean, I'm sure when Henry comes home, there'll be the patter of tiny feet again.' Janine's laughter filled the room. 'Talking of which, I'm to have another.'

'Oh, that's wonderful news.' This coming so soon after Janine's last remark stopped Beth from feeling embarrassed. She found that the upper and middle classes could be quite outspoken about personal matters, something she hadn't got used to yet. She expected it from her own class of people – they loved a raucous joke and to say anything they thought funny at the top of their voices.

'Well, stand by your bed, Beth. Henry is on his way and you won't see the light of day for a week!' Again, Janine laughed her lovely tinkling laugh. Thinking it best to join in with her, Beth said, 'Is that what happens when Gareth comes home, then?'

'It is . . . Oh, I do miss him when he's away, and that's only for weeks at a time. How you've coped with three years apart, Beth, I just don't know. Henry will seem like a stranger to you.'

'No, he won't. We've said everything in our letters that we would have said to each other if we were together.' Beth laughed then. 'Ha, I'd like to be a fly on the wall of those who have the job of censoring the letters that the men and their wives send to each other. I bet they have red faces sometimes.'

They laughed together then.

The door opening interrupted their mirth. 'I take it that you are very happy with everything?'

Beth bit her lip. This seemed so funny, given what they had been talking about, but she managed to stop herself from laughing more. 'Yes, thank you, it certainly is, and I will want to begin the process of purchasing the house as soon as possible.'

'That's excellent.'

The elderly gentleman had a twinkle in his eye as he said this, and Beth had the sneaky feeling that he had overheard her and Janine. But she didn't let this worry her. She felt an excitement grip her as the words she'd said had sealed the deal. This was a lovely home. She could feel the happiness in its walls and knew her future was going to be wonderful. She realised then that she was thinking like Jasmine would have thought and that made her catch her breath in her lungs. She hoped that Jasmine would never find her. But then, how could she?

'Eeh, me lass, you shouldn't have worried. The little ones have been as good as gold. Benny is a caring little boy. I've been proud of him today. Eeh, he's looked after little Lilly as if she was a doll. She only had to whimper and he seemed to knaw what she wanted and fetched it for her.'

Beth didn't have time to react to this as Benny came hurtling at her. 'Ma, ma! Oh, I am glad you're home, Ma. I've been waiting for you for hours.'

'Oh, Peggy's been telling me that you've been really good. Well, Ma's very pleased with you.'

Lilly, who was sitting in the high chair, yelled out at that moment, in a way that demanded attention. Benny turned and immediately ran to see what she wanted.

'Beth . . . can I say something to you, and not offend you?'

'Of course, Janine. What is it?'

'Well, it's about how Benny addresses you. I, well, I think it's charming, and as you know, I love the northern accent, but Henry is going to want his son to go to a private school and, well, any little quirk he has in his speech will make him ridiculed by the other boys.'

'Oh, I hadn't thought.' Beth sighed. There were some aspects of this upper-class world she didn't like. 'Ma' was a lovely way of addressing your mother. It was to her, anyway. 'So, I should teach him to say mama, as you do?'

'Well, look, I really don't want to upset you, but, yes. I think it would be best. It is how all his school friends will address their mothers.'

Peggy huffed and went in the direction of Beth's small kitchen.

'Oh, I didn't want to upset anyone, really. I shouldn't have said anything.'

'No, you have your nephew's welfare at heart and you're right. I wouldn't want him to be different and attract bullies to him. Thank you, Janine. And always feel that you can help me to make this transition into your world. I want to be the wife that Henry deserves. I think I have been too long in Blackpool with all those that have a northern accent. I've noticed one or two sayings that Benny has picked up.'

'Yes, I have too. Oh, I feel such a snob. I'm sorry. I don't feel like that at all, I love your family and love hearing them speak. I just feel afraid for Benny as he has to live in a different environment.'

'I understand, and I know you well enough to know your motives. Don't think any more about it.'

'I'll make it up to Peggy. I've some more of those chocolates in my case. She ate nearly a boxfull last night.'

'Well, chocolate is something we've rarely seen in recent years. I'm not going to ask how you got hold of it.'

'Oh, no, it's nothing like that. Cook makes—'

A rattle on the door made them both jump. 'That sounded ominous. Shall I go, Beth?'

'Yes, please. I don't think Peggy heard it.'

Beth waited for Janine to come back into the room with the mystery caller. She couldn't think who it could be. She didn't know anyone around here – oh, except for Amy, of course, she'd never forgotten Amy.

Thinking about her now, she wondered how she was and if her man had survived the war. Her mind went back to the one and only time they met. It had happened in a café when she'd first started to go out with Henry. Amy's soldier boyfriend had been a bit annoyed to see Henry sitting there and had challenged him about not being in uniform. The incident had passed and Amy had returned to the café after she'd calmed her man. Her explanation of her boyfriend's fear at having to go to war was endearing, and she'd liked Amy immediately. Amy had said that she worked on the railway station as a porter. A funny job for a girl, but then, everyone had had to turn their hand to whatever needed doing.

Beth made her mind up that after Janine left the following day, she'd get Peggy to push her along to the station and she'd make enquiries about Amy. She'd promised to look her up, but everything had changed when Henry had been conscripted.

All this had taken her mind off who might be at the door. When Janine returned on her own, she waited for her to tell her. But Janine was deathly pale and had a look of fear on her face. She opened her mouth but no words came out.

'What? Janine, are you all right? Who was it?'

'It . . . it was Jasmine.'

'What? No! How did she know I was here?'

'I don't know. Did she know you rented this cottage with Henry?'

'Yes, she did. But . . .'

'Well, there's nothing mystical about it then. She knew you were set to return when the war ended; she must have been watching this cottage awaiting her moment.'

'But what did she say that frightened you so much?'

'Oh, I'm being silly. She's just a woman. I actually liked her when we had your gypsy wedding. She's just vexed. I wouldn't take any notice.'

'Please tell me. If I know, I can be ready for her. I will know if it is something we needn't heed. But don't worry, I'm not going to take any of her nonsense.'

'Well, she said she'd come to beg you to forgive her, as she knows now that she did wrong, but that you have to understand that she has been shaped by thousands of years of culture. She asked me to tell you that on the night she took you, she saw that your mother wasn't capable of taking care of you. Your mother had no money, she'd been evicted from her home, and though she had come to the gypsies for help, she wasn't going to get it because they needed to protect their own. She said this was because there was a young girl betrothed to one of their finest men and their wedding was planned, but her man lusted after your mother. And so, Jasmine knew the clan would banish your mother the next day. The poorhouse would have been her only alternative. She told me that she and Roman were childless, and it seemed to them that God was asking them to take care of you and Babs. And she said that they felt that they had to do it the way they did as they knew your mother would never give you up. She asked you to remember that they loved and cared for you and gave their lives to you. And then . . . well, she said that if there is no forgiveness, then the curse she put on you will come to be. And she will put that curse on all the children you bear. I told her to go away, that she wasn't welcome and that I would call the police. But ... well, she didn't go. Her face turned ugly – evil. And her eyes ... I have never seen eyes have a look in them like hers had. And ... and she said that the baby in my womb would only survive if her wishes were met. And then she was gone.'

'Oh, Janine. Oh, no!'

'You mean ... you believe her?'

'I – I, well, no, but ... look, I have seen her predictions come true, but I don't believe that anyone but God has the powers she claims to have. I think she is just frightening us, trying to make me give in and go back to her. Oh, why didn't I listen to Babs? Babs wanted me to go to the police and to make sure that Jasmine and Roman were locked away for a long time for kidnapping us.'

'Yes, you should have done that, Beth. She frightens me. How could she have known that I was expecting a baby? You can't tell by looking at me.'

'Jasmine can, as can all the gypsies; they say there are signs. So don't set store by that. Look, we have to be sensible. There is no such thing as a curse. Often the things that Jasmine attributed to her powers had already happened. But I do believe that she is capable of making things happen, as we are, if we put our minds to it.'

'Call the police, Beth. You have to.'

Beth fell quiet. She knew in her heart that Babs and Janine were right, but the thought of Jasmine and Roman cooped up in a cell broke her heart. But then, weighing that up against years and years of them hounding her and making bad things happen, she knew that she must.

'I will. I'll get Peggy to wheel me to the police station tomorrow. I promise.'

As they hugged, Beth could feel Janine's body trembling, and felt ashamed that she had been instrumental in bringing fear to her. 'I'm sorry, Janine. I will do something about it. Please don't be afraid. Jasmine can do none of the things she claims.' But even as she said this a shiver went through Beth. For she knew that Jasmine did have an uncanny way of knowing everything and of seeing into the future. Whether she could shape that future, Beth didn't know. But she still asked herself, *What if she can?*

The police officer listened with an incredulous look on his face. 'Well, well. I read about such things in books when I was a boy, but I never believed that they happened. This is serious. I am going to have to get my colleagues in the north to question your mother to get her side of the story. But in the meantime, we will be going to apprehend these gypsies. Now, that isn't easy. We rarely catch them for the crimes they commit. They seem to know when we are looking for them and disappear in an uncanny way. Not that we mind. Just getting them out of our hair is enough at times. They're a bad lot.'

Beth wanted to protest at this sweeping statement and explain that not all gypsies were bad, and tell of how hard they worked and of their moral code and religious faith. She wanted to say that often when they did steal, they did it just to survive, and that they always asked first, or tried to sell something to the rich folk – something beautiful that they had made with their own hands – and that the kind of prejudice that he was showing was the reason they had to resort to wrongdoing.

But she bowed her head and kept quiet. If she defended them, she would be going against her promise to Janine. *Why did it take that to finally make me act? I should have done this when Ma was so hurt by Jasmine and Roman's presence, and when Babs begged me too.* It came to her then that if she could, she should go on her knees and beg her ma's and her sister's forgiveness.

'Don't upset yourself, miss. We will sort this out one way or another. We'll get those evil gypsies off your back, don't you worry about that.'

But she did worry. *Oh, Jasmine, Roman, why didn't you just go away and live your lives as I know that you were meant to – under the stars at night and travelling by day?*

Peggy's comforting hand came onto Beth's shoulder. She looked up and in Peggy saw true goodness. Why had she seen that in Jasmine, when it had never been present? Yes, Jasmine could excuse herself and make it look as though she had done the right thing, but she didn't. People like Peggy would have offered help to Ma, not taken her children from her. But then, why didn't that happen? Peggy knew Ma in those days and everyone in Blackpool knows each other, so what of others? Why did Ma have to turn to the gypsies?

Suddenly, Beth knew there was more to her ma's story. That her ma must have done something to upset her own people, but what it was, she couldn't imagine.

Once outside, Peggy asked if she was all right. When Beth was only able to nod her head, Peggy said, 'Eeh, lass, I knaw as you don't feel good about it, but it's the right thing that you've done. Look, that tea shop's open, lass. Shall we go along there and rest ourselves before we go back? Give you a moment to get your head around all that's happened, eh?'

Once they were seated and their tea was served to them, Beth asked the question that she now had a burning need to know the answer to. 'Peggy, why didn't Ma's own people help her? Why did she have to turn to the gypsies?'

Peggy froze with her cup almost to her lips. Her cough told more than any words could have done as she cleared her throat.

'Peggy?'

'Eeh, lass, it ain't for me to tell you owt about your ma, but it were a shame on us all that we took the stance we did, judging her, when we knew how bad times were for those who had a man to provide for them, let alone for those without. Well, it was our parents really. I were only a young woman, but saying that, I were old enough to have a mind of me own. I could have stood up for your ma.'

'What did she do, Peggy, that you all disapproved of enough to cast us out?'

'It's not sommat as your ma is proud of, I'm sure, and I'd beg you not to ask her. She may not have even told Tommy. She were a lost soul when it happened and all I knaw is as everything she did was motivated by her need to take care of you two.'

Beth was quiet for a moment. Whatever it was, it must have been bad – did she prostitute herself? The thought made Beth shudder. But surely Ma didn't do that? Though she had admitted to being a drunk. *Oh, I don't know. Whatever it was, it must have been bad to turn the people who'd known Ma all their lives against her.*

262

As they sat with their own thoughts, quietly drinking their tea, Beth tried to bring memories back. *There must be something that I saw or heard!*

Martha, the woman Babs had once reminded her of, came to her mind and she could see a cosy front room with a fire blazing and a table laden with food. And a nice feeling washed over her as she remembered a hazy image of Martha's face. It was the face of a woman that she knew she had loved. She could see a glistening Christmas tree and knew that she had been longing for the Christmas promised, but then . . . another memory came. Raised voices – Martha's! *Prostituting yourself and breaking another woman's heart!* Then Ma saying that they couldn't have Christmas as they'd planned as Martha was ill. Martha went out of her life and she never saw her again. She was sure she hadn't died because later, Ma was left her house, so all must have been forgiven in time.

Sighing, Beth knew that she had to accept that she may never know the full story, but she now thought that whatever it was that Ma did was responsible for all that had happened since. This thought hurt, as she never wanted to put the blame for it all on her ma's shoulders. Always she'd seen her ma as a victim of the accident that had killed her da. Now, she would forever wonder. And yes, see everything in a different light. *But I don't want it to be. I don't want it all to be a chain of events, started by Ma's own actions.*

It seemed to Beth now that even being confined to a wheelchair was part of the events triggered by what her ma did. *If Ma hadn't sought help from the gypsies, Babs and I wouldn't have been stolen and I wouldn't have ever been separated from Babs. And I may never have become a nurse as I wouldn't have been searching for a way to live my life differently from the gypsy way, which never felt normal to me.*

Anger boiled up in Beth as now she felt that a light had been turned on. It wasn't Jasmine and Roman who were evil, it was Ma! The thought rocked her world, as did the realisation that came to her that what Jasmine had said about her ma not being able to care for her was the truth, and that the love Jasmine offered her was what she really needed in her life.

TWENTY-ONE

Babs

'It's here!' Pearl came bursting into their billet hut waving a piece of paper, which Babs knew must be their orders to ship out. They'd already overseen the discharge of the last of the patients to Paris and the shipment of all of the medical equipment, medicines and tents. Now there were just a handful of nurses and themselves to leave.

Babs giggled at Pearl as she did a little dance. 'Our going home orders are here! I can't believe it. We and the rest of the staff are to make our way to Paris and report to the Red Cross by Monday. There are travel documents for everyone – well, only ours now as I distributed the others to the doctors and the rest of the nurses on my way here. All said they were going to go immediately.'

'Oh, I'm so relieved. Come on, let's get our things. I want to go right now, too!'

'Hold your horses, the courier brought a note for you. I think it's from Marc!'

Babs felt her stomach muscles tighten, and not only through fear of the fact Marc had hardly been out of her thoughts, which made her have guilty feelings. *Is it really all right for me to feel like this for another man just two years after my darling Rupert died? Does it make me disloyal to him?*

'Hey, I can see the soul-searching on your face, Babs. Stop it! So, you fancy a dashing young man. What of it? Who wouldn't? Any red-blooded female, married or not, would. Marc's a hunk of a man. So, stop giving yourself a hard time. Falling for someone else doesn't mean that you are being untrue. If Rupert was half the man you tell me he was, he'd be happy for you. Read Marc's note, and enjoy it. I have one from Bart too. He says that they have at last got their shipping orders and are set to go to a camp in the UK to await their dispatch back home, and he wants to see me before they go.'

'Oh? Are you going to delay going to Paris?'

'Of course I am. We've three days to get there and it only takes a few hours. Besides, I've thought about Bart every waking hour. He was the one with the red hair and the lovely blue eyes and long eyelashes, and a smile to melt your heart.'

Babs laughed. 'I know, you daft apeth! You haven't stopped talking about him, though I can't remember him.'

'No, because you only had eyes for Marc. Anyway, I've got to say that though I love how you're mastering the King's English, when you come out with a saying like "daft apeth" I do feel nostalgic for how you used to speak. Never lose these little sayings, Babs, though be careful with them. Make sure you are in the right company when you use them.'

Babs sighed. She didn't like not being herself, but had to accept that if it would get her what she wanted then it would all be worth it. 'Yes, I am practising all the time, but we still haven't got a solution for how to make it all happen.

'I might have. I've thought about it a lot. I really want you to have a chance to see your little son and, if we can manage it, for you to have a hand in his upbringing. It will mean that I will have to lie to and deceive my family, but though I hate doing that, I will. Besides, it's all in my own interest too, as I don't want to part from you yet, Babs.'

'Nor me from you, but I can't let you—'

'I'm not giving you the option. Let me tell you about my plan first. I'm thinking of giving you the story that you were orphaned as an infant and that your aunt, who had married a Frenchman but was widowed and had stayed on in France, took on responsibility for you and fetched you to live with her in Paris. That this aunt treated you badly, and so when the war broke out you saw your chance to escape for a while and went to the Red Cross HQ in Paris and volunteered your services. That you then trained to become a nurse. That you worked in the Paris hospital for a time, but when the fighting intensified here, you were assigned to us. And that in the last few weeks we became friends after you had the terrible news that your aunt had died, and your cousin has plans to sell the house and doesn't want you to return to it, or to be bothered with you. There! How does that sound?'

'Oh, Pearl, it could work! It really could. How on earth did you think that up? You should write novels or something. I don't know what to say . . . Well, if I could speak in my natural voice, I'd say, eeh, lass, that's grand.'

They giggled at this.

'You are such a good friend, Pearl. I'm so glad that I met you.'

'Hey, you're crying, old thing! Now, none of that. Stiff upper lip, you know!'

But even though Pearl said this as she took Babs into a hug, Babs saw tears glistening in her eyes too.

As they came out of the hug, Pearl warmed to her theme and began to ask Babs questions about Paris. None of them were a problem to her. Her trips into Paris with Rupert and with Cath had been an education for her. She could name all the main attractions and talk about them knowledgeably as she'd learnt so much on her trips there when on her days off. Besides this, she even knew a residential area where they could say that her pretend aunt had lived.

'It's perfect. No one could trip you up if they spoke to you about Paris. And if they ask why I hadn't written about you before, I'll just tell them that though we had been friends since you arrived, we only really became close after your bereavement, and it was then that I asked you home with me. So, when we get to England, I'll send them a telegram to tell them that you are with me. We have a lot to do as you will need some clothes, but mostly you need some disguises. We have so little time.'

'Oh, but I want to go home first. I want to spend Christmas with my ma.'

'Babs, I know how you feel, I do. But if you do that, you might slip back into your old way of speaking and ruin it all. If you come with me, I can help you to see a different way of life – how a house is run with servants, et cetera, as you will need all of this sort of background if you are to succeed in getting a position that will let you be with your son.'

Babs felt her tears well up again. She so wanted to see her ma and to be held by her in a hug. But she knew that Pearl was right. She would be surrounded by the northern way of life again and would drop straight back into it. She hadn't had long enough in this new guise for it to become natural to her. Beth did it, so she knew that she could. But what would she tell her ma?

'Babs. I know you are struggling with this, but you need to think about it. I so want this to succeed for you. I'll do all I can to steep you in the culture that you will have to blend into. Albeit as a servant – well, nanny – who is much more elevated than the maids, et cetera . . . But you can't do that unless you throw your heart into it and this is your best chance.'

'You're right, I know that. I'll do it. I'll write to Ma and explain, she'll understand. Ma went through what I am going through so she'll support me and I will need to go home at some point. But what do you have in mind as a disguise for me and, well, how can we be sure that I will get the job of Art's nanny when it comes up?'

'I will ask my father to help us. As I said before, I am sure he will know the Barnhams. Daddy's a good sort. He'll understand more than Mama why I wanted to bring what he will call a waif and stray home. And I will ask my sister if you can help out her nanny and be taught by her. And I have ideas of how to disguise you – change your hair, maybe get you some glasses? I know, why don't we go to Paris on Friday as that will give us Saturday to shop? There must be salons open there where a girl can get her hair done, and we could surely find somewhere where we can buy some spectacles. And we'll have to change your name. You can't keep the same one, as it is known by Rupert's family.'

It all seemed to be becoming impossible to Babs. How did one completely change themselves? Oh, she knew it was possible to change your appearance, but your name and every-thing? 'But if I change my name, I will need false papers.'

'With the war over, no one is going to ask you for your passport in Britain. Why should they? You go home as you, but then become the new you. If asked, you can say that you lost everything. Now, what about a name?'

Pearl made everything sound easy.

'You need to pick something that you know and will read-ily answer to.'

Cath came to Babs's mind. The lovely Cath – it would be fitting to her name. She'd only ever known one Cath, and would always react when she heard the name. 'I'll use my late friend and colleague's name, Cath. But all of it worries me. Can I really pull this off? Won't anyone check me out?'

'What can they check? You're from France, you've lost your papers. You know nothing of where you were born. You don't even know your mother's maiden name as your aunt would never speak about your mother. So, where do they start? Besides, everything official will be in chaos for a long time to come. The authorities will have much more to deal with than a young girl who wants to be a nanny.'

Suddenly it did all seem possible. Babs's heart soared. Yes, she could do this. Here was a wonderful chance for her to be with her Art, and she'd take it. She'd do all that she could to achieve it. Already she'd disguised her voice, and that had been difficult. If she could do that then she could do anything. With these thoughts, the hope that Babs had let die with the many obstacles she had seen rekindled.

'That's my girl. I love it when you smile, Babs, and that smile is one that I have come to know. It says that you are up

to whatever challenge presents itself. We can do this, Babs ...
I mean, Cath ... Dufort! That's it, we'll name you after that
French soldier, Andre Dufort, who we nursed. You remember
him? He was lovely. And if asked, you can say your aunt gave
you her married surname and it's the only one you know.'

'Cath Dufort. I love it. And yes, I do remember the lovely
Andre. He was one of our successes ... Pleased to meet you,
Pearl, I am Cath Dufort, a French madame pretending to be
a nanny.'

They both laughed at this and it lightened the moment.
Babs really did believe they could make this happen now, and
excitement surged through her.

'And, Pearl, I know of the perfect place in Paris for our
quest.' Though it was painful for Babs as memories were
evoked, she told Pearl about the Hotel Vendim. 'Rupert's
family own the penthouse suite, and the hotel is magnificent.
It has many salons leading off the foyer – some selling clothes,
but some devoted to beauty treatments, and the dressing of
ladies' hair. Mind, it costs an arm and a leg.'

'Well, we have plenty. Our pay has been building up for
months.'

'Yes, that's true, but how do we access it at such short
notice? I have very little left of the allowance we were given.'

'We go into a bank, darling. Oh, my dear Babs, I have so
much to teach you. We can have a money order authorisation
wired through from our banks in England. It's so simple. Let's
do it. Let's splash out on ourselves.'

The idea appealed to Babs, and would be a test for her.
When she'd been to the hotel before she'd been under the
protection of Rupert and his family name. This time she

would be going under her new guise. 'Yes. I think it's a wonderful idea, Pearl.'

'Oh, that's super! It will be such fun. So, now all we have to do is make arrangements to meet Bart and . . . Oh, you haven't read your note. Open it at once, Babs, as I know that Marc wants to see you too.'

Babs's hands shook as she opened the note. Her heart longed for it to say what Pearl thought: that Marc did want to meet up with her. But she wondered how that could be as he'd said that they were shipping out and had given her his home address in Canada.

Dear Babs,

Our departure has been delayed, and I am hoping that you will consent to meeting up with me. I would so like to see you again. I know that Bart is asking your friend Pearl to come too.

As there will be no time for you to reply, we have decided that tomorrow we will travel to Château-Thierry and will wait in the public square from twelve noon.

It will be sad to see the town again as we have memories of many comrades lost in our quest to take it back from the Germans in July, and we hope that the brave people will have been able to clear some of the rubble from the terrible destruction that was the result of the battles.

However, the spirit of my people – the French – is such that their wonderful pavement cafés and bars always remained open and there is one in the public square that threw a welcome to us like no other when we entered, having defeated the Germans. It is outside there that we will be waiting – you will easily spot it.

Please come, Babs, I haven't been able to get you out of my mind since we met.

Marceau x

Clutching the note to her breast, Babs turned away for a moment. Her eyes looked upwards, and in her mind's eye she saw her lovely Rupert. A peace settled in her as she imagined him smiling down on her. Did he know that she was doing all she could to get back to their darling son? Did he know of how she'd healed just enough to be able to feel something for another man? Would he be hurt by this? The peace she felt told her that no, Rupert would always be in a special corner of her heart, leaving the rest of her to the life that she had to live.

She didn't know if she would ever lead that life with Marc, although she knew that she wanted to. But there was something tugging the strings of her heart much harder.

The public square was bustling with people when they arrived. All seemed to have somewhere they must be, and had an eager optimism about them. This made for a lovely atmosphere, and took Babs reeling back home as the strains of an organ grinder's music filled the air. People displayed their wares on benches outside the ruins of what Babs imagined would have been their shops before the terrible battles that ravished this lovely town.

She looked around to see buildings proudly pointing jagged and broken walls towards the sky as if to say, 'I wasn't completely destroyed that day.'

This wasn't a town of misery dwelling on what happened, but a town of hope as already builders were working on some of the ruins, and the pavements, which she knew had been piled high with the rubble of the places that had represented the people's lives, were now clear and glistening with the frost the cold night had clothed them in.

When she saw Marc standing outside the café he'd spoken of, she had the urge to run to him and feel his arms around her, but she smiled and gave a little wave. As she did, she felt her barriers coming up again, and her doubts flooded her once more.

They sat inside the cramped café, their knees touching. Their surroundings were typically French – low ceilings, with the walls clad in stained wood, and the bar laden with drinks of all manner as well as what seemed to be the obligatory string of onions hanging from the four corner posts. The floor was scrubbed red tiling, but was littered with cigarette ends, and the furniture, which was mainly benches and tables, was a dark, highly polished wood.

Their conversation was polite. Babs felt that she was deceiving Marc. She wasn't the woman he thought he knew. He'd never heard her speak in her proper voice, or knew much about her at all, but she didn't feel able to tell him and he didn't ask questions. She made her mind up that in her first letter to him she would tell him all, and then he could decide if he ever wanted to contact her again.

'Babs, this is awful, and not how I imagined meeting you again would be. Will you walk with me?'

They left Pearl and Bart deep in conversation, and oblivious to others. When outside, Marc offered her his arm. After a moment she took it.

'I have thought about you so often, Babs. I know we have only met once before but something happened to me then.

274

Something quite profound. It changed me for ever. I – I, well, I don't mean to frighten you, or to seem too forward, but once we Canadians make our mind up, we don't beat around the bush. You see, I fell for you, Babs. And I have this urge to tell you of my love and beg you to come to Canada as my wife, but I know that will frighten you. So, I just want to ask, do you think there will ever come a time when you will look on me in that light?'

Thrilled at his words, in her mind she said, *Aye, I will do, me lovely lad, that'd be grand*, but aloud, she just said, 'I don't know. I do know that I . . . I feel much the same about you and if ever I am ready to marry again, you are the one I would want to marry. But my life is complicated. I cannot leave England. I have ties that keep me there and will do for a long time into the future. I will write to you, Marc, but I can't promise anything more than that.'

'Really? You mean it? You do look on me as someone you would like to marry?'

Babs nodded, her shyness making her blush now. How did she become this unsure of herself, when always she'd been a strong person who stood her own corner?

'Then I will look into emigrating to England, the moment you tell me in your letters that you are ready.'

'Oh, Marc. You know so little about me. Wait to make that judgement until I write. I can put so much into a letter that you should know, but I cannot talk about it to you now.'

Marc stopped walking and looked down at her. 'My mysterious lady. You are so beautiful. Look, there's a photography studio. It was a fellow Frenchman – for I am French-Canadian, remember – who invented the process of commercially developing photographs. He was called Louis Daguerre. Will you have a photo taken with me? I can collect it when it is ready, or have them send two copies to me and one to you. That way you will never forget what I look like.'

Babs knew she would never do that anyway. And she marvelled at how much knowledge those who had had the privilege of an education possessed. Cath and Rupert used to teach her so much, and Pearl did too, and now Marc. She loved it and felt herself growing in confidence because of it, even though her feelings for Marc were making her bashful.

Marc steered her towards the shop.

'I don't feel dressed for a photograph.'

'I told you, Babs, you look beautiful.'

Babs didn't feel beautiful and wished that for this moment that in the future would mark their history together she had worn the better of her few frocks, but she'd chosen this brown woollen one for warmth. It had a high collar which was relieved by a pretty cream lace edging and long sleeves with the cuffs edged in the same lace. Fitted to her waist, it fell to the floor, enabling her to wear her knitted long pantaloons underneath for extra warmth. She'd added a hip-length cream jacket and then topped it all off with her black wool nurse's cape, which gave a lot of warmth as she could huddle it around her. Pearl had brushed her hair off her face and coiled it into a long ringlet that hung down her back, and she wore a bonnet that tied under her chin that she didn't think very becoming, but which kept her ears protected from the biting wind.

The studio bell rang out like a church bell peeling when they opened the door. Inside was in almost total darkness, but suddenly a very bright light came on. A voice called out in

French, 'Enter. Don't let any of that unnatural light in from the street, please.'

Babs wanted to giggle as her nerves clutched at her but she managed to swallow and contain it.

Sitting on the gold-coloured chaise-longue next to Marc, Babs trembled with the feelings rippling through her as at the photographer's direction, they moved closer and held hands. The photographer was a little weedy man who moved in jerky movements that were unnerving. One minute he was in front of them, fiddling with a collar, or a wisp of hair, the next gone behind a long black curtain that covered his camera.

'*Lèvez la tête, juste un peu, s'il vous plaît.*'

Their heads lifted in unison to this command, and then a dazzling light flashed. Babs thought she'd gone blind as she blinked to try to clear the after-rays that clouded her vision.

'*Bon! Maintenant, regardez la madame, monsieur.*'

Marc moved beside her. She could feel his eyes on her, just as the photographer had instructed. 'Babs.'

Her name on his lips compelled her to look at him. She couldn't turn away. In the depth of his eyes, she saw an intense love. She longed to take what Marc was offering, but she knew it wasn't enough. She would always have this moment to remember, but nothing could ever replace being with her little Art.

TWENTY-TWO

Babs and Tilly

The hotel was just as Babs remembered it. Gleaming glass doors with the name of Hotel Vendim inscribed on them in gold. The porter was the exact one who'd greeted her and Rupert, but he didn't seem to recognise her. He opened the cab door and ushered her and Pearl inside.

Pearl took the beautiful interior in her stride – the magnificent arched ceiling with golden carvings, the multi-coloured marble floor and the Roman-looking golden urns, but to Babs, it was just as magical as when she'd first stepped inside this foyer.

She looked around her, her heart pounding. Rupert seemed to be sitting or standing everywhere her gaze fell. She imagined that she could smell his lovely musky cologne and felt as if she could reach out and touch him.

'Very nice, Cath.'

'Oh, Pearl, we needn't start calling me that now, need we? What if the receptionist wants to see my passport?'

'Oh, all right, but we must start at some point or you'll never be used to your new self.'

'As soon as we get to England and are away from the rest of our colleagues. After all, we may have discharge papers to sign, and a lot of official stuff to go through. I don't want to be getting confused.'

'You're right. Well, I must say, you did well to tell me about this place. We'll book in and make an appointment with the beauty salon for first thing in the morning and ask that two telegrams be sent ... Oh, I just thought ... They won't know you here, will they? I mean with you having been before?'

'No, Rupert never had to sign in, but in any case, that won't matter.'

'It will if they link you with Rupert and inform his family that you returned.'

'That won't happen. My name was never registered, I was just a woman that came to the penthouse with Rupert.'

'You were much more than that, Babs.'

'I meant to them that's all I was. But yes, I was. This building holds precious memories for me. Some of the happiest moments in my life. And it was here that I became pregnant with Art, I'm sure of it.'

'Well, never let go of those memories, but never be afraid to make new ones.'

They were in their room when Pearl shocked her by saying, 'I may have made a baby with Bart myself.'

'What? How? When? Oh, Pearl!'

Pearl crossed the bedroom – a large room with twin beds covered in gold satin bedspreads – and sank into one of the ruby-red Queen Anne chairs. 'I couldn't help myself. We kissed and then the landlord came over and whispered something to Bart. It all sounds a bit seedy now, but it wasn't, it was wonderful. Anyway, Bart gave the landlord some money and he showed us through to the back where there was a bedroom.'

'Oh, Pearl.' Babs didn't question the action of the landlord as what he'd done was normal practice and part of many bars' services. And not just if a soldier had his own girl with him, as often they supplied the girls too. 'What if you are pregnant? Oh God, your father might send you to a convent! I couldn't bear that for you, Pearl. They'll take your baby away from you.'

'You sound as though you know a lot about it?'

Babs sank down on the edge of one of the twin beds. 'I do, but I'm not up to telling you about it, not yet. But, Pearl, this news is devastating.'

'I may not be pregnant yet, we don't know. I only did that which makes you so. And jolly lovely it was too.'

Babs could never get over how the rich girls she'd met talked so openly of such matters, but she supposed it was because they had spent a lot of their lives in all-girl boarding schools, and then so many had become nurses because of the war – that profession alone lowered your inhibitions!

How Pearl would solve this latest problem was a worry. She didn't seem aware of what could happen. There were many girls from wealthy families in the convent, and most had a very sad story as their choices were taken from them, and they knew if they did any other than give their baby up and return to the family home, keeping the pretence of having been to Europe for a year, they would be banished with a very small allowance. She couldn't see Pearl giving a child up. 'Pearl, whatever happens, you will always have a friend in me. Never be alone. Promise me.'

'Oh dear, you're frightening me now, when I'd taken the prospect in my stride. Besides, I trust Bart. He has promised to make contact before he is shipped out to Canada. So, if I am pregnant, I will be able to tell him and I just know that he will marry me.'

Babs knew from this that though worldly-wise in many things, Pearl didn't have a clue what her action could lead to. Yes, Bart seemed a lovely young, honest man, but most men would say and do anything to get their own way.

Shaking this thought away from her, Babs determined not to try to disillusion Pearl. It wasn't fair to do so, but she would make sure that if the worst came to the worst and Pearl had to go into a convent, she would go to the convent where Sister Theresa and Daisy were. Thinking of them, she also made her mind up to write to tell them that she had to delay her visit. She couldn't face them with the deception she was planning as she didn't know how they would take it, no matter what her motive. Nuns could be very strait-laced at times – right was right and wrong was wrong in their eyes.

The arrival of the telegram felt like a kick in the gut to Tilly. And to get it on Christmas Eve of all days.

Sorry, cannot be home for Christmas. I will write to explain. My love, Babs.

Everything was almost ready, despite the upheaval of two funerals and Tilly still not feeling back to normal. All that remained was to get a tree, and Tilly had wanted to wait until Babs got here to begin to decorate it.

Coping with having extra folk around most of the time wasn't helping, as Alec was still unwell too, and though out of danger and no longer suffering from the flu, he was left with a chesty cough that had weakened him. And so he was still living with them, which meant that Molly was always bringing Mary over, and often Vera too.

Not that Tilly minded. She loved the girls and was happy to see Mary and Alec so caring of one another. She just wished that she felt better and that she had her Babs and Beth here for Christmas.

Beth had only written once in the last couple of weeks, and that had upset her as the letter didn't sound as though Beth had written it. It contained the facts of what was happening in her life, and that was that. Even the signature wasn't as loving as it had been in the past.

This niggled away at Tilly, but Tommy just passed it off as Beth being really busy getting everything ready in her new home in anticipation of Henry returning. 'At least it is that she took time enough to write to you.'

But when Beth's parcel had arrived, the feeling of something not being quiet right had deepened. Eliza's card spoke of Beth's love for her and how she would miss her over Christmas and wanted her to visit. But for Tilly, there was a short message hoping she enjoyed Christmas, with just 'Love Beth x' at the end.

Tilly hadn't told Beth that she'd been ill, though she had now written in a letter she hoped wouldn't arrive until after Christmas about losing Ivy and Ma Perkins.

The house was quiet at the moment. Alec was lying on his bed in her work room – though nowadays no work went on in there as the shop was closed until further notice. Tommy was out with Phil cutting down the Christmas tree. The only occasional sound came from the kitchen as Cliff worked away preparing the Christmas food. This was usually Eliza's job, but she'd felt duty bound to open the shop today to make sure she fulfilled all the Christmas orders.

Eliza was coping well and Tilly had seen in her the makings of a very strong young woman emerging and this made her proud. All women needed to be strong these days, just to survive.

Sighing, Tilly wished that some of her own strength would come back to her. Although the younger ones who had fallen victim to the flu had suffered stronger symptoms, they did seem to be able to recover quicker than she and others of her age did. Except Alec, but then, he wasn't the strongest of young men.

Shoving the telegram into her pocket, Tilly made her way to the kitchen. 'Can I give you a hand with owt, Cliff? By, lad, it all smells good. I've thought to ask you before, but haven't done – when did you learn to cook how you do?'

'Naw, I'm fine, I don't need any help. It were me ma who taught me. Da didn't like it, he said as it weren't a man's job and that I'd be a laughing stock, but I reckon as Ma knew she'd be leaving us and wanted me to be able to look after me and me da. And I don't hear him complaining now!'

'Oh? He seems very glad to come to us at Christmas.' Tilly laughed as she said this.

'Ha! That's because the first Christmas we came, Ma had only just died. After that, he hopes every year that you'll ask us. I don't think he can face Christmas at home with just me and him.'

'Well, you're allus welcome here. Have you heard from Babs?'

Cliff was quiet for a moment and then parried with a question rather than an answer. 'Have you heard then?'

'Aye, did Tommy tell you as she ain't coming back here to live? And that telegram that came says she won't be here for Christmas either.'

'Awe, I didn't knaw the last bit, but I did the first.'

'And you don't mind?'

Cliff stopped in the action of basting the roasting pork and looked at her with shock on his face.

'Eeh, I'm sorry, lad. I thought, well, I . . .'

'Naw. There's nowt like that in mine and Babs's friendship. We're best mates. And I'm sad that she ain't coming back here to live, but she said she would be here for Christmas. Is she all right?'

For the first time, Tilly realised that Babs might not be well and this was the reason. *It must be that! What else could keep Babs from me? Oh no. Not me Babs.*

'Tilly?'

'I don't knaw, the message was very brief.'

'Maybe she's just tired and decided not to travel all the way up here. I wouldn't worry. Babs is as strong as an 'orse. I'll miss her, though. I were looking forward to seeing her.'

This sounded a lot stronger than someone who was just a mate, but Tilly left it there as Tommy was coming through the door and his and Phil's antics were a sight to see as they tugged a huge tree in.

Cliff's actions, though, took her aback. He snatched at a folded tablecloth and threw it over the food he was preparing. For all the world, his movement reminded her of a ballet dancer or circus act, but she thought better of teasing him.

'Just sit there, Mammy.' There was no arguing with Eliza. Not that Tilly had the strength to do so, and was secretly glad to have someone take charge. 'I'll do the tree. Eeh, I wish you could feel better, Mammy. I feel really worried about you.'

They were in the Sunday best room; decorations for the tree were strewn over the floor and a fire blazed up the chimney. At such a time there would usually be a happy, light-hearted atmosphere, but tonight, everything was just happening because it had to.

'Aye, I must say that I'm for being of the same mind. Tilly, you're going to see the doctor once all this is over, and no argument!'

Tilly couldn't remember Tommy being so firm about anything before. And she didn't have the energy to argue, though she wanted to. She didn't want the doctor poking her around. She'd never forgiven him for not sending Tommy to the hospital after the accident, and had made her mind up to only go to him in emergencies.

Christmas had its moments, but for Tilly, the day couldn't pass quickly enough. The house was full of guests and felt stuffy. Cliff and his da, Molly, Will, Mary, Gerry, Vera and Alec, besides herself, Eliza and Tommy. Then in the afternoon, Florrie, Reggie and Phil came.

The usual games went on around her, but there were moments when Mary and Vera shed tears, and this started Eliza off. But even then, Tilly was unable to feel anything. It was as if she was too tired to take on sympathy for others.

'Tilly, lass, I've never seen you like this.'

'I've never felt like this before in me whole life, Florrie. It's as if me stuffing's been drawn out of me body and left me with a shell that doesn't want to function.'

'You could do with a break. You allus seem to be coping with sommat – if it's not your own lot, it's others that you're fond of who are tugging at your heart. You cannot take on the pain and troubles of the world, lass.'

'Is that what I do, Florrie?'

'It is. And it's a lovely, kind trait that you have, but over the years it has drained you and left nothing for yourself when you need it. Why don't you, Tommy and Eliza take yourselves off after Christmas? Go and visit Beth. Stay a while and let everyone up here get on with their own troubles. Between us – me making the cushions and things, and Mary ready to take up the running the shop, Alec making the baskets and Molly overseeing us – everything on the business side is covered for when the shop reopens. Then here on the farm, Cliff and Phil can manage. Eliza can let Ma Perkins' solicitor knaw that she's taking a week off. You've nowt to worry over here, lass, and it would do you the world of good, and Beth and Eliza an' all.'

The idea began to warm Tilly's heart and worm out the feeling that had descended on her that nothing would ever be the same again.

'Don't mourn the past, Tilly. Rise up and make a future out of it.'

'Eeh, Florrie, I reckon as you're right. Me girls can't come to me, but I can go to them. There's nowt stopping me, is there? And by that time, I'll knaw where me Babs is going to be and can visit her an' all. It sounds just what we all need.'

As if a tap had suddenly been turned on allowing her energy to flow back into her, Tilly felt herself lifting and the tiredness draining away to be replaced by hope for her future – a new and different future to what she'd planned, but a good one.

'Now, that's made my Christmas, Tilly, to see that lovely smile on your face.'

'Ta, Florrie. I suddenly feel so much better.'

'That's because what was wrong with you wasn't physical, but mental. You'd fallen into the doldrums and shut yourself down. It's called depression and my, if it takes hold, you're in trouble as it's worse than any physical ailment. Your whole body stops as if it has no purpose and all troubles weigh you down.'

This made sense to Tilly. Triggered by the flu that had weakened her, she'd let everything get on top of her. She hadn't even left herself open to change, and everything in life changes. She knew she just had to make the best of it and that's what she would be doing from now on.

With this new resolve, Tilly rose from the chair. There was a lull. Everyone had been play-acting Christmas and had run out of energy in doing so. Well, Tilly had something up her sleeve. Something that she'd purchased months ago when she'd seen the hope of the war coming to an end. She'd thought to throw a party for when peace was announced, but that had come and gone with not much to celebrate after the initial hugging and dancing on the promenade, as none of the young had made it home as yet. So, then she'd thought to leave it till Christmas when she'd have all her family around her; she hadn't reckoned on the destruction of the flu virus and her girls not coming home in time.

She crossed the room to where stood the beautiful cabinet in mahogany, with its legs bowed in a lovely curve and its doors adorned in each corner with carvings of leaves. Tommy had been bemused by it, especially when, considering her past problem and the problems that Babs had had, she told him that it was a drinks cabinet. But he had just laughed, and had never asked her why she hadn't filled it with bottles of gin and such.

A few minutes ago, its presence had seemed like a mockery to her failed plan for Christmas; now it was the object that would rescue it.

'Right, everyone, I've a treat for you all.'

Tommy's face was a picture. It was as if she'd suddenly become someone he didn't recognise. She smiled over at him, a smile that turned into a little giggle. She was rewarded by seeing his face light up. She'd been lost to him, but now she was back.

Going to the sideboard, she pulled out a flat case. Everyone was watching her. 'In here, I have a surprise for you. It's me present to me Tommy.'

Opening the case, she pulled out a record. Black and as large as a dinner plate, she held it up and read the label. 'This is a recording by the Peerless Quartet. Push the chairs back and roll up the rug, we're going to have a dance!'

'Tilly? That's for being amazing, but what is it you are planning to be playing it on? For sure, it is that we don't have a gramophone!'

'Ah, but we do!'

With this, Tilly lifted the lid of the cabinet with a flourish a magician would display. Everyone gasped.

'Eeh, Mammy!' Eliza jumped up from where she'd been sitting crossed-legged in front of the fire. 'A gramophone, a real gramophone! How does it work?'

'Well, now. I've to fit this handle into the side and we have to wind it up, then pop the record on, put the needle in the first groove and that's it.'

There was a round of applause as everyone came to life, getting up off their seats and crowding around the magical gramophone that no one had suspected was there.

Soon the uplifting song 'I don't know where I am going, but I'm on my way' blasted out and the room became animated. Furniture was shifted to the walls, and the huge carpet rolled up and dragged into the hall by the men. The stage was set, and all to the lively sound of everyone singing along. It was a moment Tilly thought she would never forget.

As the record came to an end everyone was laughing and clapping.

'What else have you got, Mammy? Or shall we play that again?'

'Naw, Eliza, lass, I've a few records. Look in the case and pick one.'

The evening after that was full of fun as songs blared out one after the other and then all were played again: 'By the

Light of the Silvery Moon', 'Let Me Call You Sweetheart' and 'I Want a Girl Just Like the Girl that Married Dear Old Dad'.

When 'Let Me Call You Sweetheart' was played for the third time, Tommy took hold of Tilly and they waltzed around the room. Not quite like they had been used to doing in the past, as Tommy struggled still with a limp, but to Tilly, it was a moment she wanted to savour.

'Me Tilly, me little Tilly. You are for being the most wonderful person in the whole world, and I love you. What was it that suddenly made you feel better?'

'Coming to terms with me lot, Tommy, and embracing change. I had change forced on me once a long time ago and I found a way to cope. I'd got a silly idea in me head that once me and me twins were reunited, everything would be put right and we'd never be parted again. I saw them living with me, or nearby to me forever. That were shattered and it seemed like the end of the world and sommat I couldn't cope with, but I can. I can let change happen and adapt to it.'

'Well, it is for being the best news I've heard in a long time, as it was bound to happen, you know, lass. Babs and Beth are independent young women with their lives to lead.'

'I knaw that, and I knaw sommat else an' all. Me and you and Eliza are going on a trip, Tommy.'

'We are?'

'Aye. Soon after Christmas is over. We're going to Margate, and then we're going to wherever Babs has made her home.'

Tommy held her close. 'That's for being wonderful news and something we dearly need. Oh, me Tilly, I'm so glad it is that you're well again.'

'Tommy? Tommy, don't cry. What's wrong?'

Waltzing her through the door, his tears wetting her hair and her neck, Tommy took her hand and led her outside. The howling wind didn't have any effect on her as he enclosed her in his arms. 'I was for thinking that something terrible ailed you, Tilly, and that I was going to lose you. I couldn't bear it. I've been so worried, so afraid.'

'Eeh, Tommy, lad. I'll never leave you. You are me saviour. Me bright shining light. Me man.'

They hugged as if they would never let each other go again, and Tilly felt that was so. Yes, she'd lost her way for a time, brought low by illness. She'd let in demons that had made her think differently about everything. But now she felt stronger and ready for her new life ahead.

TWENTY-THREE

Babs

Christmas for Babs was like none she'd ever celebrated before. Surrounded by strangers, other than Pearl, and all of a class that she had no knowledge of.

Everything was on a grand scale in Pearl's home; it had so many rooms Babs wondered if some were ever used. In each one, the ceilings were vast and hung with glittering chandeliers, and they were all filled with sumptuous furniture and had carpets that you felt your every tread sink into.

The land of her family estate was beautiful as it stretched for miles into sloping hills – nothing like the rugged hills of the north, but gently giving way to flat fields and then rising again like waves of the sea that could be seen in the distance.

Babs was overawed by it all, and found herself going into her shell, only speaking when spoken to, afraid of putting a foot wrong.

Naturally everyone was inquisitive about her and questions were fired at her ten to the dozen. Sometimes, if she felt herself getting lost, she would begin to speak in French and then apologise, and this would make her inquisitor realise that they were intruding too far and upsetting her.

With this strategy, she coped well, as long as she didn't look at Pearl, who was intent on making her giggle and would have spoilt the smokescreen she was trying to hide behind.

Christmas Day itself seemed regimental; the traditions of it were nothing like she'd known at home – more in keeping with her convent life. Church in the morning, a light lunch of ham, pickles and hot potatoes, after which had come the present-giving. Then most of the thirty guests retired to their rooms and left herself and Pearl with Pearl's sister and brother and their partners and children.

This was when it all changed and the day became enjoyable for Babs. She'd found Pearl's sister Elaine to be just like Pearl – fun and easy to get on with – and her brother Ian a tease, who enjoyed playing with the children.

During a lull when the children were resting, Ian suggested they play some music. This turned into a jolly time of silly games, and was when Babs felt most relaxed. There were a few hairy moments when Ian said, 'Catherine, I think you should teach us a French game – something you played as a child.'

Babs cringed for a moment. She had no idea what the children in France played as opposed to what they did in England – if she even knew what English children played, as most of the games so far today had been new to her. Nothing like them ever figured in her childhood. But suddenly, one that Jasmine had taught them came to her and she hoped that it could be considered French. 'Well, for the one I loved, we will need five small stones. You put four of them on the floor and then you throw the fifth one in the air. Before you catch it, you have to pick up one of the stones and then next time two and so on.'

'Oh, you mean snobs! I love that game. We played that here too. Let's play it, it'll be fun.'

Babs almost let out a sigh of relief, but she just smiled at Elaine, Pearl's sister, as she said this and then joined in the silly banter that took place as they got into the game.

A few times her mind wandered to what might be happening at home. Would everyone be there? Eliza would, of course. Oh, how she longed to see Eliza, and Beth, yes, she longed to see Beth too. And maybe Henry had made it back. Aunt Molly and, well, all of them, but mostly she pictured Ma, and she felt a longing for her stronger than the pull of any of the others. She closed her eyes and tried to imagine her ma holding her, and could hear her laughter and see her lovely smile. For a moment, she was transported back in time to when she was separated from Ma and didn't know where she was. It was her ma's smile that had kept the desire burning inside her to find her. *If only I was with you now, Ma. How hurt you must have been to hear I wasn't coming home.*

This thought swamped her and she felt tears pricking her eyes. She had to get away, spend a little time alone.

When the next round of the game finished, she stood up. 'Pearl, I'm sorry, but I need to rest a while. I suddenly feel very tired.'

'All right, Cath, I'll come with you.'

'No, I'll be all right. I just want to sleep.'

'I know how you feel. It's been hectic. All right, old thing. I'll give you a knock around fiveish so that you can get ready for dinner.'

Glad to escape, when she entered the bedroom that she'd been given for her stay, she made for the chair in the window, passing the double bed, draped in a cream counterpane, and the lovely cream-painted kidney-shaped dressing table. She'd intended on sitting in the window and just having a good weep, but decided she would undress and get into her robe and hope that this gave her time to compose herself.

The first thing she removed were the spectacles, which she hated. Round and framed in wire, they were bought in Paris from an optician and were what he used for fitting, hence they had plain glass in them, which didn't interfere in any way with her vision. She thought they looked hideous.

Next, she carefully took off her lovely frock, one of those bought at the Hotel Vendim and chosen by Pearl for her to wear today. She lay it on the bed. A pale primrose colour, it had two layers, the top layer having little capped sleeves and falling in a straight line to her thighs and the bottom layer flowing in a fusion of pleats to her ankles. Made of a satin, it had a sheen to it that caught the light when she moved. Babs loved it and thought it more of an evening dress until she'd seen the other ladies, who all looked to Babs as if they were dressed to meet the King!

With her hair now cut into a bob that fell just below her jawline and make-up that was more stated than she'd ever worn – black pencil lines drawn on her eyelids and her eyebrows thinned and elongated to be level with the corner of her eyes, and the awful rouge brushed onto her cheeks, making her look like a clown – she did feel like someone different. More a Catherine than a Babs.

The notion that she looked like a clown left her as she caught a glimpse of herself in the mirror. The rouge had settled down, making her think that maybe she'd put too much on in the beginning. She pouted her ruby-red-lipstick lips at her image, and actually thought she looked rather beautiful. This boosted her confidence as she had to admit that the transformation, and in particular when she had the glasses on, made her feel self-conscious. Though she knew it all worked as she wasn't even recognisable to herself!

Cheered by this, she set about cleaning the make-up off – she'd apply it freshly a little later, only this time be more sparing with the rouge. With this done, she sat in the window looking out onto the sweeping drive lined by poplars and lit by a row of gas lights. Babs marvelled that she was actually here doing such a thing. *How did this happen? How did I get from the gypsy camp to this luxury and behaving as if it is my normal way of life?* A little giggle escaped her, but without warning it turned to tears flooding her face. She needed her ma – her family. She'd been two long, long years away from them and she wanted to go home.

Dinner was over and the ladies had left the men to smoke cigars and drink brandy, a custom, like many Babs was learning about, that felt strange and yet fascinated her.

Pearl's mother, a tall, slim, lovely lady who wore her years well, clapped her hands to bring everyone to attention. Babs thought she was the picture of elegance, with her thick grey hair coiled into a chignon at the back of her head and her twinkling blue eyes making you think that she was about to announce something of great fun. 'Ladies, shall we play bridge?'

A series of oohs and ahhs signalled their assent. Babs was relieved it was something she knew, as Pearl had taught her to play and they had often played with a couple of the VADs. Especially lately when there hadn't been much to do. She was quite good at it as it happened, much to Pearl's chagrin, who'd been playing for years and found that Babs had mastered the skill in just a few weeks, and better than she had.

They hadn't been playing many minutes when Pearl's father burst in. 'Forgive me, ladies, I must speak with my wife.'

Pearl's mother's expression went from shock to annoyance, then measured composure in just a few seconds. Pearl looked at Babs and shrugged her bottom lip. The room gradually went from silence to noisy chatter again and Babs felt that whatever the crisis, these ladies would handle it in their very feminine way and carry on with their chit-chat.

'What's wrong, Pearl? You don't think that someone has realised that I'm—'

'French? No, they all know that, dearest Cath. It will be something or nothing.' This Pearl accompanied with a warning frown, which made Babs realise that she'd been about to blow her own cover as ears were listening, despite the pretext of nothing having disturbed them all.

When the door opened again, a maid entered and came over to Pearl. 'Miss Pearl, your mama and papa would like to talk to you and to your friend. They are in your papa's study.'

'Thank you, Kitty. Come on, Cath, we're soon to find out what's going on by the sound of things.'

Once in the vast hall, that was so imposing it couldn't ever make anyone feel welcome, with its arched beams, many portraits of family through the ages and highly polished wooden floor that echoed every footstep that crossed it, Pearl showed that she was just as nervous as Babs felt. 'I don't know what this is all about, old thing, but try not to drop your cover. We have to stick to our story.'

This increased Babs's nerves and she felt for a moment that she couldn't remember a single detail about where she was supposed to have come from and who she was meant to be.

When they reached the study and the door opened, they both gasped.

'Pearl, Catherine, I believe you may know these young men?'

Babs had never felt anything like the mixture of feelings that took her at that moment. Joy, astonishment at the beauty of Marceau, combined with a fear that he would expose her. He stood with Bart, both towering over Pearl's parents, and both wearing full-dress uniform. She couldn't speak.

Pearl gasped. 'Bart! Oh, Bart. Mama, Papa, this is Bart, and Marceau. They are Canadian – French-Canadian officers, whom we met in France and are our friends.'

'Yes, so they have been telling us. I am surprised, Pearl, that you didn't have the good manners to tell us about them, nor to extend an invitation to them to join us for Christmas. They tell me that they are housed in billets near to Portsmouth, that they only arrived there yesterday, and because of how drab it looked, they set off to come here in a borrowed army vehicle. I am ashamed that you could let this happen to our Allied troops!'

'Sir, no. It really wasn't like that. We all had to go where directed. Pearl and . . . her friend didn't know where that was, just as we didn't until we arrived. We had exchanged addresses,

298

though, so once we saw where we were, we made our minds up to try to get here to be with a family, where we knew we would be made welcome.'

Babs nearly died when Bart began this speech, but was surprised how well he covered up.

'Very well, my boy, I am glad to hear it, and of course you are welcome. We have our Christmas evening ball very shortly, but first, we shall see to sorting out a bedroom for you both and a meal, which I am sure you are in dire need of.'

'We are. Thank you, sir.'

Marc hadn't spoken yet, but his eyes hadn't left Babs's. She waited to see what would come next, but then was very happily surprised as Pearl's mother said, 'I will see to all of that, Edgar, you go back to the gentlemen. And Pearl and Catherine, we will leave you to say hello for a few moments.'

When they had left, Pearl went straight into Bart's arms. 'Bart, you did it! I didn't believe you would. Oh, it's so wonderful to have you here.'

'You knew, Pearl? You didn't say anything.'

'Sorry, Babs, but, well, I didn't want to believe it, it was only something we laughed over. But don't worry, I told him what we had talked about. Not the details as we hadn't finalised them then, but that we had a plan to disguise you and change your name.'

Babs felt her colour rise. If Pearl had told Bart this, what else did she tell him? Had she disclosed everything? *She must have as she would have to give a reason why I had to pretend to be someone else.* But as this thought died, Babs was reassured that Pearl hadn't told all as Marc asked, 'What's this all about, Babs?'

'Don't call me that. I – I have to remain as Cath.' As she looked at him she suddenly knew that she could tell him. Had to. There was no other way. To surround herself with more lies would be too confusing. And besides, what she read in his eyes told her that this was a man she could trust as his love for her was clear for her to see.

'I will try to get used to it. Those glasses suit you, especially when you are cross.'

'Oh, I forgot I had them on.'

'And your hair! Though I did love your long curly mess. How on earth did you straighten it?'

This wasn't what she wanted to be talking about. She wanted to go into his arms as Pearl was in Bart's, and hold him and tell him of her feelings for him. With her not answering, he put out his hands to her. She took them and then almost jumped as she felt an emotion zing through her that took her breath away.

'We will talk, B – Cath. Whatever the reason for you doing this, I'll help you, I promise.'

The knock on the door stopped any more conversation. Both girls moved away from the men and Pearl called, 'Come in.'

To this, one of the manservants entered. 'The gentlemen's rooms are ready, Miss Pearl. Shall I take them up? And then a meal will be laid out for them in the breakfast room as the dining room is ready for supper.'

As Babs walked with Pearl, they began to giggle. 'Pearl, you daft idiot. Why didn't you tell me? That was a massive shock and frightened the life out of me.'

'I didn't know, honestly, but isn't it amazing? I'm so happy. Bart truly loves me, he must to have done this.'

'But you discussed it with him. You discussed me.'

'I didn't, honestly. I just prepared him, really. Our plan was only hours old when we met up with Bart and Marc that day. But I knew that Bart was going to play a big part in my life, just as you know that Marc is. Oh, I've heard of love at first sight, but this is ridiculous. Not only did I fall instantly in love, within such a short time I gave myself fully. I cannot understand it. I never thought such a thing would happen.'

'Well, it has, and you may have to face consequences yet, Pearl. But I know what you mean. This is the second time it has happened to me. But it is so complicated. Just how much do they know?'

'All I said to Bart was, well, it was after we made love and he'd said that he must see me again. He'd thought then that there might be a long delay in getting them all home but knew that they were coming to this country to await that happening. We planned that wherever he was he would contact me and we would meet. I told him then what we were up to. I told him that it wasn't my place to tell him why we had to do it, though. He accepted this, and then we talked about Christmas and if we would get to England in time. It was then that he said he wanted to spend it with me. From that we just talked silly, really, about ways that he could do that. I never dreamt in a million years that he would be shipped out the next day, land in Britain and start to plan how he could be with me. Or that he would bring Marc too.'

After changing once more, this time from a mauve-coloured frock with a ruched top and slightly flared skirt into one that Babs loved – a full-length pale blue chiffon gown of many flowing layers. With this she wore elbow-length gloves, and added a black velvet band to her neck with a single dropped pearl sewn to the centre of it.

All of her clothes and the few items of jewellery that she'd bought had cost her a small fortune, though most were not as elaborate as those she'd bought for today, but were more practical day dresses and formal outfits.

As Babs paraded herself in front of the long mirror, she had never felt more beautiful in her whole life. The style of the frocks suited her hour-glass figure, and this one in particular as it was cut in such a way as to remind her of a fish tail. *Eeh, I look and feel grand.*

Giggling at herself, she did a twirl. Then spoke sternly to her profile: 'You're not to even think in your Blackpool accent if you're to pull this off, Babs, me girl . . . I mean, Catherine.' With this, she had a sudden urge to scream out in her natural voice against all that had happened to put her in this deceitful position, but then she thought of Marc waiting downstairs for her and she smiled. If she told him everything, and he was on her side, she could pull this off.

Looking up at the sky, she said, 'I know that I already have you on my side, Rupert, my darling.'

With this, she thought of how different everything could have been for her if she'd been born into the same class as Rupert. 'This class,' she said out loud as she lifted her hands to the room. 'I would have been acceptable to the earl then, and be protected and with my child.' Sighing, she took a deep breath and went towards the door.

The ballroom was breathtaking. To Babs, it was a wonderland, hung with even bigger chandeliers that glittered with

302

the candles burning inside them. The walls were a series of arches into which had been fitted benches, and the trim to these and the ornate carvings that ran from floor to ceiling were gold. In each corner of the room was a marble column, and occasional tables were marble-topped. The floor was a dark mahogany that shone so deeply that it reflected the lights, giving the room a fairy-tale appearance. A band was assembled on the stage and were playing soft music.

As soon as she entered, Marc came over to her. He still had his dress uniform on, which at first glance was the same as the British one, but Marc's cap, that he carried under his arm, was slightly bigger, and he wore a green tab on his shoulder.

'You look so beautiful, Catherine.'

She smiled up at him.

'May I have the first dance?'

'I hope you have all the dances with me, but I don't know what the etiquette is for that.' Giggling, she whispered, 'I'd only read that word in books when I was a girl, until I came here. It sounds so strange to be saying it now as if it was natural for me to.'

Babs didn't know why, but she felt so relaxed with Marc that she was able to make a few jokes that hinted at the real her.

The evening had been one that Babs would never forget. She'd danced most of the night with Marc, glad that she'd learnt a few basic steps from Pearl, and with the natural rhythm that the gypsy dancing had given her, she managed really well. But today – Boxing Day – was giving her a chance to really be on her own with Marc and talk to him.

Everyone was free to do what they wanted to and they had taken themselves off for a walk. They hadn't gone far when Marc asked, 'Can you tell me now what this is all about, Babs?'

'I can, but you will be shocked. My life hasn't been an easy one. Things have happened to me that should never happen to any child or young girl.'

'I'm here for you, Babs, and whatever it is, I won't judge you.'

As they wandered the lanes outside the estate gates, Babs told him her story. Marc just listened. When she finished, he was quiet for a moment, then he stopped and faced her. '*Puis-je te tenir?*'

Babs nodded, and then went into his open arms. She wanted to shout, *Yes, you can hold me. I want you to for ever and ever.* But she just let her spirit join with his and experienced the happiness of the moment.

When he pulled away from her and looked down into her eyes, he said, 'Your story tears at my heart. I want to kill all those who hurt you. Rupert sounds like a lovely man, and I wish I could have met him. But I will honour him, Babs, by helping you, as I know he would want me to. There has to be a way to be with your child that won't take you away from me for years and years. I'll find a way, I promise.'

Somehow, Babs knew that he would.

And this was sealed when his lips came onto hers, as then her world burst into a flame that lit her whole body, and she knew it would never extinguish. When they parted, he whispered, '*Je t'aime.*'

'*Je t'aime aussi.*'

Once more his lips covered hers in a kiss that sealed the love they had just spoken of.

TWENTY-FOUR

Tilly

The journey had been a long and tiring one for Tilly, Tommy and Eliza, as the train was held up many times due to snowdrifts, but once they left the Midlands behind them, the weather became milder.

But nothing could dampen Tilly's spirits as she thought of how she would soon see Beth, and then would come their visit to Babs.

She still hadn't taken in all that Babs had told them, but was hoping against hope that it all worked out for her and at last she understood all the mystery and why Babs couldn't come home sooner. Now, she felt confident that she wouldn't drop back into her northern ways just by being with them – a real threat to the success of her mission, as she'd never lost her accent from birth and was now retraining herself so this new way of speaking became normal to her. Tilly couldn't wait to see her and to give her the support and encouragement she needed. *If only I had been given such a chance to be near to my girls.*

'That was a big sigh, Tilly, me little lass. The journey's nearly over now.'

Tilly smiled at Tommy and cradled the sleeping Eliza to her and tried to keep her mind off thinking about her worry over Beth's coldness of late.

By the time they reached Margate after two days of travel, they were all very tired, but cheered when they saw Henry standing on the station to greet them.

Eliza ran into his arms. 'Henry! We were so glad when we heard that you had made it home for Christmas!'

'Only just, but it seems like a long time ago now, even though it is only a few weeks. Beth and Benny have kept me busy. But oh, it's good to see you all. Thank you for making this long journey.'

He greeted Tommy next and then Tilly. 'Eeh, lad, is everything all right with Beth?'

'Tilly, it is that you said you wouldn't mention this feeling that you have.'

Henry didn't answer either of them, but turned away and called a porter to help with their trunk.

'By the looks of our luggage, you'll be for thinking we're moving in, Henry.'

'Ha, I wouldn't mind. But, well, Beth is a little . . . Look, let's go and have a cup of tea in the café that's just down the road from here.'

Tilly's heart dropped. She knew that there was something wrong and it seemed she was about to be warned what it might be.

Henry didn't say any more on the subject, but led the way off the station.

Once they were in the little café, with its steamed-up windows, packed with folk wearing heavy coats, they were soon served. The mug of hot tea was welcome to Tilly, though more to warm her hands on than anything, as she didn't know if she could drink it, her stomach was so tied in knots.

Henry looked embarrassed, but spoke in a straight manner. 'Ma, I found a change in Beth from what she was like before I left, and from what her letters had told me. You see, she has this notion that . . . well, that all that has happened to her and Babs may be because of something that you did.'

'What? Why? Eeh, lad, I did nowt more than love them and yearn for them.'

'Is it that we shouldn't have come, Henry?' Tommy took Tilly's hand as he spoke and squeezed it as if trying to reassure her, but nothing could do that. Her mind screamed at her that once more Beth was at odds with her and she couldn't bear it.

'No. It is better that you do. You see, I think that seeing you will bring Beth back to her senses. I don't think she is right in what she thinks. And even if she is, we cannot undo the past, we have to forgive and go forward. For that, you all have to face up to what it is that she has on her mind – her too – and so it is good that you are here.'

'But what is it that she thinks Tilly did?'

Tilly held her breath.

'Well, she asked Peggy why your own people didn't help you, Tilly, so much so that you had to turn to the gypsies, which led to her and Babs being stolen.'

Tilly gasped. 'Oh naw!'

'What is it, Tilly? Tilly, you're shaking.'

'What did Peggy tell her?'

'Nothing, except that what you did you were judged on and the people who knew you would have nothing to do with you. But she has since tried to make Beth see that you were always looked on as an angel, that you helped anyone who needed it. How you nursed your mother-in-law, even though the woman had shunned you for years, and the woman Beth and Babs called Aunt Liz, and a lady called Martha, who had also shunned you, but needed you in the end and you forgave and took care of her. And Florrie when she was sent to the poorhouse, and how once you found out about it you did everything you could to help her to get out and get back on her feet. But Beth is fixated on whatever it was that happened that caused you to go to the gypsies. She is a great believer in people shaping their own lives by the decisions they take and she now thinks the decision you took, Tilly, was what led to her and Babs's downfall.'

Tilly felt panic rising in her. Was she going to be made to tell of the most shameful time in her life, that she hadn't even told Tommy of? Could she face doing that? And if she did, would it help? Would it? She didn't think so. For it was a sordid tale that she'd lived with for such a long time.

She closed her eyes, hoping it would all go away, but instead pictures flashed into her head – of Joe, the man who owned the greengrocery shop and gave her employment, but at a price. Of how she was desperate for money, to keep a roof over the twins' head and to feed them. And how she didn't feel that she had any choice.

Her heart had been split in two on hearing the news that her Arthur had been killed in an accident. She was reeling from shock, feeling desperately alone, and what Joe offered began to feel like a way of getting comfort for her sore and broken heart, but more than that – survival for her children. Now, as images often came to her during the night, and never really gave her peace, she wished a thousand times that she'd taken the path to the poorhouse.

Her body shuddered.

'Mammy? Mammy? It's all right, Mammy. You don't have to tell owt to anyone.' Eliza's voice, soothing, kind, unjudgemental, seeped into Tilly and steadied her. When she opened her eyes, Eliza turned on Henry. 'Whatever Mammy did is her own business, Henry. And whatever it was, or how bad it was, I knaw as she must have been forced into it. And I ain't going to allow Beth or naw one to put Mammy through any more. I'll be telling Beth that an' all. Naw one suffered more than Mammy has, and I'm not going to let her suffer any more. What difference will it make to Beth if she knaws? She either loves Mammy or she doesn't and that's that.'

Henry took Eliza's hand. 'Eliza, you are right, but when you have been through what Beth and Babs have, then you do question the reasons why. You do need answers to enable you to find a way with living with your past.'

'Mammy found a way, and so has Babs. Why can't Beth?'

Henry didn't seem to know what to say to this.

'I'll talk to Beth. I'll tell her everything. I don't knaw how I'm going to do it as it is a part of my life that I am ashamed of, but what I did was done solely to protect my little Beth and Babs. It wasn't a good path, but all I can say is that I had only two choices at the time – take this chance offered to me, or go into the poorhouse, where conditions were so terrible that children died in their hundreds, and it was almost impossible to get out of such a place.'

'No, Tilly. It is that those of us who know and love you don't need you to explain yourself. I am for suspecting that Jasmine and Roman are behind this. Well, Beth chose them once; if she is choosing them again, so be it. I'm for knowing what you have been through, and how you rose up out of that by your own courageous battling for a better life, not only for you, but for Liz. Henry, we will be for booking into a hotel tonight and returning to Blackpool tomorrow. Please be telling Beth that she knows where we are and that we will be waiting with our arms open when it is that she can open her heart and see the right path she should be taking. Me Tilly is not going to be put on trial by her or anyone else. This is an end to it.'

'Naw, Tommy, naw!'

'Yes, Tilly. I am for putting me foot down. You have nothing to atone for. Jasmine and Roman do, and until Beth is for seeing that, I for one don't want to hear from her.'

'Pappy's right, Mammy. Let's go back home.'

Tilly felt the world she'd put back together shatter into splinters once more. Part of her knew that Tommy and Eliza were right, but if she left now, would that mean she would lose Beth? The thought was unbearable to her. She looked pleadingly at Henry.

'Ma, I cannot go against Tommy. I, well, I shouldn't say it, as it feels disloyal to Beth, but I think both he and Eliza are right. You have nothing to atone for. Beth has no right to ask you to do so. You are right, Tommy, it is Jasmine and Roman who are influencing her. They have travelled down here and made

310

contact with Beth. Well, I have had enough. I've done wrong in standing by Beth in this, I'm sorry.'

Though ashamed for it to happen in a public place, Tilly broke down. All her yesterdays had crowded in on her. She had been forced to face things that she had long found a way of living with, now they were coming back to bite her with the bitter truth that they truly could ruin her life. But why? She had long settled herself by telling herself that she had been young, alone in the world, and desperate to keep her children. Joe had offered a way for her to do that and in her weakest hour, she'd taken it. But worse than that, images of Joe lying with blood pouring from his head came to her, and she flinched against the truth of them.

'Tilly, me little lass, no, don't, Tilly.'

'Mammy, Mammy. It's all right, Mammy.'

Henry stood and went around the table to Tilly. Putting his arms around her, he told her, 'Beth loves you, Ma. She loves you so much that she is suffering terribly over this new revelation. She's battling with demons all the time. We need to save her from Jasmine and Roman. Jasmine has some sort of hold over her. If we could break that, then we could help Beth. I need your help, Ma.'

A lady who Tilly thought might be the owner of the café came over. 'Is there anything I can help with, missus? Only you're upsetting me customers. Would you like to go through to me back room where you can have privacy? I don't open it in winter, on account of trade not being good.'

Tilly composed herself. 'Naw, I'll be all right, ta. I'm sorry, I had some bad news. We're leaving now. Pay the bill, Tommy.'

'You have them on me, love. Sadness abounds these days, what with all the death and destruction. I've not been able to do me bit, except give the odd cup of tea when it's needed. I'm sorry for whatever has happened, missus.'

Tilly didn't think to find such kindness down south; she'd always heard that they were a toffee-nosed lot. Henry went to protest, but Tilly stopped him. Wiping her face with the hanky Tommy had given her, she thanked the lady. 'Ta, lass. A little kindness goes a long way so I reckon you've done more than your bit. I'm sorry about causing a scene in your café.'

The woman smiled and nodded her head.

Once outside, the cold didn't penetrate Tilly, but she could see that Eliza was shivering.

Henry took charge. 'I'll get my car and take you to the hotel. There's a number of them along the promenade, and some remain open during the winter months. We can easily find one as they display their vacancy signs in the window.'

Once they arrived at the Belmont Hotel and they had checked in, Henry told them, 'I'll talk to Beth. Thinking she may lose you might open her eyes to what she is asking of you. I hope so. I hate to see her suffering as she is, but I know that it is only herself who can make that better. She needs to do what she should have done a long time ago. Bring Jasmine and Roman to justice. But she is afraid. She is steeped in their culture and believes that they can harm us – well, Jasmine; not Roman so much.' Henry was quiet for a brief moment. Expressions went across his face that Tilly couldn't fathom, then he said, 'I think I might try one more way of ending this. I'll try speaking to Roman. You get some rest now. And, Ma, Tommy, I'm so very sorry.' With this, Henry held his arms out to Eliza. Eliza went to him and Tilly saw that thankfully, the deep bond they had formed in the short time that Henry had been with them wasn't damaged.

Eliza looked up at Henry and told him, 'Eeh, Henry, I missed you, and prayed for you to be kept safe every day – well, that's when I had time. Ma Perkins ... well, she ran me off me feet, but by, I wish as she could now.'

Henry held her to him. 'I know. There're often people in our lives who are thorns in our side, but they also get under our skin and we love them. I was sorry to hear that Ma Perkins was taken by the flu. It's a terrible scourge that is killing so many. I live in fear of Beth or Benny contracting it.'

This zinged through Tilly. It was what she feared the most, one of hers being taken by this flu pandemic. Suddenly, her strength came back into her. There were a lot worse things done than what she'd done, and a lot worse happening in the world. And yes, she'd atoned for her sins. Years and years of not knowing where her beloved children were, the period she spent in the asylum and the terrible loss of Ivan were punishment enough. She wasn't going to suffer anymore. Not by the whims of one of them, and definitely not by the evil workings of Jasmine.

'Henry, take me to Beth. Tommy, Eliza, stay here, I will come back. I am going to stop this once and for all. I want you to take me to Beth, and then both of us to Jasmine. It ends here. One way or the other, it ends here!'

Whether it was how she came across, Tilly didn't know, but all agreed with her.

Her nerves shook her as Henry drove through the surprisingly quiet streets of Margate. Wanting to say anything to break the silence, she said, 'It's not as busy as Blackpool, is it?'

'No. Blackpool is unique. Here there is a definite season for holidaymakers, and we get very few visitors through autumn till Easter . . . Ma, you will go carefully, won't you?'

'Naw, lad. I'm going to go all out to save me Beth. I'm sorry, but me blood's boiling. I've been made to feel shame this morning, and not deserved. I've paid for owt that I did. This thing will only fester if it's not sorted. I'm here now, and I'm going to sort it.'

Henry sighed. She could feel how afraid he was, but she didn't care. She was on a mission. And she hoped to get the outcome she wanted. If not, she would find a way of living with it.

Beth greeted Tilly with a surprised look. 'Where's Tommy and Eliza? I thought . . .'

'They—'

Tilly forestalled Henry and ignored Beth's open arms. 'I want no cuddles from you, lass. I want an honest love that doesn't blackmail me into doing what you want me to do. That accepts me as I am, faults an' all. Not holds me to account for things in me past, or blames me for what was out of me control. You've done that to Babs, because she chose to look for me and you didn't. Aye, she were reckless, but she followed her heart. It wasn't her best decision, I'll give you that, but shows me the love that she had for me was greater than her reasoning. And that's all I've ever done – carried so much love for you, me little girls, that I threw reason to the wind and took wrong paths, but all with one aim – to save you both. To stop you having to live in the poorhouse where they take children from their parents.' Now she'd started, she couldn't stop. 'I don't know what lies that Jasmine told you, but I'm going to find out. And you're coming with me an' all. You owe me that much. I've been through more hell since you came back into me life than I did in all the years I were longing for you. At least then I thought that you were still mine. And looked towards the day you were old enough to come and find me. But you didn't, did you? You got free by using the fact that Jasmine had lost Babs and didn't want to lose you. But when you got your freedom, did you come and find me? No. You could have done. Yes, nurses were needed, but you could have tried to find me first.'

With this last sentence, Tilly broke.

'Ma, Ma, oh, Ma. I'm sorry, I'm sorry.'

'What's to do? Eeh, Tilly, lass. I dreaded this happening. It wasn't my fault, Tilly, I tried and tried. I'm sorry. Eeh, Tilly.'

Where Peggy had come from Tilly didn't know. She'd noticed that she wasn't around to greet her, but hadn't thought further than that. Now she knew that she'd gone too far. Said things she hadn't meant to. Things she hadn't even thought, until the tirade broke loose from her. Her body slumped onto the nearest chair, that stood in the large hall just inside the door. 'Oh, me Beth, I've lost you. How can you forgive what I just said?'

'Ma, no, no.' Between sobs, Beth told her that it was her that should beg forgiveness. 'Of you and of Babs, Ma ... Oh, Henry, what have I done? Help me.'

Henry, who had stood as if in a stupor, now moved to gather Beth into his arms. 'Nothing, my darling. You dealt with things how you saw them. How they have been fed to you from a very young age. You can undo everything. But,

Beth, you must start by getting Jasmine and Roman out of your life.'

Beth's sobs didn't confirm whether she would do this or not.

'That's got to happen, or me and you are finished, Beth! Aye, I'm sorry for all I said, but that don't mean as I can go on like this. I can't. I can't.'

'Naw, don't say that, Tilly, lass. I knaw you don't mean it.'

'Oh, Peggy, I do. Me heart has been hardened with the shock of hearing that I were invited down here under false pretences. That I was going to be put on trial. Those who knew me when everything bad happened to me have long forgiven me for what mistakes I made, but how can I fight years of lies that have been fed to Beth? I can't. I can't.'

'I'll fight them too, Ma, I will.'

'Then start by coming with me to see Jasmine now, Beth. This has to end, lass. I don't feel that I can claim you as me daughter until it does, and I need to see it end. See it with me own eyes.'

'Ma, I can't let that happen. Beth is distraught and so are you. Let me fetch Tommy and Eliza and let's all have the dinner together that Beth and I had planned.'

'Naw. I'm sorry, Henry, but I don't want to be here. Not with a daughter who holds accusations in her heart. I tell you, Beth, what you've been through in losing your ability to walk is nowt! Nowt! Not when you compare it to what me and Babs have been through. Give me a wheelchair, a kind nurse, a loving husband who can provide for me and the advantages you had to make your way in life and I'd take it any day rather than the load that I've had to bear.'

'Oh, Ma, how can I make it up to you? Help me, Ma. Help me!'

'Not until you've helped me.' Tilly couldn't believe how her heart had hardened against her darling Beth. But something compelled her to make this stand. 'If you can come with me and finish this once and for all, the love I have for you will knaw naw bounds, lass. But if not, then a piece of me will die. The piece that holds you dear to me heart.'

'I'll do it. Henry, help me to do it. I have to.'

As Henry rushed to get Beth's coat, not heeding Peggy saying, 'Naw, this ain't right. Stop this, Tilly,' Tilly couldn't help thinking that Henry was well and truly wrapped around Beth's little finger. *Eeh, why am I thinking like this? This is me Beth. Me timid one. Me kind and caring one.* But as she thought this, she knew she was wrong. Babs had always been the outspoken one of the twins, self-assured and knowing her direction. Never in a million years did she think it would be Beth who would turn out to be the strongest, and the least feeling.

As she sat in the back of the car, Tilly's heart was thumping a mountain of emotions around her body. Regret – what had possessed her? Fear – how was this going to turn out? And pain – how was she ever to get Beth back after this?

Jasmine came running out of her caravan with her arms in the air. 'Me Beth, and Henry. It is good that you visit me. How I have waited for this ... Oh ... I ... Roman! Roman, you should come ... Roman!'

Tilly got out of the car. 'Roman nor anyone else is going to help you today, lass. Your day of reckoning has come, you lying, thieving, kidnapping bitch!'

317

From the open window of the car Beth called, 'No, Ma. Not like this.'

'Oh, yes, Beth. I'm going to have me say. I've waited for this day for a long time.'

'What is this? What is it that you are here for, Tilly?'

Roman was now standing by Jasmine's side.

'I'm here to make you confirm the truth to Beth. You knaw as everything didn't happen how you say it did. Tell her how Phileas and Jonas robbed me time and time again. Tell her how Phileas ran into me with his horse and ripped me shoulder out of its joint, leaving me unable to make me baskets. Tell her how Lilly Lee encouraged me to go to the camp for help, then stood by as I was given a lethal drink of almost pure alcohol. Tell her how I passed out and how Phileas raped me, and how you took advantage of all of this and snatched me babbies. I never knew owt about it till three weeks later when I came to in the hospital. By then you were long gone.'

A painful sound coming from Beth had Jasmine crying out, 'No, it wasn't like that, me Beth, she lies! She's made all of this up.'

'No, Jasmine.' This came from a distraught and tearful Beth. 'I remember! Oh, Ma! I remember. I've always remembered seeing you on the floor and in so much pain. I've seen you in my mind, dancing a lovely dance with one of the gypsy men and then collapsing on the floor. I remember you, Jasmine, taking us to your wagon, and assuring us that Ma would be all right by morning, and then me and Babs waking in the night to find the wagon was moving. You stole us, Jasmine! Ma would never have given us up. Oh, Ma . . . whatever the reason that you only had the gypsies to turn to, you didn't deserve what happened.'

'I curse you all!'

Tilly leapt forward and slapped Jasmine so hard across the face that she reeled backwards. 'Don't you start with your curses, you evil woman.'

Roman stepped forward. His fist in the air. Tilly lifted her foot. She felt it squelch into his crotch, saw him go down like a baby, squealing like the pig that he was. Tilly put her head back and laughed as the exhilaration of doing something she'd dreamt of doing filled her with euphoria.

Henry was by her side in a flash. 'Ma, no more. This ends it. Go and get in the car with Beth, she needs you.'

Tilly realised then how Beth was sobbing her heart out. And for the first time since Henry had dropped the bomb-shell, she felt the love she had for Beth overwhelm her. As she went to get into the car, she heard Henry telling Jasmine and Roman that he was going to fetch the police.

Jasmine turned and ran for a box on the side of the wagon that had its lid wide open. In a movement that was so swift Tilly hardly realised what was happening, Jasmine pulled out a rifle. Pointing it at Henry, she screamed at him to leave.

Henry tried to reason with her. 'Put that down, Jasmine. Don't make this worse than it already is. Please, for everyone's sake. You've done wrong. And now it is time to face the consequences.'

With the loud click of Jasmine cocking the gun, Beth's scream pierced the air.

In what seemed like slow motion, Henry lunged at Jasmine. The crack of the gun resounded around them, birds screeched their protest, and then there was a silence that held the suspension of time.

Tilly looked in horror at the blood spurting from Roman's neck as he fell to the floor. Henry went on his knees and tried to stem the flow. 'Ma, come and help me! Jasmine, get a towel, hurry!'

But Tilly couldn't see Jasmine. As she stepped back out of the car, she shouted to Jasmine to do as Henry says, but the only answer was a second loud crack as the gun was fired once more.

TWENTY-FIVE

Beth

Beth clung on to Henry as the policeman scribbled in his notebook. Finding out that she was unable to get out of the car, the constable had allowed Henry to sit in with her to help to calm her while he asked questions. Beth didn't think her body would ever stop shaking.

Ma stood outside the car leaning on the side, her eyes staring. She seemed to have closed down.

It was the farmer whose land Jasmine and Roman had been camping on who had fetched the policeman. He'd been riding his horse down the lane when he'd heard the shots, and thought that he'd catch Roman poaching again.

He'd told them that he would go to his home and await the constable, who did a regular rural round once a week and today just happened to be the day for his visit.

Henry had done all he could, but both Jasmine, who had shot herself in the head, and Roman were dead by the time the police arrived.

The bodies still lay on the ground. Beth couldn't look at

them. That it should all end like this just wouldn't sink in with her. Part of her mourned their loss, but a big part of her felt released as in her heart she'd known that they would always have had a hold on her.

'Well, it seems to me that it all happened how you said, Doctor, a tragic accident and a suicide. They got off light, if you ask me. We should have acted when your wife reported this a few weeks ago, but we had to wait till we had gathered evidence and that hadn't arrived from the police up north. But I can assure you, we were looking into it, and had asked the farmer to let us know of any movement of the gypsies. Anyway, I think you should get your young wife and your mother-in-law home out of this cold now. They've both had a shock. Everything will be seen to here.'

'Henry, there's money in a trunk under the bed at the back of the wagon. Do you think we ought to take it to the other gypsies so they can arrange a proper funeral? Otherwise they might just get a pauper's funeral.' Beth couldn't believe how calmly she said this, or how no sadness was provoked by saying it.

'What do you think, Constable?'

'I shouldn't worry, I'll have to inform their clan and they will see to everything. I know where they're all camped. These two always camped away from the rest of the clan when they came here.'

Ma looked up then. 'Beth, is it the same clan that I knew?'

'No, Ma. Jasmine told us that they went to Ireland; these are Romanies and related to Jasmine.'

Ma nodded, but didn't say any more. But she did show signs that, at last, she was feeling something as she pulled her coat around her, whereas before she'd been like a statue. Henry had spoken to Ma to try to reassure her. He'd told Beth that she just wanted to be alone with her thoughts and he'd advised that it was best to leave her until she was ready.

'I would be grateful if you could see to their effects getting to their clan, Constable,' Henry said, and then asked. 'And, well, if you can possibly keep them from knowing we were involved . . . I fear they may take reprisals; it is the gypsy way.'

'They won't know. I'll say it is a mystery why the wife killed her husband and then herself.'

'Thank you. Only I really think that for my wife and her mother, this should be the end of an ordeal that has stretched for most of my wife's life. Well, here's my card just in case you need us further, but I will get off now. Thank you again.'

'I don't think you will hear further. I can't see that anyone will be interested in finding out any more details after I file my report. They were gypsies, and their demise means we have two less to worry about.'

Though Beth knew of this attitude, she was shocked to hear it voiced, and by a custodian of the law. Didn't the gypsies deserve his protection too? But then, this attitude wasn't new to her. It was something she'd lived with all her life.

Henry knew her feelings and squeezed her hand. Once they were driving along, all three sitting on the bench seat in the front of the car, he said, 'Forgive me for not saying anything to the policeman about his remark, darling. I know how you feel about it all, but I didn't see any point. Just admonishing one man isn't going to change the world, and he has taken a huge weight off our shoulders.'

Beth just patted his hand. Her heart was in turmoil.

'Ma? Are you all right?'

'I am, me little Beth. I just can't take it all in and feel responsible. I keep thinking that if I hadn't insisted on going to their camp, they would both still be alive.'

It was Henry who answered. 'You can't blame yourself, Ma. You did the right thing. All you wanted to do was to sort out the mess we were all in once and for all. That has happened in a way that is more final than you could ever have thought. And that was down to Jasmine, not you. She was going to kill me. I saw it in her eyes, in a look I will never forget. I had to lunge at her.'

Beth gasped.

'Yes, Beth, never forget that. Whenever you feel that you are sorry, or miss them, remember that Jasmine, who you set so much store by, was going to kill your husband. And killing herself was her own choice. I know I shouldn't say it, but I for one feel a sense of being free from a great burden.'

This shocked Beth. Up until now she hadn't thought that Jasmine would have killed Henry. She'd thought she meant to frighten them all away but that it had all gone horribly wrong. A feeling of hate welled up in her. She'd felt this before for Jasmine, but always it was tempered by her feeling sorry for them. Now she felt only hate. 'How will you all forgive me? I have done a terrible thing.'

'I have nothing to forgive, darling, and I don't think that your mother has either. You were a victim as much as anyone was. Jasmine was a powerful woman, who could cast a spell on anyone.'

'But this thing that I got into my head that led to all of this happening . . . I'm sorry, so sorry.'

When her ma put her arm around her and asked that they start again, putting all this behind them, Beth knew that she had to speak up if the air was ever going to be truly cleared between them. 'Ma, can we? With all that was said? I'm not what Babs thinks I am, and it hurts that you have come to think like that too.'

'Beth . . . I . . . well, I'm sorry.'

'No, I must speak, Ma. I want you to know that I'm not manipulative. I know that it looks like that and that it also looks as though I use situations to my own advantage, but I didn't – I don't. I have been weak, I know that . . . well, unsure of myself. When Babs left me to try to find you, and I didn't have her to lean on anymore, I did grow in confidence. I had to. But I was more alone in the world than I had ever been. The illness that I went through at that time gave me a direction. I had a wonderful nurse . . .' As she continued to tell her ma how everything had happened, Beth found a new determination to change how she was perceived. If she didn't, then her ma and her sister would always be wary of her, and she didn't want that, nor did she deserve it. 'You are wrong, both of you. I didn't use Jasmine's sorrow at losing Babs to get what I wanted. I had to fight them both all of the way.' She told then of how Jasmine set her up on the gypsy grabbing night – a time when the male gypsies take a girl, even against their will, and are violent if they have to be, to get the kiss that seals the girl as his future wife.

'Oh, Beth, naw. Eeh, that's wicked, I knaw what it is like. It happened to me.'

'Really? Oh, Ma, we know so little about each other.'

'We'll change that, me little Beth.'

'We will, but right now I have to carry on explaining. I didn't tell you before as I had this stupid, misguided notion that I couldn't put Jasmine in a bad light. But she did that to stop me leaving to become a nurse, so you see, far from manipulating her into doing what I wanted to do, I had to struggle to be allowed to leave and promise that I would be back. Roman helped in this. Roman was different to Jasmine, but he too was under her spell. He'd been appalled at her and very angry for putting me in that situation with the grabbing, and it was him wanting to make up to me that led them to at last let me be schooled. And I did see me doing that as a way of getting to find you, but, well, maybe I have a better decision-making process than Babs. Yes, I could have left my training and set off for Blackpool, but what if you weren't there any longer? If I was trained as a nurse, I could come back and find work as I had a skill. But then war broke out, and I wanted to do my bit, so put off coming to Blackpool – as Babs must have done, as she could have once she was trained, just as much as me. But then, she may have had circumstances that stopped her. But for me, my life changed and my desire to find you became something I thought I could never achieve.'

Henry spoke for the first time then. 'I can vouch for that, Ma. As soon as we knew our love, Beth told me of her life, and her dream to find you. I wish you could have seen her happiness when I told her we would honeymoon in Blackpool and look for you together. It was a moment I will never forget.'

'Oh, Beth, Beth, I had it so wrong, and so has Babs. She loves you, but couldn't forgive you for keeping in touch with Jasmine and Roman and, not only that, but expressing your love for them.'

326

'I don't know if I'll ever forgive myself, Ma. I can't explain more than I have tried to. I can only ask you not to put an old head on the shoulders of a child. Babs and I were so young when we were taken. A child needs love and care, and we did get that. That should make you happy, not angry that we returned that love, because although we did, we never forgot you. Most very young children would have done. We talked about you all the time and longed to be with you. How much worse would it have been if you had to find out that we were cruelly treated?'

'I feel so ashamed. Sorry isn't enough. I took on what Babs believed of you and it did seem that was how it was.'

'No, Ma, it's all right. All that has to stop – apologies, guilty feelings, recriminations, blame. We have to forgive and forget, and we have to take responsibility too. I do. I am not going to feel guilty, but I do know that most of what has happened is down to me not letting go of Jasmine and Roman. But that is the person you gave birth to, Ma. A little weak, needing guidance and loving those who give it to her.'

Henry once more let go of the wheel and squeezed her hand. 'A lovely person, Ma. A daughter you can be proud of. I am. And I admire how she stuck with Jasmine and Roman, and know that though she is saying all of this, underneath she is suffering because of what just happened. All you wanted, darling, was for Jasmine and Roman to accept they had done wrong and that they now had a chance to put that right by going away and living their life in freedom.'

Beth felt her tears well up. 'It was. I couldn't bear to think of them caged in a prison. I knew they should be punished, but I thought their punishment was to have lost me and Babs.

If they had accepted that and gone away, they wouldn't have ended up how they have.'

'Don't cry, Beth. Think of them as free at last, because now they can't feel the pain of being childless, or of losing you and Babs. And think of yourself as being free, because Jasmine would never have given up, and I was afraid of what she would do in the end.'

Henry was right, Jasmine would never have set her free. 'I know, and I can't explain how I feel. I have mixed emotions, mostly of hate for Jasmine and Roman, but sorrow too.'

'You wouldn't be me daughter if you didn't feel sad at them having gone. In a way, in Jasmine's last act, she showed that she was letting you go. I knaw that she must have realised that Roman would die, and maybe she couldn't live without him, but I think her thoughts, too, were that she had to let go now. Let it all finish. The only way she could do that was to take her own life.'

Beth leant her head on her ma's shoulder. 'I love you, Ma. So much that my pain has been so deep that it was unbearable, but now I do feel we can begin again.'

Ma just held her tightly to her. It was enough for Beth as Ma's love encased her, as that was all she'd ever wanted. 'I'll make everything right with Babs, I promise. She'll be better for knowing what you have told me. She loves you very much and misses you. And ... oh, I've good news about her – you will never guess in a million years.'

When they reached the hotel, Tommy came out of the foyer. He must have been waiting and watching for them to return. He ran towards the car as fast as his hobble would let him. As Beth watched him, she felt a surge of love and respect

328

for him. Hadn't he lost so much and yet risen above it? He was an example to them all.

And as she watched him cuddle Ma, she so wanted to be able to get out of the car and join them, but then the thought came to her that Tommy may be thinking of her as Ma did and Babs still does. This hurt her deeply.

'Shall I help you out, darling? Or see what is happening before I do?'

'See what's happening first. I ... Oh, Henry, that they should all think that of me.'

'I know, my darling. I felt so terrible as you were explaining. I wanted to shout at Ma that I was disgusted with her and Babs, but that wouldn't have helped. You coped so well, my darling, I am proud of you. Let's hope that as your ma put it, this is the end of it all. And, darling, no one else will say this, but I am very sorry about what happened. I am relieved they are out of your life as I was genuinely afraid for you, but I didn't want it to happen like this.'

'Hold me, Henry.' When he took her in his arms, Beth knew she could cope with anything as long as she had him by her side.

Tommy came to the car, opened it and slipped in beside Beth. She could see the love he had for her in his expression, and went willingly into the cradle of the arm he extended to her. 'It is that you have been through a lot, me Beth, but all will sort out now. I'm sorry to the heart of me that it ended this way, for I know you must be hurting.'

'Thanks, Tommy. I am, but I'm not, if you can understand that. But nothing can spoil the happiness I feel that you are all forgiving of me. Where's Eliza?'

'She's away to her bed for an hour or two. She's exhausted and sad, as she thinks our trip is all spoiled when she was so looking forward to seeing you, but we'll let her sleep and have a rest ourselves. Me little Tilly looks all in. Then if you can fetch us in a couple of hours, Henry, we'll have a proper reunion, so we will.'

Beth put her other arm around Tommy's waist. 'I do love you, Tommy. Thank you for being so understanding.'

Tommy smiled down at her. 'Well, me joy is filling me. I need to help me Tilly now so we will see you later, lass.'

As they drove away and Beth looked back, she saw Tommy with his arm around her ma, and she knew that she could rest easy. Tommy would help Ma to come to terms with everything and when they were all together later it would be a happy time. She couldn't wait to hear the news about Babs. *Everything will come right for you and me, Babs, I just know it.*

TWENTY-SIX

Babs

Babs felt jittery. Ma, Tommy and Eliza were on their way and she didn't know what their reaction would be to what she was going to tell them. *Oh, why didn't I keep them up to date when I wrote to them?*

Somehow it had seemed to her that she needed to keep Marc secret for a little while. The love they shared was still a wonder to her. And she didn't know if it might be too much of a shock for her ma and Tommy. She hoped they would understand. But would they ever understand that she would have to go to live in Canada? Or accept the plan that she and Marc were still talking about: to snatch little Art and take him with them?

She sat on the platform, praying that these couple of days would go well. There was so much to talk about that it worried her. Pearl had made all the arrangements, telling her parents that she and Catherine wanted to have a couple of days shopping in Brighton. The Bedford Hotel where she had booked them all into was a grand place where famous people came to stay, not at all somewhere she felt comfortable, and neither would her family.

Pearl had thought this nonsense. 'They will have a lovely time here. I'll look after you all, I promise.' And with saying this had promptly asked for a cab to take Babs to the station and kissed her goodbye. *I have to get over this silly shyness that has taken me with my new guise, and assert myself with Pearl.* But she just couldn't think of upsetting Pearl, who'd done so much for her and was about to do even more.

The announcement of the arrival of the train filled Babs with mixed emotions. She so longed to see everyone; it had been a long time — almost two years — since they were last together. Yet she feared that her resolve would be weakened if Ma was distraught at what she had to tell her.

All of her fears disappeared into a fusion of cuddles and kisses, tears and the wonderful love of the greeting they gave to each other.

'Babs! Oh, me wee Babs, you look lovely. That haircut suits you. Eeh, I love you, and have missed you so much.'

'Eeh, Ma, it's good to see you. I've missed you too. And you, Eliza, me lovely little sister . . . Oops! Ha, I'm not with you all of two seconds and I become me old self.'

'It is that it is lovely to hear, Babs, but we understand as you have to be this other person, so you can be her when around us — you'll not be any different in our eyes.'

'Oh, Tommy, thank you . . . There, I did it! I didn't say ta.'

Tommy stood back from hugging her and put his head back and laughed out loud. They all joined in. Eliza took the opportunity to get closer to Babs. 'I love you, Babs. I've so needed you.'

'Ah, poor Eliza. Your world has been turned upside down, but Ma says that you have plans, so you'll have to tell me all about them. And I have plans I need to tell you all about, so let's get a cab and get to the hotel, shall we?'

When they reached the Bedford, Ma's jaw dropped as she looked out of the cab window. 'Eeh, we're not stopping there, are we, lass?'

'Yes, you are, and you are the honoured guests of Pearl Hartshore, my very best friend. Don't worry, Ma, everything will be fine. Oh, here's Pearl now. You'll love her, Ma.'

Pearl came down the steps with her arms open. 'Mrs O'Flynn. I'm so pleased to meet you.'

'Aye, and me you an' all, lass. You've been a grand help to me Babs and I'm grateful to you.'

'Oh, Mrs Flynn, it's so nice to hear you talk. I really miss hearing Babs speaking like you! I love your accent.'

Ma beamed and Babs could see that she was beginning to feel at ease.

'And this is Tommy, my step-father.'

'Pleased to meet you, Tommy. You're from beautiful Ireland. I have visited and loved it. I'm sorry about what happened. My uncle is a landowner, and I'm always telling him off about how things are.'

Tommy smiled and shook Pearl's hand. Babs felt this was a bit awkward and though in the long hours she and Pearl had spent together with no other entertainment but to chat to each other she'd told her all about Tommy and the rest of her family, she should have warned Pearl not to say anything about Ireland.

The moment passed. 'And this is my lovely sister, Eliza.'

Pearl put her arms out. 'And I heard that you give the loveliest of hugs, though I must say, I didn't realise that you were a young woman. Babs talks about you as if you are a child!'

Eliza went into Pearl's open arms. 'Aye, well, I've grown some since Babs left. But you know, being the youngest, I reckon as I'll always be looked on as a child by them all.'

'I know what you mean, I have exactly the same from my lot. Well, me and you can be buddies against them all.'

Eliza giggled and went with Pearl, their arms around each other. For Babs, it was a moment of revelation and she looked at Eliza with fresh eyes. Yes, she had grown into a young woman. She would be eighteen this year and it was time that everyone did start to treat her as such, but oh, she would miss the impish Eliza who she'd left behind when she'd gone to France.

'Well, Babs, it is that you have something to tell us? Now, don't be beating around the bush, your ma needs straight talking. She's been through a lot and she's worried that you have more to put on her shoulders.'

'Why, what's happened, Ma?'

They were in the suite booked for Tommy and Ma, with an adjoining bedroom for Eliza. Eliza had gone for a walk with Pearl and Babs knew Pearl would spoil her. Take her to tea and maybe buy her a couple of presents. Pearl had really taken to Eliza, and a few treats is just what her lovely sister deserved, but Babs just wished that it was her doing the treating. She turned her body to face her ma, who was sat next to her on the sofa, with Tommy sitting in the armchair opposite.

As she listened to ma, Babs couldn't believe what she was hearing. Jasmine and Roman, dead! Pictures of them came to her, so alive, so much in love. How did it come to end in this tragic way? But as more of the story unfolded, she was glad. Beth would never have been free of them. And they could never be as they once were together while Beth was under their influence.

'So, how is Beth? Her letter to me was very strange.' Babs didn't want to say that Beth had begun to question Ma. She'd only had the one letter from Beth since she'd been here and it had upset her. Getting letters from her family had been made possible by another plan devised by Pearl. They were sent in an envelope addressed to Pearl, so that her father, who was the first one to look through all the mail and distribute it to each of them, wouldn't become suspicious of Babs receiving letters from England. Also, it meant that her family hadn't had to address her as Catherine when they wrote to her. 'You should have gone into the secret service,' she'd told Pearl, and they had laughed together at how easy it was to pull off their deception.

As she listened to her ma, Babs began to feel great joy. 'So, I was wrong? Oh, Ma, I'm so pleased. I didn't want Beth to be the person that I thought she was. If only she had explained. All this protecting two people who hurt our family so much has caused a rift between us.'

'Well, lass, she's sorry now, and so am I. But we can do nowt about what has passed, we can only go forward. But I've gone on long enough. Tell me all about you, me Babs.'

'Before I do, I need to hear about Benny. I know you have avoided speaking of him, and I love you for it, but I do miss him so much. My only memory is of him as a small baby, but he engraved himself on my heart. I want to hear about him. I didn't before, it hurt so much, but now I do.'

'Eeh, Babs, he's grand. He's like a little man. Henry is besotted with him, and Beth dotes on him. She had a picture taken of him. Would you like to see it?'

'I would, Ma, oh, I would. And how's Peggy? And Henry?'

As she searched in her bag, Ma brought her up to date with how everyone was.

'It's good to hear. But poor Peggy, hating it down there and yet not wanting to leave Beth. That must be so difficult for her.'

'It is, but she wouldn't have it any different. Oh, and I forgot, I have this letter from Cliff for you an' all. You knaw, I thought he was the one for you, Babs.'

'No, I love him as a friend, as he does me. I would so love to see him. I had to laugh when you told me in one of your letters about him doing the cooking. But oh, Ma. I was so upset to read of how the flu devastated you all. Thank God you survived and it didn't reach the farm ... My goodness, Benny! He's beautiful, Ma.' A lump came into Babs's throat, but she swallowed it down. *So, this is what you will look like, my lovely Art. A little person. I wonder if you still look like your da, just as Benny looks so like his.* Her thoughts went to Rupert. The time was on her to tell about her second love and though she was at peace with Rupert locked in a corner of her heart, she couldn't help wondering what Ma and Tommy would think.

'He's a lovely boy. So friendly and loving. But soon you will be with Art, me lovely Babs, and I knaw as you'll find him to be the same. Has everything been finalised yet?'

'No, but there is a plan. Elaine – that's Pearl's sister – is going to let me work alongside her nanny to learn the ropes. All of Pearl's family think it is a wonderful idea for me – Catherine – to take up that profession, and are trying to steer me towards becoming a governess as they want me to stay on to teach their little ones French. But I have told them that I have my heart set on being a nanny and Pearl's mother has promised me that when I feel ready, she will ask around her friends to help find me a position. Pearl is scouring a magazine that the family get in the hope of coming across an advert for a nanny for Art. If she does, then she will ask her father, who knows the earl, to recommend me.'

'Well, that sounds so hopeful, lass. I'll pray that it works.'

'Thank you, Ma. I'll come up to see you as often as I can and you can visit too. I write to Rupert's old nanny now – she's from the north. She will do anything to help me, and knows the situation. And, more importantly, Art's nurse is keeping me informed. We've become good friends in our letters to each other. I can't thank Cliff enough for making that connection for me. I know so much about my Art that I wouldn't have had a chance of knowing. And I'm bound to hear from her of when she will hand over to a nanny to take care of him.'

'By, lass, I can't see this failing. And I'm so excited for you.'

'I hope not. I'm doing all that I can and can think of nothing else I can do to make it all happen. Anyway, is there any more news from home, other than what you have written to me about? It's really good news that Molly's Brian is home. That must be such a help to Vera, with her and Mary still grieving for their ma, but Mary's news is exciting too, and

Alec sounds lovely. There's so much hope for the future for us all. It's wonderful.'

'He is, and Mary, though still very upset at losing her ma, is a different person. So, what's your other news, lass, as nowt you've said so far gives me the impression that we know it all yet?'

'Well, there is more, Ma.' Telling about Marc and being in love was the easy part now, but about her plan . . . well, she had held back a bit on that.

'Eeh, me little lass, that's wonderful news.'

'Aye, so it is, Babs. To see you happy is all we are for asking. But how is it that this Marceau – Marc – will fit into your plans to be a nanny to Art? Isn't it that nannies have to be unmarried?'

Babs drew in her breath. 'Yes, it is, Tommy. Look, there's no easy way to tell you this. It breaks my heart to think of it coming about, and yet warms my heart too, as it means that I have a chance of having my Art back. Really back and to be with Marc as his wife. But all must be kept a secret and when the time comes you are to deny ever knowing where I am.'

'Babs? I don't understand.'

'When I tell you, Ma, try to have in your mind the lengths you would have gone to to have me and Beth with you – maybe even the lengths you were forced into to try to keep us – and open your heart to this being my only motive of even thinking of carrying out Marc's plan.'

She saw Ma's worried expression, but carried on, telling her of what Marc had proposed. To Ma's gasp of pain, she assured her, 'It won't be for a couple of years, Ma. Marc has to go home as a soldier, with the rest of his regiment, to be demobbed. Though it seems now that they are thinking of taking all the stranded Allies home in order of priority. Being an officer, Marc can more or less choose when to go once the arrangements are in place. But he plans to come back and that is when we will carry out our plan.'

'Oh God, Babs. Eeh, lass, it's so risky. You could end up having to spend years in prison if you are caught. Not that I'm saying don't do it, lass, and aye, it is sommat I would have done and that I understand. But wouldn't just being with Art be enough?'

'It would, Ma, and I suppose I can't expect to have me cake and eat it. But I want to. I want to be with Art and Marc and live like a proper family.'

'I'm for understanding that, and your ma is too. It will take us a while to get used to the idea, but I for one are for you, Babs. And it will be as you must go abroad or you will be caught and then your fate would be one that I'm not for wanting to think about.'

'If I get the position of his nanny, I will have every opportunity to pull off the plan; I can't see anything going wrong with it, Tommy. But I don't want anyone else to know, not Beth and Henry, or Eliza, or anyone.' They both looked doubtful at this. 'I want you to promise me that, please. I will tell them that Marc is American, so that when it happens they think that is where I have gone – no one would even try to find me there. But most of Canada is British and the earl may have influential friends there. Even in the French quarter, as Marc told me that a lot of the monied folk came to England to go to university. Then there is the ambassador, who is bound to know the earl. So you see, it is far better that very few people know the truth. Once everything calms down and the family give up looking, they can be told then and hopefully come to visit me. Otherwise there is a chance that they will slip up if put under pressure while being questioned.'

'By, lass, it all sounds so frightening. But I think you're right. We'll keep this between us. And I'll pray that another way presents itself to you and Marc. One that won't take you away from us, lass.'

'I don't think there will be, Ma. If we tried the legal route, then I would have to expose my deceit, presuming I do get the job as Art's nanny, and that would go against me, besides all that is known of me already. And we have to face it: all the bigwigs who sit in judgement will be friends of, or influenced by, the earl. I think this is my only way. And, Ma, don't think of me as gone forever. You and Tommy can come to visit us and stay for a long time, once you are both retired. Marc tells me that Canada is beautiful, and though it takes a long time by sea, it is something you can undertake.'

'It is that we will, lass. We want to travel when we retire. We've already spoken of it, and your ma's really keen. So, if it is that this all happens, we'll be over there like a shot, so we will.'

Before Babs realised it, they were in a huddle. She saw a tear in the corner of her ma's eye, but she ignored it. Many tears would be shed by the time her dream was realised and many after it too, but Babs couldn't think about this or about how she would feel being so many miles away from home once more. She just knew that having Art with her and being Marc's wife was all she dreamt of.

★　　★　　★

The next day, Babs had a chance to be alone with Eliza. 'Well, lass, how have you been?'

'Eeh, Babs, are you allowed to call me "lass"? You knaw, I can't get used to how you speak now, you seem more like Beth than Babs.'

'Well, I suppose I must. We are identical, and now that we speak the same, it will get confusing.'

'Not with your hair cut like that, it won't. I do love it, Babs. Eeh, I'd love mine done like that. It's all the fashion.'

'It is. Why don't you? I'll treat you. There's a salon in the hotel.'

'I'll see what Mammy says.'

'No, if you want it, then just do it, Eliza. You can make your own mind up and choose to look how you want to, Ma won't mind.'

'I've never done that yet – gone and done something without asking Mammy.'

'Well, it's time you started. Surprise her. And your pappy. I'd say that he'd be the one to be the most surprised.'

'All right, I will. Eeh, I feel like a naughty girl now. But it is time I took the plunge and did sommat without permission. Do you reckon as it will suit me?'

'I do. You are so like me and Beth that it's bound to. Anyway, it will grow out if it doesn't.'

They stood on the promenade looking over at the sea. The waves were wild and had a different sound to those that smashed onto the coast at Blackpool. 'I ain't much for those pebbles, Babs, I bet they don't half hurt your feet if you tried to get to the sea with no sandals on. I prefer our lovely sand.'

'Yes. Oh, Eliza, I long to come home. But I can't. I have to keep my cover. Here' – Babs delved into her pocket – 'look, this is the completion of my disguise. What do you think?'

'Eeh, glasses. Well, I reckon they suit you. Anyone who saw you at that horrid time would never know you, Babs. You're so different. You had weight on your hips then, and you're much slimmer now.'

'Ha, yes, I hated that look, but Peggy said that was mother's fat and what supplied the milk for our babies. So that helped me to live with it. Until Art was taken, of course.'

Eliza's hand found hers and she squeezed it. 'I love you, Babs. I wish that bad things didn't happen. You heard about Ma Perkins, didn't you?'

'I did. I'm so sorry. I would have written but you would have been on your travels by the time it got to you, so I just waited until you were here and you mentioned it. I know how much you thought of her. What will you do now? Is the shop closed?'

'It is. I'm not sure what will happen with it, it's all to do with legal stuff. Naw one knew if Ma Perkins had any relatives – I never knew of any. So, we'll just have to wait and see.'

'Something will turn up for you. Besides, you always wanted your own cake shop. Have you thought about that?'

'Mammy and Pappy'd think I'm mad. I told you, they think of me as a child.'

'I don't think so. They have recognised that you're in love. You are still, aren't you?'

'Aye, I am. I'll love me lovely Phil till I die. But, well, I'm not ready to marry yet. I'm still keeping Phil in check. Sometimes I think he only wants one thing. Men!'

Babs wanted to giggle, but she stopped herself. This was probably Eliza's first woman-to-woman chat and she didn't want her to think that she was mocking her.

'I know. And it is more difficult for them as they get powerful urges, but as long as he respects your wishes, that's what's important.'

'Well, I get them urges an' all, but I don't try to maul him. He's like an octopus sometimes.'

Babs did laugh out loud at this. 'Oh, Eliza, never change. You're so lovely.' With this Babs hugged Eliza to her. When they came out of the hug, she asked her, 'Are Phil's advances really too much for you, lass?'

'Well, naw, not really. I can cope. It's more me. I – I, well, I'm scared that I might say yes one of these times.'

'Don't do that, Eliza. It will spoil your future, especially if you become pregnant.'

'I won't. I reckon he'll be better now, anyroad, as I told him if he don't show me more respect by the time I get back, then he'll be walking up the lane, with naw job and naw girlfriend.'

'Good. Only you can handle this, Eliza. It's bound to happen. Phil is a young man. He will experience a strong need to show his love for you, but he will grow up and realise that he is doing wrong. Carry your threats out if you have to. Well, I mean, not his job, but fall out with him to bring him to his senses.'

'Awe, Babs, I do miss you, it's so nice having a sister like you. I can't talk to Beth the same, though I did find her so changed and we did have a couple of long chats.'

'Well, we all got Beth wrong, and I feel responsible for that. I think you will find that now there's nothing between us all and Jasmine and Roman have gone from our lives, Beth, too, will be the sister you always wanted … And, Eliza, you may need her one day, so work on that. Write often to her and build a good relationship with her.'

'Why do you say that, Babs? Eeh, you're not leaving me, are you? I mean, you will be back to visit?'

'I will.' Babs held Eliza again. 'But life has a tendency to get in the way of our plans. I know that you know all about mine to be with my little Art, but, well, one day I might leave these shores. Anyroad, I have someone I want you to meet.'

'Eeh, is it someone nice? Have you fallen in love again, Babs?'

'I have.' She told her about Marc. 'Ma and Tommy know, but I wanted to tell you myself. He, well, he's an American.'

'By, I'm that pleased for you, Babs. I've allus felt so sad that you were alone. I can't wait to meet him … But … Eeh, is this why you said … Will you go and live in America, Babs?'

'Well, it's possible. But we will write, and one day you will visit me. And you will meet him as he's coming to dinner tonight, and so is Pearl's young man.'

'Pearl told me about him. She says she's going to marry him and I was to keep my fingers crossed that her father agreed.'

Babs thought about this and hoped that he did, as she was afraid for Pearl, who'd already missed her monthly.

'We'll both keep our fingers crossed. She will know soon, as Bart is asking her father tonight before he brings her to dinner. Come on, let's get that haircut.'

As they crossed the road back to the hotel, Babs physically crossed her fingers. *Let everything come right for my lovely friend,*

God. Please let Bart's credentials – which is what he will be judged on – stand up to the scrutiny of Pearl's father.

Bart had told them that his family owned a huge estate, as did Marc's family, and that as the eldest sons they would one day inherit. If Bart and Pearl did marry, she would go to live in Canada too. Something that Babs prayed for as it would make her life away from home so much easier. But what if Pearl's father refused to let them marry? Babs knew if this happened, all her own dreams would be shattered. For she would never abandon Pearl.

TWENTY-SEVEN

Babs

Marc was wonderful with her family and Babs didn't think she could be happier. Everything in her relationship with Marc, now that he knew all there was to know about her, was so easy-going. She remembered how things had never been like that with her lovely Rupert. Always they'd had to be clandestine when meeting, and even after they had wed, their time together was tainted by them having to meet in secret, and by the attitude of his family, not to mention the bloody and horrifying war that intruded on their daily lives.

When he chatted about this and that with her family Marc was careful to put his family life in a vague context, only once mentioning America and never Canada. Even to Eliza's questions, when she asked what it was like in America, he gave a description of his own home, which Babs had heard, but didn't confirm or deny that it was in America. As for his slight French accent and occasional French words, he passed this off by saying his mother was French, which was the truth, and that she made him speak French whenever they were alone.

This and being in France for so long had made him lapse into that language more than he used to. Not that Babs thought Eliza would imagine anything different to what she'd been told as she was such a trusting person.

'So, I'm to gain a young sister when I come back to claim my bride? I like that idea, and now I've met you, Eliza, I like the idea even more.'

Eliza blushed. 'Well, you should make your mind up on that when you knaw me more. I can be a tartar.'

They all laughed, but then laughed even harder when she added, 'Ha, that's funny, I make tarts, so that does make me a proper tarter!'

'Eeh, our Eliza, you're a one. She's like this all the time, Marc. We're allus saying that she should be on the stage, but all she wants to do is bake cakes. She'd be a marvel at it an' all.'

'Well, I wish that I could sample some of your cakes, Eliza, and I'd love to visit your farm . . . Oh, but that won't be possible.' Turning to Babs, he had an appealing look on his face. 'Would it? Is there no way we could go there without you being seen?'

'No, well, not unless I let everyone in on my secret.'

'Well, I can't see why you have to, lass. You could be you, but with a new haircut. Naw one would ask any questions of you then. Look how easily you slipped into being the Babs we knaw when we arrived. And naw one from the earl's lot would see you, they live miles away.'

The idea began to appeal to Babs. To be able to share her beloved Blackpool with Marc and to see her home and everyone she loved would be so wonderful.

'Aye, we'll do it, lad. We'll take ourselves to Blackpool and have some fun. Eeh, Ma, it'll be grand.'

Everyone clapped their hands at this and to see Ma's face light up did Babs's heart good. Excitement bubbled up inside her and she couldn't wait. Nor could she breathe for the hug that Eliza was giving her. 'Ha, let go, lass, you're strangling me.'

When they settled down Tommy struck a more serious note. 'Is it that you won't be worried that you might slip so comfortably into your old skin that you make mistakes when you return here, Babs?'

'No, I did worry about that happening at first, but now I do something that Pearl advised and treat the two accents as I do when speaking French, as if they are two different languages, then I can switch from one to the other very easily and know when to use them or to think in them. I didn't know that would ever happen, but needed this time with those who speak the King's English to get a really good hold of it. Now I am ready to come home, and do you know what, Ma? I'll be able to do that on my leave days if everything works out for me and no one in Blackpool need ever know that there is another me.'

'That'll be grand, lass, grand as owt.'

Ma had a tear in her eye, but her face was a picture of happiness. Babs reached over for her hand and took it in her own. No matter what happened or where she landed up, Babs knew that her beautiful ma would always be her guiding light.

The moment was shattered by Pearl bursting into the hotel lounge where they were sat waiting for her. 'Babs! Daddy gave his permission. Oh, you have to be my bridesmaid! I'm so happy.'

Babs jumped up and ran into Pearl's arms. She wanted to squeeze her lovely Pearl so hard, but was gentle with her, knowing that she had been feeling delicate lately. 'Oh, Pearl, that's the best news. When? Will your wedding be soon? Oh, I'm so happy for you.'

When they broke free, Marc was shaking Bart's hand. Babs went to them and told Bart how pleased she was. 'Ooh, come and sit down and tell us all about it.'

Once everyone had congratulated Pearl and Bart, they listened to how Pearl had been able to persuade her father to let her marry very soon. 'I told him that Bart is going to look into paying his own passage back home.'

At this, Babs breathed a sigh of relief. She was on edge that Pearl and Bart may forget that they must not mention Canada in front of Eliza.

'And so, Mama said to post the banns immediately and have what is still considered a war-time marriage – a quickly arranged, small affair which suits us very well – and so, we will marry in just three weeks' time. But of course, Bart won't go, he will pretend to be continually thwarted – which may be true in any case, with the possibility of not getting transport. You see, I need to get used to the idea of going to live over-seas and will need to make a lot of preparations.' With this, Pearl gave a sideways, smiley glance at Babs.

'Oh, I'm so pleased. And yes, I would love to be your bridesmaid.'

'Oh, I wish that I could ask you all to the wedding, but, well, I have to think at all times of Babs's cover, and, well, other than saying you are Babs's friends, or family, I just wouldn't know how to get away with it.'

'You don't have to, Pearl. You can come to us for your honeymoon. Blackpool has some lovely hotels, and me and Ma'll put a do on for you. You can taste some of me cakes then.'

'That's a great idea. What do you think, Bart? Blackpool is a very popular northern seaside resort; most of my friends have been there to take the waters for their health. I would love it.'

'Anywhere you want to go, honey, I'll leave it up to you. But those cakes sound tempting, and would be what I would go for.'

Babs felt good to hear her family laughing and relaxed with Pearl and Bart. 'That would be perfect. We have just been talking about us going up. I would have to drop my cover, and can introduce you as who you are – a dear friend that I met while in France. We can drop our guard and just have a wonderful time.'

'Ooh, that's even better. When are you planning to go?'

'Well, not yet. I need to get started with my work, so maybe May time, but if it looks like Bart and Marc are going back before, we'll do it at a minute's notice!'

The waiter came over to them then and asked to show them into the dining room. He looked very surprised as Eliza told him, 'Eeh, that'd be grand. I'm ready for me tea.'

'Oh, but this is for dinner, Miss. Tea was served hours ago, but I can arrange to have you served tea if you prefer.'

'Naw. Dinner or tea, it's just the same, only we have our dinner at midday in the north and our evening meal is our tea. But it all goes down the same way, so dinner it is.'

Babs held her breath, not knowing whether to laugh or give into her embarrassment, but the day was saved as the waiter smiled. 'I have family in the north – Yorkshire. By gum, they'd frown at me serving a Lancashire lass.'

Eliza laughed her lovely laugh. The waiter joined in with her, but received a stern frown from the maître d'. 'I beg your pardon, this way, please.'

They were all chuckling as they followed him to the dining room and Babs felt herself relax once more.

The evening went so well, the conversation flowed and there was a happiness around the table that everyone settled into. Babs felt so proud of her family and all her worries about them not being comfortable left her.

When Ma, Tommy and Eliza went to their room, Bart ordered a bottle of champagne. To Babs, it still felt strange to realise just what money could buy. It was if the shortages of the war hadn't affected the rich. She thought of all those who were struggling. But then, for all their money, Pearl, Bart and Marc had done their bit and had all suffered fear, hunger, cold and despair, so they deserved to have some of the finer things in life now.

'Here's to my darling wife-to-be. On that day in France, when we heard this motorbike roar to a halt outside the café, little did Marc and I suspect that it would bring the loves of our lives to us. But it did. Cheers.'

When Babs clinked her glass with Marc, she thrilled at the look in his eyes.

The chatter that followed the toast made it seem as if they hadn't a worry in the world and Babs began to believe that she didn't. The champagne left her feeling light-headed and gave her a devil-may-care attitude.

She sobered a little when Marc whispered in her ear to ask if she would go for a walk with him as a nerve in her tingled its response to the feel of his breath on her neck, telling her that she wanted more than to walk out, but she nodded. Once in the foyer she took hold of his hand. 'I'd rather walk to my bedroom than outside.'

His eyes clouded over. 'Really? Are you sure?'

'Yes, I've been sure since the moment I met you.'

'Oh, Babs. I love you. I would never have pushed you.'

'I know. I knew it would be down to me to make the first move.' She winked at him, 'So, shall we go then?'

'Together? Do you want to go first and I'll make out I am going to my room?'

'Well, yes,' she giggled. 'Maybe it would be better to behave properly – well, pretend to. I'll see you soon.' Whispering her room number to him, she leant in close and kissed his cheek. The lovely woody-fresh smell of his cologne, tinged with the scent of the oil that he'd tamed his hair with, heightened the need that had taken her.

When in her room, Babs began to wonder what she'd done as a sense of shyness came over her. With it came the idea that she was being unfaithful, which made her clam up. She wished with all her heart that she'd just gone for a walk. The tap on the door put her into a state of panic. But she breathed deeply. She could tell Marc that she had changed her mind, he'd understand.

When she opened the door, all her misgivings dissolved as she went into Marc's arms. Guiding her inside while still holding her, the moment the door closed, his lips touched hers in a light sensual kiss that deepened to a passion, taking away any last shred of doubt and making Babs certain that this was meant to be.

They didn't speak. Their kisses said all they wanted to express – tender kisses that deepened to a passion that consumed them as they caressed each part of their bodies as they helped each other to undress.

When at last they lay on the bed, their naked bodies entwined, but not yet joined, Marc's hoarse whisper, 'My Babs, *C'est maintenant que je te fais mienne,*' thrilled her.

'Yes, yes, I want to be yours. *Tu es mon monde, mon chéri*, my world.'

When he entered her, Babs was filled with joy. Holding him close and wrapping her legs around him, she cried out with the feeling that swept through her whole body and released so many emotions. Emotions that carried her to a place she remembered being in before. A place that only true love can take you to and she allowed the splintering of her soul, the shattering of who she was. Her beloved Marc would rebuild her. Make her his as she accepted the love in his every movement, his every sigh and in the sound of his moans of pleasure.

With him now deep inside her, his thrusts took her to the exquisite plateau from which there was only one descent. When it happened, the feeling that took her gripped her whole body in wave upon wave of sensations so strong that she didn't think she would be able to bear it. She begged Marc to stop. Clung to him, called out his name and her love for him until, spent, she lay back.

'My darling Babs. I love you.' As he said this, Marc lifted his head and kissed every part of her face. When he reached her lips, he ground his body into her. His movements quickened, and his moans became more intense, then he was gone from inside her, but clinging on to her, his face wet with tears, his arms holding her close to him. So close she could feel him pulsating as he reached his climax.

They lay there, not moving, not wanting to break apart. And Babs knew, this was just the beginning for them. That they had a lot to go through, but they would face it all, together or apart, and she would never forget this moment.

TWENTY-EIGHT

Babs

The wedding had been lovely. Though Pearl's mother had said a 'quiet affair', it was anything but, with fifty guests for the morning breakfast and another twenty joining the party for a ball in the evening. Babs had felt exhausted by the end of it, so couldn't imagine how Pearl felt, but she, as usual, seemed to take it all in her stride.

Babs hadn't been able to take anything in her stride as emotions had churned her insides. Lady Barnham had returned from a trip she'd taken a week before the wedding and had the most wonderful news.

Now she, Pearl, Bart and Marc were in Blackpool. Babs just couldn't believe it when they pulled up outside the farm. The journey had taken hours and hours on each of the two days they had been travelling, but she hadn't minded as when they'd gone to their rooms in the lodging house outside of Manchester where they'd stopped off, it hadn't been long before a tap on her door heralded Marc coming to be with her. Once more they had given of their all to each other, hungrily taking and giving in a frenzy of lovemaking that rekindled the feelings they had experienced the last time in the hotel in Brighton.

But although she felt bathed in love, what they had just done evoked a sadness, as the time was coming when they would part.

'So, what is it you cannot wait to tell me, my darling?'

Watching the smoke from Marc's cigarette curl above them, she told him. 'It's just such amazing news, Marc. Pearl's parents went to a winter ball held by the Earl of Barnham – Rupert's father, and the man who has custody of my Art.'

'Oh, I'm already fearing what you're going to say.'

'I know. It's the only downside to my dream to be with my son coming true, that you and I will have to part. But I long to be with him, and the pull on me to do so is too strong for me to turn away from.'

'I understand and wouldn't stand in your way. I'm happy for you, but sad for me.'

Babs wished it could be different; she dreaded parting with Marc.

Kissing his cheek, she told him, 'Nothing's certain yet, but Pearl's mother got into a conversation with Lady Barnham about the aftermath of the war, and she mentioned me as a case in question – at least, what she thinks I am: a young woman displaced by circumstances and now having to try to make a life for herself. She also told her what I was going to train to be.'

'When she came home, she told Pearl about it and asked Pearl if I would consider moving to Kent as she thinks that Lady Barnham is interested in retaining my services once my training is complete. I just can't believe how easy it was for my dream to come true.'

Marc was quiet for a moment. 'I don't know if I can stand being away from you, Babs. But I know that you have to do this. Would you marry me first? I so want to have you as my wife. I don't want to go home as me. I want to go home as your husband and await the time that you come back to me.'

'Oh, Marc! Marc! Yes, yes, I will. But it has to be in secret. Just me and you and a stranger for a witness – or maybe Pearl and Bart. But no one else must know. I would never be accepted as a nanny if anyone knew that I had a husband.'

'Thank you, my darling. So I haven't wasted my money on a licence then!'

'What! You have a licence? How? When for? Where?'

'Yes, and through a solicitor, and for this next week, in Blackpool!'

Babs couldn't believe it. Fear clutched her for a moment as she thought of the possibility of being found out, but how could that happen? How could anyone in Kent connect Catherine Dufort from France and living with Mr and Mrs Hartshore of Brighton with Babs Barnham from Blackpool, who married a Canadian officer? As this seeped into her, she jumped up and in all her naked glory danced around the bed. 'I love you, Marceau Rugely, I love you with my life.' Her dancing reminded her of the gypsy dance as she twirled and bent her body. But before she could feel any emotion about this, she was caught in Marc's arms and carried back to the bed. There, if she'd ever thought she'd experienced the ultimate sensations that lovemaking can give, she found this wasn't so as Marc took her with such passion, tenderness and extreme love.

On the hoot of the car horn, Ma, Tommy, Eliza, Phil and, finally, Cliff, came running from all directions and before she knew it, she was encased in hugs that showed her that she was truly home. Cliff was the last one to hug her. 'Eeh, lass, it's good to see you. I've missed you.'

'And I've missed you, Cliff. We'll catch up with one another later. I've to see to my guests.'

'By, that sounded posh!'

Babs quickly covered up. 'Eeh, I'm mixing with monied folk now, lad. But there's nowt posh about them. They're lovely. I knaw as you'll like them.'

Pearl, who stood just behind her, laughed out loud and clapped her hands. 'Oh, Babs, it's so good to see you again. Goodbye, posh Cath.'

Cliff looked bemused as they giggled. 'It's just an old joke. I'll explain later. Let me introduce everyone.'

After a welcome cup of tea, the men went on the grand tour of the farm with Tommy. Feeling the tug of Marc, Babs would so love to have gone with them, but Pearl said that she was tired, and so she decided to look after her and went with her up to the bedroom that Ma had got ready for her and Bart.

It was a lovely room. Pearl loved it and kept finding something to delight in seeing when looking out at the farm, visible from the small windows.

'This is just how I imaged a farmhouse would look inside. All homely. Everything looks as though it has been hand-made. I love the rustic feel.'

'Well, it has, Pearl. The basket over there holding fresh towels was made by Ma. The cushions by my Aunt Molly, and that goes for the covering on the chairs and the bedspread.'

'And all matching the lining of the basket and those other baskets on the dressing table. They will be so handy for holding my jewellery and make-up. It's a lovely room.' Stretching herself, Pearl added, 'I know I will sleep well in here. Mind you, right now I could sleep on a clothes line. How come you are as fresh as a daisy? It isn't fair.'

'That's your condition. Being pregnant makes you tire easily.'

'What? Even this early in the proceedings? What's it like when you're like a barrel then?'

'Oh, don't worry, you'll have more energy later. It's just while your body gets used to its extra responsibilities. Well, I'll leave you to rest. I'm going to find Cliff. I need a chat with him.'

'He's very handsome to just be a friend. How come you didn't fall for him?'

'You can't turn feelings on just like that. Cliff and I have a lovely relationship – a deep friendship that I value very much. I can talk to him how I can talk to you. I'll see you later.'

When she got to the bottom of the stairs, Ma was waiting for her. 'Eeh, lass, let me have a proper hello now that everyone is out of the way. I've missed you, me Babs, and wish you were home to stay.'

They held each other close. 'It's so good to be home, Ma. I wish I could stay and that everything was as it should be. But, well, you knaw what I have to do. And, Ma, I have news that I haven't shared with anyone yet. I wanted to tell you first.'

Ma stood with her hands over her open mouth and her eyes filling with tears. 'Married! And here, with me? Oh, me Babs, me Babs.'

Another hug followed that was peppered with laughter and tears.

'That's not all, Ma. I'm hoping against hope that when we get back I may have news.'

'Oh? Is there sommat else happening then?'

Babs told of what had occurred at the earl's ball.

'Naw, naw, I can't believe it! I knaw as you said that you had a chance, but I really didn't think you had. Eeh, these monied folk are in a league of their own. They seem to make anything and everything happen that they have a mind to . . . But what about Marc? Eeh, why am I even asking? I knaw what I'd have done and I knaw what you will do, me lass.'

'Aye, I'll carry on with me plan, only I will have the lovely knowledge that I am married to Marc, and when the time comes, me and my son can go to him and then I will be complete.'

'By, Babs, I'm proud of you. All of this holds heartache for me, but that don't matter. To see you fighting for your son, it's like you're doing it for me. I mean, I could never achieve finding you and Beth, but to see one of your children achieving what you couldn't, it somehow makes up a little for that.'

Finding Cliff in the cowshed, Babs skipped over to him.

'By, you look happy, and so you should with such a nice man to love you. Eeh, I'm that happy for you, Babs.'

'I knaw, ta, Cliff. Are you all right?'

'I keep on keeping on.'

'Cliff, you never did tell me what was troubling you. You can, you knaw.'

'You might be shocked.'

'Naw, lad, nowt can shock me after what I've seen in France.'

'Well, this ain't nowt of the kind you would have come across. I – I well, I have a vocation. I want to follow a religious life.'

Babs was shocked, but only because she'd thought he was going to tell her that he fancied men rather than women! She never dreamt that he would say this in a million years. Though why she hadn't, she couldn't imagine. Cliff never made any bones about his religious beliefs, and he was the most likely candidate she'd ever met. 'Come here, I need to hug you.'

As they went into a hug, Cliff asked, 'You're not shocked then?'

'Naw. Just very surprised.' She giggled at what her thoughts had been.

'Why are you laughing then?'

'It's the relief and happiness for you. All sorts have been going around in me head ever since we were up in the Bowland hills.'

'Oh, aye, I can imagine.'

'Not that any of it would have mattered, but this will be an easier and safer path for you than what my imagination had dreamt up.'

'I knaw, but, Babs, I did expect you to laugh. I expect everyone to. I mean, who do I think I am? I'm not good enough for such a calling.'

'Eeh, you are, Cliff. You are the best good person I've ever known. So, what are you going to do about it?'

'Nowt. Just live me life as best as I can, and become an old bachelor.'

'Oh, naw you're not. The Church needs good folk like you. People need good folk like you. And they say as God does the calling and deciding, so you'll be going against his wishes an' all. Besides, I want you to do it. I have a nun rooting for me – Daisy, one of me other best friends – and I want a priest an' all. I'll have the full set then.'

They both laughed at this and the moment lightened.

'But I ain't educated enough, Babs. I've looked into it and there's a lot of studying to do. You have to be a theologian, whatever one of them is.'

Babs was having none of this. She got quite cross with him as she went through all that she and Beth had to do to become nurses. 'And we'd never been to school! So, if we can do it, so can you!'

Cliff had kept his head down while she'd been talking. When he lifted it, tears were streaming down his face. 'I didn't want to be different. I didn't, Babs. I didn't want to be chosen. I wanted to be like everyone else and marry and have kids. I don't knaw how to cope with how I feel sometimes. I've been in a lonely place, afraid as I'd be made a mockery of.'

'Eeh, Cliff. I'm sorry, lad. You mean that you have those feelings as well? For a woman, I mean?'

'Aye, I do. But I allus control them. I've never . . . you knaw. I've been too scared to in case it's all I think it is and I don't want to stop. And yet, I knaw I can't go down that road as I'd allus be on me wrong path.'

'Oh, Cliff. I never realised. I thought it was simple to take up the religious life, that priests and such were different . . . Well, you knaw . . . that they didn't want to do things.'

'I reckon that's the biggest sacrifice they make. It will be for me.'

'You are going to do it then?'

'Aye. Talking to you has made me realise that I can. I'm going to see about starting me studies. There's an old priest, Father John, at St Cuthbert's church where I attend. He's easy to talk to, and he ain't one for buttering up to anyone. He's a good, holy man. I'm going to talk to him and see if he can help me.'

'Eeh, Cliff, I'm that pleased, lad. Come here, I need another hug.' As she held him, she told him, 'I'll allus be here for you, Cliff. You can write to me and share your feelings with me. And, aye, maybe even visit me one of these days, eh?'

As he wiped his face on his hanky, she told him her news about the wedding, and about how she had hopes of the dream she'd written to him about coming true.

'I'm glad for you, Babs. By, I can't believe how your life is turning around for you. I haven't seen much of Marc, but what I did, I liked. But there's allus a sting in the tail for you. To think you won't be able to be with him for a long time must be breaking your heart. When will you go to him, when Art goes to boarding school?'

Babs bowed her head. 'We'll see. One step at a time, eh? Just keep hoping for me that this comes off, and that Lady Barnham takes to me and gives me the position, as that's a start – the best start I could wish for, if I can't be together with both Art and Marc.'

'Why don't you get your feet under the table at the earl's place and settle into the job, and then, when you're trusted, just go? Take Art on a day out or sommat and don't go back, but instead, get on a boat and go to wherever Marc lives. I'd help you.'

'By, I don't think a priest should be suggesting such things, but, Cliff, I am thinking of doing that. You wouldn't think bad of me then?'

'Naw. You have been sinned against. You're not the sinner. God intended a child to be with his mother, and that's how I'll look at it. Look, the way I see it, you could get a passport under your married name, once you're wed, as well as owt in the way of paperwork that you might need, before you leave here. After all, you have the best reason for wanting to emigrate and a right to enter your husband's country. You can say that you want everything in place so that you can join him later. Then you'll be all ready for when the time's right. I will help you all I can.'

'Cliff, you're a genius. I can't believe that you've come up with the same plan that I have, but not only that, you've dotted the "I"s and crossed the "T"s, as many a matron has told me that I should do. And yes, I may need any help I can get. How do you think that you could help me?'

'I have a lot of hobbies and one of them is shipping. I go to Liverpool on me days off, and I check what ships are going where, and sometimes watch out for them on the horizon in Blackpool. I've thought many a time about emigrating, but I knew it weren't for me really. Anyroad, I could find out when there's a boat going to where you'd need to go. And I could pick you up and take you to it. I've bought a van of me own, that's it out in the yard.'

Suddenly, it seemed to Babs that everything was possible. How would anyone connect her with Catherine Dufont? She wouldn't even have to travel as Barbara Barnham, a name they do know, but as Barbara Rugely. 'Eeh, ta, Cliff. You're a true mate.'

Cliff smiled at her. 'And so are you, Babs.'

Blackpool the next day lived up to all Babs knew of it as she walked with Marc a little ahead of Pearl and Bart. The promenade was alive, as the sun bathed it in warmth. Music blared out from the Wurlitzer and from a beggar who stood on the corner of Manchester Square, playing the same song on a violin, whilst a woman sang along with him in a cackling voice that made them laugh as she tried to hit the high notes. A shout of, 'Shut up, Minnie, you'll make the sea turn tail and never come back,' had them doubling over.

'Eeh, there's naw folk like Blackpool folk.'

'I could get used to you talking in your accent, Babs, I love it. Hold on a mo.' With this, Marc crossed over to the woman and Babs heard a few coins tinkle as he dropped something in her man's hat. 'Ta, love, God bless you and yours.'

When he came back to Babs's side, Marc was looking serious. 'It makes me sad to see that. People having to beg.'

'It's a hazard of the seaside. They don't all need it, it's just what they've done for years.'

'Well, just in case. I feel better for giving.'

'I love you, Marc. I love everything about you.'

'Well, if it gets that reaction, all the beggars are going to be rich today!'

They linked arms, giggling at this.

'I've never seen anything like this, Babs. I love it. It makes you feel alive. The colours of the different tents, the music, the men and women shouting their wares and the delicious cooking smell.'

'That will be the fish and chips, we're famous for them. Let's get some and sit on the sea wall, I need to talk to you.'

None of them had ever had fish and chips, and their enjoyment of them gave Babs a warm feeling. Marc was right, there was nowhere like Blackpool.

While they ate Babs told them about how Cliff had fitted the pieces of the jigsaw together. She didn't tell them what he'd shared with her. One day, when he was ready he would tell the world. And she hoped everyone would be as happy for him as she was.

'So, you needn't come back here, or be involved at all, Marc. I will come to you, with little Art.'

'It could work. It really could.' Pearl's excitement further infused Babs's growing confidence. 'Oh, Babs, we'll all meet you at the dock. What a wonderful sight it will be to see you walking down the gangplank with your son. We'll have to get a move on, though. You have two weeks in which to marry, and get all the papers that you need. You'll need a solicitor too.'

Babs thought of Mr Fellows, then thought better of it. The fewer people involved who knew her background, the better. As it was, Ma, Tommy and now Cliff knew what she intended. But she could do it, couldn't she? *I can, or I'll die trying.*

As she thought this she felt a new sense of determination. Yes, her plan had flaws, and if it went wrong, she faced a very long sentence in prison, but she'd not think of that, she'd just think of how one day she would be with Marc and with her Art.

TWENTY-NINE

Tilly and Babs

Within a few days, Babs found herself getting ready for her wedding day. Nothing could mar her happiness.

'Eeh, lass, I don't knaw where you thought you were going to wear that up here. Did you have an inkling that you would be a bride then? It's beautiful.' Tilly stood back and admired Babs's frock in a lovely primrose colour. She hadn't ever seen one like it with its many layers and its satin sheen.

'I bought it for last Christmas, and I tell you, Ma, it's nowt to what the others were wearing. And naw, I didn't knaw. But we had all planned on having a special night out in Manchester, so I packed it just in case. Now, I am wearing it for one of the most special days in me life.'

'Awe, love, I reckon that all your troubles will soon be behind you and it won't be long before Marc is back carrying out your plan.'

Babs didn't say that her plan had changed since she'd had a chat with Cliff, as she wasn't sure that it had. Marc had agreed that the new plan could work, but he didn't want her going through with it without him, nor did he want her travelling all that way on her own, so as things stood, he was still set on returning.

As she stood outside the registry office with Marc, Babs looked up into his eyes. 'Thank you, Marc. You've made me very happy.'

Marc pulled her closer to him. 'We'll soon be together, darling, and never be parted. I will be back at Christmas time, I promise. In the meantime, we have our time in Manchester. We catch the train later this afternoon so, before that, let's celebrate in Blackpool's way.'

Tilly felt as though she was brimming with tears – some happy, but some sad as she knew that today marked the beginning of a time when her Babs would go to live on the other side of the world and she wondered, despite Tommy's assurances, if she would ever see her again.

'Eeh, Tilly, lass, what are you doing in here on your own? I've looked everywhere for you, and never expected to find you in your work room.'

'Oh, Molly. I'm that emotional, I had to escape for a moment. Have I been missed?'

'Naw. Everyone's very happy. By, it's a shame that Beth couldn't make it.'

'I knaw, but it's lovely that Babs and Marc are going down to stay with them for a couple of days, while Pearl and her young man go off to Bournemouth to spend a short time on their own.'

'Life's funny, Tilly. Here we are, our young 'uns all flown or flying from the nest. Well, not Eliza, of course. Has she heard any more about the shop yet?'

'Yes. I were going to tell you and Florrie when we had our next day out.'

'Tell Florrie what?' the door opened and Florrie walked in. 'Ha, you don't miss much, lass.'

Florrie smiled at Molly. 'Says the one that's here before me. So, come on, what is it?'

'Well, Ma Perkins has only gone and—'

The door opening stopped Tilly in her tracks as a cross-looking Eliza came through it, 'Mammy!'

'Eliza! Eeh, I was only telling Aunt Molly and Aunt Florrie, lass.'

'Well, I told you that I was going to make an announcement and I came to find you as that time has come. Babs and Marc are about to cut the cake that I made for them. Come on. You knaw as I want to be the one to tell everyone.'

Tilly looked at the others. 'Well, I consider meself told.' Molly and Florrie laughed with her as they went out of the room like three naughty children following an indignant Eliza.

'Eeh, you found Ma and her buddies then?' Babs laughed as she said this, and then winked at Tilly, which told her that Eliza must have made a fuss about them being missing from the room. She smiled a knowing smile at Babs. But then they were all brought to attention by Eliza. 'Right, as chief bridesmaid, I announce that the bride and groom are going to cut the cake.'

Everyone clapped and a toast was proposed to the bride and groom and a few minutes taken to congratulate them with hugs and kisses.

To Marc saying how lovely the cake was, Eliza said, 'Aye, well, I have an announcement to make.' Everyone fell silent. 'I were told yesterday by Mr Fellows, who called me into his office, that Ma Perkins has left me the shop and quite a bit of money, so Ma Perkins' Bread and Cakes will be reopening.'

Everyone cheered and Tilly felt so proud of Eliza. Everyone wanted to know about her plans and Eliza chatted with them all, filling them in. When Babs got to her, they hugged. Tilly could see the love they had for one another as she had many times and it did her heart good. And, she thought, so much was falling into place to put everything right for her young 'uns and she was happy for them.

'Now, was that for being a happy sigh, me little lass?'

'Yes, and naw, Tommy. I've learnt in life that everything has a price and often happiness has the highest one. Everything seems to be panning out for everyone, but for me their happiness has a large tag on it – my time with Beth and Babs at home was so short, and mostly spoilt by Jasmine.'

'Aye, it is how life goes. Not the spoiling by an evil person, but the parting of the ways. They all have their lives to carve out. And we should be happy for them.'

'I am, Tommy, I am. I'm just finding it hard to come to terms with it all. What mother wouldn't?'

'I know, and it is for being the same for me as a father, as I feel that is me role.'

'It is, Tommy. But mostly you are my man, and nothing will part us, so we're to get on with it and lean on each other as we allus do.'

'On that note, I have something to liven things up a bit.'

Tilly didn't have to ask what, but smiled as Tommy began to play his mouth organ. Will crossed to the piano as if this was his cue and before long the party was in real swing.

Tilly allowed herself to be caught up in the happiness that surrounded her. Today wasn't for sadness – there was always plenty of that waiting around the corner. She mustn't go to meet it, but fly in the face of it.

When Babs arrived at Beth's, having had a wonderful time in Manchester, her happiness was such that she felt fit to burst.

'Beth, oh, Beth.'

They held on to each other as if they were the only people in the world. When they parted, they found that everyone must have crept out as they were now alone in Beth's back room – a lovely room, furnished in soft blues and greys, and with the sunlight beaming through the French doors which led on to her garden. They were both crying.

Wiping Beth's tears with her thumb, Babs sighed. 'It's been a long rocky road for us, Beth.'

'It has, and none of it should have happened to us. But it's all behind us now, well and truly behind us.'

'It is, Beth. Well, everything that was coming between you and me is.'

'Yes, but you know, I feel that all will come right. Keep strong, Babs. Your strength will get you through.'

They hugged again.

Beth giggled then. 'You just don't sound like you, Babs. But you know, listening to you makes me realise now how I must have come across to you. Speaking differently, and apart from my injury, having had everything in my life fall into place. I can understand how you felt. But I'm glad you know the truth now.'

'Oh, Beth, I'm sorry.'

'Let's forget it all and enjoy this new beginning. And that is what it is – for us both. And I am so happy for you. You look wonderful, Babs. I love your hair. I might have mine cut like that.'

'That will be three of us then, as Eliza has this style now. And you look so well, too, Beth. Oh, Beth, I do love you. And when I move to Kent, I'll come and see you all the time.'

'Is it certain? Have you heard?'

'No, not about the job, but I am moving anyway. You remember I told you about Rupert's nanny? Well, I am going to move in with her if my plan doesn't come off. It will be fine now as the nurse who looked after Art is moving on, so I'm not likely to bump into her and have her recognise me. But it's not what I want, as that will mean that Art has a new nanny and it isn't me.'

'Oh, Babs, I don't know how you bear it all.'

'I'm all right. I'm the happiest I've been for a long time. I have my wonderful new husband, and hope for my future.'

'Babs, how is this all going to work? Ma said that once Marc is demobbed you will probably join him. What about Art then? How will you cope having seen him again and then having to leave him?'

Babs smiled, but behind the smile she felt so deceitful. But she had to protect Beth. And herself. Henry and Beth may not approve and may take measures to stop her – well, how can anyone approve who hasn't been through it? And with Henry's standing, how can they sanction a criminal act? No, better they are left ignorant until the deed is done, then they can deal with it.

'I'll find a way. I cannot go without a small piece of him to take with me. Even if it is just one memory of a glimpse of him. Then I will await his coming of age.'

'You are so brave, my darling Babs.'

'Ha, I don't know about that, but brave or not, I am impatient. I need to see little Benny right now. Where is he?'

Beth laughed and rang a bell beside her. Faithful Peggy came through the door, a little boy, two years and a few months old, toddling by her side. He looked at Babs, and then at Beth, a query on his face. He must be wondering what was going on, as here was someone who looked just like his mummy but wasn't her. Then his face lit up with a smile and he ran to Babs, showing her his wooden soldier. 'You have.'

Babs's heart overflowed with love. 'Thank you. Can I have a hug as well?'

His little arms reached up to her, and Babs scooped him up. 'You're a fine boy, Benny, and I am your Aunty Babs.'

'Babs?'

'Yes, that's right. Aunty Babs, and I love you.'

He looked at her again and once more his face was full of questions. Then he smiled and said, 'Babs.'

Babs laughed and tickled his tummy. 'Yes, that's right. That's me. Hello.'

Benny laughed with her and then put his chubby arms around her neck and hugged her. Babs's eyes filled with tears. To her, the hug made her feel that she was one step nearer to her Art as memories came to her of how the two little boys had bonded, and now she wondered if they would ever meet again.

'Come on, Benny, lad. I'm to get you ready for tea.'

Benny put his arms out to Beth. 'Cuddle Mama first.'

Handing him to Beth, Babs's heart ached at the sight of them together and to see the love they had for one another. *It WILL be like that for me. My son will love me. I know he will. But somehow, I am to keep my emotions in check. I will have to treat him as if he is nothing more to me than a charge. Oh God, will I be able to do that?*

Saying goodbye to Beth, she promised to come to see her again soon. The two days had been a wonderful time for them all and Babs had thought that Henry was lovely, and she was so happy to meet him and to know that Beth was safe, wrapped in the love he had for her.

And not only that, but she was overwhelmed by his determination to make Beth better. Babs couldn't get over how Henry talked of Beth one day being able to walk. She'd asked him to explain, not believing it possible. To this he'd talked of Beth's condition only giving temporarily paralysis – something he'd always known. He told her that the medical profession were learning all the time of new techniques and treatments. 'I'll get her there. But I don't know how yet. I'm meeting with some eminent professors who studied in America before the war and have continued to work on what they learnt there. They are fascinated with my own paper on neurology and eager to meet me to study Beth's case.'

'Well, Henry, you have added to my hope for the future.' With this, she'd hugged him and been rewarded with a lovely

374

smile. She liked Henry and knew she could grow to love him as a brother-in-law, and prayed that he was right in his theory, for Beth's sake.

As they drove back towards Brighton, Babs asked Marc what he thought.

'I think that your sister has every chance, Babs. I liked Henry very much. And he is passionate about what he does and even more so about getting Beth well. I think he will succeed.'

'Oh, that will be wonderful. And what did you think to Beth?'

'How could I not love her? She is you.'

'Yes, we lost our way for a long time, but I feel that too. Beth and Babs are one. It is going to be so difficult to be thousands of miles away from her. From them all. I feel as though I have only just found them again.'

'I know. I feel your pain, darling. I miss my mom and dad, and my brother, and all the family. It is hard. But we will be together, and nothing can top that.'

'Yes, my husband, we will.'

'Babs. I haven't told you yet, but we will be shipped out in just a few weeks. But as soon as I get home, I will make arrangements to sail back to be here by Christmas. I'll book the return sailing for mid-January for us both and a child. I want you to be ready then. Do you think you can be?'

'Yes, I will make it so. Oh, but so much hangs on whether I get the job as nanny to my little Art.'

'Pearl is confident that you will. Her father is giving you a reference and so is her sister and Pearl said that being a qualified nursing sister, you will only need a few weeks to pick up the guidelines of what is expected of a nanny. I think you are home and dry, my darling. I think in a few weeks you will be with your son. I will pray for that to happen.'

Babs drew in a breath. Emotions attacked her. Sorrow at being parted from Marc, but mostly sheer and utter joy at the prospect of being with Art.

When they reached Brighton, they booked into a small bed and breakfast in the back streets. Cosy and clean, it was just for the one night. The night of goodbyes.

Pearl and Bart arrived not long after them. They'd decided between them that this was where they would meet up before going home together the next day, Babs returning to her status of being Catherine Dufont, a single woman, and Marc as the friend of Bart.

Babs was dreading it, just as she was dreading saying goodbye to Pearl and Bart very shortly as Pearl was sailing with Bart when he left for home.

Part of Babs hoped that she could go to the dock to see them off, but a bigger part hoped that she was in Kent by then.

They none of them wanted to stay up late. So, after an adequate dinner served by the landlady of pork chops and vegetables, they retired to their rooms.

Babs snuggled into Marc, exhausted after their lovemaking. 'Babs, are you all right?'

'Yes and no, darling.'

'I feel the same. How am I to say goodbye tomorrow?'

'Does it have to be that soon?'

'It does. Before, I visited Pearl's home as a friend of Bart's, but he will be living there now and I will have to go back to the camp. I have no reason to give for not doing so.'

'When will I see you again, my darling?'

'We have to think of tomorrow as goodbye until I come back at Christmas. I don't see another way, then you can get on with your plan. Focus on succeeding, my darling, as I know you will never be happy if you don't.'

His arm came around her and he gathered her to him. His tears wet her hair, hers dampened his chest. They didn't go over it all again but lay silently like this until they drifted off to sleep.

PART THREE

The Healing of Hurts

1920–21

THIRTY

Babs

The rhythm of the train drummed in Babs's brain as she sat in a closed carriage with Pearl. So many things tugged at her heart. Her joy as at last she was going to her son, and yet her pain at parting with Marc, which had broken her heart.

He had come to visit, when he hadn't thought he could. Bart and Pearl had taken up temporary residence in a lovely little cottage on the estate and they had invited him. It had been wonderful to be there too, and for two blissful days and nights to be able to be his wife. No one had questioned her staying at the cottage as everything looked as though it was being conducted properly with Pearl and Bart chaperoning them.

Now she was on her way to Bexleyheath in Kent. A car would be waiting for them at Bexleyheath station to take them to the earl's estate, which stood between Bexleyheath and Dartford.

As she looked out at the countryside, dotted with oast houses, whose pointed roofs gleamed in the early May sunshine, memories caused her heart to thump in her chest as she was taken back to a time when she had run away from the gypsies, and Rupert – just a young boy at the time – had come across her while he was riding his horse. He the son of an earl, her an urchin, stinking from the filth of the ditch she'd tried to hide in, and yet he hadn't been disrespectful to her and she'd never forgotten him. He hadn't known the fate he was sending her to when he'd directed her to the nearest farm to seek shelter and work.

What she'd suffered at the hands of the monster who owned the farm shuddered through her and she thought of how what he did marked the beginning of the downward path she'd trod, which the child that she had been had no control over.

Meeting Rupert again on the hospital train had been a massive coincidence, but once more, he was only meant to be a brief encounter in her life. A time that gave her a deep love, and their child.

'Are you all right, Babs?'

'Yes. A lot of what I told you of happened around here.' It had been on the way here that Babs had finally told Pearl about her young life and the terrible things that had happened to her. The fear of visiting this area again had prompted her to share with her dearest friend what was causing most of her anxiety about this journey.

Pearl crossed over the carriage and sat next to her and took her hand. 'It's all in the past now. And you have a wonderful future to look forward to.'

'I know. But I'm splintered inside as I have been many times. Part of me is dreading what I have to do. Part of me wants to run back to Marc and board the boat with you all when you go next week. And yet another part is visiting the past and being shredded by it once more. And through it all I am trying to hold my emotions in check, as soon I am going to see my son for the first time in three years. He has had three birthdays without me. I don't even know what he looks like. And yet, I have to do that while pretending I don't know him. How? How?'

'I don't know. Of everything that you have to do, I think that seeing him for the first time is going to be the hardest. You are going to need great strength. And I know you have that, Babs, you do. Think back over all that you have over-come – a lesser person would have crumbled. Hold on to that courage that you were born with, passed on through your beloved ma. A wonderful woman whom I admire so much. You can be her, Babs. You can be Tilly O'Flynn.'

Babs felt the strength coming back into her as she took this on board, something she'd been trying to achieve since they had returned to Pearl's home over a month ago and heard that she was to meet Lady Barnham a week later to be inter-viewed by her. Pearl had told her the haste involved was because the nurse had disgraced herself by being caught walk-ing out with the footman, and had been banished. Babs hated the thought of her dream coming true on the back of the misfortune of someone who had been so kind to her over the years. But she could do nothing about it. If she tried to find and help her, she might be recognised by her. She couldn't take that risk. As it was, she dreaded coming across the earl's solicitor, the only other person who knew her. But she didn't think that likely.

The meeting with Lady Barnham took place in Brighton, where she'd told Pearl's mother she was taking the opportunity to visit a cousin she hadn't seen for a while. It appeared that she wanted the matter of a nanny for her grandson settled as quickly as possible as he was being cared for by a temporary nurse, and they wanted to get him settled once more. Babs imagined him missing his nurse, and wanted to console him.

She'd found Lady Barnham to be just what she had expected – a cold person – and had so wanted to slap her for how she had cruelly treated Rupert, her son. And since the meeting Babs had felt more determined than ever to take Art away from her. Nothing in her manner suggested that she was fond of her grandchild. Babs had thought her incapable of loving any child as she knew that Rupert hadn't felt loved by her. Poor Rupert had told her so much of his heartache that had been caused by his mother. And how she spoke of 'my son's child' was in the terms of a nuisance that she had to deal with.

'I want you to see that he is disciplined well,' she'd said in a way that you might speak of a dog. 'His manners are to be impeccable. He is to know his place and when he is not to interrupt his elders, and that he is to be seen and not heard. I don't want him mollycoddled, or made a cissy of. He is to show that he has a backbone. And he is to be prepared for boarding school, where he will go at the age of seven.' She'd hardly taken breath before she said, 'I understand that you are well educated and I want you to be part tutor as well as to see to the child's welfare. I want you to teach him to speak French, and I am informed you are well versed in French art?'

Though she wouldn't say she was knowledgeable about French art, Rupert and Cath had taught her a lot and given her a love of art on their trips into Paris on their days off from their work on the hospital train.

Lady Barnham had also said that the whole family would like to take a trip to Paris, and that she would accompany them and be their interpreter and show them the sights.

This had appealed to Babs as something she would very much like to do. To see Paris in peacetime, and to remember Rupert, though the latter didn't appear to feature in Lady Barnham's mind. Babs would have expected any mother to want to go to see where her late son worked and maybe where he died, and to honour him in some way. However, Lady Barnham hadn't been a mother, but a heartless woman who had wanted little, if anything, to do with her son, and had banished his beloved nanny – not because of her northern accent, but, Rupert believed, because he had loved her and she him.

This thought gave her a sudden insight into what may have been the true reason that the nurse had gone.

'Pearl, I can be strong. I know that now, and I also know that I have to do something harder than anything else I've had to do in my life.'

'Oh, what's that?'

'I have to be professional with Art, but not affectionate. As I think I know the reason that the nurse suddenly left.' She told Pearl how Rupert's nanny was banished. 'I think Art's nurse has suffered the same fate.'

'Hmm, you could be right. Well, it will be a fine balance, but maybe you could show him love, but teach him not to let his grandmother see that he loves you. I mean, if we weren't planning to get him away from her, I would never advocate teaching him such deceit, but I do think for him to be happy when you leave with him, he will need to know that you love him and he will need to love you, otherwise he is going to go through a terrible ordeal, and he doesn't deserve that.'

'Yes, you're right. How I will do that, though, I can't imagine.'

'Don't try to imagine it. Until you know what Art is like, how intelligent he is, and if he is someone who can keep a secret, then you can't plan for him.'

'No, but your sister's nanny told me that the way to teach a small child is through play. So, I could do that, make it all a game that we love each other, but Grandmother and Grandfather don't know that.'

'I think you are going to do fine, Babs – Cath, I mean. I must call you that from now on as I have slipped up lately ...'

'No! How?'

'Oh, I haven't actually done it. But I have so nearly called you Babs when I shouldn't have. It was having the old you back while we were in Blackpool that did it ... You know, I loved our time in Blackpool. And your family and friends, and your home. I loved your home so much. When I am making my own home, I'm going to model it on yours. I have looked into shipping goods to Canada, and I have my eye on a few things that your ma and Alec and Molly and Florrie make. Once Bart and I have bought a place of our own and I know the layout, I'm going to write to your ma and order quite a lot to be sent over to me – baskets, basket chairs and stools, curtains, cushions, counterpanes and, oh yes, some of the unique ornaments that Molly's husband makes too. I can give them all the instructions of how to crate and dispatch them.'

'That's wonderful! I can do the same. It will be like having Ma and all of them in our homes with us. Oh, Pearl, she will be so thrilled, they all will. And you know, Ma may know quite a bit about shipping her goods as she told me that when she and Tommy lived in Ireland, she used to still make her baskets and have them shipped to Liverpool to be picked up for the shop.'

'That's perfect then. Oh, I can't wait. I will miss my family and England, but I know that you can get used to that; we did when we were in France. And besides, as soon as I have some-where, Mama and Papa will visit ... Oh ... Oh my God! I never thought. None of us did! But they will know by then that you have taken Art!'

Babs's heart dropped like a stone. Why hadn't this occurred to them? Why hadn't they planned for that happening? Suddenly it seemed that her quest was hopeless.

'Oh, Babs ... Cath, how can we get around that? Nothing we do – telling them you are away, or you are visiting without Art – will cut it as it will be obvious that the girl they took in and found a job for had stolen their friend's grandchild!'

Babs felt as though she was drowning.

After what seemed like a long silence, Pearl said, 'I suppose we could come clean with them and tell them who you really are, and your story. My mama and papa are very compassion-ate, they may decide to go along with it. It's our only way really, or they will be hounding me in letters to tell them who you are and where you might be.'

'That's it! Where I might be . . . they won't have an inkling that I am in Canada with Marc. They know we are friends, but they don't know that it went any further than that.'

'Oh, I don't know what to think anymore. I'm so sorry to put this panic on you just as we are arriving. But look, we have time. We can think of something as nothing is going to happen until Christmas. I'll give it thought and you do the same.'

'That's all we can do. But, Pearl, please don't do anything until we talk over the options we come up with. I mean, don't go ahead and try to tell the truth to your parents or anything like that, as something much better may occur to us that will make that a huge mistake.'

'I promise. We'll write often. You have Bart's address. Letters will take a time to get to me, but we'll make it a priority to think of something very quickly.'

The train began to slow, and Babs felt a tremble ripple through her as fear of her coming ordeal increased. They both stood to look out of the window. When Babs caught sight of a chauffeur in a uniform of a similar colour to her own – light grey – she took a deep breath. 'This is it. Oh, Pearl, I am so glad that it was agreed that you should accompany me. I couldn't do this on my own.'

Pearl took her in her arms. 'I'll always be by your side. Even when I am thousands of miles away, you only need to think of me and I will be with you. And I will do the same, as parting from you is breaking my heart.'

Babs felt a surge of love for Pearl. They had been through so much together – the blood, sweat and tears of field hospital life, and yes, the hope of that time too, when they saved a life, or limited someone's life-changing injury. Their friendship had been her salvation. That it should continue now with a huge class divide between them was a measure of its strength.

Barnham Hall, the earl's home, was a huge, rambling building at the end of a long drive lined with trees, the symmetry of which was broken every now and again by the placement of a bench or a statue. It had two wings, one on either side, and its walls were covered with ivy.

When the car pulled up at the bottom of the steps leading to the front door, the class divide between herself and Pearl was never more marked than when the chauffeur opened the door to the side Pearl sat, then closed it and unloaded her luggage before returning to the driving seat.

A butler came out and greeted Pearl. Babs waited, but then the car went around the island between the two wings of the house. Looking back, she saw Pearl standing staring after them, not heeding the butler picking up her luggage and waiting to escort her into the house.

When they reached the other side of the wing, the car stopped. No opening of the door this time. Babs sighed and got out of the car. Her baggage was dumped beside her and the driver, in not an impolite voice, told her to ring the bell on the gate ahead and someone would show her in.

The someone was a maid, who did a little curtsey – even downstairs folk had their own class system and Babs had learnt from her short time at Pearl's sister's house that the nanny was looked on as having a lot higher status than the maids.

'Good afternoon, miss. I'll take your luggage and take you to the housekeeper. She will see to you.'

'Thank you, dear, that is very good of you.'

The maid relaxed and smiled up at Babs, showing a mouthful of blackened teeth. This shocked Babs. Surely in a household such as this the servants were taken care of? But she had no time to ponder this as she was soon in the company of the very formidable Miss Pratt, who dismissed the maid, giving Babs a jolt as her name filled her with memories of her lovely friend from her days in the convent.

'That will be all, Daisy, and if you haven't blackened that stove by the time I come back, you will be packing your bags. You're flipping hopeless!'

Babs gasped.

'Well, she is, and I am plagued by having many like her. You will find that this house is run on a very tight budget and one that doesn't allow for me to get decent, well-trained staff. Now, come this way, Miss Dufont. I will show you to the nursery and introduce you to your charge, and then to your room. Your bag will be taken up for you.'

Babs felt her heart in her throat. The moment was on her. Biting her bottom lip, she followed Miss Pratt.

As she went, Miss Pratt gave her the rundown of how her day would be. 'You can choose when and where to have your meals. They can be served in your own dining room with Master Rupert's . . .'

At the small noise involuntarily released from Babs, Miss Pratt turned and looked at her. 'Are you all right?'

'Yes, thank you.' She offered no more explanation, thinking that to do so would make things worse. *Why didn't I realise that Art would naturally revert to his first name?* But then, his grandmother hadn't referred to his name at all, and so nothing had given her a hint of this obvious conclusion. She'd only called him Art because his father's name was too posh for a lad who was meant to be brought up in Blackpool.

Not having time to think about it more or to compose herself for the next hurdle, she listened as Miss Pratt took her along a number of corridors and up a flight of stairs and continued with a list of how and when she could have her meals, and the general outline of the parts of the day that would concern her. There was nothing about the route to give Babs any other impression than this was the servants' quarters, until they went through a door at the end of the last corridor and light flooded the large landing they stepped into. 'This is part of the main house, Miss Dufont, and is where you are housed.'

To the left of Babs was a wide descending staircase. 'You will take Master Rupert down that way to his grandparents if you are required to. The nurse in house at the moment knows the ropes and will talk you through them, barring any changes by Lady Barnham, of course.'

They turned to the right. This vast landing was papered in a very regal pattern of browns and golds, and light came from a skylight in the ceiling, a magnificent dome made of beautiful stained glass. 'Right, through here.' Miss Pratt opened two double doors and swept through. They were now in a corridor with doors on the right side only. The brown and gold flocked paper continued to adorn the walls here, and again, this was a light and airy space as on the left side there were a number of windows looking out over immaculate landscaped gardens. 'Now, here we are. Here is the key. That door there leads to your bathroom and is for yours and Master Rupert's use only.'

As she said this, Miss Pratt pointed to a door a few feet from her bedroom. 'We'll go along to the nursery now and you can acquaint yourself with your apartments afterwards.'

Babs's legs turned to jelly.

Just a few steps along they passed another door. 'That leads to Master Rupert's bedroom, but you will find when you enter yours that you have a door that leads directly to his, and an inner door to your bathroom, and that Master Rupert's bedroom leads through to your sitting room and dining room and then to the nursery at the end of the wing – well, we call it a nursery, but it is where you and he carry out activities as the cot has long since gone.

'Here we are.' Miss Pratt gave one sharp knock and then before she could be summoned to, she opened the door and entered. 'Miss Dufont. The new nanny.'

This didn't give any respect to the young nurse sitting in an armchair by the fire of a large room that held no cheer. Cream-painted walls gave a clinical impression and weren't relieved by any paintings. A small round table stood in the centre and a bashed old rocking horse occupied one corner. To her left was an array of cupboards and Babs assumed that this was where Rupert's toys were as, but for a pile of books, the horse and the height of the table, you would never guess that this was a room for a child to be amused in.

'Oh, hello. I'm Jane. Master Rupert is asleep at the moment. Come on in. You can leave Miss Dufont with me now, Miss Pratt. Thank you.'

Miss Pratt turned with a humph and left.

Jane, a tiny girl, which belied her standing as a children's nurse, who Babs thought were always buxom, motherly figures, came over to her. 'Well now, Miss Dufont, I'll just start by taking your coat and pouring you a cup of tea. I've only just made it.'

'Nice to meet you, Jane. I understand you are going to talk me through the ropes.'

'Yes. I'll soon run through the routine with you.'

'Is the routine a set one then? I thought that was down to the nanny to organise.'

'Oooh, don't even think you can make changes. Lady Barnham is a tartar. She has set Master Rupert's routine, and only she can change it. Mind, this being my last day, and him being overtired today, I have dared to change it and put him down for a nap before I should do. Would you like to see him? He's adorable.' She laughed. 'That is, when he's asleep. He can be a scamp when awake. But then, can't all little boys? Follow me.'

Babs's legs felt as though they were made of wood. Somehow, she followed. But then to her relief, Jane stopped at the door at the end of the row of cupboards. 'Creep in, he's a light sleeper. I'll pour our tea.'

With a prayer of thanks for this opportunity to see her baby son on her own for the first time in just under three years, Babs stepped inside.

Tears welled up in her eyes as she looked down on the angelic child, sleeping on his side with his thumb in his mouth. *Oh, my darling, my baby.*

Her hands reached out, but a voice behind her stopped her. 'You'll rue the day. Let him wake up in his own time. He can be very fractious if woken before he's ready.'

Babs jumped back as if she'd been caught red-handed doing something she shouldn't.

'Sorry, I didn't mean to boss you, I was just pre-warning you. If you want to wake him, feel free.'

Annoyed at herself more than anything, Babs said, 'I will.'

Jane scurried away.

I have to. I can't just stand looking at my son and not touching him. Shaking him gently, she called his name.

A small moan came from his beautiful lips – his father's lips, full and protruding slightly. As he rolled over, still in a dreamy state, she could see just how his features were so like her lovely Rupert's. *Our son is just like you, my darling.* But his hair and, when he opened them, his eyes were hers. 'Hello.'

The tears were flowing freely now. Tears full of joy.

Little Rupert stared up at her, but showed no fear. His eyebrows creased. His little head went to one side. 'Are you crying?'

His voice was beautiful.

'Yes, with happiness at meeting you.'

He frowned again, then sat up. Babs sat next to him. Holding her arm, he lifted himself onto his knees. His chubby hand reached out and he wiped her face. 'Happy tears?'

'Yes. Everyone can cry sad and happy tears.'

'I cry sad tears.'

'Oh, what about when you giggle? Don't you cry happy ones then?'

Rupert nodded. Then slipped off the bed and came to stand in front of her. Looking up into her face, he studied her. She wanted to clutch him and hold him close.

'Where did you come from?'

'I'm to be your nanny. Do you know what one of those is?'

He put his elbows on her knee and held his head in his hands, still looking up at her, then he shook his head.

'Well, I am like the nurse you have, only I will do more than care for you, I will teach you things. How to read a book. How to speak in a different language. And we will go for walks and I will teach you what all the wild animals are, and what the birds are called.'

'I like animals. What's a lang . . . gage?'

'It's the way that we speak and let each other know what we want to say. We are speaking English, but in other countries, they speak in a different way.'

Rupert shrugged as if what she was telling him was too much for him.

'Don't worry about it. It will be very gradual, and like a game. You will enjoy it, I promise. Would you like to sit on my knee?'

Rupert scrambled up.

As Babs enclosed him in her arms, she closed her eyes against the powerful onslaught of emotions that were unlike any she'd felt since he was handed to her just after his birth.

Putting her head gently on his, she was rewarded with him snuggling into her.

'That is something I would advise you against, Miss Dufont. That little boy is starved of love, and if he is shown any, he grabs it with both hands, to the detriment of those who love him. His nurse did that, and once his attachment to her came to the notice of Lady Barnham, she was up the road with her suitcase.'

Babs kept her head down. 'Yes, I realised that as soon as he woke and I smiled at him. But how can anyone not love him?'

'I know. He tugs at your heart with those eyes; they are pools of loneliness, poor little soul. Anyway, I will have to go soon. Baker – the chauffeur – is taking me to the station, so if you want to come and get your tea, I can tell you what you need to know.'

'Yes, I'll be out in a moment.'

Hastily wiping her face with her free hand, she whispered to Rupert. 'Happy tears are our secret.'

With the intelligence of a much older child, he nodded. 'I like secrets. I had secrets with my nurse.'

'That's lovely. I think your nurse was a very nice nurse because some secrets are good. I expect one of them was that she loved you.'

Rupert nodded.

'Well, that will be our secret too, because I love you, Rupert. With all my heart. But you must never tell anyone.'

Rupert looked at her with the same quizzical expression that his father had often used and Babs's heart did a little flip and nearly somersaulted as he tugged her hair, pulling her face closer to his. He put his hands on each of her cheeks and kissed her.

To Babs, her dreams came true in that moment.

THIRTY-ONE

Beth and Tilly

Beth looked at the contraption in front of her. The huge iron construction resembled more of an instrument of torture than something which would give her back her life.

The banging and clanging as the workmen assembled it in the spare bedroom over the last week had nearly driven her mad, and she'd had times when she wanted to scream that she would stay in a wheelchair all her life if only they would cease. But a big part of her was hoping against hope that it would work.

Henry had said that his theory was based on reconnecting the mind with the muscles and strengthening them at the same time so that when this miracle happened, she was able to walk on her own.

He'd explained many times that her paralysis was only temporary and if he hadn't gone to war, he would have been able to help her before now. 'The problem is that a lot of doctors don't believe in my theory. The professors I have been working with of late do. They have had their successes, darling.

But it also takes a lot of work and determination, and a great deal of courage from the patient. You have that in abundance, my darling.'

Looking at the frame, which reached to the ceiling and supported strong, thick ropes on pullies and a sort of brace that she would be strapped into, all of the courage Beth might have had deserted her.

'Darling, this is it. This is going to be a major help to you. Are you ready?'

Henry had spent hours with her telling her it was possible that she could walk again, because her paralysis wasn't as complete as it would be if her spinal cord was damaged. 'You have sensation in your legs and feet.' Then he'd winked at her. 'And in other places too.'

They'd giggled, and the moment had led to Henry lifting her and taking her to their bedroom to demonstrate what he meant – as if she didn't know. His demonstration was very sensuous, and when they could resist no longer and began to make love, she called out in ecstasy, oblivious to them having left a surprised Peggy sitting in Beth's sitting room.

When they'd finally gone back Peggy wasn't anywhere to be found. A note was propped up on the mantelshelf saying that she'd gone for a walk.

They'd collapsed in giggles, and had just let the moment pass when Peggy returned as if nothing had happened. But thinking of it now brought a blush to Beth's cheeks as Peggy spoke. 'Eeh, I don't like the look of it, Henry.'

'Now, Peggy, it's our job to help and encourage Beth.'

'I don't knaw if I can. I'd be terrified she was going to get hurt.'

'You have no need to physically do anything, Peggy, or even be in here while Beth is on the machine. Just encourage her if she is flagging and saying she doesn't want to go through with a certain scheduled session. I have two nurses coming who are familiar with it, and will see that the exercises are carried out correctly.'

Beth reached up and took Peggy's hand. Seeing her fear helped Beth to be brave once more. 'Don't worry, dear Peggy. I'm ready now. Let's do this.'

As if on cue the doorbell rang. 'Ah, that will be them now.' As Henry passed her to go down to let his nurses in, he caught hold of her other hand. 'It starts today, darling. The beginning of your road to recovery. I'm so excited.'

His excitement conveyed itself to her. 'I am too, darling. Let's get started.'

None of what she feared happened. The nurses, Prudence and Marion, were strong and knew how to lift her. In no time she was strapped in and being gently bounced onto her feet and off again. This caused her legs to bend and then, when she went up in the air, they would straighten them again. Her part was to breathe deeply when she went up and exhale when she was lowered. And though after a while it was tiring, the exhilaration at just standing upright when she was on the ground made up for that.

For the first time ever, she had hope, and with this a determination that this would succeed. Henry had said it would take a while, but that she must work with it. And she would. She willed her legs to take her weight as he said that would help her brain to once more send the messages to them.

After fifteen minutes, which seemed like a day, the nurses got her into a hot bath and then lay her on a table on the other side of the room and massaged her muscles.

'I must say, Marion, it feels good to be 'elping one of our own.'

'It does, Pru. I ain't ever met anyone who went to nurse overseas, Beth. I'm in awe of you.'

From the moment they'd taken charge of her, Beth was reminded of Amy as they had the same accent. She'd never yet made it to the station to see if Amy still worked there. She made her mind up that she would get Peggy to push her along there later.

'Well, it wasn't easy, and I still have nightmares about it, but you did your bit here. We had to have nurses to send them home to.'

'Yes, and I were glad you sent my Pete home. He came in the 'ospital near to death, but went out wed to me. Poor bugger!'

Beth joined Marion in giggling at this from Pru. 'I bagged one as well. I mean, what else could you do? All the doctors were meant to be retired, they weren't marriage material at all, but the soldiers ... We eyed them up, then stitched them up, mended them, made sure everything worked and then married them!'

Beth collapsed with laughter. These girls were a tonic.

'Well, my Pete weren't all in working order, but he's getting there. It's the nightmares that bother him. Are yours bad, Beth?'

'They are calming down now. Especially now I have Henry home. So, how do you get away with still nursing if you are married?'

'We can't, can we, Pru?'

'No, that's why we do this job. We work in a rehab clinic; this is extra money for us.'

'Oh, so that's where Henry met you. He's kept most of the details away from me, as I haven't looked forward to this, but now I am. I'm going to look forward, not only to the treatment, but having you two here as well. I don't see many women of my own age, and definitely not of my own profession. I'm going to love having you here.'

'Well, we've made a good start then. I think that calls for a cup of tea, Marion. You go and find the kitchen and put the kettle on while I help Beth to dress.'

Beth didn't know how Peggy would take this, as she felt that the kitchen was her realm.

She was surprised, and very pleased, when Peggy came into the room with Marion. 'Eeh, lass, we've fallen on our feet with these two. I'm going to look forward to their visits. Marion here is a card.'

Beth inwardly sighed with relief, but outwardly she just smiled.

It was the next morning when Beth finally made it to the station, but Amy wasn't there. All the women staff had been laid off and men were once more in the positions of porters, guards and ticket collectors.

'I'll ask one of them, they might knaw your Amy, lass.'

When she came back, Beth was disappointed that no one knew Amy. 'Well, that's all we can do, Peggy. I'll never forget her. She was coping with her man having to go to war when we met her in that café along the road, and was so embarrassed at how he'd gone for Henry. I liked her, and promised that one day I would come to find her if I came back to live in Margate.'

'Well, you still might meet her one day, lass. For my part, I'm really happy that you have Pru and Marion calling on you. I've allus worried that you only had me for company since we came down here.'

'Are you happy, Peggy? I mean, would you like to go back?'

'I can't lie. I would. Look, I'll push you over there so that I can sit a while.' Once Peggy had sat on the bench she began looking out at the sea. 'You'd think one seaside town would be like another, but there's naw place like Blackpool. It gets into your heart.'

'I'm sorry, Peggy. I miss it as well, so I have an idea of how you feel. It's the people, how they all chat to you, and the liveliness.'

'And the fish and chips. What they serve here don't come anywhere near.'

'And most of all family. I had such a short time with Ma and Babs and Eliza.'

'For me it's friends. It's knowing everyone. Even if they aren't your close friends, they are still your folk.'

'Peggy, when I can walk, you must go back.' Beth knew it was no use suggesting this happened now, though she felt that was what Peggy needed. She would never go, not while Beth needed her.

'I'll find it hard to leave you, Beth. I feel like you're me daughter sometimes – awe, not in the way that Jasmine did, but just in how close we are. It'd be a wrench to go.'

Beth put out her hand and took Peggy's. 'And for me too. And yes, you are much more than my nurse to me. I love you very much.'

Peggy's face creased in her lovely smile, which she rarely let see light of day, and tears glistened in her eyes. 'And you knaw that I love you, lass. Come on, we're getting all maudlin when this is a good day. The day you stepped on the ladder to recovery.'

Beth caught her breath. Could it happen? Somehow, she knew it could.

Tilly drove along the promenade. She'd been held up for a good ten minutes as the crowds spewed out of Central station. It always surprised her just how many folk came to Blackpool, but pleased her too.

When she reached the shop, she was amazed to see a new design in the window. Always there'd been shelves with baskets and a few cushions in the opposite corner, and bigger baskets in the centre. Nothing special, just a way of showing what the shop sold. Now, it looked beautiful. Everything was set out as if it was a room. Two basket chairs were each side of a beautiful occasional table, which had a glass bowl in the centre that sat in a basket that fitted it perfectly. The bowl was of red glass and it shone through the basket. Each chair had a lovely cushion in a flowery, country-looking pattern. The shelves were still to the side, and they were arranged with all kinds of baskets.

Opening the shop door, she was greeted by Mary. 'Eeh, Tilly, what do you think?'

'I love it, lass. Who did it and when did Alec make that wonderful little table?'

'Ha, we wanted to surprise you. Molly's coming in a few minutes an' all. And Florrie. Will's fetching Florrie. She has worked so hard on those cushions.'

'Well, you have surprised me. And in a lovely way. I need to talk to Alec, I want one of those tables meself.'

'He'll be so pleased. He's been making it in the evenings. I've been here some of the time with him. He didn't want to share it, so it was allus put in his room behind the door. He wasn't sure that he'd got the design right.'

'Well, he has.' As she said this, Tilly felt the time was coming when she could retire fully. And she and Tommy could do some of that travelling they always talked of. She'd loved visiting Beth. Well, once all was sorted, she had. 'And he needn't hide them from me any longer.'

'Who's hiding what? Eeh, lass, that window display looks lovely. Did you do that?' Will asked, as he and Molly arrived at the shop door.

Molly had walked in, and after having a hug, she asked, 'What do you reckon to it, Tilly?'

'I love it. These young 'uns are taking our shop onwards and upwards, Molly. Oh, and here's Florrie.'

'All the gang's together then. What was it that was hiding?'

After greeting Florrie and Will, they all chatted about the window display. 'You've a real talent in shop management, Mary. Well done.'

'Ta, Tilly, that means a lot.' Going to the bottom of the stairs, she called out to Alec to come down. When he did, Mary said, 'We have sommat to tell you all. Go on, Alec.'

'We've set a date to get wed. Christmas Eve.'

Everyone clapped their hands. 'But why wait so long, Mary?'

'Well, Vera came in earlier. Have you seen her, Molly?'

'Naw, I were going to stop by the stall, but there were that many folk about I came straight here.'

'Well, I should leave it to her and Brian to tell you, but just to say there's going to be an event in September, and until after that, Vera won't want to be wearing a bridesmaid frock.'

'Naw! Naw! Oh, that's grand news.' Molly grabbed Will and they danced about. When they stopped everyone was laughing. Molly went up to Mary and took her hands. 'I mean both of the bits of news that you've given us, Mary. We'll be so happy to see you and Alec married. I'll get right on with making your frock.'

When everyone had congratulated Mary, Alec and Molly, Tilly said, 'I still think Christmas Eve a funny day to wed. Are you sure that the priest will accommodate you? It's a busy time for them.'

'Aye, we've already spoken to him. And the reason is that we want everyone here. You said, Tilly, that both Babs and Beth were hoping to be here, and Peggy too. And I didn't want to wed without them, especially Beth. I do miss her.'

Tilly knew how well Mary and Beth had got on, and was glad to hear Mary say this. She didn't say that they were expecting Marc to come too. She didn't want questions, in case she slipped up. As far as they all knew, Babs was working as a nurse with her friend and near to Beth, until the time that her husband was demobbed and could come and fetch her.

Linking in with Florrie and Molly, she said, 'Right, lasses, now that we're all together, let's go around to Eliza's and see how she is doing. By, she'll have her work cut out this Christmas by the sound of it.'

Molly kissed Will and sent him on his way. 'See you later, love. It's women's time now.'

Will laughed. 'Well, that's means as I'll not see you for hours then. Eeh, you lasses can chinwag when you get going.'

As they walked along to Eliza's shop, they chattered on about the news and all they had to do. 'Well, it's months away yet, and they've given us plenty of warning. Eeh, I'm that happy. By, I'm to be a granny again, and Mary's settled an' all. I reckon as everything's going to come right at last.'

'It is, Molly. Though how do you feel about your girls being so far away from you once more, Tilly? I feel so bad for you.'

'Naw, Florrie. It's nowt like last time, at least I knaw where they are. And, well, I reckon that I at least can fully retire soon, and then me and Tommy plan on going to see our girls wherever they are.'

Tilly couldn't believe herself how she was accepting of all that was happening. She'd always dreamt that her girls would take over her business, but now she couldn't see that happening.

'Well, I might do the same. You manage all the sewing now, Florrie, but if ever you want to let up, we can get an apprentice in and get that side of the business sorted an' all.'

'Aye, well, that'll be a long time coming, Molly. I'm all right. I love what I do and being able to do it at home suits me. I loved seeing me cushions displayed in the shop window how they were. Mary's done a grand job.'

They had reached Eliza's shop.

'Eeh, ain't it grand that Eliza has achieved her dream an' all, Tilly?'

'It is, but I worry about her. It's too much for her on her own.'

'Well, there's plenty of lasses looking for work now the men are back. It shouldn't be too difficult to find an assistant.'

'I heard that, Aunt Molly.' Eliza came out of the shop. 'I was just coming to stick this notice on the door. So if you hear of anyone, let me knaw.'

'Eeh, Eliza, lass, them cakes in the window look delicious.' Florrie said. 'I'll have one to eat on me way home.'

'And me,' Molly and Tilly said in chorus.

'Well, you can come in and eat it if you like. I had an idea today, and I'd like to hear what you think of it.' They followed Eliza in. 'There.'

In the corner of the space in front of the counter was a table and chairs with a gingham cloth covering it.

'Why, that's grand, and can we get a cup of tea an' all.'

'Well, you can, but I ain't sorted for customers to do that yet. I want to set it up, though, but just one table ain't going to be enough. I'd love to move the counter and make this a café as well as a cake shop. What do you think, Ma?'

'I think as you are a clever and lovely daughter, lass. And that you're going to go far. I'd say, get yourself a good worker, and then let's get Cliff and Phil here for a morning. Tommy can spare them, then they can move everything around for you. By, Eliza, lass, I'm proud of you, I am.'

Tilly gave her a hug, and then Eliza told them that as she didn't want to use the flat upstairs where Ma Perkins lived, she'd one day like to turn that into an upstairs café.

'By, there's naw stopping you, lass. Never mind your ma being proud of you. We are an' all, ain't we, Florrie?'

'More than proud.'

Tilly looked at her lovely, grown-up Eliza, and knew that she was now a strong young woman. All that had happened in the family had given her that strength. She was a very special person.

'Well, christen me first table then. Come on, sit yourselves down. Eeh, if Ma Perkins were here, she'd say you were making the place look untidy.'

They all burst out laughing. Tilly looked at her friends and winked. 'That's me Eliza for you.'

'Aye, and we'd not have her any different. She's allus been the same, naw matter what gets thrown at her. It's nice to see her settled in what she's allus wanted for herself.'

'It is, Molly. It really is.' Tilly swelled with pride.

THIRTY-TWO

Babs

Babs looked out of her sitting-room window. The garden was now clothed in its gold, brown and red autumn colours and still looked as beautiful as ever.

Today she would have to endure the ordeal of having tea with Miss Pratt, who, since Babs had been here, had taken to coming up once a week.

Babs didn't mind. She liked the company, as none of the others were allowed to visit her because they were seen as being below her station, and it was frowned on for Rupert to spend too much time in their company – one of the many rules which Babs hated but she stuck to, not wanting to do anything to upset Lady Barnham.

Thankfully, she had little to do with that lady. Sometimes they would be summoned and Lady Barnham would coldly ask what Rupert had learnt since she last saw him. Babs always schooled him in what to say. Not often, but every now and again, Lady Barnham would raise an eyebrow and begrudgingly give her grandson a little praise, but always it had a sting in the tail. Yesterday, Babs had prepared him to greet his grand-mother in French. He practised on the way. He stood tall with a beam on his face and in a clear voice said, '*Bonne journée, grand-mère.*'

Looking up at her, Lady Barnham had asked, in an irate voice, 'What is the boy saying?'

Shocked that such a lady didn't even know the basics of how to say good day in French, Babs told her. In reply, there was a 'humph'. No praising Rupert's massive effort. And, 'Speak only in English to me, boy.'

'I beg your pardon, Lady Barnham, it is my fault. I thought you would like to hear his progress in the French language. He is doing very well, and can now ask for any basic things that he needs.'

'Very well. And I want you to continue with that. How is his reading coming along?'

How Babs longed for her to direct a question to Rupert, or even to use his name. But she never did. 'Master Rupert can say the alphabet and make the sounds of all the letters, ma'am.'

'Good. Very well, you may take him back to the nursery.'

Babs had been seething as she'd walked out of the sitting room where they had been received.

A tap on the door interrupted her thoughts. Running to open it, not daring to call out, Babs prayed that Rupert wouldn't be woken from his nap. She didn't want the housekeeper or anyone to see the love they had between them that gave her such great happiness.

This was getting difficult as every day Rupert told her that

410

he loved her, and she him, but she so worried that their deep attachment would be noticed and reported, and she suspected the first one to do that would be Miss Pratt.

As always, Miss Pratt didn't greet her but waded in with whatever was on her mind. 'I'm telling you, Nanny, if I come to this room a thousand times, I will always have the same memory of Master Rupert's father as a boy.'

This shocked Babs. She'd often wondered why no one spoke of her Rupert. He was the son of the mistress and master of the house and had been brought up here, and yet she'd never seen a photo of him, or heard him referred to.

'He was such a lovely boy, and so lonely after Elsie, his beloved nanny, was banished ... Oh, I beg your pardon, I'm talking of things that I shouldn't. Forgive me, but, well, I have wanted to tell you about him before, but I had to be sure of you. Anyway, I don't know if you know or not, but Master Rupert's father was also called Rupert and we lost him in the war. Broke all our hearts. May he rest in peace.'

Babs had thought that she was ready for Rupert to be talked about, but she didn't feel it at the moment. Remembering what she and Pearl had practised, she responded in the way that would be expected of her. 'I'm sorry to hear that. So, what happened to Master Rupert's mother?'

'We were told by the mistress that she died, but, well, we know different.'

Babs trembled. Swallowing hard, she braced herself.

'Well, like I say, we're not supposed to know, but Annie, you know, Master Rupert's nurse before you came, well, she knew all about it. She said that Master Rupert's father married a girl from a much lower class. That was typical of him, he had no

411

side to him. Anyway, the poor girl was forced to give her child up.'

Babs waited, hoping against hope that Miss Pratt – a gossiper about the household, and her mistress and master's business – didn't know any more about 'the poor girl' but thankfully, she didn't offer anything further.

'That's very sad, but I expect it was necessary. After all, Master Rupert is the earl's heir.'

'Yes, that's how we all look on it, and glad to have him we are too. He's a ray of sunshine and looks just like his father, though his hair isn't his father's. Funny, but come to think of it, it's just the same as yours, isn't it? You don't often see hair that colour. A sort of blue-black.'

Feeling her colour rise, Babs held on to her control and kept to the script. Pearl had thought of every situation she might find herself in. 'Oh, I get mine from my French ancestry. And my poor eyesight from her too, or so I have been told.'

'You know, I thought you would have a French accent, not a posh one.'

Again, all of this had been practised. 'Well, I can't go into all of my history now, but I was born in England and taken to France to live with a British aunt who had moved there. She spoke the King's English and insisted that I did too while I was in her company. It was only when in school or visiting friends that I spoke French.'

'Ah, well, the French have very dark hair, don't they? You'd think that Rupert would have married a French girl as he was out there so long, but no, he married a nurse according to Annie.'

Babs clenched her fingers till her palms felt sore as she waited for what might come next, but Miss Pratt didn't mention her having been a nurse.

'Oh, well, there's no accounting for love, and Rupert Senior was not like the rest of the family. Like I say, a lovely boy.'

You were a lovely lad, Rupert. My first love.

'Anyway, what are you going to get up to on your days off?'

Thankful to change the subject, Babs told her that she was just going to take a train along the coastline. 'I thought I would enjoy looking at the sights through the train window. From what I saw of the area on my journey from Brighton, it looks so lovely.'

She didn't say that she would go to Margate, she didn't want anyone knowing that. And now, with her new plan, she couldn't wait for tomorrow to come. *If only I could take little Rupert with me now. Beth would so love to see him.* She hated leaving him.

Babs hated the thought of Helen, the head girl of the upstairs maids, taking care of little Rupert while she wasn't here. But this was the procedure and little Rupert was used to it and liked Helen. Though apart from these times she wasn't allowed to show an interest in him, which Babs thought was harsh.

For a little boy, he had learnt some strange rules, but took them in his stride. Babs had realised this when they had come across Helen one day as she polished the banister of the stairs they used. Rupert had looked up at Babs and said, 'We mustn't talk to Helen, only when she comes to the nursery.'

Miss Pratt had informed Babs of this, so she didn't question it. She just smiled at Helen and was rewarded with a lovely smile in return.

When Miss Pratt left, having gone through all that had happened in the house in the last two days, Babs sat back. Her thoughts were in turmoil. *This atmosphere will stifle my little Rupert. I cannot wait until Christmas. I have to get him away. I want to be his ma, not his nanny!*

Beth came to mind. *Would she help me? Would it be too risky? Did Earl Barnham's solicitor know of Beth's existence?* As the idea took hold, Babs let her mind go over that painful day when Art had been taken from her. Nothing she remembered told of anyone having made a reference to Beth. And she knew Rupert hadn't said anything about her family or of her having a twin sister in the letters he sent home that told of herself.

The idea began to form in her mind. She could do it! She would wait until December – two months away, that's all – then take her little Rupert to Beth's. Live there with him until Marc came to pick her up, and then they could sail to Canada and to safety.

The morning wasn't easy. Babs was packed ready to go, but Rupert was fractious. 'I don't want you to go. Me come with you.'

'You can't, darling. Now, be a good boy.' Babs hated threatening him, but knew she must do. 'If you aren't good and just wave me off without crying, I may never come back.'

His bottom lip quivered and Babs gathered him into her arms. 'Oh, my darling boy, that will never happen. I will always find you, I promise, but it will be so difficult if your grandmother makes me leave.'

With understanding beyond his years, he snuggled into her.

'Rupert will be a good boy, but it will hurt here.' He patted his heart. 'Please come back, Nanny, please.'

Feeling terrible at making him so unsure of her, but desperate to have him behave as if it didn't matter to him that she was going, she hugged him. 'Help me to always be with you, my darling boy. Help me by being very good for Helen, and not crying for me.'

How could she expect such a little mite to understand? 'Look. You know how much I like my lace handkerchief that a friend gave me, don't you? And how I would never leave it behind?'

Rupert nodded. A tear plopped onto his cheek. Babs wiped it away with her thumb. 'Well, I'll leave that with you and that will tell you that I will be back. Now, where shall we hide it, where no one will find it?'

As only children can, Rupert brightened as if someone had switched a button in him from sad to happy. 'I have a secret place, but you must not tell anyone.'

'I won't. But hurry, Helen will be here soon.'

Taking her hand, he led her into the nursery and over to the shelf where there were a few items he wasn't allowed to touch. One was a china doll, which Rupert pointed to. Babs didn't know its origin, but imagined it had belonged to a little girl who used these rooms long before even Miss Pratt was here as she'd never ventured to talk about it.

'We take off its head.'

Curious, Babs did as he said. To her surprise, when she unscrewed it she saw a folded paper inside. Pulling it out, she read, *I will always love you, little Rupert. You can look at this whenever you think about me. But never tell anyone. Annie x*

Babs wanted to cry. Poor Annie.

'I know what it says. Annie read it to me, but she won't mind me showing it to you, Nanny. And Nursie said I could always look at it, but I can't read it yet. Nursie said that I would when I am a big boy.'

'You will, darling. And now I know of it, I will read it to you whenever you want me to. Now, let's put it back carefully and fold my hanky in with it and you will know that I will come back.'

This done, Rupert took her hand and led her back into her sitting room. There she picked him up and held him to her, vowing to herself that one day he would see Annie again. And though she hadn't dared go to see Rupert's old nanny, Elsie, despite longing to, she still wrote to her, even though she couldn't receive letters back, so she would ask Elsie to tell Annie that Rupert still loved her.

As she left the house and got into the car that would take her to the station, Babs wondered if she dared ask the driver to drop her in Bexleyheath. There was a later train she could catch, which would give her time to go to see Elsie. But at the last minute, she didn't. She didn't know who she could trust, and the driver had been told to take her to the station. What if he gossiped that she'd asked him to do differently? *Eeh, I daren't do owt to put everything in jeopardy.* At this thought, she almost laughed out loud. How did she suddenly go into her own skin? Stopping herself resulted in a kind of snort, which earned her a strange look as the driver turned to look at her. Patting her chest, she made the excuse that she had a cold, but had the devil's own job to stop from going into a fit of giggles. *If only I could be me all the time.*

As she relaxed back, she gazed out of the window, but her thoughts weren't on the scenery. As always, they turned to Marc. He wanted her to be herself; he'd loved their time at Ma's when she'd just been Babs. Not daring to think how much she missed him, Babs hoped against hope that when she got to Beth's there was a letter from him. And she hoped, too, that it would say that he had been able to confirm his plans.

'Beth! Oh, Beth, it's so good to see you.'

Being held by Beth healed some of her pain. 'You look so well, Beth. And you had your hair cut. I love it.'

'And yours is growing again. I thought we would look the same.'

'Ha, there's naw stopping our hair. Do you remember when it reached our bums?'

They giggled. But then were quiet for a moment, Babs realising that she had stepped onto a delicate area – their past.

Beth broke the silence. 'It was good to hear you using your proper voice. But tell me about Art, I can't wait to hear about him. Have you a photo?'

'We'll have to call him Rupert, Beth, like I told you in my letters. Or I might slip up when I go back. And no, I can't get him away from the house. Well, only for walks. I mean, I daren't ask really. I know Annie, his nurse, did because she used to tell me about going to see my Rupert's old nanny, but I'm afraid to do that myself, let alone take little Rupert. He picks up on such a lot and asks so many questions, and I can't put the onus on him to keep any more secrets.'

417

She told Beth about the doll's head. 'And he keeps his love for me a secret, bless him. Anyway, where's my little bundle of joy?'

'Sleeping. He'll be up soon, but I have so much to tell you, Babs. Do you feel like taking me for a walk?'

'I'd love to.'

'My coat's all ready. I'll ring for Peggy.'

When Peggy came through the door from the kitchen, it was so good to see her and to hear her voice, 'Eeh, Babs, I saw you come up the path, but I thought I'd let you alone for a while. How are you, lass?'

Babs felt her eyes sting with tears. 'Eeh, give me a hug, Peggy, you bring Ma to me. I can hear her when you talk.'

Peggy wasn't good at hugs, but she held Babs for a moment. 'By, you lasses, you'd think you were starved of love.'

'I am, Peggy, I am.'

'Ah, Babs, that's so sad. Well, you're not here, love. You're loved all the world.'

When they were outside, they chatted about this and that, and Babs wondered what Beth's news was; she felt impatient to know. 'Look, there's a tea shop. I'll take you there and then we can chat.'

Nothing prepared Babs for what Beth said as they took a sip of their hot tea.

'We're moving back to Blackpool.'

'What? When? Oh, Beth, I so need you down here. I'll come more often, I promise, but I have to be so careful. I daren't be seen to be doing anything on a regular basis.'

'No, it's nothing to do with you, Babs. And you'll be going away for good soon, don't forget. It's to do with how I feel. And Peggy, she's so homesick. I want to be near to Ma.'

'I know how you feel. I long for that too. But how is all of this going to happen? What about Henry's job?'

'We think it might be Christmas time. I haven't said anything to Ma yet, I don't want to get her too excited.'

Babs's hopes lifted.

'So, you see, not long before you make the break. Henry has been promised a position in the Lancaster hospital. It will mean him travelling, and stopping over some nights, as it's a good two hours' journey by car, but there might be a good train service, we don't know yet. The job doesn't start until the new year ... Oh, Babs, I can't wait. I'll tell Ma on Christmas Day. We'll turn up as normal, then tell her we aren't going back! Then we will look for a house while we're staying there. I think it will be a wonderful Christmas present for her, besides what else I might have for her, but I'm not saying a word about that.'

Not taking heed of all of this last, Babs knew the time was on her to ask. 'Beth ... I'm happy for you, I am. I wish with all my heart that Marc and I could do the same. But, well, I wanted to ask if you would consider something.'

'What? Oh, Babs, I'd do anything, anything.'

'Wait until you've heard me out. I ... well, I haven't been truthful with you.' Beth's face as she listened to Babs telling of her true plan went from shock to softening, to an excited grin. The last gave Babs the encouragement she needed. 'So, you don't disapprove?'

'No, I don't. Art is your child and you have a right to him. And I hope with all my heart that you succeed, but how can I help?'

'Well, as I said, my plan was to wait for Marc, but I've been thinking of taking Rupert before Christmas, and I wondered if I could stay with you?'

Beth looked stunned. 'I – I, oh, Babs, have you thought about this, I mean really thought about it? The answer is yes, of course, but what about the implications? Going sooner than when you can go to the ship and get right away leaves the earl so much time to hunt you down. And they can, you know. They have access to resources we have no idea of.'

'But I can't bear it much longer, Beth.'

Beth held her hand. 'Babs, you can. You are with Art – I mean Rupert – every day. That will help you to bear it, surely?'

Babs knew that Beth was right. She made her mind up that she would forego any more leave; she'd say that she had nowhere to go and just wandered around aimlessly. But really, she just couldn't stand these separations from her darling son.

'Babs?'

'I'm all right, it was a daft idea.' She told Beth her conclusion.

'I understand. But what about your post?'

'I'll write to everyone tomorrow while I am here and tell them all that they are not to communicate with me until I contact them.'

'What are your plans, Babs?'

'Well, I hadn't been completely truthful with you, Beth, but only because I wanted to protect you from any questions that you couldn't answer truthfully, but you haven't taken the news of all I am going to do how I thought you might and you and Henry have encouraged me all along in my decision to become a nanny to my son.' Telling Beth the truth of where she was going to live was a relief.

'That sounds wonderful. I'm glad you've told me, but I understand why you didn't. Now I can write to you openly

420

without going through Ma, and we'll come out to visit. That would be so lovely. I love travelling. Must be the gypsy in us ... oh, I mean ...'

'No, you're right. I have many traits that we learnt from Jasmine and Roman, and we must talk about them and that time, that way we will heal.'

Beth squeezed her hand. 'Yes, I believe that. I'll never speak of them with love, because I don't hold any love for them any longer, but to talk about our childhood would be good.'

'Like that time when we went missing? Ha, we were devils at times. We hid in the farmer's barn but then the cockerel came pecking around and must have been spooked by coming across us and flew in the air going mad. We screamed and ran out!'

They giggled. 'Oh yes, and when we ate those crab apples and had tummy ache all night and had to swallow the horrid potion ...'

'Oh, Beth, stop it.' They laughed like only those who were there and it happened to could. It was healing laughter, that increased every time someone looked at them with disdain.

'Come on, Beth, let's go. I'm dying to see Benny, and read my post, and besides, if I don't, I'll do Ma's trick and pee myself.'

'Stop it! Oh, Babs, I love you.'

'And I love you, Beth.'

THIRTY-THREE

Babs

The day was on her. It was 23 December and Babs felt sick.

The bitterly cold weather blew northerly winds across the flat open fields surrounding them. But this didn't deter her as she had long insisted on being able to take Rupert out for his daily walk no matter what the weather.

She'd only just won a battle on the matter with Lady Barnham a week ago, prompted by the meddling housekeeper who had brought her walks out with Rupert to Lady Barnham's attention.

'Are you doing the right thing for the boy, Nanny? The housekeeper reports that no matter what the weather you have him out in it.'

'I am, your ladyship.' A little trickle of fear had told her that if she was stopped, she would never be able to get him away. The letter from Marc which she'd read over and over this last few weeks stated that he would be in the area she'd told him about, parked on the road that ran through the wood. She could access the wood from the bottom of the garden and had found that there was a smooth enough path to push the carriage through.

Walking such a distance was far too much for Rupert; besides, she needed to conceal a few things in the carriage for him – his favourite toy, the contents of the china doll, and a few bits of clothing to tide him over.

Once they met up with Marc they would drive to Liverpool. Marc told her in his letter that he was to arrive just one week from now, two days before Christmas. The ship he came on would dock for several weeks before turning around to go back. They had to be on that ship when it did. In the mean-time they would stay in a hotel – no one would think of looking for her in Liverpool.

Her only sadness was missing Christmas. And she couldn't let her ma or Beth know that, as she was no longer able to send letters. The thought of not saying a proper goodbye to them was breaking her heart.

Lady Barnham had gone on to say, 'I'm not so sure. If he catches a cold, it could be very serious. You must know that. I cannot understand your folly. You are to keep him indoors and warm at all times.'

Never speaking back before, Babs had been compelled to: 'May I speak, your ladyship?'

'Oh, if you must, but I will not be persuaded. The earl himself has expressed his concern.'

Babs had never met the earl, but had seen him in the distance. Her Rupert had taken after him in every way. Tall and good-looking in a rakish way that held charm. The earl was rarely at home. Babs didn't find this surprising, as she remembered her Rupert telling her that his father had a mistress whom he loved very much and spent a lot of time with. The thought disgusted her and gave her a small amount of sympathy for Lady Barnham.

'Your ladyship, as a qualified nurse, I know from experience that it is opposite to what you imagine. A child who is cosseted and kept away from the world becomes delicate and unable to fight off any virus that comes his way. Whereas lots of fresh air and exposure to the elements builds their inner strength. I make sure that Master Rupert is kept warm at all times. We walk at a brisk pace for him and I even make him run for a time so that he keeps his circulation going. As well as these measures, I take the carriage so that I can wrap him up in a blanket in it once he gets tired, or if I think he is getting cold.'

There had been a moment when Lady Barnham had pondered her words. Babs had begged of God to make the answer be that she could carry on with her regime. 'Very well. But I do hope that you know what you are doing. One sign of him getting a cold and not only will you be in extreme trouble with the earl, but I will sack you and not give you a reference!'

Babs suspected that Lady Barnham had wanted her to give in at the prospect of losing her job, but Babs had a lot more to lose than that.

Checking that everything was as it should be, and looking in her bag for the umpteenth time to make sure she had her passport, Babs called Rupert. He came running, carrying his coat. 'Oh, Rupert, I have told you not to climb on the chair to get your coat.'

Rupert stopped in his tracks, his bottom lip quivering. 'Am I a naughty boy, Nanny?'

'No. Come on, Nanny didn't mean to snap.'

Feeling bad, Babs scooped him up and held him close. The door opened at that moment and Miss Pratt stood there. She stared and then gave a look of anger, before closing the door.

Babs hurried Rupert into his coat and fastened his bonnet. What she needed was already in the carriage. She'd only to grab the blanket. She'd been taking things with her over the last few days, always wrapped in the blanket or in her handbag and storing them in the compartment in the bottom of the carriage.

In no time she was collecting the carriage from where it was left for her, just outside the side door. She wanted to dump Rupert in it and run, but she walked at her normal pace, pushing the carriage with one hand and holding Rupert's hand with the other. She had to hope that the housekeeper wouldn't go straight to her ladyship and even if she did, that she wouldn't get an audience with her straight away.

'Look, Nanny, a robin.'

'Good boy, yes it is. We will draw one when we get back and you can paint it.'

'What if I get paint on me?'

'I shall laugh at you if you do, because you will look funny. Shall we walk a little faster, Nanny is getting cold.'

Rupert picked up his pace. Babs was desperate to get to the woods. She couldn't wait to see her darling Marc. And yet, she worried he wouldn't be there. He had no way of letting her know if he was delayed, and she would have no knowledge of when he would come another time, if he didn't make it.

Her stomach churned. Everything hung on this next half an hour or so, as then the staff would begin to worry. She never stayed out longer than that.

Making it to the wood, she scooped Rupert up. 'We're going on an adventure, Rupert.' Hold on, as Nanny will be pushing you very fast.'

'Where to, Nanny? Will we see Toad of Toad Hall?'

Babs laughed and some of her tension eased. Rupert loved the stories from *The Wind in the Willows*. 'We may do, keep your eyes open.'

'I never shut them unless I am in my bed.'

'Ha, you do, you went to sleep in this carriage once.'

'Did I, Nanny? Was I a very little boy then?'

Babs wanted to pick him up and hold him to her, but she hurried on. Her emotions were vying for prominence and had her in a whirl. *Will I soon be in the arms of my beloved? Will anything go wrong? Don't let it, please God, don't let it.*

When at last she came out the other side of the wood, there was not a car in sight. She mentally checked the time and knew that she had it right. Trying not to panic, she let her mind wander over the possibilities. She was still within the time that she would normally be out with Rupert and could make it back without raising suspicions. But she didn't want to. She wanted everything to work out for her. This day could change her life forever. She would be loved and cared for, no one could hurt her again. She deserved that chance, didn't she?

A noise different to the sound of the wind made her turn around. Was it a car engine? She didn't breathe, her heart banged against her chest. She peered this way and that, not sure which way Marc would appear from. And then in the distance she saw a car. *Please, please let it be my darling Marc.*

The car slowed. And in that moment, Babs's hope of finding the happiness she sought died. It was the earl.

'What are you doing? You are my grandson's nanny, I believe.'

He couldn't fail to know this from her uniform. 'Yes, sir. We are out for a walk and Master Rupert likes to watch the cars go by. Not that many do, but it is amusing to him and lets him see the outside world.'

'But it is freezing. Bryant, get out of the car and hand the boy in. You can walk back, Nanny, and I will see you in my office later.'

'My lord, I beg your pardon, but I sought permission from Lady Barnham, who expressed your concerns. I explained that a child needs exposure to all weathers to grow hardy and to be able to fight off anything that comes along. I am from a farming family, and they rarely get ill. Besides that, my nursing background has taught me the benefit of fresh air and exercise. Master Rupert walked to here, I only put him in the carriage as we planned on being still for a few minutes.'

'Humph. Very well, we will talk more about this when I summon you, but I will take the boy home now.'

Another engine sounded in the distance. Babs panicked as to what to do. Somehow, she kept a calm exterior. She knew that nannies did have a certain amount of power over what happens with their charges and she hoped that the earl respected that.

'May I explain to him, my lord? I have promised Master Rupert that I will take a detour on the way back to see the hens in the kitchen garden; he is learning where our food comes from and how the gardeners and farmers work hard to produce it. He is also very amused by the hens and has been promised that he can feed them.' Babs didn't know where she was finding the courage; her only hope was that the earl had the heart that his son had and was open to the wishes of others.

The car in the distance slowed its pace; she was certain it was Marc. *Please God . . . Please . . .*

'Oh, very well. You can continue as you planned. You certainly seem to have a different approach and one that I am not unfavourable to. Most want to mollycoddle him and that won't do. But I would still like to see you in my study tonight. I would like to catch up with my grandson's development and your methods of child raising, which have piqued my interest.'

'Thank you, my lord. I will await your summons.'

She wanted to scream at him that a must in a child's development is to be loved and to be noticed and acknowledged, but most of all she wanted to tell him to just go, but she just said to Rupert, 'Now, Master Rupert, say good day to your grandfather, and then we will visit the chickens.'

'Good day, Grandfather.'

'Good day, my boy. Bryant, drive on.'

Babs was shocked. Had she seen a tear in the earl's eye? Had she got it all wrong? After all, he'd lost his only son. Maybe it was too painful for him to now look upon his grandson. But no, as she turned around, she thought, grieving or not, would any man or woman reject a child and simply have him schooled to take their place when they die? Not the men and women she knew. And not the gypsies from her childhood, who loved and cared for all their children. There was something very different about the aristocracy.

She was a few feet into the wood when the other car passed by. It didn't stop. Marc wasn't coming. Her own tears dripped onto her cheeks, as her hopes died inside her.

As she walked on, she was glad that the carriage was one of

the first that she'd seen where the child faced away from the person pushing. At least little Rupert couldn't see her.

'Nanny, I wanted to go in the car. Have you been in one? What does it feel like?'

She wanted to say, *You have been in one. On the day you were taken from me . . . your ma*, but she just said, 'Oh, I'm sorry, I thought you would prefer to see the hens.'

'It doesn't matter. I like the hens. I hope one lays an egg again, it was funny seeing it come out of its bottom.' Rupert laughed his lovely laugh, and Babs thought, *If I never see Marc or any of my loved ones again, I will have my Rupert. My darling Art. And I will never leave him.*

Tilly thought she was destined from now on to forever prepare for Christmases without all her family around her as Babs would go so far away straight after, and Beth may not make it up to the north as her family grew. Though there were no signs of that happening yet. And so, she determined to make this one a Christmas that none of them would ever forget. One that partly centred on her two little grandsons, giving them a memory to treasure.

She stopped in the act of spreading lard over the chest of the huge cockerel as her heart skipped a beat. *Am I really going to see me little Art? Or is my grandchild destined to be with others, just as my girls were?* Life is so cruel at times. And something could go wrong with Babs's plan. Not hearing from her was torture, but she understood. Babs had to do everything that she could to get her child back. Tilly didn't want her to live with the agony that had been her own constant companion for years and years till her girls came home – as surely if this failed, Babs would go with her husband, wouldn't she?

'I think that cockerel is larded enough! Tilly, are you all right?'

'Aye, I am, I just went into me thoughts, that's all, lad. Eeh, what would we do without you, Cliff, now that Eliza's so busy she can't help much at home? Tommy would never manage the farm with just Phil, and the help you give me at times like this, well, like I say, what would we do?'

'Tilly, have you thought more about fully retiring?'

'It's in me plan, I'm just waiting for those that are learning to get to the standard that they can relieve them as are skilled, and let them just concentrate on the more intricate stuff. That Frank, the young man who lost part of his face in the war, seems to be really taking to the basket work, and is making a lot of the smaller stuff now. Problem is that they are our bestsellers, so it still takes some of Alec's time to keep the levels of stock up. But I don't think it will be long now before that sorts itself, and then I can give up. I never thought I would say it, but I can't wait.'

'And young Jack has turned into a fine lad and loves the farming, so, well, if I should leave, I think Phil could manage the farm, as Jack's brother is wanting more hours now.'

'Eeh, it was an ill wind that Christmas Day, Cliff – but one that blew in a lot of good as well. Yes, it changed me Tommy's life, with his gammy leg, but it brought you to us, and look at Rita Rawcliffe now. When you met her outside the church that day she was down and out, now she manages what we still call "Liz's House" for me. She sees that those who are housed there can get a second chance in life, and she has two of her sons in work here and her daughter doing well at school ... Eeh, I just realised what you said. You're not leaving us, are you?'

Cliff concentrated on kneading the bread he was preparing

and didn't look up. 'I, well, I was just sort of talking about if things changed. They aren't going to yet, but if they did.'

Tilly could see that Cliff had something on his mind, but she could also tell that he wasn't ready to talk about it yet. 'Right, let's get this cockerel in the oven then, lad. By, we've a busy time with Beth coming later, and the wedding tomorrow. We need to be on the ball.'

'Is Babs definitely coming for Christmas? Have you heard from her?'

'Naw, it's like I told you, Beth said that until she gets here naw one knaws owt. She had to stop visiting Beth as they both got scared that her regular visits to one place would be noted and looked into. And that meant that she couldn't write letters. You see, she'd have to give her letters in with the rest of the household's to be taken to the post office once a week, and she couldn't let them think that she had any other than Pearl to write to.'

'Couldn't she post them herself?'

'Naw, she's miles from Bexleyheath, she'd need a lift. And Beth said she feels her every move is being watched. She's terrified of losing her job as all her hopes would go with it.'

When Beth arrived, the hug they had helped Tilly to forget all her worries over whether Babs had managed to get away or not, as they all knew that today was the day.

'Well, me lass, you look well. There's sommat different about you.'

'Just happiness, Ma. I'm so glad to be here, though worried about Babs.'

'You and me both. This has got to work for her, Beth, it's got to.'

'I think it will. I know it has been planned with very little contact, but Marc's letter said that he had everything in place, so it is just down to Babs being able to do her bit today. And knowing Babs, we shouldn't worry.'

'But will they get away with it?'

'They will need a lot of luck and, Ma, well, don't pin all of your hopes on them coming here. Marc's letter talked of them being safer going straight to Liverpool and staying in a hotel for a few weeks.'

'Naw! Why didn't you say, Beth? I've never thought that they wouldn't come here, lass.'

'Sorry, Ma. Henry cautioned me about dashing your hopes. Babs is strong. If she wants to come here, she will, even if it's just for five minutes.'

'Why wouldn't they? What's unsafe about it all?'

'Well, no one knows, do they? I mean, all our friends know bits, but not Babs's plan to snatch her baby. If they come here, they will. And the more that know, the bigger the danger. This is the first place that the earl will try. It has to be. I'm not saying that they will think that their nanny is Babs, but that they will think that Babs has somehow kidnapped their grandson and their nanny. She is the obvious one to do such a thing.'

Tilly felt the bottom drop from her world. All of this made sense; Babs coming here didn't. She sat down on the kitchen chair. Something told her that she'd seen the last of her Babs and little Art for a long, long time. The thought was unbearable.

'Ma, you will be all right. You will know where Babs is and that she is safe and loved. You coped when she was in France and you can cope again.'

Henry came into the kitchen then, clapping his gloved hands to ward off the cold. 'Hello, Ma.'

Tilly looked into his smiling face and smiled back. She loved Henry. 'Eeh, lad, it's good to see you.' And it felt good to be hugged by this lovely young man.

'Ma, do you think I could borrow Cliff for a mo? I need a hand bringing in our cases.'

'Cases, lad? How long are you staying? I thought it was only for a couple of days.'

'Henry, I think it's the right time to tell Ma. She's very upset over Babs possibly not making it on Christmas Day.'

'Tell me what?'

'Well, ask you really, Ma, you and Tommy.'

'Ask us what, Henry? And where's Benny? Eeh, I forgot about him with all me worries. How could I do that?'

'Ha, we like to forget him when we put him to bed! He'll exhaust you, I'll tell you, Ma. He's always up to something, getting under your feet, and his questions . . . He can drive you crazy.'

Beth was laughing as she said this.

'Beth's right, but we wouldn't have him any other way. He's with Peggy. He spotted Tommy and went over to him, so Peggy went with him. Ah, here they are now.'

Tilly didn't have time to speak as Benny ran towards her shouting, 'Grandma! Grandma! We've come to stay!'

Tilly bent down and hugged him. 'Eeh, lad, me little Benny. I knaw, but not for long enough. But we're going to have a Christmas to remember, lad.'

'But we are, Grandma, we've packed all our things.'

Tilly looked up at Beth. Beth laughed. 'Well, that's one way of finding out.'

'What? You're staying? But . . . ?'

'If you will have us, Ma, and you, Tommy.'

'And me, Tilly lass.'

'Peggy. Eeh, Peggy, come here and let me hug you.'

Peggy came more willingly than she'd ever done to get her hug, and Tilly felt her face wet with tears against her own wet cheek.

'So, what is all of this about, Beth? How long is it that you want to stay? Not that it matters, for you are welcome here in your own home for as long as you want to make it so.'

Beth couldn't answer. Tilly could see that the emotion of the moment had got to her. Benny was by her side, looking concerned. 'Mama, wasn't I supposed to tell?'

Tilly watched Beth pat Benny's hand. 'It's all right, darling, these are happy tears, and I can't think of a nicer way to tell Grandma and Granddad that we are coming back to live in Blackpool.'

Tilly screamed. She couldn't help herself. It wasn't a horrified scream but a scream of sheer joy as happiness surged through her and burst out of her mouth before she could stop it.

They all hugged one another as they laughed and cried in equal measures; even Cliff joined in. It was a few minutes before Beth could explain fully. 'And, well, we thought to keep it a secret and tell you on Christmas Day. But there was no better time than now. I'm so glad that you're happy about it as we may be living here with you for at least three months; it could take us that long to find the right home.'

'And we have another secret, don't we, Mama?'

'Benny, shush.'

'Sorry, Papa.'

Tilly wondered what this secret was, but thought better

434

than to ask. They would tell her in their own time. Instead, she laughed it off by saying, 'Awe, when I was a nipper, I couldn't keep a secret either, lad.'

'What's a nipper, Grandma?'

In this, Tilly felt the difference between herself and the class this grandson was being raised amongst. And she knew it would be the same with little Art. She'd schooled herself for it, but now she wasn't handling it as well as she thought. Henry saved the day. 'Ha, you'll learn even more about the lovely north of England and its wonderful folk off your grandmother than you have already from Peggy, lad.'

Benny laughed. 'You've never called me lad before, Papa.'

'No, and you've never called me Da, but I have a strong feeling that you soon will do and I'll love it.'

'Really, Henry? You won't mind him picking up northern ways?'

'How can I, Ma? Some of the best people I know and who I love very much are northern – well, Lancastrians, actually. No, I'll go one better than that: Sandgronians. As most of you are born and bred in Blackpool.'

'That's for being a grand thing to be saying, son, and I hope you're for including the Irish in that.'

'One in particular, Tommy.' With this, Henry shook Tommy's hand, and they laughed together and Tilly thought that this young man was special. For hadn't Henry been instrumental in smoothing over many a doubt in Beth's mind? But then he came from a very special family.

When they all calmed down, Tilly asked about Philomena, Henry's mother, and about his sister and her family.

'Mother is very well. She's a busy grandmother to Janine's

children, and we've heard the lovely news that Janine is pregnant with her third child.'

'That is grand.' Tilly looked at Beth when she said this, but Beth was smiling. She obviously wasn't worried about not being pregnant herself. This put Tilly's mind at rest, as it niggled at her that Beth and Henry might have wanted to increase their family, but that it wasn't happening for them. 'Well, you and Cliff get your luggage in, and we'll all go through to the living room. I've a roaring fire in there. Mind, naw one's to go into the Sunday best room until Christmas morning.'

'Where is the Sunday best room, Grandma?'

'Don't tell him, Ma, he'll not be able to resist going in.'

Tilly laughed at Beth, who now seemed to have fully taken on motherhood – it had always been Peggy who would have said such a thing. Taking the big iron key out of her pinny pocket and waving it at Benny, she told him, 'You can come and see where it is and you can turn the key in the lock, lad. But then, when it is locked again, this key here will keep out the most inquisitive boy in the world.'

'Even Peter Pan?'

Tilly wasn't sure who that was, but she laughed and said, 'Even Benny, you mean, lad.'

With this Benny giggled and took hold of her hand. 'I like it in your home, Grandma.'

'It's your home an' all, lad. It's your home an' all.'

Her heart swelled as she walked towards the Sunday best room with him. At last she was going to be just like Henry had said Philomena was – a busy grandmother and she knew that she was going to love every minute of it.

THIRTY-FOUR

Tilly

Mary and Alec's wedding yesterday had gone off without a hitch. Everyone was in a happy mood, and the excitement of the proceedings was added to by the anticipation of Christmas being the very next day.

It had been lovely to see Beth and Mary laughing together. And to hear Beth saying that one day, she would come back to the shop to work. Beth had spoken of all the ideas she had for the expansion of the business, such as another shop in Lytham, and Tilly had felt the gladness of it all, as she could see this next generation taking her little basket shop to new heights.

Gerry hadn't forgotten Benny, and was soon taking charge of him. Benny loved it and the two were insepar- able all day.

Eliza had been a picture to watch as she was so happy with her Phil, and they both spent a lot of time playing with the children. It was good to know that all her plans were coming together, as she had found a helper in a lovely homely lady who didn't live far from the shop and, though a lot older than Eliza, respected her. 'Patsy's a gem, Ma. She used to allus come into the shop and we got on well then. Eeh, Ma, it's going to be grand.'

Eliza had hugged her, and Tilly had felt so happy for her, and knew that in this daughter she was lucky. She couldn't see a day when any heartache would befall her where Eliza was concerned.

Now, Christmas Day had dawned and Tilly lay awake thinking about the day ahead and tried to imagine what it would feel like if Babs didn't make it, because she still held hope in her heart that she would.

A noise in the house had her listening; someone was up and about. She smiled, wondering if it was Benny. This made her glance at the key to the Sunday best room; it was still there. *Eeh, Benny, lad, I saw yesterday how mischievous you can be, but by, it's going to be grand having you live nearby.*

Tilly still couldn't believe that was going to happen and was struck by how life can throw so much at you. On the one hand she had had the most wonderful news of Beth coming back to Blackpool, and on the other, even if Babs did make it, she would have to face her going far, far away.

The noise came again. Throwing the covers back, Tilly jumped out of bed and grabbed the extra present that she had for Benny – a toy train that Tommy had made out of wood. He'd made one for Art too, and painted Benny's blue and Art's red.

Downstairs she found Benny listening at the Sunday best room door. Smiling, she asked, 'And what are you hoping to hear, lad?'

Benny jumped round. 'Oh, Grandma, you scared me. Do you think that Father Christmas has been? Mama said he always comes down the chimney in the Sunday best room.'

Tilly laughed. 'He has. Come and give Grandma a cuddle.' As he did, Tilly's heart warmed. She didn't think there was any feeling like having grandchildren.

With his little arms around her neck and Tilly sitting on the bottom step, he asked, 'How do you know for sure that Father Christmas has been? Shouldn't we open the door just to check?'

'Naw, we don't have need to do that. He left you sommat to be going on with until all the grown-ups get out of bed.' Tilly and Tommy had decided that this idea would help the little ones to follow their usual tradition of waiting until after breakfast to open their presents.

'Ooh, let me have it, Grandma! What can it be?'

'Naw, Father Christmas said that Granddad Tommy has to be there an' all, as this is our first real Christmas with you as a big boy. Hold your nightshirt up and take me hand. We'll go up the stairs, and you can jump on Granddad to wake him up.'

When they got into the bedroom, Tilly knew that Tommy had heard every word as he was hiding under the covers. Benny giggled, then climbed onto the bottom of the bed and shouted, 'Granddad!' only to be sent into a fit of laughter when Tommy shot from under the covers saying, 'Boo.'

To see them cuddle made a tear come to Tilly's eye, and to see Benny's reaction to his train was something Tilly thought she would never forget.

In no time both him and Tommy were on the floor playing trains, warmed by Tommy rekindling the embers in the grate. To Tilly, it was part of her dream for Christmas coming true.

After breakfast, the house was in uproar. Brown wrapping paper was everywhere, and all the men were playing with Benny's toys when Molly and Will, Vera and Brian, Mary and Alec, Florrie, Reggie and Phil arrived. Peggy fussed over them, taking their coats and getting everyone a drink.

'Well, no more farmyard playing for me. I've to see to the dinner now.'

'I'll come with you, Cliff. Everyone, take your seats. It doesn't matter where you sit.' Tilly whispered to Henry to take the two place settings away from the table that she'd laid for Babs. 'We don't want any empty places, lad.' And though she felt sad about this, Tilly didn't mope over it. Instead she threw herself into helping Cliff.

The chatter around table was jolly, and the meal delicious. After the main course, Henry banged the table. 'Can I have silence for my beautiful wife, please. She has something to share with you all . . . Beth?'

Everyone looked at Beth. Tilly felt an excitement stir inside her. Was Beth expecting another grandchild for her? She hoped so. But nothing prepared her for what happened next. Henry pulled out Beth's chair, and then gave Beth his arm.

And there, before her very eyes, Tilly witnessed her daughter stand up properly for the first time since she was a child.

'Beth! Oh, me Beth!'

'This is my Christmas present to you, Ma.'

'Oh? When? How?' As she said this she raced around the table to Beth. 'Can I hold you, me lass? It won't make you fall, will it?'

To everyone clapping and cheering and, yes, with tears running down their eyes, Beth and Tilly hugged like they

440

hadn't been able to for a long time. Tilly never wanted to let her beautiful daughter go, but Henry gently took her from Tilly's arms and helped her to sit again. 'Well, I think we have some explaining to do, Beth.'

Beth couldn't speak; she was overcome.

'Mama's happy tears again, Grandma.'

Everyone laughed at Benny, including Beth.

'And I didn't tell the secret, did I?' These words were muffled as Benny had shoved a huge potato into his mouth. When he bit on it, the part that escaped landed flat in the middle of his gravy, splashing Gerry, who'd insisted on sitting next to him on a board with cushions on that was laid across two chairs.

'Benny, you don't change, do you? By, you're a lad.'

This from Gerry had the room in uproar.

When they quietened, Henry explained the treatment that Beth was undergoing and that they had every hope that she would walk again.

Tilly couldn't believe it. Nothing, not even her worry over Babs, could spoil the feeling that she had. 'That's the best news I've heard in a long time, Beth. Ta, Henry. Ta from the bottom of me heart, lad.'

Henry held her in a hug as the noise levels increased with everyone excited over the new turn of events.

'Eeh, Beth, lass, I wish Babs could knaw before she sails away.'

'She does know, Ma. I was having treatment when she visited. At least, she does know that there's hope. As soon as she settles and sends us an address, we'll write and tell her. And maybe I will have a photo of me standing by then.'

'Eeh, that'd be grand.'

'How are you holding up, Ma?'

'I'm fine. Nothing can mar the news that I've just had. I'm so happy, I could do a jig, and probably will after we've had the plum pudding.'

The rest of the day was funny, happy and had its moments. One of these being when the drink Pete, Cliff's dad, had consumed seemed to tell him that he could dance, as everyone was doing to music coming from the gramophone. He suddenly stood up and took hold of Peggy. Well, to say neither of them could dance was an understatement. But somehow it didn't matter, as Cliff told them, 'Eeh, that's the first time I've seen me da happy since me poor ma died. And I'm glad to see it. And, aye, so would she be an' all.'

This set the gossiping off as Molly and Florrie huddled together on the sofa and Tilly heard them speculating as to whether anything would come of it. Tilly laughed at them. 'Hey, you two, stop marrying poor Peggy off, bless her.' They all giggled.

'Wouldn't that be a turn-up for the books, eh?'

'It would, Molly.'

'So, are you happy, Tilly? Eeh, I knaw as you've not got Babs here like you hoped, but happen she couldn't get away.'

Tilly just nodded and changed the subject, and soon the three of them were laughing their heads off about their antics of the past.

'Eeh, me lasses, I'll never be sad for long with you two around me. I do love you both.'

'And we love you, and you'll never have to do without us, lass. We'll allus be here for you.'

442

Tilly knew this without doubt. She'd been through such a lot in her lifetime, but all of it had been lightened since she'd met these two. Her lovely Blackpool lasses.

Everyone had gone except Cliff, who, though he'd been working hard making the dinner, had volunteered to shut all the animals down for the night. Benny was in bed and Tilly, Tommy, Beth, Henry and Eliza were sipping cocoa, sitting around the kitchen table, when suddenly Cliff burst in. 'They're here! Eeh, Tilly, they're here.'

Tilly nearly dropped her mug. 'What? Who? Ba . . . Babs!'

Cliff nodded, his grin wider than she'd seen it for a long time. 'Oh, Beth, Eliza, Babs is here!'

Tilly had only just finished saying this when Babs ran in carrying a small sleeping boy. 'We are, Ma, and you'd better have saved some dinner for us, we're starving. Merry Christmas, everybody!'

After a flurry of kisses, hugs, tears and questions, they all at last sat around the table again. Tilly was holding little Art on her knee. 'He's beautiful, Babs. Eeh, me little Art, wait until you wake in the morning and meet your cousin. By, you're going to get on like a house on fire, lad.'

'Eeh, Ma. I know they are. I've been telling him all about you all on the way. He's so excited to be starting a new life, and so far hasn't shown a bit of concern about leaving his grandparents, but then, they were nothing to him, bless him.'

Babs smiled at her ma, and then at Beth. She couldn't believe that she was here. Ignoring the churning of her stomach, she clung on to her darling Marc's hand.

Her mind went back to two days ago and how her heart had clanged with her despair as she'd trudged back through the woods – her dreams in tatters. But then a noise behind her had made her turn, and there he was. Marc. Her Marc.

Neither could move. They just stared at one another for a moment, then Babs had let go of the pram and had run into her beloved's arms. It was a moment of sheer joy. A coming together of her two worlds to make them one again and she'd had the feeling that now, her life could begin.

Ma's voice brought her back to the present. 'Eeh, me Babs, you look worn out, lass. I'll plate you both a dinner up. There's loads left, and I'll pop it on top of a pan of boiling water, it'll soon heat up.'

'Ta, I am tired, Ma, but, well, we—'

Marc interrupted her. 'I'll tell them, darling.'

Babs felt glad of this; she didn't think she had the strength to.

Beth, seeming to sense that Ma was in for a shock, held out her arms. 'Let me hold Art, Ma. Oh, Babs, he's lovely, and he's the same size as Benny, and the same colouring.'

Babs could only nod. Extreme sadness had gripped her and threatened to engulf her.

'You see, we have to leave, once we have eaten and freshened up.'

'Naw, Marc. Naw! Eeh, Babs . . .'

'I'm sorry, Ma.'

Eliza was by her side in an instant, holding her as if she could prevent it happening. 'Don't go, Babs. Please don't go. I thought as you'd be staying a bit.'

'I have to go, Eliza, love. I wish that it was different, but it isn't. I'm not safe here. In the eyes of the law, I have done something really bad. I've kidnapped a child from his legal guardian. This could be the first place they will look for me. They may even be on their way now.'

Eliza's eyes brimmed with tears.

'Be happy for me.' Suddenly Babs felt her strength coming into her. Ma was holding on to a chair staring at her. Beth was heartbroken and Henry and Tommy looked shocked.

'Try to be happy that I at last have my child and my husband. I have a big sacrifice to make, I have to leave you all. But remember that you will visit me. And one day, I will come back.'

Marc squeezed her hand.

'We shouldn't have come, but Babs so wanted to see you all before she left. And I'm glad we have, but what we need is your support and help to do this.'

Tommy crossed the room and grabbed Ma as she swayed. 'Tilly, me little lass, if ever it is that you need your strength it is now. And you can take hold of it. I know that you can be for doing so.'

It seemed to Babs that Ma grew inches in moments. 'Aye, I can do this for me Babs, and me lovely little grandson, and you, Marc. It's wonderful what you've done for me Babs, lad.'

Babs looked over at Cliff then. He hadn't spoken since they'd hugged on her arrival.

'Cliff, can we trouble you to get us some dinner, please? Only I think Grandma should sit with Rupert for as long as she can.'

'Rupert?'

'Aye, Ma. He uses his proper name now and I love it.'

Tilly nodded and took the still sleeping Rupert from Beth's arms.

'Shall we take him into the front room, Ma? I want to hold him an' all and we're crowded in here.' Babs watched Eliza go with Ma. She wanted to run after them and tell them she wouldn't go, but she knew she had no choice.

'So, what are your plans, Marc?'

As Henry engaged Marc in conversation, Babs slipped off her chair and went over to Beth and kissed the top of her head. 'I won't be long, Beth.' Beth took her hand and they looked at one another for a moment. 'I'll just go and have a word with Cliff while he's out in the cold room.'

Beth nodded.

When Babs entered the pantry, a large cold room just through a door in the corner of the kitchen, she found Cliff holding on to one of the shelves with both hands and his head drooped between his arms.

'Cliff?'

'Babs!' He stood straight. 'So, this is it then? You're on your way? By, I can't tell you how happy I am for you, and I'll be praying for you – praying that you succeed.'

'Thanks, love. But what about you, Cliff? Have you made any decisions?'

'I have, lass. But the time has to be right. I feel the tug of me da's needs and of your da's an' all.'

'Cliff, those feelings will always be there, but you have your life to lead the way that you must. Everyone copes in one way or another; they have to. And for all we know, we might be hindering those we love from getting on with their own life by thinking we have to be there for them all the time.'

'I never thought about that.'

446

'No, and you never talk to anyone about your own needs, and that's a mistake, Cliff. What I'm about to do will hurt so many, and yet because they know everything, they will find a way to cope. We all will. You will, too. So, what are you going to do? No maybes now.'

'I'm going into a monastery, Babs. I haven't got the brains to be a priest, but in any case, since I've looked into this side of religious life, I knaw it's for me. And I have all the skills an' all – farming and cooking. With them and me desire to serve God, I'm fully qualified.'

Babs couldn't take this in for a moment, but she didn't show her surprise. 'Oh, Cliff, I'm so happy for you. I could see as you told me the happiness that your decision has given you.'

'So, this is goodbye, lass. I'm not going into a closed order, so I can write to you. But you'll be gone a long time and I can never visit you as we dreamt.'

As she'd said to him many times, Babs said now, 'Give us a hug then.'

They hugged for a few moments, then Babs gently pulled away. 'Now, if you're any sort of a friend, you'd get me some dinner. I'm nearly fainting with hunger.'

They parted on a giggle, and Babs knew her friendship would always be like that with Cliff – easy, with them both able to say what they wanted.

As she rejoined the others she went to Beth and put her arm around her once more. 'I'm going to miss you, Beth.'

'And me you. But, Babs, you've given me a goal . . .'

Babs felt the joy she'd found at being reunited with her Marc, and which had left her as she thought of saying her goodbyes, flood back into her as Beth told her of her progress and how she would aim to come to see Babs the moment she could walk. 'That'd be grand, lass. Grand as owt.'

Beth laughed. 'By, it will an' all, Babs.'

They giggled, but to Babs, in that moment, she felt as though she'd truly got her sister back.

Several weeks later, with a smile on her face, Babs walked up the gangplank of the ship that would take her away from all she knew. Marc was beaming too, and little Rupert was jumping up and down holding both their hands as eager to get aboard as they were.

Once on the deck they stood holding the rail and waved with everyone else. Not to anyone in particular on the dock far below them, but because their happiness at finally reaching safety was realised. Marc's arm came around her. 'Happy?'

'I am, my darling, so happy.'

'I'm happy too, Mama.'

Babs hugged herself. Yes, she had pain in her heart, but mostly she had joy.

It had taken about a week to get Rupert to call her Mama; now he did as naturally as if he'd done so for ever. She'd wanted to be called 'Ma' really, but she knew she had to prepare him for his future. For one day he would be the Earl of Barnham and when that day came, they would all return to England and she would once more be with Ma, Tommy, Eliza and Beth and her family.

EPILOGUE

LETTERS DON'T GIVE HUGS

1935

Tilly

Fourteen years later, Tilly stood on Liverpool dock with her arms folded, hugging herself. The huge ship manoeuvred into place. Hundreds of passengers were on the deck waving and a huge cheer went up. An arm came around her and she looked into Tommy's dear face. Like hers, his lovely hair was grey now, but it was still thick and curly, and his Irish eyes hadn't lost their twinkle, though now they glistened with tears. He didn't speak; she knew that he couldn't.

Beth stood on Tilly's other side. She linked her arm through Tilly's, her body trembling with her excitement. In all the years since it had happened, Tilly couldn't get over the miracle of Beth being able to walk. Now she was a mother of two: Benny, a strapping lad of eighteen, and Martina, twelve, both of whom stood with Henry, Benny teasing Martina and making her giggle. Eliza and her Phil stood next to them, with their ten-year-old twins, Susan and Sally.

Tilly had realised her dream of being a busy grandmother, but though they were a joy to her, always there was something missing from her life – from her brood of grandchildren. And now they stood together – two-thirds of her family, waiting for the moment they had longed for for years.

Just a little way away, giving them space but ready to support with a love as solid as a rock, were Molly and Jim, and Florrie, now in a wheelchair because of her weak heart but still strong in spirit, and Reggie. And with them, the surprise of her life – Peggy, married at last, and to the lovely Pete, Cliff's da.

She wondered about Cliff; would he make it? They hadn't seen him for years, but always had news through Pete and Peggy of him and his wonderful work with the poor. They were able to visit him often as Cliff wasn't in a closed monastery. It would be wonderful if he was here too.

These thoughts disappeared in the even louder cheer from the crowds around her as the first passengers stepped onto the gangplank, but still they couldn't pick out Babs and Marc.

Beth took Tilly's attention away from staring at every tiny form. 'Look, Ma, he's come!'

Tilly turned. 'Cliff, eeh, Cliff, lad!'

Coming towards her, his brown robe flapping around him, Cliff waved. 'Hello, Tilly. I'm sorry I'm late. By, in this gown you can't get anywhere for folk wanting to bombard you with questions about your life. Some of their perceptions make me smile.'

Cliff hugged her then. Tilly hadn't expected that. She hadn't thought he would be the same lad, but reserved and all holy, preaching about their wrongdoings. She hugged him back. This was their Cliff, and she knew he would be the icing on the cake for Babs.

'Ma, Ma, I can see them!' This from Eliza came as Cliff was still making his rounds hugging everyone.

Tilly turned, and there they were, waving with every step they took down the gangplank – her lovely Babs. Tilly's eyes filled with tears.

Marc was by Babs's side, and Rupert followed them, tall and handsome and, though still a lad, looking every inch an earl, and ready, with Marc's help as manager, to take the title and run the vast estate he now owned.

Behind Rupert came Babs and Marc's brood of four. Matilda, thirteen, Arthur, eleven, Eliza, nine, and little Beth, three. Tilly and Tommy had gone over to Canada for each of their births, enjoying their time there, and also catching up with Pearl and Bart and their family of three.

Tilly had written often in between visits, and loved receiving letters back from all of the children. Seeing their handwriting improve over time – a marker, with the photos that they sent, of their growing years – was always a joy, and yet a sadness as she and Tommy were missing spending time with them. Tilly would often think to herself, *Letters can't give me hugs.*

But now, she would have all the hugs she wanted, as she could go to Rupert's estate as often as she liked, and was already planning on making that once a month. She and Tommy had checked out the trains and had made the journey once already. *Eeh, I can't wait.*

Rupert's grandmother had died first, which Babs had written was of no consequence to Rupert; he just felt sad that she couldn't have been a better mother to his father and grandmother to him. But then when the earl died, Babs wrote that Rupert seemed to grow up in an instant, and he spoke of him being a decent man at heart. After all, when he'd tracked them down in Canada, he had relented and given his permission for Rupert to continue to live with his mother, on the proviso that Babs saw to it that Rupert had a good education so that he was suitably prepared for his role.

Rupert had been writing to his grandfather over the years, letting him know his progress, and they had built a kind of relationship between them. Babs had said that the earl's letters were often full of instructions for the running of the estate and for the duties Rupert would carry out in the House of Lords. He'd also written of his approval of Marc managing the running of the estate if Rupert hadn't come of age by the time he inherited. Not that Rupert needed his legal approval as when it came to pass, he was the earl, but it had pleased him to know that his grandfather hadn't objected to his plan.

Tilly had hoped when this first contact was made that Babs would come home, but she was afraid that it was all a trick and Rupert would be taken from her, and so years of separation had continued.

At that moment, Eliza came around the back of Tilly and put both arms around her waist and squeezed her, leaning her head on her. 'Eeh, Ma, at last, at last!'

'Aye, lass. The day has come.'

And then they were there and all thoughts, regrets and longings disappeared amongst hugs, tears and happiness.

'Ma, hold them both. Your twins. Since I had mine, I've felt your pain. I want to see you healed of that. Take Babs and Beth in your arms together.' Tilly smiled at lovely Eliza and did just as she said and held her twins close to her.

As she did, Tilly felt all the pieces of herself knit together once more and she determined that nothing, and no one, could ever tear her apart as life had done so often in the past. And the thought came to her that *By, Christmas this year was going to be the best ever.* With that thought she realised how often Christmas had marked a turning point in their lives – not always for the good. But the one coming up would mark the day she'd longed for all of her life – all of her family and especially her beloved twins would be together and nothing would ever mar their happiness again.

LETTER TO READERS

Dear readers,

Thank you for choosing my book. I hope that I have been able to give you hours of enjoyment with The Sandgronian Trilogy as you followed Tilly and her family.

If I have, I would very much appreciate it if you can take the time to put a review on Amazon and/or Goodreads and Facebook for me.

Reviews are like hugging an author – as they help us to progress in our career, they give encouragement to us as we sit alone writing the next book and they are the biggest thank you in the world that you could give to us. And for me, they make me want to hug you back.

A Blackpool Christmas is the last in The Sandgronian Trilogy, but though a series, each book is a standalone. So if you missed the first two books, don't worry; you can still enjoy reading the backstory of Tilly and her life in the first in the trilogy, *Blackpool's Angel*, and then the second book, *Blackpool Sisters*, in which Tilly's story carries on, but we are now with Beth and Babs as the story unfolds of their escape from the gypsies who stole them, and how the rift between them came about. As always, you will need tissues at the ready for each instalment.

Oh, and in case you are wondering why the books are called The Sandgronian Trilogy, Sandgronian is the name given to a person born and bred in Blackpool – which Tilly and her family are.

The name has many spellings, and I was taken to task by one of my old bosses, who is herself a Blackpool-born lass, as she spells it the popular way – Sandgrown'un – and yet others have told me it is Sandgrownian. So in order not to take sides in this friendly debate, I have chosen to use the version given on the internet as the official one.

I myself am a proud Blackpudlian, a name given to anyone living in Blackpool, whether born here or not.

If you would love to read more of my books, besides the The Sandgronian Trilogy, there are two further titles in publication – *Blackpool Lass* and *Blackpool's Daughter*, and more on the way.

All current and back titles are available online or to order from all good bookshops and in your local library – also look out for current and new titles in your local supermarket.

And finally, I love to interact with my readers and would very much like to hear from you. I can be found at:

Facebook: www.facebook.com/HistoricalNovels or search on Facebook for BOOKS BY MARY WOOD AND MAGGIE MASON.

Here you will be able to chat to me, enter my numerous competitions for giveaways of signed books and themed merchandise, and even have a chance to win a tea party with me and my husband.

On my website, www.authormarywood.com, you can receive all my news first-hand by subscribing to my regular newsletter and join in competitions and contact me through email on a one-to-one basis. You can also read first chapters of all my published books. And finally, you can also book me as your speaker for an event, or meeting.

Twitter: Follow me @Authormary.

I look forward to hearing from you

Much love to all

Maggie x

RESEARCH

I like to research in the area that my book is set in, so it's lovely for me that I write books set in my home town of Blackpool.

This makes it easy for me to find street names and local places for my characters to live and work – I just go walk-about till I find the setting that I need.

For historical facts for my books – and my goodness, Blackpool certainly has a fascinating history – I rely on the internet and the following books, the authors of which I am very grateful to for their wonderful work in compiling:

Blackpool's Trams – James Joyce, 1985

Blackpool at War: A History of the Fylde Coast During the Second World War – John Ellis, History Press, 2013

The Story of Blackpool Rock: An interesting account of how it is made and who made it – Margaret Race, 1990

Blackpool History Tour – Allan W. Wood and Ted Lightbown, Amberley Publishing, 2015

ACKNOWLEDGEMENTS

Many people have a hand in bringing a book to publication and I want to express my heartfelt thanks to them:

My agent, Judith Murdoch, who stands firmly in my corner.

My ex-editor at Sphere, Viola Hayden – I miss you already. You were always there for me and I loved your sensitive construction edits. I wish you every success in your new venture and am now looking forward to meeting your successor.

To Thalia Proctor and her team of copy editors and proofreaders, who tailor the words to sing off the page and check my research for flaws, always mindful of keeping my voice and bringing my story to its polished best.

To my son, James Wood, who reads so many versions of each book, advising me what is working and what should go – suggesting edits to the draft manuscript and then helping with the read-through of the final proofs when last-minute mistakes need to be spotted.

To Millie Seaward, my publicist, who works to put my books on the map.

To the sales team, for their efforts to get my books on to the shelves. To the cover designer for my beautiful covers. Thank you. All of you are much appreciated, and do an amazing job.

I thank, too: My family – my husband Roy, who looks after me so well as I lose myself in writing my books, and is the love of my life. By my side for almost sixty years, I couldn't do what I do without him or the love and generous support that he gives me. My children, Christine, Julie, Rachel and James, and their husbands and partners, for your love, encouragement and just for having pride in me. And to my grandchildren, and their husbands, wives and partners. And my great grandchildren. You are all loved so very dearly and all give me love and cheer me on. To my Olley and Wood families, for all their love and support. Thank you to each and every one of you – you all help me to climb my mountain.

Lastly, but by no means least: I want to thank my readers. Without you, I couldn't do what I do. And a special thanks to those who follow my Facebook page and my webpage, and me on Twitter, for the love and encouragement you give me, for making me laugh, for taking part in all my competitions, for pre-ordering all of my books, for taking the time to post lovely reviews, for supporting my launch events, and for just being my special friends. You are second to none and keep me from flagging, I love you all. Thank you.